The Winner of Sorrow

Brian Lynch was born in Dublin in 1945. His first book of poetry, *Endsville*, was shared with Paul Durcan. *New and Renewed: Poems 1967-2004* was published by New Island in 2004. His feature film *Love and Rage*, starring Greta Scacchi and Daniel Craig, was directed by Cathal Black in 1998. *Caught in a Free State*, his 1984 RTÉ/Channel 4 series about German spies in Ireland during World War 2 has been seen in more than 40 countries. Also an art critic, he compiled the acclaimed *Tony O'Malley*, now in its third edition from New Island. A long poem on Northern Ireland, *Pity for the Wicked*, with a preface by Conor Cruise O'Brien, was published by the Duras Press in 2005. On the nomination of Samuel Beckett he was elected to Aosdána in 1985. He lives in Dublin.

The Winner of Sorrow

BRIAN LYNCH

NEW ISLAND

for Camille

The Winner of Sorrow
published 2005
by New Island
2 Brookside
Dundrum Road
Dublin 14
www.newisland.ie

ISBN I 904301 80 0

Typeset by New Island
Cover design by Fidelma Slattery @ New Island
Printed in the UK by Biddles

10 9 8 7 6 5 4 3 2 I

Sacrifice is self-elaborating guilt. It transforms murder into suicide. It enables us to see murder from a perspective in which the vanishing point is suicide – a point that is so far away we find ourselves gazing at the origin of all things. Where we encounter divine suicide: the Creation.

from The Ruin of Kasch, Roberto Calasso

I

It was the first day of a new century and in East Dereham the Christians were going to church. Amongst them, but not of them, was an old man, William Cowper, who believed in Christ and his infinite mercy, although he was also convinced that God hated him personally and was intent on sending him to hell, soon, for all eternity. That the belief and the conviction contradicted each other he understood clearly. He understood, too, that he was completely insane, or rather almost completely, but not quite. In the same nearly perfect way, he was sure that he had always been too contemptible to be loved by any living creature, but that loving him had destroyed the lives of four women, three wild hares and a linnet. These were passive destructions, but he had once actively killed something – he had cut the head off a big snake with a garden hoe. Apart from that, he had never been physically violent, except to himself.

The jangling bells of the church of St. Nicholas were falling over each other as if in a hurry to welcome in the new era. Newness, however, did not sit easily on Dereham. It was a pretty little town in Norfolk, but even in 1800 it was considered old-fashioned – the streets were unpaved and some of the houses were still roofed with thatch. Cowper, too, although he was elegantly dressed in knee-breeches and a linen chamber-cap, looked like something left over from an earlier age. As he was a recent arrival to the town and rarely left his lodgings, only a few of the churchgoers knew him by sight, and even fewer — such is literary fame — that he was a famous poet. One of these was a broken-nosed army officer called Borrow — he had occasionally glimpsed Cowper peering from the upstairs window of a house in the market square, and recently he had seen the death-like figure one frosty dawn in the churchyard. Now, when the hulking captain saw the spectral poet shuffling along the pavement, clutching the arm of his young cousin, the Reverend John Johnson, he tipped his hat in respectful salute.

Cowper saw a hand raised against him. He broke free from Johnson and hurried out into the middle of the street.

'What is it, Mr Cowper? What is the matter?'

'That man is mocking me.'

'What man?'

'The brute in the red coat. He's been following me now for weeks.'

'Captain Borrow following you? How could he? You haven't been out of doors this past month.'

This was not quite true. Some days before Christmas he had stolen out of the house and gone to the church to mark a private anniversary. There, under the slabbed floor of a side-aisle, someone he had known intimately was buried. But, of course, the doors of the church were barred against him, as always, and not just because of the early hour. So he had stood outside, bowed and mourning, in the sun-dial shadow of the Clocker, which is what the locals called their bell-tower.

'And as for being a brute,' Johnson said, 'really, he is the gentlest of men.'

'What did you say his name was?'

'Borrow. Thomas Borrow.'

'You amaze me, sir. '

But why he was amazed he would not explain. Instead he abruptly turned round and followed the crowd into the church. Johnson was himself amazed — they had only come out to take the air, and his cousin, though a saintly person, had not set foot in a church for more than twenty years. But a sudden conversion, or re-conversion, to religion, much as Johnson had long wished for it, was not the reason for Cowper's about-turn: all he wanted to do was to take a closer look at the Captain Borrow who had gone down to London to fight with Big Ben Brain, the champion of all England. There, in Hyde Park, after an hour of combat the exhausted boxers had shaken hands and declared a draw. And four months later when Big Ben had died, worn out by the dreadful blows he had received throughout his career, he had done so in Borrow's arms.

So, Cowper thought, this was the man they have sent to follow me even unto the edge of my Mary's grave. A hero!

But what else, apart from spying, had the captain been doing in the cemetery? The blood-splash of the red coat had startled Cowper and he had shied off like an arthritic deer and hidden behind a yew-tree. But Borrow had stood staring at the ground for a long time before putting on his tricorn hat and going away.

Cowper had waited until he was sure the churchyard was empty and then he had hurried back to his lodgings, merely glancing at the spot where the captain had been standing: it was a grave, not quite fresh, marked with a crude wooden cross bearing the name Jean de Narde. The previous summer this lieutenant in the army of Napoleon, along with a score of his compatriots, had been held captive in the Clocker awaiting transportation to the prison camp at Norman Cross.

There was history in the name of Norman Cross. Ancient history and new fatality. After more than a thousand years the Normans had again come to a divide in the English road. Love your country, beat the French and never mind what happens next! That was the cry of all England, and it was Cowper's cry too. The French were a despicable people, lawless and unlovable. But, he thought, that is my own fate and condition: to be despised is my destiny.

What a funereal sight the camp at Norman Cross had been! A monumental collection of five or six immensely tall wooden casernes, and in each one a thousand Frenchmen, starving, fed on rotten carrion flesh and bread the hounds would not eat; and the guards, battalions of them, were constantly searching their quarters at bayonet point in case the prisoners had somehow procured for themselves any of the comforts of existence, the which being found they burned in great bonfires in the barrack square beneath the glaring eyeballs and the cursing mouths of the captives. But worst of all was that the buildings, high as they were, had no windows. The walls were blank. And the prisoners in the attics had removed tiles and protruded their heads through the gaps, looking like what in truth they were – the terrible brain-blossoms of war.

Had he really seen that himself? No, it was merely a rumour, a report, the sideways talk of Norfolk, and then it became a dream which he could not sleep for the dreaming of.

Perhaps news of the horror of Norman Cross had reached Jean de Narde in the clock-tower, or perhaps it was simply that, being only twenty-six-years-old, he imagined escape was an escapade, an adventure, but whether for dread or for daring he had been shot to death while fleeing through the cemetery on a warm midsummer night. And now he was buried there.

It is extraordinary, Cowper thought, that I lay awake in my bed just one street away and did not hear the musket thundering forth the bullet that ended a man's life. Shivering in a pew at the back of the church, he felt, yet again, the amazement of revelation, a joy indistinguishable from an agony, a sensation in his chest like a wick torn out of wax. Captain Borrow had slain Lieutenant de Narde – that was the revelation he had now received.

But had the English hero gone to keep a vigil at the grave of his French victim out of remorse, as he had gone to Mary's? That was a question that could neither be asked nor answered, if only because since the day she had died, Cowper had never once uttered her name.

2

A beam of sunlight was striking silver from the Reverend Edward Olden's grey head. Every word he uttered from the pulpit hawed out as a cloud of hoar-frost.

'We are in the darkness of the world and there is shone upon us the gift of an otherworldly light which cometh from the father in heaven. We are mutable here and we are promised immutability there. We stand in the shadow of our own turning, but we shall pass into no shadow. The father of lights will not turn from us. He is steadfast. He is immovable and unvarying, and yet, although He changeth not, He changeth us. In the words of the poet,

> God moves in a mysterious way
> His wonders to perform.
> He plants his foot upon the waves,
> And rides upon the storm.'

Mr Olden faltered. Someone at the back of the church was crying, 'No, no!' Then two men were scrambling out of a pew and hurrying away down the aisle.

Cowper struggled weakly to pull open the door, and Johnson helped him, but Cowper was not for helping and would not look him in the eye. Outside, they walked up the hill in silence, or rather, Johnson was silent while Cowper, stopping frequently to get back his breath, muttered to himself. Eventually he concluded that it was fantastic to imagine that Captain Borrow would feel remorse about shooting Lieutenant de Narde, that is if he had shot him, and also it was vile, perhaps even a blood libel, to suspect that Borrow and Mr Johnson, obedient to the Olden world, were in league with one another.

They had climbed the hill and come into the High Street when Johnson felt Cowper's hand slip into his pocket. He held it, a small bundle of cold sticks.

'Do you know, Mr Johnson, what a familiar is?'

'Something to do with witchcraft?'

'A familiar is the servant of a sorcerer, yes, but also of a Roman prelate. Sorcery and heresy, they go together. Magic and cruelty recognise each other. Does that not distress you, sir?'

'Oh, yes,' Johnson said.

'Why do you smile then? Are you with the French? I think you are. But who I'm with I know not. Poor wretch.'

He had tottered away a few steps, to be safe, but now as speedily returned to take Johnson's arm, thinking him the end of safety, yet his only hope of it in the world.

'Oh, my dear friend,' he said, 'take me home and don't kill me.'

By now, after five years of living with him every day, Johnson was used to Cowper's conversation, and what he could not catch he let go. But this sudden mention of France disturbed him. His cousin was under the impression that, given the opportunity, the French would do to him what they had done to Marie-Antoinette. Moreover, in Johnson's experience, mention of disturbance was likely to cause disturbance. They had been wandering around Norfolk like a pair of genteel gypsies for years, so any further moving was out of the question. Johnson had recently become rector of the nearby hamlets of Yaxham and Welborne, his first living, and he was determined that they should settle in Dereham, though settle was hardly the word since they had already moved house twice. It was not that Cowper was capricious or wilful — quite the contrary; these last years he had become as biddable as an old horse, but betimes he grew restless and bolted. No, Johnson thought, horse is not right, nor is he a bolter; he is like an old hare that suddenly goes capering across the heath not because danger is near but because of watching for it for too long.

In the drawing-room of their lodgings, the curtains were drawn and a slacked-down coal fire glowed in the grate. As Cowper was being helped off with his coat, he said, 'Well, that's final. I shall never go to church again.'

'Oh, sir, don't say that.'

'But I do say it, Mr Johnson. I am a private gentleman and I'm entitled not to have my name bellowed forth from the pulpit.'

'Mr Olden merely quoted a verse. He didn't say who wrote it.'

'And why not? Is my name not a respectable one?'

'Well, of course it is, and I think you're pleased.'

'I am most certainly not pleased.'

'Why are you smiling then?'

'It is a rictus, entirely involuntary. Would you like me to make you some toast?'

'Let me hang up your coat and I'll see to it.'

'Would you like me to poke the fire for you then?'

'No, sir,' Johnson said and he set about making the fire hot enough for toast. This was the way his cousin operated: he offered you a kindness in order that you would do it for him.

'Next thing you know,' Cowper said as he sank into the sofa, 'the rogues will be quoting Gilpin instead of the Gospel, the which would be a worse scandal than today's.'

'A scandal, well, that's sweet!' Johnson said. Normally his cousin would not hear mention of 'The Diverting History of John Gilpin'. It was just a year since the publication of the collected poems, an accomplishment Johnson had marked by reading aloud the entire two volumes, but Cowper had jibbed at hearing 'Gilpin', because he was ashamed of having written it, or so he said, although it was more likely, in Johnson's opinion, that he rejected the poem because it was too popular, as if he had not produced anything serious, which was irritating, but less so than when boring persons quoted back to him, with a twinkling air of discovering their own wit, lines that had long grown hackneyed, 'Variety's the spice of life', or 'I am monarch of all I survey', or worst of all, 'the cup that cheers but not inebriates', always in the singular when it should be plural, and invariably said when the blessed tea was being poured.

'Speaking of sweetness,' Cowper said, 'where is Miss Perowne?'

'Still a-bed and in a mighty ... She's in a mighty fit of sleeping. Will you have your tea now, sir, or will you wait on the toast?' Johnson had been going to say 'in a mighty fit of temper', but a second thought had stopped him.

'Poor lady,' Cowper said. 'I'll bring up a cup to her when she wakes. But as for myself, since it's a holiday I believe I'll sip a small glass of port. Will you join me, Mr Johnson?'

'No, thank you.'

Cowper had asked this a little defiantly, but Johnson at that moment did not mind defiance. For one thing, Cowper hardly ate anything at all these days except for toast sopped in port, so to keep up his strength he needed to drink a great deal, which he did. For another thing, Johnson was relieved to have avoided explaining why the Old Maid was in a mighty temper.

3

'*He* was talking to a snail!'

'Peggy, I implore you, keep your voice down,' Johnson said.

'And he knocked over the looking-glass. Did you not hear that? Does it not matter I was frightened half to death? It's not good enough.'

Although dawn had broken, it was still dark in the kitchen. Peggy drew her flannel dressing-gown more tightly about her gaunt person and began to cry. These tears, he thought, spring not from grief but mere vexation at being woken. 'There, there,' he said and patted her bony shoulder.

Miss Margaret Perowne was, in Johnson's opinion, a vinegary old whinger and a scold. Since he was, strictly speaking, her employer – she was paid, or rather fed and kept, to keep his household – he could have dismissed her. It was within his power to do so. On second thoughts, which Johnson had many of, there were few things in life that he wished to exercise less than power. Anyway, she was a kinswoman and – more to the point – Mr Cowper could not do without her, day or night. Especially night.

To Cowper she smelled of rosewater. Although it was underlaid with the acidity of withered virgins, the scent was exactly that of his mother. Almost every night he dreamed of Margaret and his mother as if they were one and the same person, and always they abandoned him. That was why Miss Perowne slept in a little settle bed beneath the bay window in his bedroom.

The disturbances that had brought her running down the stairs to cry at the kitchen table had been spread out over many hours of that New Year's Eve. For Cowper, they began as soon as he closed his eyes.

Immediately, he remembered, with the force of a blow from a fist, the sound of his mother's voice.

'Roses,' she was saying. 'Roses and violets. Pinks and jessamine.'

Then his arms were around her neck and he was kissing her cheek, the rosy warmth and glow and perfume of it.

'Here, you try,' she was saying from miles away. 'Try the jessamine.'

They were in her bed and she was showing him how to prick out onto paper the pattern of flowers on her brocaded dressing-gown.

'Jessamine,' he said. 'Jessamine. I like that word.'

While he concentrated, she reached under the pillow, took out a confectionery plum, unwrapped it from its twist of paper and touched it against the back of his neck.

'A sugar-plum,' he cried. 'My favourite.' And then she pressed his head against her soft breast and he closed his eyes.

When he opened them again, he was a sixty-nine-year-old man, lying rigidly on his back with a pain in his side. A beam of moonlight was shining onto his mother's portrait. It hung on the rail at the end of the bed so that it was the last thing he saw at night and the first thing he saw in the morning. His cousin Mrs Bodham, Anne Donne that was, had sent it as a gift ten years before. He remembered the date, the tenth of March 1790, as if it were Resurrection Day, and the piece of old white satin it came wrapped in were the winding-sheet of Lazarus, iridescent in the candlelit room. Until then, the only image he had of his mother was stored dimly in his memory, but this portrait, oil on copper, the work of some itinerant dauber, was her to the life, and he had crept up to it and kissed the cold metal with the same trepidation as if it were flesh and blood, the original she.

Closing his eyes, he was a boy again. Outside the house there was a noise. He got out of bed, went to the window and saw a great beast trampling the earth and striking sparks from the stones. It was a horse. A man slid off its back and the door of the house opened a path of light to him. His father was coming out carrying a lantern. The lantern was making the path. He heard his mother's voice briefly crying out from her distant bedroom.

Then he was sitting on the floor with baby John. Using a scarlet crayon, he was colouring in the pattern he had pricked out from Mother's dressing-gown.

Standing at the window was Nursie. She called him over. He did not want to go – there was a lump in his throat – but he went. Her skirts were jessamine red, like Mother's, but her smell was not so nice.

Outside, a long box was being lifted on to a cart. It was Mr Slocum's cart – Father called him Mr Slowcoach – but now it was draped in black cloth. And the people watching also wore black. But Father was wearing the long white shirt he called a surplice, and that meant Divine Worship.

'Where is Mummy?' he asked.

Nursie said, 'Your Mum is going to heaven. You can wave to her now.'

Mr Slocum's cart was moving off and the people were following, led by his father. William waved goodbye. Another word for heaven was paradise.

'My mother is dead, isn't she?'

'Yes.'

'When will she be coming back?'

'Oh, William, I can't say.' But when he demanded to know when, when, when, she said, 'Tomorrow.'

'Tomorrow?'

'I think so. Tomorrow. Yes, tomorrow.'

He heard laughing and turned and saw John scrawling all over his pattern with the crayon.

'John, you bold bad boy!' he cried, and ran to save what could not be saved.

He opened his old man's eyes. The moon was shining on his mother's portrait. Words came back to him:

Oh that those lips had language! Life has passed
With me but roughly since I heard thee last.
Those lips are thine — thy own sweet smile I see,
The same that oft in childhood solaced me;
Voice only fails, else how distinct they say,
'Grieve not my child, chase all thy fears away!'

It had cost him a great deal of argument with himself to write
'Voice only fails', but now he could not remember what it meant.
It made inexplicable sense, which was the way of poetry. Another
fragment troubled his memory:

My mother! When I learned that thou wast dead,
Say, was thou conscious of the tears I shed?

That was more than a question, it was a terrible truth: as soon
as she was dead, she knew his grief, but death allowed no signal to
pass between them. And yet he was no longer alone. In her portrait
Mother was moving.

Shawling himself with the eiderdown, he crawled to the end of
the bed. And stared and stared.

Miss Perowne stirred in her sleep and half-heard him say, 'It is
a most unseasonable time for you to be abroad.' Then she was fully
awake and he was speaking to her. 'It is New Year's Eve, my dear,
and where you are, you should not be.'

'What?' she said.

He was coming towards her with his hand held out, saying, 'He
is not a demon, Miss Perowne, but he would have drunk from my
mother's eye.'

She shrank back against the windowsill as she saw by the light
of the moon a snail in the palm of his hand. She knocked the snail
to the floor and sprang out of bed, scrambling for her dressing-
gown.

He wandered away muttering and, before she could get out of
the room, he banged into the mirror and it fell with a crash.

He did not notice the commotion. Sometimes he was fortunate
in the midst of chaos. He climbed into bed, burrowed back under
the bedclothes and forgot about the mirror. It was meant to be

propped up on a chair so that if he woke and felt forsaken, he could look at it through the curtains and check that Mr Johnson or Miss Perowne was watching over him. It was a visionary scheme to have come up with, but he forgot about it now.

4

There was another snail in his head. And a cart-horse was clopping along the road ...

No, they were bowling along in their whiskum. The horse stepped high in it. It was called a whiskum because it whisked them here and it whisked them there. He was wearing his plum-red velvet cloak and cap. He wore them going to school when his mother was alive, and now when he was going to a new school she was dead. These truths were linked somehow with the twist of the clasp that bound them and the crushed valleys of the textured folds of the velvet.

'Why is Berkhamstead called Great, Daddy?'

'Because it is grand.'

'And why is it grand?'

'Because the Cowpers are in it.'

We are great and we are grand, William thought.

'We have,' his father said, 'connections. The Cowpers are connected to the Donnes through your mother, and the Donnes are a very considerable family too.'

One Donne was a Dean. He said that again in his head. It went up and down the way hills did. The Dean of St Paul's was once John Donne. One Cowper was an Earl and a Lord Chancellor. One was Speaker of the House of Commons. Great Berkhamstead was a village, yet it had streets, and Markyate Street, the place they were going to, was also a village, so how could it have the name of only one street? 'Well,' his father said, 'I'm sure I don't know that.'

Then the whiskum turned sharply, whirling up an avenue to a brick building with diamond panes of glass in the windows. The knocker on the front door was a cat's face. His father banged the face. Almost instantly the door was opened by a slatternly young woman with a baby at her breast.

The hallway was cavernous and silent. The slattern led them across the hall and opened a door. In a high-ceilinged room two dozen buzzing boys were eating at a long table.

A giant was coming towards them. His name was Mr Pittman and his huge paw was warm, soft as a plush cushion. He said, 'What age did you say he was?'

'Six and a piece. He's an obedient child, but I'm at a loss to know what to do with him.'

'We'll take him out of himself. That's what he needs, taking out of himself. Now, Master William, it's time for tea. Tea and toast, and before you know where you are, we'll have you tucked up in bed.'

It was dark because he had the bedclothes over his head. Suddenly they were billowing back like sails and a piggish boy was standing over him. The other boys in the dormitory were quenching their candles and getting into bed.

'We have a sniveller,' the pig was laughing. 'The girly boy is snivelling. Cowper wants his mummy's titty. Titty, titty, titty!'

Then, as the pig heard the footsteps of the giant clumping up the stairs, he threw back the bedclothes over William. The bed was wet. His heart was pounding. It was not a dream.

But it was like a dream. When he opened his eyes, he saw a wildly running figure bearing down on him. The figure dived to the ground and slid past him, feet first, and then leaped up, holding his arm aloft triumphantly.

Only when the fielder was throwing the ball back towards the wicket did William realise that he was lying in the grass of the Paddock where the big boys were playing cricket. The giant was the umpire and he was calling out, 'Well played, mister. Well played.'

William walked away through the trees. The sun hurt his eyes.

The light showered like coins through the leaves, gold coins falling and green leaves spangling. That was a word he had learned in reading class. He liked the hiss, spit and ring of it. Ssss-pang-ling. A fieldmouse, foraging in the leaf-mould, heard a sudden voice and scurried off. William looked towards the voice and saw smoke rising from a dip in the ground. He went towards it. He had to. Often now he felt summoned.

Down in the dip the piggy boy, Bulstrode, and two other boys, Edwards and Slaughter, were sharing a clay pipe of tobacco.

'What's this?' Bulstrode said. 'A spy. I believe we've caught a spy.'

'A mighty small one,' Edwards said.

'You won't tell on us, will you, boy?' said Slaughter.

'He's not a boy, he's a girly girl.'

'He's a boy, Bulstrode,' Slaughter said.

'No, he ain't. Look at that cloak. Velvet! Velvet's for girlies.'

'Hey, boy, want a smoke?' This was Edwards, and he tried to put the pipe in William's mouth. It would not go in at first, but when it did, Slaughter said, 'He's a boy all right.'

'Let's have a look then. What? What?'

'No, Bulstrode,' Edwards said.

Bulstrode knocked Edwards aside with one arm. With the other he pulled William to him. 'He's too pretty to be a boy. Come on, Slaughter, let's have a look.'

Slaughter pinned him by the arms and Bulstrode dragged down his breeches.

Edwards said, 'Don't be afraid, Cowper. We only want to see your thing.'

Then his small-clothes too were down around his ankles, and when Slaughter let go of him, he fell over.

Startled by what they saw, the boys stood for a moment in silence.

'Well,' Bulstrode said, 'look at that.'

'Hell and damnation,' Edwards said.

'It's tiny,' Slaughter said. 'His tiny is tiny.'

'No bigger than a snail's foot,' Bulstrode said. 'Let's give it a pinch.'

Suddenly there was a roaring, and a slap from a great hand on the back of his pig-head sent Bulstrode flying on top of William.

Then the bad boys, covering their faces with their hands, were running out of the trees towards the school. William was high up and beneath him the giant's voice was roaring, 'I'll thrash you, ye miscreants! I'll thrash you, ye cursèd devils!'

William was in the giant's arms. He saw the chaps from the cricket team watching him, and his secret voice was saying in his head: I am a different boy, I am a different boy.

He was hot and he was cold at the same time, rising and falling at the bottom of the sea. The sea was the undulant air in the gloomy dormitory. The slattern was wiping his brow with a damp cloth. She smiled at him. He closed his eyes. His mother was sitting beside the bed reading to him from the Bible.

He sat up suddenly. His mother was gone and in her place was the slattern and, standing behind her, the giant.

'I know something, Mr Pittman,' William said.

'Yes? And what would that be?'

'I fear nothing that man can do unto me.' That was what his mother had been reading to him from the Bible.

And, as he spoke, a sudden beam of sunlight shone in through the window and illuminated him in the bed. The giant and the slattern opened their hands in a gesture of surprise.

'That, too, was biblical.'

The sound of his old voice startled him. The image had been in a book. It showed a woman surprised in her bath. Was it Judith? Or Susanna? And the man spying on her with his hands outstretched in surprise had a red cloak, a beard and was bald. Sixty-three years had passed and he had remembered a picture from a book of engravings seen once in his mother's bedroom.

His cry was an imitation of hers the night she died.

Childbirth had killed her. She had died giving birth to John, so who was the boy who had scribbled on his jessamine pattern? Mother had had six babies in nine years, but they had all died in infancy. It must have been Nursie's son. Or was it an imp, his first familiar? There was sorcery around him even then. But now all that he had was his memory and his own stale stink. He huddled under the bedclothes, but they were cold and clammy. Had he wet them? No, but he was young again. There was a carriage plunging through the darkness; the horse's hooves were striking sparks from the stones, trampling the enemy and crying Ha! Ha! to the trumpets. Bulstrode was being borne away into outer darkness, expelled from school, and he was following him, safe with Father in the whiskum.

But he had been seven when that happened. Now he was eight and there was another carriage creaking on the road, the horse clopping away into the distance. He was back in Great Berkhamstead, walking alone through Saint Margaret's cemetery carrying a lantern against the twilight. The sky was livid with low clouds. One last shaft of sunshine had broken through and was striking the hill beyond the town. The rooftops were leaden and dumb.

His foot struck something. In the long grass, laired as in a hare's nest — no, not nest, the proper word was form — was a yellowed skull. He picked it up. In the corner of one eye-socket there was a snail. He saw what the skull saw, and he thought, This is death, and this will happen to everyone else, but of all the people in the world, I, William Cowper, I alone am fated not to die.

With the lantern in one hand and the skull in the other, he was immortal.

No, that hadn't happened at Great Berkhamstead. It had happened in the cemetery near the Disneys' house. I was dizzy, so Daddy sent me to the Disneys. He liked the sound of that, then he hated it, but he couldn't stop saying it. He had been sent away for two whole years. There were tiny bothersome spots floating in front of his eyes like flies, and Mr and Mrs Disney were oculists. They made spectacles. Their house smelled of boric acid. Or was it peroxide? Mrs Disney despised him because he cried all day. But in the evening when she bathed his eyes she was motherly, and for that while he wasn't any longer the boy who came out from his bedroom onto the landing at the top of the tall stairs and stood there in the dark looking down at her. He hadn't called for help. He was only waiting. The candle she was holding threw a big shadow on the wall. When she saw him, she stopped in mid-stride, and he said, 'I want something.'

5

Arabella Lady Higham Ferrers wore a wig like a monstrous snail, no shell, only the body, dredged in grey powder. Her long bony face, thick with court plaster, was dead white, her thin mouth a rouged wound.

It was Morning Assembly at Westminster School and Vinny Bourne, the Latin Master, was taking prayers when a sedan chair was carried into the Great Hall by four drunken, sweating men. Vinny jumped down off the dais and ran to greet the visitor, waving his fingers in the air as if marmalade was stuck to them. The men stopped in the middle of the aisle and out of the chair stepped the horror.

'Howja do?' she said. 'Where's me son then?'

'Lord Higham Ferrers,' Vinny called. 'Your lady mother's here, milord. Come forward please.'

'He can't,' Cowper said.

'What?'

'He can't come forward. He's sick. In the infirmary.'

Downstairs in the kitchen Margaret Perowne said, 'Do you hear that, Mr Johnson? Am I expected to sleep with a maniac cackling in the middle of the night?'

Upstairs, snail-contracting with shame, he saw the expression on Mr Bourne's face as that awful lordling, mincing around in his mother's lavender silk dress, humiliated him. Vinny was the finest Latin poet since Propertius and he had not deserved such treatment.

In the back-room of Milligan's chophouse in Holborn, the Nonsense Club met for dinner, and Cowper was its chairman and secretary. Ned Thurlow, a schoolmate from Westminster, was reminiscing about Higham Ferrers.

'He was a bum-bluffer then and he's a bum-bluffer now. I saw him in Vauxhall Gardens not a week ago, wearing skirts. And I have it on good authority he's grown himself bosoms.'

Was that the night they adjourned to the Bethlehem Hospital? It was a long, low-ceilinged dungeon, smelling of urine, stale sweat and terror. A madwoman on all fours played horse for a dwarf riding on her back. Her breasts spilled out of her dress.

'Look at those titties,' Ned Thurlow said.

'Poor beasts,' William Russell said.

'Poor beasts, my cods,' Cowper said.

Afterwards he and Russell had walked arm-in-arm as far as Southampton Row. He was not insensible of the misery of the poor captives they had seen in Bedlam, but their madness had such a humorous air, it was impossible not to be entertained. But he was angry with himself for being so vulgar, imitating that thug Thurlow. Disappointed, too, that his new friend Russell wouldn't come in and meet Theadora and Harriot. They were his first cousins, glorious girls, odd as ants, and, why, even if it was three o'clock in the morning, they didn't give a straw for sleeping. But Russell had given him a strange look and left him alone in the street. Still, he had agreed to come to Theadora's birthday party.

'You jig like a dancing-master,' Uncle Ashley said. 'Where on earth did you learn it?'

'I taught him,' Theadora said.

'So she did, Uncle, and you must allow no dancing bear was ever so genteel or half so *dégagé* as myself.'

'Young women nowadays,' Ashley said, 'they do whatsoever they please. England is a paradise for them.'

'A paradise for horses and a hell for women,' Theadora said

sharply. 'Now, if you don't mind, I'll show my mount how to make a graceful exit.'

She dragged him away into the dining-room. The chandelier had been extinguished and on the damask-draped table the few remaining candles were guttering out. She scooped a glass of punch from the silver bowl and drained it.

'Do you know, despite appearances, I think my poppy approves of you.'

'He's a very tolerant soul.'

'Ah. And does the nephew approve of his cousin?'

'He likes her, despite appearances.'

'Yes, they always counted against me dreadfully.'

'But the dress does make up for a lot.'

'Does it?'

'It does. He, you know, adores your dress.'

'Does he then?'

He dropped to his knees. 'He kisses the hem of your garment.'

Theadora held out her foot. 'And the ankle?'

'Dear ankle.' He kissed it.

She raised the skirt to her knee. '*Et le petit genou aussi?*'

He stood up. She kissed him on the mouth. But after a few seconds she said, 'Do you call that a proper kiss?'

'As I'm not receiving it, I can't judge.'

'Then I shall have to teach you.' She took hold of his ears and drew his face to hers, but then the door was opened, light streamed through it and Miss Perowne and Mr Johnson came in with a candle each. Did they know? Had someone told them?

Miss Perowne sat on the edge of the bed and Mr Johnson in the chair. They were warning him. But her gaze wavered as Thea's never did.

During all the summers they had spent together on the beaches of Norfolk, Theadora had never sought attention, but then she had suddenly grown shockingly beautiful and he could not look at her straight, especially now that she had stolen into his room in Southampton Row in the dead of night and was sitting on the edge of his bed.

'What's the matter, sugar-plum?' she said, lying down beside him. 'Haven't you ever had a lady in your bed? I'm sure you've had harlots aplenty.'

'Thea, please don't look at me like that.'

'And your poor little hand. It's like a leaf. And so cold. Sssshh. Don't you know what I want you to do? *Doucement*, Billy, *doucement*. Don't you know how warm a lady's bosom is?'

She was whispering in his ear, almost kissing it. But when she put his hand on her breast, he pulled it back as if it had been bitten by a serpent and flailed himself, ridiculously, out of the bed. He stood with head bowed, arms pressed tight against his sides. Although she was bewildered, and offended too, a cold part of her eye noticed a detail and the correspondingly cold part of her intelligence said: I can see his thumbs; he doesn't even make a fist like a man.

Mr Johnson sighed, 'Please, sir, do get back into bed.'

'What *is* he doing now?' Miss Perowne was saying.

He was running away into the bushes and trees that were growing thickly by the Thames at Windsor. Ahead of him, he saw Theadora and Harriot. They were standing at the mouth of a cave. He was fearful and they embraced him. Theadora had her arm round his waist and her forehead was touching his shoulder. Both girls wore Grecian robes. Harriot's face was blotted out by a black veil. On his own head was a turban, with ribbons flowing down his back. He held out his fist and opened it. On his palm was a snail.

Theadora was too afraid to look but Harriot took the snail and leaned into the cave, offering it to the darkness.

'I'm never too afraid!' Thea said. 'Anyway, the snail should properly have been an eye.' The dream was classical. She knew these things. But he had translated Vinny Bourne's poem about the snail, and it was true to the life:

> Give but his horns the slightest touch,
> His self-collecting power is such
> He shrinks into his house with much
>
> > Displeasure.

The stone in the ring he gave her was a carnelian.

'A what?' his father said.

'A carnelian. The engraving depicts Omphale draped in the skin of a lion. The reference is to Hercules, meaning, I suppose, myself.'

'Goodness,' Thea said, 'what an educated young person you are!'

'It was you who designed it,' Cowper said. 'And your Greek is better than mine, almost.'

'Excuse me,' his father said. 'Am I to understand that this signifies you propose marrying your cousin?'

'Oh, I expect so.'

'I never heard such nonsense in my life. You haven't two ha'pennies to rub together.'

Theadora said, 'He's going into the Temple to be a nice fat lawyer, ain't you, William? And if he doesn't like that, you'll make him Clerk of the Parliaments, won't you, Poppy?'

'*I* am the Clerk,' Uncle Ashley said. 'Do you think my father paid £18,000 for the patent in order that I should give it to my nephew?'

'No, but there are other positions. The Clerkship of the Journals is a nice one. It would suit him. He's fanatically grammatical.'

'Well, I don't know about that, but I do have the giving of it.'

'Blessed are those who give,' Cowper said.

'Yes,' Uncle Ashley said, ' but the present incumbent has to die first.'

'Why then,' Cowper said gaily, 'I shall pray for him to be taken up into the light *quam celerimme*.'

His father frowned. 'Blasphemous boy.'

Theadora kissed him. 'You're so kind, Uncle, and I'm sure you will always keep an eye out for my Billy.'

'He wouldn't dream of it,' Cowper said.

They smiled at each other. They were so quick together.

'It's you, Theadora, who are the dreamer,' her father said. 'Marriage is a serious business, my girl. What on earth would you do with your time?'

'Why, I'd wash all day and ride on the great dog all night.'

Theadora sometimes said the wildest things, and even in the presence of a clergyman like her Uncle John she could be outrageously ribald. But forty years later, huddled in his bed, Cowper was still wondering what she had meant. And how was it she had recognised, as no one else had, that he was in some respects the Great Beast?

His memory whorled sickeningly, like rainbowed oil in water.

'Rebecca, Rebecca!' he cried out and woke Miss Perowne again.

'What? What?' she cried from her own nightmare, but then she slipped back to sleep.

Rebecca Marryat was the real Great Beast. His mother had hardly been four years dead when a sour, crippled, ugly widow was put in her place. Father had betrayed Mother. That was unforgivable. Never to be forgiven. Being sent away to Westminster School had been a deliverance out of Egypt. And then Rebecca had died. She had left everything she owned to be divided equally between him and his brother John. It was a division, he told Harriot, not very unlike the splitting of a hair.

But Father had bought him chambers in the Inner Temple in London when he had qualified at law. That was compensation, but not atonement.

On his first night there he had shivered between musty sheets as he was shivering now in East Dereham. But then a marmalade cat had jumped up onto the bed and lain beside him. In the other room a cinder from the meagre fire fell into the grate and a cold draught came down the chimney.

Before leaving, his father had presented him with the family Bible. On the flyleaf he had written a verse from Matthew, *If thine eye offend thee, pluck it out*. It was a strange choice.

'I haven't offended you, Father, have I?' he had asked.

'No, this is a general truth. You're a light-headed boy, but your heart is good.'

'Well, if my head is light, I shall float it away like a thistledown.'

'What?'

'On the other hand, although I could spare an eye, if I dispose of my noddle I should be literally dead.'

'You seem to think you can mock Scripture and doubt everything else.'

'Well, I do doubt that Scripture advocates suicide. After all, a chap who commits self-slaughter can hardly be saved, can he?'

'Who knows these things? A man may kill himself to save himself. Perhaps it is God's will. Indeed it must be.'

Cowper saw into his father. He was fundamental and strange.

'Now,' he said, 'let us pray.'

They went down on their knees and recited the Lord's Prayer to the staring cat and the collapsing embers.

That was melancholy. The Inner Temple was miserable. And he was, as ever, briefless, a lawyer without the law. But most melancholy of all was the separation from Theadora.

He had told Russell, 'Uncle Ashley effected the closure for monetary reasons, but there were more reasons than those that turn on a coin; for we, and I more than she, are gauzy creatures and couldn't hang so long in the air of dreaming and not find a dismal awakening.'

This had been borne in on him most clearly when he went down to Berkhamstead to bury his father. Then, and not until then, he had felt for the first time that he and his native place were fated to be disunited for ever. So too with Theadora.

'We see each other, but rarely, and prefer not to, and are friends,' he told Russell and, really, Russell was a good consoler. Almost every day they walked round the city talking and laughing, and not always nonsensically either. Russell was modest, upright, joyful, and he despised cynicism. Besides, with his stiff brush of blond hair, his muscular athlete's body and startlingly white teeth, he was lovable. William loved Russell, yes, and he had told him so too. And he had invited him down to Kent to meet Harriot's fiancé, Lord Hesketh.

He could hear his name being called faintly in the distance and ran towards the edge of the cliff and the abrupt blue sky. It occurred to him that if he kept on running, he could float off like a sea-bird and hang in the air. Beneath him he saw Russell raising the sail on a small yacht. He hollowed his hands around his mouth and shouted, 'Wait, wait. That's our picnic basket, you robber.'

Russell shouted back, 'I'm going to swim first.'

But Cowper did not hear because Harriot was saying, 'Do come back from the edge, cousin.'

'I'm not afraid of a little cliff, Harriot.'

'You are afraid of everything, William, and the only thing that's frightened of you is money. What are you going to do about these debts of yours?'

By the time the sun had gone down, a gale was blowing. Out in the bay fishermen in boats lit by lanterns were casting nets for Russell's body. On the shore a fire had been lit and was being fed with driftwood by barefooted boys. Showers of sparks rose and were blown against the cliff.

Cowper was calm. It was true, as Harriot said, that he was afraid of everything, and yet when danger came he was not frightened. Disaster is like fast bowling, he thought: one must look at it slowly. There might be an essay in that conceit for *The Connoisseur*. The magazine had already printed his pieces on Billy Suckling, the mollycoddle, and on Christopher Ironside, who kissed a girl and found his upper lip transfixed with a large corkin pin hidden in her mouth.

'William.'

'Yes, Harriot?'

'You're talking to yourself.'

He was about to tell her what he was thinking when he heard screaming. Women, their arms stretched wide and their shawls flying behind them, were running along the shore. A rowing boat had come up unseen out of a deep trough and was riding broadside on the crest of a huge wave, spilling men into the foam. He saw Russell for a moment, seeming to stand upright, his head to one side, quizzically, before he was thrown down again into the water, arms loose as a rag doll's.

Cowper dashed into the retreating wave. It was like trying to run across a falling cliff of stones and water. Immediately his feet were swept away from under him. While he was falling, the capsized boat whipped round and, as it came towards him, he felt its weight and suddenness as a great and indifferent force. Then he had hold of Russell, the keel of the boat was passing over them and a new wave threw them back into the dribbling cliff. Men ran through the surf, high-stepping like horses, and dragged them clear.

He lay trembling on the sand. All his strength had vanished in a few seconds. Beside him, Russell's face was peaceful. From his mouth a few strands of seaweed hung loosely, like bootlaces. He tried to clear them away, but when he pulled, long lengths of the weed came out with a gush of water, and kept on coming.

Quietly, quietly, he slid out of bed, wrapped himself in a sheet and crept down the stairs to his study. Yes, the book was where it was meant to be. He sat at the table and by dawn's early light read the passage.

> Still, still I mourn with each returning day
> Him snatched by fate in early youth away
> And her through tedious years of doubt and pain
> Fixed in her choice and faithful – but in vain.

When he looked up he saw himself in the mirror over the fireplace. Standing behind him were two men. One of them was Mr Clarke, his lackey in the Inner Temple, a carbuncled ancient with a clay pipe clamped between blackened teeth.

'God's truth, sir, he'd pass for a girl,' Clarke said, hacking off his locks with a tailor's big scissors. 'Look at him. I've seen more meat on a butcher's apron. When did you last eat a chop? Tell your uncle that.'

'Yesterday.'

'Hah! Yesterday! Well, he must have found it under the bed. To my certain knowledge he's hardly been out of here this twelve months. Do you know my opinion?'

'No, Mr Clarke, but I believe I soon will.' Uncle Ashley was irritated.

'In my humble opinion, he's a natural-born idjit, like all the Cowpers.'

'Thank you, Mr Clarke. I am obliged to you.'

It was entirely wrong to say that he had not left his rooms for a twelve-month. Although he mourned Russell, he saw his remaining friends often enough. He had written for *The Connoisseur*, quite amusingly. He had read a great many books. Every day, or almost, he went walking, thither and yon. And now, unexpectedly, here was Uncle Ashley, paying him a visit and – really, it was quite comical – having to put up with being insulted by his lackey.

When Clarke had removed himself, Ashley said, 'I called to

the courts, but they told me you were at home, so I came over *instanter.*'

'Is something wrong?'

'On the contrary, my boy, your prayers have been answered.'

'Prayers, what prayers?'

'You may be able to afford a decent suit of clothes anyway. Look at you, you vagabond.'

'Uncle, please, tell me what you're talking about.'

'My dear boy,' Ashley paused, reluctant to hurry the moment of revelation. 'My dear nephew, the Clerk of the Journals has died.'

'What?'

'Died. He's defunct. Dead. Gone to the bosom of Abraham. Left a vacancy. It's one of the neatest little sinecures in all England, and I have the giving of it, and I mean you to have it. What do you say to that now?'

He made no reply. Clarke looked in the door and stared at him. His uncle was staring too. They had come to judge him for wishing a man dead. Time and all other dimensions, including the air, had turned solid. Motes of dust in a beam of sunlight ceased their wandering. For a moment he saw himself in all the power he had prayed for, transfixed in the authority of the Temple, and the glance from his eye was a great silvery wooden beam.

'Have you nothing to say?'

He had, but the words were unutterable: 'It's a judgement on me. And I shall die for it.'

He shrugged off the sheet and went over to the mirror. Then he had been a Samson with a ridiculous haircut. Now he was a Samson wearing a stocking nightcap with a bobble on the end.

6

'Don't tremble, man, you're not going to be hanged,' Uncle Ashley said. 'It's the merest formality, I assure you. At least you look the part.' He flicked an imaginary mote of dust off the silk lapel of his nephew's new navy blue coat.

As they were ushered into the office, the Lord Chancellor, dressed in a gold-embroidered gown, looked up from his desk. It was an enormous room and in the distance higher officials and lowly clerks sat at a long table writing.

'Ah, Cowper,' the Lord Chancellor said.

'Lord Chancellor.'

'I take it this is your boy?'

'Nephew, milord. William.'

'Yes. How old are you, William?'

'Thirty-one.'

'What's that?'

'He's thirty-one, milord.'

'And where were you born?'

'Born? I was born, sir, I was born in Great Berkhamstead. In Hertfordshire.'

'Indeed, that's where it is. You have Latin and Greek?'

'Yes, milord. Both. I have both.'

'Excellent. Well, Ashley, I'd say he'll do. However ...'

The Lord Chancellor had risen from his desk and come round

to inspect the candidate. Now he took Ashley by the arm and drew him aside. As they talked, Cowper was aware of the clerks watching him. One of them, almost a boy but wizened and anciently sly, approached the desk to put some documents on it. He whispered, 'You have Latin.'

'Beg pardon.'

'*Respice finem.*'

'Excuse me?'

'Look to the end, Mr Placeman.'

Cowper turned to see Uncle Ashley and the Lord Chancellor looking at him and shaking their heads.

As they were being driven out of the gates of the Palace of Westminster, Uncle Ashley was saying, 'You have enemies. That's natural in this world. A party has formed against your appointment. Rest assured, you're of no account to them personally. It's me they wish to drag down. My power, my privilege. I have the giving of this clerkship and they may go hang if they think I'll surrender it.'

'Who are these people, Uncle?'

'God knows and I can guess. But it's politic, I think, to keep you in the dark. What you don't know can't hurt you.'

'But what I don't know does hurt me.'

'Don't talk nonsense, boy. All you have to do is go down to the House for a few days, read the Journals and in no time you'll have the whole thing off pat.'

'Pat? For what reason?'

'For the examination. It's the simplest thing in the world. No writing. A *viva.*'

'A *viva voce*? An interview?'

'I do believe that's what *viva voce* means.'

'Forgive me, Uncle, I am a little dismayed. Who is to be the examiner? Not the Lord Chancellor himself?'

'If only, if only. He's on our side. No, it's before the Bar of the House.'

'Before the House of Lords? Before the whole House of Lords?'

'Have you discovered some virtue in repetition, William? A thing doesn't double its meaning because you say it twice.'

'Forgive me, Uncle.'

'Anyway, when the time comes, you'll find that the most of their lordships will be asleep, particularly if it's after luncheon. In any event, it's child's play; there's no law involved, and you have a good six months to mug it up.'

'Six months!'

'Long enough for me to flush out these enemies, and when I do, I shall smite them, hip and thigh.'

7

The barber was stropping his razor on a leather strap. Cowper, his face covered with lather, watched the bright steel intently.

The barber began shaving him. 'Winter's in the air,' he said. 'The whoreson will be on us before we know it.'

'I fear so.'

'I do hate the season. I hate that black wind that comes up the river. Still, what can we do?'

A customer sitting with a towel over his face said, 'We could go mad.'

'We could, we could.'

'There's comfort in madness.'

'How is that, sir?' Cowper asked.

The towel was lifted and he saw an old man with a drooping moustache and a drinker's blood-injected eyes.

'A madman, we say, is out of his mind. That's a comfortable place to be.'

The barber chuckled. 'You're a philosopher, sir, a philosopher.'

'I am, but I'm a blue one. I have the blue mulligrubs.'

'The blue mulligrubs?' Cowper said. 'I think I know them.'

'Know them?' the barber said. 'They've eaten us all. But I have a cure for those gentlemen. Look here.' He opened a drawer and took out a small box.

'What is it?' Cowper asked.

'It's from Africa, sir. Hold out your hand there.' He poured brown pellets into Cowper's palm. 'Hashish, that's what they are; hashish pills, sir. The blackamoors use them. Fourpence a piece. A sure cure for the melancholy.'

Haggard and unshaven, he was standing at his bedroom window holding up a lighted candle and staring through the flame at the cold red disk of the rising sun. Everything was shining and lifted up.

Smiling to himself, he went into the drawing-room. On the floor lay an open trunk packed with clothes and books. He put the candle on the table and sat down to look at it. An hour later, as it guttered down to smoke, Clarke came in carrying a jug of hot water. 'Up early, are we?'

'With the lark, Mr Clarke,' he said and burst out laughing.

Clarke stared at him, then put the jug on the table and went into the bedroom.

Cowper observed the steam coming out of the jug, thinking, steam and smoke, entirely different, yet the same.

Clarke returned. 'The bed hasn't been slept in,' he said accusingly.

'Really?'

Clarke indicated the trunk. 'What's this?'

'That? *Ça c'est un grand valise.* Or is it feminine? *Une grande.*'

'Where are you off to?'

'That, Mr Clarke, is a secret I alone have the knowledge of. But you I shall tell. I'm going to France. It's the only way. *La langue* is a difficulty, I admit that. Why is it the word *langue* always reminds me of a cat's tongue? But I suppose if I enter a silent order, I won't have to speak French.'

'What are you blithering about?'

'It's quite clear, Mr Clarke. I cannot present myself before the Lords, so I shall cross the Channel and become a Papist.'

'You a Papist?'

'Yes, yes, yes. Roman Catholicism is an abomination, but you see, they have monkeries. One can become a monk and withdraw from the world. It's quite the most honourable solution for me.'

'You've been eating those pills again.'

'Oh, I have, Mr Clarke, I have. The sensation is very pleasant I assure you. It's like, it's like . . .'

Clarke went into the bedroom and found the box of hashish pills, almost empty. He heard Cowper calling and went back to him.

'Mr Clarke, I've found the . . . You disappeared and I found the words. The sensation is like having a thousand butterflies under one's skin.'

Clarke pinched the flame of the candle with thumb and fore-finger, sat down and put the pill-box on the table.

'Mr Cowper, I'm taking these away from you. They're the devil's potion.'

Cowper stared aghast at the smoking wick. 'The devil's potion. Do you think so? Yes, I believe you're right. What shall I do? What shall I do, Mr Clarke? I'm all one wound. I don't know what to do.'

'Go to bed, man. Go to bed. I'll sit with you a while.'

'Oh, Mr Clarke, I want to thank you. You've always shown me the greatest consideration. And I'm such a selfish and ungrateful wretch.'

He took Clarke's liver-spotted, horn-nailed hand and kissed it, holding it against his lips to still the trembling that now possessed him.

The next day he felt better. But it had taken, he thought, more courage to swallow the pills than to stop swallowing them. The lifting of depression at the start, the disappearance of it into a glowing cloud of fine distinctions, which were amusing by reason of their being so momentary, and the delicious slumbers that followed, all these had soon faded and been replaced by insomnia and a sense of having entered a mysterious region of dreadful knowledge.

> A little onward tend thy guiding hand
> To these dark steps, a little further on.

That was John Milton's voice and he had followed it until he knew what Milton saw, and saw what Milton knew:

O dark, dark, dark, amid the blaze of noon,
Irrecoverable dark, total eclipse
Without all hope of day.

But Mr Clarke had been right to take away the drug. Fleeing to France to become a monk for the sake of silence was impractical: one could not hide amongst the enemy. And now that he had stopped the hashish, he could read Milton without being too afraid.

'Here we are, Mister C. Hot chocolate and a roll.'

Cowper closed the book. The waiter in Richard's coffee-house, where he usually took his meals, was serving him breakfast. At mid-morning, the place was almost empty, and yet the only other customer, a respectable old man, had chosen to sit at the next table.

'When is our big day then?' the waiter said.

'Next week. This day week in fact.'

'Not to worry, you'll fly through it.'

'Me, fly?' Cowper laughed. 'Which way I fly is hell; myself am hell.'

The waiter looked at him strangely, but the man at the next table said, 'Unless I'm greatly mistaken, that's Milton.'

'It is, sir.'

'Can you go on?'

'I have it here.' Cowper opened the Milton, removed the bookmark, a piece of House of Lords embossed notepaper, and showed the man the lines he already knew by heart:

Me, miserable! which way shall I fly
Infinite wrath, and infinite despair?
Which way I fly is hell; myself am hell;
And in the lowest deep a lower deep,
Still threatening to devour me, opens wide,
To which the hell I suffer seems a heaven.

'Is that not a capital passage? Capital! Allow me to shake your hand, sir. It's a pleasure to meet a young man so familiar with our greatest poet. I wager you write verse yourself.'

'Mr Cowper's been in the papers, sir.'

'I knew it. You said the line with such conviction, I knew it on the instant.'

'Oh yes?'

'One can recognise a gift without having it. Such is the world, sir, such is the world. And yet we can fly. That's our final freedom.'

'How do you mean?'

The man's face now seemed terribly large and Cowper saw that one eye was blue and the other one brown.

'I mean we can fly out of this hell if we've a mind to.'

'Can we?'

'If we have the courage. But that's a Roman virtue. Young men nowadays, they're not noble, not like you, sir. Poltroons, the lot of them. Poltroons clinging to life, *Eyeless in Gaza at the mill with slaves* as the poet puts it, and not a Samson amongst them.'

Cowper stood up suddenly, saying, 'You've given me a gift, sir. And I thank you for it. Indeed, I thank everyone,' and rushed out.

Then it was evening. For nearly an hour he had been walking up and down outside an apothecary's shop in Lambeth. He went in.

'If you please, sir, I should like to purchase some laudanum.' His voice was high-pitched, a bat-squeak.

'Laudanum? What for?' The apothecary had a bark like a dog. He was grinding medicine in a mortar with a pestle.

'What for? I believe — that is I have been told — it mitigates any pain.'

'Aye, it does that. But do you know what laudanum is, sir?'

Cowper did know. He had read what Paracelsus said it was, a compound of gold leaf and pearls, and that was part of its seductiveness, but to be Roman was to be silent too. And now he was silent.

At last the apothecary spoke, 'It's a tincture, sir, a tincture of opium, and opium is a deadly draught. It's not small-beer or ginger-wine.' He stopped grinding. 'How much do you want?'

'I don't know. How much will I need?'

'How much is safe, sir, that's the question. A small amount is safe. A large amount is safer still. Do you see what I mean? I think you do, and I think you don't, so I'll give you the half-pint.'

He reached under the counter and brought up a brown bottle with a label on which was stamped a skull and crossbones. Cowper took the bottle and headed for the door.

'That has to be paid for, sir. This isn't Liberty Hall, you know. Everything has to be paid for here.'

Cowper turned. As he fumbled for his pocket, the bottle slipped out of his shaking hands, but he juggled with it for a long moment, all wrists and elbows and sideways heels, and prevented it from smashing onto the sawdusted floor.

The apothecary smiled at him in a ghastly way.

Six days to go. It was too soon. The bottle was in his breast-pocket, a small weight against his heart, its touch cold and warm. Dead-alive. When he took his hand out of his pocket and opened his eyes, Theadora was walking around the drawing-room inspecting the furnishings with distaste. She had brought him presents: a caraway seed cake and a bottle of old Madeira. In twenty minutes she had nibbled a small piece of the cake and drunk three glasses of the syrupy wine.

'I'm not suprised you wouldn't invite me here. What a dingy cave. But now you can buy yourself a *maisonette* on the river. And a little boat. Then you can sail down to Westminster and cock a snook at the lawyers.'

'If I pass the examination.'

'Of course you'll pass, William. You have more brains than a gooseberry.'

'And about the same consistency at the moment.'

'Moment, moment, why do you let moments bother you? I don't. I don't let any thing or any person bother my head.'

'I can see that.'

'Can you? Can you indeed? Well, Poppy says the honour of the Cowper family is in your hands. So you'll do the honourable thing. You always do.'

'Not always.'

'Well ... I'm not sorry about us, Billy. Are you?'

'Yes. I think both of us are, but you shouldn't be.'

'I said I'm not, though it might be thought I have the more time for sorrow, being as I am an idler. Idle as a needle in a box. But I'm not the seamstress type, as you know.'

'I know.'

'Let them sew on their own blasted buttons is what I say. But you, darling, what reason have you for sorrow? Why look so wan?'

'It's the thought of the future. I've always been the dupe of tomorrow, even from a child.'

'Oh, you poor little beast. Don't think of yourself so much.'

'Yes, it's selfishness, I know that.'

'You're not selfish, Mister C; you're bothered, that's all. Think about money, think about happiness, think even about me. They're prizes worth having, ain't they?' She kissed him on the cheek, then broke away to continue her inspection, opening the door to the bedroom. 'Hey, lookee here! The monk's cell. Is this where you gamahuche the boys?'

He didn't know what the word meant, nor did he want to. He waited for a moment, then went in after her. She was sitting on the edge of the bed, head bent, hands in her lap, and when she spoke her voice was different.

'You do like me, William, don't you? Say you like me.'

'Thea.' That was all he could say.

'Look how bright the moon is,' she said. It was bright, and her profile, now turned to it, was lit up like a newly minted silver coin. But then, as she turned away, her features were invisible, and again the tone of her voice was different, lower and yet somehow business-like. 'You can examine me if you want.'

She lay back on the bed. The moonlight flooded down the length of her body. She clasped her hands behind her head, and again her voice changed, this time to mockery, but mockery with a plea in it: 'It won't take long. I promise you that.'

For a moment she was abandoned to his gaze. But he did not move. He could not. She stood up, even more businesslike now than before, but as she went past him, she put her hand, fleetingly, on his cheek.

He was lying, old, in his bed. And he remembered her helpless caress. It was too condensed for words, delivered, incapable of being returned.

The cat was watching him. Its eyes were like Theadora's: dark honeyed almonds. Someone was tapping lightly on the door.

'William, it's me. Let me in.'

'Theadora? Just a moment.'

He got out of bed. What was this? The key was in the lock and he turned it.

Theadora was standing there holding up a lantern. Her hair was loose and she was dressed in a loose gown.

'It's late, Thea. It's too late, darling.'

She laughed and brushed past him. Now her voice was unacountably coarse, 'This won't take long, I promise you. I promise you that.'

In the darkness of the drawing-room he saw a rat sitting on the table. Its eye was gleaming. He closed the door and turned the key. The key was cold, as cold as glass, and yet alive. When he turned, he saw that Theadora was lying on the bed. There was no moonlight now, only the yellow glow of the lantern which she had hung on the bedpost. It glistened on the silk of her gown, a silk so thin he could see the outline of her legs through it and where her legs met a blot too dark to be merely a fold in any material. One breast had freed itself, or been freed, and he could see that she was touching its brown-pink nubbled nipple with the long oval tips of her fingers. Now she was pinching it hard and saying, 'Gamahuche me, boy. Gamahuche me, boy.'

Then he saw that her other hand was quivering between her thighs. All her body was quivering, and her head was moving back and forth on the pillow as if trying to free itself, and she was saying, 'Kiss me, kiss me. Say my name, say my name.'

But as the commands dissolved to a sobbing, his attention was attracted by another sound, a laughing that became a cackling that drowned out Theadora's pleas. A creature was sitting on the bedside table. It was hunkered down like some kind of monkey and its face too was monkey-like, needle-teeth bared in a desperate grin. Theadora was shuddering on the bed and groaning, 'It's you, Billy, it's you.' And the beast's face was indeed his.

A violent pain pierced him, like the turning of a knife in his innards. He woke up and threw back the bedclothes. There was a small stain on the sheet, still wet. He knew what it was; this had happened before in his nightmares. It had happened once when he was fourteen, shinning up a flagpole at Margate, and afterwards he had felt weak and ashamed. Then he had not known what it was, but at Westminster there was a time he saw boys rubbing each other in the privies, and he understood that this was what the Chaplain had warned against: 'robbing yourself of your seed'. It was quite wrong. William Russell had been a good fellow and no robber, but he remembered one night after a Nonsense Club dinner – they had been talking, deliciously, long into the night – how strangely Russell had laughed when he told him he had never done such a thieving thing. The sin of Onan.

There was no sign of Theadora. How was it she had gone and then come back? He got out of bed and went into the drawing-room. Of course, it was not a rat's eye he had seen but the gleam off the bottle of Madeira on the table. The bottle was empty. She had drunk it and gone away laughing. He had walked with her across Pump Court to her carriage, led by a link-boy with a lantern. The driver and the boy watched as she embraced him, violently, for a moment, got into the carriage and sat there looking straight ahead, not turning to wave as she was driven away.

He remembered and rushed back into the bedroom. Under the bed his fingers touched something cold, glassy, alive. It was the bottle with the skull and crossbones.

How long had he lived with that two-boned man laughing at him?

Clutching the bottle, he lay down, pulled the covers over his head and fought to reassemble the broken pieces of what had happened.

He had gone for breakfast to Richard's. It was wonderful to be hungry. He had ordered tea, toast and two eggs. That had a nicely comic sound to it. As he was contemplating the taste of the words, the waiter came over.

'Mr Nunally said you'd be interested in this.' 'This' was a newspaper.

'Mr Who?'

'Mr Nunally, sir. The gentleman from Didcot you were talking to last week, sir. He was in yesterday.'

A piece of verse on the bottom of a page in the newspaper was ringed with red crayon. In the margin, written in black ink, were the words, 'A cricket is a stool but a fool wrote this. And the nobility, where is that?' The verse was headed, 'A Receipt to Cure a Love Fit'.

> Tie one end of a rope fast over a beam,
> And make a slip-noose at the other extreme;
> Then just underneath let a cricket be set,
> On which the lover must manfully get;
> Then over his head let the snecket be got,
> And under one ear be well settled the knot.
> The cricket kicked down, let him take a fair swing;
> And leave all the rest of the work to the string.

The waiter, who had hurried to rescue the bread, which had fallen off the trivet into the brazier, now felt something strike him on the back, and when he turned around with the blackened toast smoking on a fork in his hand, he saw the newspaper lying at his feet and his favourite customer standing at the door onto the street, shouting, 'Your cruelty shall be gratified. You shall have your revenge.'

That was not the last of the final signs. A carriage had taken him to Tower Wharf. Why had he asked the cabdriver to wait? That was unreasonable and, worse, unmannerly. But manners no longer mattered. What mattered was finding stones with which to fill his pockets. Then there was a flight of mossy steps and he was, carefully, clumping down towards the brown swirling waters. But a dark man in a dark cloak looked down at him, shook his head and walked away. No, if he went out with the tide, he could not come back. Somehow coming back was a necessary condition of suicide.

Then he was back in the carriage. It was jostling him from side to side, like a sweetmeat in a jar. The laudanum ran down his chin and stained his shirt. His mouth would not open. Some force, some third hand, drove down the bottle into his lap. Again and again he tried to drink. Each time the third hand prevented him.

Then he was in the Temple. He locked the bedroom door and poured the laudanum into a bowl. Tore off his coat. A button on his shirt hung on a thread and its two eyes watched him.

'Oh, you coward; you rank coward!'

That was his own voice reproaching him for being afraid of the pain of death. Not death itself but the mere pain of it. And still, another voice, also his own, was saying, 'Think what you are doing, consider and live.'

As he lay there musing, he heard the outer door opening. He hid the bowl, unlocked the bedroom door, coughing to mask the sound, walked casually into the drawing-room and said, 'Ah, Mr Clarke, good day to you, or is it evening? I was resting, as you see. How is the weather out? Very cold I think.'

Clarke said, 'Three shirts, four pairs of drawers, assorted stockings and the nankeen breeches, sponged.' He put the laundry, neatly folded and ironed, on a chair beside the dead fire. Then he said, 'The examination is nigh.'

'It's tomorrow. Long threatening comes at last.'

'Have you a needle?'

'Beg pardon?'

'A needle and thread. That button's hanging there. Or do you want me to do your mending and darning, as well as everything else?'

'No thank you, Mr Clarke. I shall see to it. And I'm most obliged to you for the laundry.'

Clarke went out. William was indeed obliged to this messenger from the laundrywoman, this cleaner of the privy-closet, this maker of fires, this barber, this bearer of hot water. And to think that he should thank him for his kindness with a horrible crime. Furious with disgust, he ran into the bedroom, lifted the lid of the commode and poured the bowl of laudanum into the urine there. Foul waters both! A witch's brew! He went down on his knees and found the empty bottle beneath the bed. The two-boned man, what was he but the heraldic sign of Satan? And now, there he was sailing through the evening air, turning over and over, on his way back

> To bottomless perdition, there to dwell
> In adamantine chains and penal fire.

Milton knew how deep hell was, for no sound issued from the bottle as it smashed on the ground, though a passing gentleman was startled and looked up. But as soon as his eyes were raised — sooner — the window was closed. Ah ha! Ah ha! Too quick for him!

The clock struck six. No time to be lost. His cousin Joe Hill was calling to bring him to Westminster at half past nine.

The cat had come to lie on his chest. He stroked her. 'Now is the time, my dear. No more dallying with love of life. But first I must lock the door.'

The cat jumped a giant leap and led him through the drawing-room. There was no one on the landing — there never was. The cat sat on the threshold and would not move. 'Come along, puss. Don't look at me like that.' But he had to put his toe under her bottom before she would go.

In the chest of drawers there was a scarlet-coloured garter with a sliding buckle. He tied it around his neck. He took a second garter, a blue one, and looped it on the first. It was extraordinary how interesting this was. Between the chest of drawers and the bed was a plain with mountains. One mountain was a chair, another was the cork of the laudanum bottle lying sideways on the crack between two floorboards. The cork was as mountainous as the chair, more looming even, but somehow more forlorn. It would be a kindness to pick it up and put it somewhere safe, and yet he left it lying there unbefriended because, before he could do anything, the pilgrimage was accomplished: he had arrived at the shrine. The shrine was the bedstead; it was made of iron, and at each corner, high up, was a wreath of carved iron flowers. He looped the loose garter over one of the wreaths. But his feet were still on the floor. He drew them up and hung there, like a monkey, for a few seconds until, slowly, slowly, the iron bent and, slowly, slowly, the garter slipped off the wreath.

A botch!

But the canopy over the bed, the tester, was also made of iron and, being braced, was much more stable. He stood on the bed and tied the garter to it, once, twice, very tight. Now then, step back.

He was hanging.

With a loud crack, the tester broke and he was lying on the floor, tied to a length of iron rail and flailing at it.

The botcher botched again!

Sitting cross-legged, he undid the garter from the tester. Curious how easily a thing done was hard to undo. Even more curious was the ability to sit there unknotting the knots and at the same time contrive and foresee the actions he intended.

And here they were, done. Bravo! He had opened the door, exactly as foreseen, and fetched a chair and now he was standing on it. He looped the garter over the top corner of the door and slid it in until his cheek touched the wood. Curiously, it was only when he felt the cool of the white paintwork, when the colour white was the feel of it, that he realised that he was about to die. He had not thought about that for such a long time. All this botchery was actually being engaged in for the purpose of achieving the death of William Cowper Esquire, aged thirty-one years, late of Great Berkhamstead. But just as he summoned up the memory of his mother's face, he pushed away the chair with his feet and an unknown voice was saying quite distinctly, "'Tis over. 'Tis over. 'Tis over.'

His bent arms were beating, like a dying chicken's wings. His hands clutched at the noose, then loosened and slapped and scratched at the door, then clutched at the noose again as it tightened. His legs kicked convulsively so that the door swung to and fro, jerking the knots even tighter. Then he ceased kicking; his hands fell to his sides, twitched and were still. His eyes flickered and closed. It was over.

8

'He had me in His eye. It was a feeling all made up of flashes. And so I thought I was in hell.'

'Sir, can you speak to me?'

This was decidedly odd; he had just spoken and yet it seemed he had not been heard. Was this not his cousin Joe Hill, who had arrived to bring him down to the House of Lords?

He had bolted the door fast. He was sure of that. But there was in his memory a tiny gap, infinitesimal yet huge, between the bolt closing and his turning to hurry back to the bedroom. He must not have done it quite. Else, how had they forced the door? So, not shooting home the bolt was deliberate, a deliberate avoidance of destiny. Not bungling; nothing was bungled. Everything was to a purpose, and his purpose was cowardice.

Someone said, 'What have you got on your neck, you fool?'

He smiled and answered, '*Whosoever shall say, Thou fool, shall be in danger of Hellfire.*'

It was strange that, weltering in the abyss, he could still remember the Word, and yet forget who it was had called him a fool, so tenderly.

'Help me,' he said faintly and the stranger replied, 'I will, Mr Cowper, I will.'

Cowper sat up suddenly and said gruffly, 'What's that?'

'What's what?'

This man, whoever he was, did not realise that he was speaking with the voice of his Uncle Ashley and that he was pointing at his garters on the floor of his bedroom in the Temple. The scarlet one had snapped and he had fallen. The blue one was unknotted.

The laundress was screaming and Mr Clarke was choking him, but only to get his finger under the knot. Yes, it was he who had called him a fool. Then Uncle Ashley, grey as his name, was striding towards him and in his hands were two dead snakes, a blue and a scarlet, and he was saying, 'My dear Mr Cowper, you terrify me.' There was no reason to call him 'mister', they were kinsmen, and yet he had. And now he was saying, 'To be sure, you can't hold the office at this rate. Where are the papers? Where is their lordships' deputation?'

'I gave him the key.'

'Which key?' the man asked, but Cowper did not answer.

Now the heads of the dead snakes were hanging out of Uncle Ashley's pocket. He had put them there while he was opening the drawer and taking out the deputation requesting the Lords to appoint him to the Clerkship. Uncle Ashley thrust the paper into his pocket. And as it disappeared, so too did the snakes. One action, two results.

'Is something amusing?' the stranger asked.

It was no longer comical to think that as Uncle Ashley went out of his life there was, in the hell of his deep pocket, two snakes and a paper. He had departed for ever, furious because his nephew was a self-murderer who had destroyed the Cowper family in the eyes of all England.

After some minutes, Cowper grew calm and said, 'Thus ended all my connection with the Parliament house. *Nous ne parlons plus.*'

'Oh, you're a rogue, my friend, a rogue beneath it all.' The stranger wagged a finger in Cowper's face and left the room.

How do you know you can leave me alone? he asked of the retreating figure, but no words came out of his mouth.

At the start he had never been left alone. On the first night, when he arrived on the coach from London, he had struggled with four men. It was very dark. There were no torches. A loud wind was blowing. And when they opened the door of the coach, he had

had to fight them. Everything was so narrow. And when they bore him in through the gates and he saw the lighted windows, he thought they were the fires of hell flashing.

They had put him in a strait waistcoat. They had taught him compliance. But they forgot their own lesson. Because he grew quiet, they took off the waistcoat. Ah ha! he thought, I have carried my point. The fire had died down. Something shone in the cinders. It was a stocking-needle. The watcher did not see him pick it out of the ashes. He stuck it into the wallpaper behind the bed curtains. And woke in the darkness and remembered his purpose. Felt for the needle along the wall and found it. Lay on his left side. One finger on the heart-pulse. Thrust. Nearly to the head. No good. How deep in is the heart? Again. And again. Ten or twelve times. Then the point broke on a rib. Oh, I give up! And the laugh brought the watcher in. Hardly any blood. And no scars remaining. I am, he thought, a sentence without punctuation. Was there ever anything more melancholy? Oh, I give up.

And was it then, with that laugh, he wondered, that I stopped killing myself?

But now he was alone again. Everything spoke to him. Outside the window a sycamore unfolded its fingery leaves. During a storm, long long ago, a branch had tapped upon the glass an admonishment, and he had cried out and pointed his own finger against it. Then there was a fellow with a saw in the tree. Now where the branch had been, there was only a greying wound, cut clean for better bearing. Such power he had in pointing!

He saw himself hunting like a pointer dog through the grey arrested desert of a London Sunday afternoon. Near the river at Hungerford he came upon a barrow full of old books. He opened a ragged copy of Tillotson's Sermons and the first thing he saw was the parable of the barren fig tree. It was meant for him; he was all leaves and no fruit, and when the Saviour pronounced a curse upon it, a cry came out of him, 'He had me in His eye!'

Two men were standing over him. One of them had a candle in his hand.

'John! Is that John?'

'Yes, William. How are you, brother?'

'It must be the night-time.'

'Yes.'

'When I began it was morning. Have you come far?'

'From Cambridge.'

'*Bene! Benvenuto.*'

The other man was saying, 'You see, he's too quick for us all. He knows you are at Benet College.'

Cowper drew back from him.

'I know you.'

'You do?'

'You're Nathaniel Cotton and this is the *Collegium Insanorum* in St Albans. Is that not so?'

'It is.'

'How long have I been here?'

'Don't you remember?'

'Seven years.'

'No, Mr Cowper, seven months.'

'Yes, I remember now. I remember every day.'

'That's good,' John said. 'Remembering is good.'

'Is it? If so, it must be then that good is evil. *Evil, be thou my good.*'

'You shouldn't say such things, brother.'

'I know that, but it's written in a book, and if I am alive, it must be so.'

'Would you like a sleeping draught, Mr Cowper? I'll fetch it for you directly.'

When the doctor had left the room, Cowper said, 'He gives me laudanum, you know. The cure is the disease.'

'Dr Cotton is the kindest of men.'

'That's true. But it's such torment to know as much as I do and yet to know nothing. I'm damned, damned below Judas, more abhorred than he was.'

Dr Cotton, coming back down the corridor with the laudanum bottle, heard his patient howling in despair.

9

*H*e was writing feverishly with the stub of a pencil on a scrap of paper. When he stood up suddenly, other scraps fell from his lap. Reading what he had just written, he began walking erratically around the high-walled garden. A man followed, checking the gate to make sure it was bolted. Cowper went to him and said, almost angrily, 'I see.'

'What's that, Mr Cowper?'

'You are the watcher at the gate.'

'Yes, sir.'

'Is your name Pluto or Charon?'

'No sir, I'm Sam.'

'You're a wise man, Samuel. Tell me, I'm not let out, am I?'

Sam shook his head. Cowper went off a few paces, then returned, his fists pressed against his temples. 'I'm in a tomb, Sam. I'm in a fleshly tomb. I'm buried above ground.'

'Ah no, sir. Look around you; it's a garden you're in.'

From the window of his office, Dr Cotton saw Cowper sobbing on Sam's shoulder.

'As the seasons change, so his spirits rise. I've seen this in other cases, and in our friend there is undoubtedly a marked improvement, but—'

Dr Cotton, pouring tea for the Reverend Martin Madan,

stopped speaking as Cowper came into the office. Madan had seen his cousin in London when he was mad but otherwise unchanged physically; now he saw a white-faced, almost translucent old man who gave the impression of having stood aside from himself; his handshake, too, was a gesture from memory, cool as ivory.

'William, I'm so glad to see you.'

'Hello, Martin.'

'Mr Madan has just now been telling me your brother John has been made a don at Cambridge. At Benet College. *Bene*, remember? *Benvenuto?*'

Cowper was often surprised by Dr Cotton's attentiveness to what he said, but he showed no reaction.

When the doctor had gone, there was an awkward pause, which Madan filled by pouring tea for his cousin.

'How are you, William, really? Dr Cotton says you're better.'

'I wonder. If only ...'

'If only what?'

'If only I had been a proper rake, perhaps all this might have been worth it. But my punishment hardly seems to fit the crime, whatever it is.'

'You've committed no crime.'

But Cowper knew that Madan, for all his natural sympathy, believed, like everyone else, including himself, that madness was at best a sign of moral weakness and at worst a criminal depravity.

'Anyway, I suppose some years must pass yet until I go through the gates of hell, so I might as well make the best of them.'

'The best? The best? How can you say such a thing? This is despair, cousin. This is worse than madness.'

'I'm sorry to upset you, Martin, but it's the truth.'

'It's not the truth. It's a falsehood. I protest against it, and so should you. We are Protestants; it is our faith that saves us. All else is a lie and a delusion.'

'Oh, if all this is a delusion, then I am the happiest of men.'

Was it not better, he thought, to be deluded than to continue paying for the incomprehensible sin of being himself? Of course he was damned, but somehow the gigantic demons of the night had lately dwindled into the dwarfish anxieties of the everyday; and besides he was exhausted, as tired as a stone. Madan's passion made him eloquent, but wasn't he only a consonant short of being himself a Madman? These Methodists were neither commonsensical and mildly observant, as gentlefolk should be, nor sceptical and urbane, as his London friends were, and they even knelt at prayer, which was an abandonment to passion, quite Italian.

Yet, to be deluded and the happiest of men? It was a remark he had made with a flat dryness, and now he regretted it. Then there came suddenly into his mind the image of an emaciated lion dragging itself across the burning wastes of an immense desert, and when the lion lifted its shaggy head, it saw in the distance the fresh green of an oasis.

Madan fell silent. Cowper was sitting immobile with the tea-cup half-raised to his lips and, one after another, tears were slowly spilling down his face. He got up wordlessly and left the room. The long corridor outside was emptier than before, grey-real without the fever of significance.

The sorrow he felt now was new, since it arose from an image of the future, and with it came an awareness that his melancholy had involved others, especially Theadora. She had written, but he could not read her letters. The illness was not his alone – it was hers too, and had long been so. Money, although it had been given out to be the reason, was not why Uncle Ashley had forbidden the marriage. He had done it to save Thea from madness. But Thea had not been saved. Ever since the night of her birthday party in Southampton Row when she had come to his room, they had fought with each other constantly and always on the same subject, which could never be mentioned. She was, of course, strange in herself and, as she said, 'very wicked' – it was she who had had the carnelian ring carved to her own design: she liked to think of herself as the Omphale who had bought Hercules as a slave, kept him for three years, made him spin wool and do all the other duties of a woman. In the early days of their courtship, the idea of being her slave amused them both; it was part of their private code, and it excited him obscurely. After the engagement was called off, it was the explanation for her sending him a broken spindle held together with some dark red threads – he knew Thea well enough to guess that she wanted him to think they were dyed with her blood, but ironically. Some months after that, she had gone missing all night from Southampton Row and had been found the next day in Oxford Street, her hair unbound, like a flaming bush, her eyes crackling.

Harriot, too, had written, but he had read her letters. She blamed Thea for being wilful and wayward and cold-hearted, when the opposite was the case, and she had wanted to visit him to discuss his finances, but he had said no. The allowance that came quarterly from his father's estate was just about enough to support sanity, but his family were paying extra for the madness, and he was also dimly aware that Joseph Hill had been collecting gifts of money for him. It was best not to think about such things.

In the same way as he forgot them, he was no longer frightened of the other inmates of the asylum. At first they had been embodiments of his demons and he had hidden from them; then they were ghosts shuffling along the dark corridors or encountered at meal-times. In the early weeks he had been force-fed in his cell, then he had been allowed to feed himself with a blunt spoon and soon after that he had started to take his meals at the big table in the dining-room – there were never more than ten patients at any time and sometimes just three or four. Even those who stayed for a short time had become identifiable individuals, and with identity came fellow-feeling and a sort of pride that their difference, the suffering that each felt was unique to himself, had badged them in common.

Terror had declined into apathy, but now, as the warm May air in the high-walled garden was filled with bird-song and the hum and drone of insects, apathy gave way to nervous excitement. Restless, uncertain, talking to himself, he walked and walked. In one corner there was an ancient bush of dog-roses and the way it scrambled up the wall and overcame the dark red brick with a flood of pure white blossoms filled him with compassion. He wanted to give himself up to it but did not dare to; he was afraid of the consequences.

He was not afraid of Sam Roberts. Sam was strongly built but diminutive, bow-legged from childhood rickets; beneath a thick thatch of hair, which was already grey, he had a face like a withered yellow apple; widely spaced buckteeth made him look like an open-mouthed idiot but, though he was illiterate, he was far from gorm-less – that was why Dr Cotton had put him in charge.

They worked together in the garden. This patient liked digging, sowing, planting, weeding – anything that was physical and out-of-doors and day-lit. The nervous excitement made it difficult to rest, and when he did sleep he had terrible dreams, all the more unbearable because they often began as visions of paradise. Once he saw a towering temple built with beams of the purest light, and in the dream he thought he could draw inferences from the vision that were favourable to himself, but then Satan quickly persuaded him, as the towers came crashing down in clouds of smoke and dust, that it had been deliberately constructed in order to increase his regret for the glory which he had seen only a glimpse of, irrecoverably lost and gone.

'Well, sir,' Sam said, 'a temple made out of beams of light, it wouldn't stand long. But anyway it was only a dream.'

That night Cowper became aware of a dim light glowing in his bedroom. Bright as it was, it revealed only itself, and the room was kept in darkness. Then the light took on the form of an angel child. The child approached, wings wide, and said, 'Mercy, there is mercy, there is mercy for you.'

When he awoke, the room was empty. There was a feeling in his chest, a heavy emotion long forgotten, the weight of an old tenderness.

Sometimes, however, the visions were visible by day. Once when he was setting onions in the vegetable garden, a storm had blown up from the east. Taking shelter in the house, he felt compelled to go up to the top corridor, the better to see the storm from the long window there. The rain had not yet begun to fall and the air was fevered, dry, leaden. Thunder crashed like huge pieces of furniture thrown about in the attic. Amongst the roiling clouds he noticed one in particular. It hung immobile, isolated, deeply black, over the nearby woods. Suddenly in the midst of it a fiery hand appeared, clutching a bolt of lightning. This, he thought, deserves watching with my utmost attention. Then, all of an instant, the hand was lifted up and let fall again towards the earth, as if transfixing an enemy.

'Auspicious is perhaps a good word,' Dr Cotton said. 'But a hand brandishing a bolt of lightning and an ominous cloud – have I not seen such an image before somewhere in a book?'

'Well,' Cowper said after a long pause, 'this is yet another crime I am guilty of.'

'What crime?'

'The worshipping of graven images.' And then, realised that the strange sound coming out of his mouth was laughter.

Dr Cotton poured more claret and said, 'Oh, I too am guilty of that offence. I collect pictures, you see. The Dutch disease I call it. It's an affliction I caught in Leyden, while I was studying under Boerhaave.'

Then he launched out on another reminiscence. They were sitting in the study, looking out over the darkening summer garden. He believes, Cowper thought, that my smile is sincere, as well he might, since I have not smiled for months, and I am glad to give him this pleasure in order that he will go on believing that my recovery is well-nigh complete. But in truth this seeming alteration is like the green mantle of a morass – pleasant indeed to the eye but a cover for nothing but rottenness and filth.

10

awn was warm but grey. A dream had sent him down to the garden. All he could remember of it was that he was naked, the usual disgrace, and in public too. The dog-roses flooded up and over the red-brick wall. If I, he thought, if I go out of the world in mourning and not in glory as these white roses do, I will not have been ... He did not know how to complete the sentence; there was a condition in it he could not allow himself to think of. It required him to be, somehow, properly insane.

As he walked, leaving behind him slurred footprints in the dewy grass, he noticed a book on a bench. It was a Bible. Dr Cotton was, in his own quiet way, a devout Christian and, for the sake of improvement, Bibles were left lying around all over the Collegium.

Cowper found himself reading about the raising of Lazarus. A memory came back to him.

Once upon a time in Southampton Row, William Russell had said, quite seriously, that he thought the Lazarus story was, of all Gospel texts, the most suitable to be read at a wedding. Harriot had groaned; Thea had shown him one of her cat-like smiles; but Cowper's father, who was not given to amusement, especially about anything concerning religon, had laughed uproariously. And yet, he thought now, it was a wonderful idea. Christ's pity was not solely engaged with eternity but also with the present, so much so that he bestowed on Lazarus the greatest of all His miracles, as it were to remarry him to human time. Coming upon this story now was not chance; it was prefigured. But in what sense? Could it be that such compassion extended to himself? 'No,' he said aloud. 'Dead as he was, Lazarus was worthy.'

He put the Bible under his arm, took out his watch, saw that it was eight o'clock and went back into the house. He was hungry.

Breakfast was served in his room. It was a considerable convenience, although in recent weeks the meal had become a disjointed affair since the servant who brought the tray was so puny he had to return to the kitchen to fetch the heavy old silver teapot. Dick Coleman was only eight years old, one of those boys with a feather of hair constantly sticking up from the crown of the head no matter how often it is slicked down with spit, a service which his father would not and his mother could not do for him, he because he was a feckless drunkard, and she because she was dead.

'Dick,' Cowper said as the boy was laying the dishes, 'what will you do when you grow up?'

'I suppose I'll cobble shoes, like Dad.'

'Is that trade to your liking?'

'I reckon it's all right. The tanyard smells rotten, but the big punch is famous.' And he made the sound, very accurately, of an eyelet being punched through leather.

When Dick went off, he had a silver sixpence in his pocket. Sam had warned against giving the boy money, since his father immediately stole it to buy gin, and often enough gin was all that Dick and his many brothers and sisters had for their supper. Had he not noticed that the boy was sometimes light-headed in the morning? And the yellowish bruise under his eye, did he think Dick had got that from falling out of bed?

Cowper flung himself into a chair near the window. Crime or not, he had given the boy sixpence and made him glad. That was good. My gift, he thought, is not my own. The sun had burned away the mist and was now shining brilliantly through the window. The cloud of horror that had so long hung over him was at every moment passing away. He was blinded by the sunlight, as Lazarus must have been, emerging from the cold and dusty tomb, and he could not fathom where the gift was coming from that he was now being offered, and he felt weak. Then he saw the Bible on the windowsill, knew instantly that comfort and instruction were pre-figured there for him and opened it. The words leaped into his eye:

> *Whom God hath set forth to be a propitiation through faith in his blood, to declare his righteousness for the remission of sins that are past, through the forbearance of God.*

He who had been set forth by God was, of course, Jesus. Immediately he felt himself receiving the strength to believe. Which book was he reading? It was Saint Paul writing to the Romans and the apostle was asking,

> *Is he the God of the Jews only? Is he not also of the Gentiles? Yes, of the Gentiles also. Seeing it is one God, which shall justify the circumcision by faith, and uncircumcision through faith.*

'I am made whole again,' he said aloud. To say the word 'again' meant that there had been wholeness before. The Atonement Christ had made on the cross was sufficient.

When Dick came to take away the breakfast dishes, there was no answer to his knock. He opened the door and what he saw sent him running back down to the kitchen for Sam. The man who was always trying to pat down his hair with spit was kneeling on the floor with his arms stretched out. Then, Dick said, he turned, 'bawlin' and dribblin', like a baby', and sobbed, 'My pardon is sealed with His blood.'

II

The man's head was thrown back and his eyes were closed. He wore no shirt and his open coat showed a fleshless ribcage and a caved-in stomach. He was propped against a post at the bottom of a flight of steps, and beside him an intelligent-looking dog was gazing at the tipped-over goblet in his slack fingers, as if wondering when it would fall.

'Do you see what is written there?'

Dr Cotton was pointing at the dying drunkard's other hand; it was holding the neck of a demijohn to which was attached a scroll.

'It says *The Downfall of Mister Gin.*'

'And indeed he has fallen,' Dr Cotton laughed. 'The man is in spirits, but there is no spirit in the man.'

They were in the doctor's office, looking at a copy of a William Hogarth engraving which a patient, in gratitude for the return of his sobriety, had given Cotton.

'And yet the man is more fortunate than the child.'

Cowper could hardly bear to look: a baby had wriggled out of the arms of its bare-bosomed and sottishly oblivious mother and was flying over the edge of the steep steps to fall on its head.

'You're very silent, sir. Don't you approve?'

'I hope I'm not a prig, but I don't like to see such scenes of corruption.'

'Liking hardly comes into it. Mr Hogarth paints corruption in order to point us towards redemption.'

'All I see is viciousness and taking pleasure in it. Well, that's typical of London, and with the grace of God I shall never look upon it again.'

Sam looked in the door. 'The coach is at the gate, sir.'

'Thank you, Sam. We will be down directly. Are you all right, Mr Cowper? You seem a trifle nervous.'

'Do I? Well, if the truth be told, I am a little anxious about the journey.'

'Oh, Huntingdon's not such a great distance. Fifty miles and a dry road with a stop on the way at Cambridge? You'll be very comfortable.'

'No, no, it's not that. It's that I've been out of the world so long, I'm afraid I won't know what to do.'

'Do, Mr Cowper? You don't have to do anything. Just, well, sit there.'

'But it's the other passengers.'

'The other passengers? What about them?'

'What if some one of them should blaspheme?'

'Oh yes?'

'People do take the name of the Lord in vain, I know that. And if they do, they should be reproved – in the politest possible manner, of course. But will I have the courage to do it? – that's the anxiety.'

Dr Cotton turned away to look out the window. Down on the road the entire establishment, patients and servants, were watching as Cowper's trunk was being hefted up onto the top of the post-carriage. The sole passenger, Sir Arthur Pond, was leaning out the window of the coach smoking a long clay pipe. Dr Cotton knew Pond's wife professionally. She had borne Sir Arthur ten of his children – he had fathered as many again on almost as many women all over the county – and she was convinced he was in league with the devil. It was an unlikely alliance: Satan, according to Sir Arthur, was something worse than a milquetoast. He was a Whig. What a pity, the doctor thought, as Sir Arthur began beating the door of the coach impatiently with the flat of his hand, that he could not go a little piece of the journey with Mr Cowper. It was an unworthy thought and he put it out of his mind, but, like a dog burying a juicy bone, he did so with a degree of pleasurable anticipation, since he knew he would return to it in the evening over dinner with Mrs Cotton.

There was another matter he would rehearse with his wife: the insouciant manner in which Cowper had announced that he was taking Sam Roberts and Dick Coleman with him to Huntingdon, as if that were of as little consequence as removing two lumps from the sugar-basin and popping them into his tea.

'Well,' Dr Cotton had said, 'I suppose every gentleman should have a manservant.'

'A manservant? Oh, I had not thought of it in that light.'

'No? In what light have you thought of it?'

'In the light of the Gospel. I believe, you see, that Sam is on the road to conversion. Laying hold of our salvation together, that's what's important.'

'Of course. But Dick Coleman, what of him?'

'Oh well, that is somewhat different. The boy will be very useful I'm sure, and in a year or two I shall have him apprenticed. Not to cobbling, of course, like his wretched father. Perhaps he may be taught the trade and mystery of a breeches-maker.'

The moment of departure had arrived. Cowper embraced everyone, including Sam, then he shook Dr Cotton's hand for almost a minute and finally, overcome with emotion, kissed it, at which the assembly burst into applause. Then, covering his face with his hat, he mounted into the carriage as if ascending the scaffold, and was driven away.

Between St Albans and Harpenden, where his journey ended, Sir Arthur did not once blaspheme and when he heard Cowper uttering the name of Jesus, he bowed his head. There was nothing else for it.

That evening Dr Cotton, after reviewing the events of the day, posed a question to his wife. 'I wonder,' he said, pouring himself an unusually large brandy, 'I wonder was our friend saner when he was mad, or is he madder now he's sane?'

12

Dear Cousin Josephus,

The only recompense I can make you for your kind attention to my affairs during my illness is to tell you that, by the mercy of God, I am restored to perfect health both of mind and body. This I believe will give you pleasure, and I would gladly do anything from which you could receive it.

I left St Albans on the 17th, and arriving that day at Cambridge, spent some time there with my brother, and came hither on the 22nd. I have a lodging that puts me continually in mind of our summer excursions in Norfolk — we have had many worse, and except the size of it (which, however, is sufficient for a single man) but few better. I am not quite alone, having brought a servant with me from St Albans, who is the very mirror of fidelity and affection for his master. And whereas the Turkish spy says he kept no servant, because he would not have an enemy in his house, I hired mine, because I would have a friend. Men do not usually bestow these encomiums on their lackeys, nor do they usually deserve them; but I have had experience of mine, both in sickness and in health; and never saw his fellow.

He frowned. Was it entirely truthful to tell Joe Hill that the lodging was sufficient for a single man when two men and a boy, even if a very small boy, were sleeping therein?

He was still considering the matter when he was greeted in the High Street by the town's only peruke-maker. Doffing his hat was difficult because of the large blood-stained parcel he was now carrying. When the brief and friendly conversation ended, the maker of wigs, an elegant and worldly gentleman, turned to look after Cowper's retreating figure and paddled his lower lip with an index finger.

As Cowper was opening the front door, two ladies greeted him frostily and hurried on. The daughter was a pretty girl, quite statu-esque, and the mother was also a substantial figure, both in herself and in the community. She had invited this young man to her house for supper, a game of cards and a little dancing. But he had declined – declined with the utmost politeness, but with an expression on his face as if she had asked him to put his hand down the front of her daughter's dress and fetch out one of her lovely bosoms. He was, he told her, obliged to refuse on the grounds that games of chance and polkas were incompatible with the Christian way of life.

In the chamber that served as kitchen, dining-room and parlour, he put the parcel down on a table piled high with books, writing materials and dirty dishes. Then he set about examining, somewhat speculatively, the fire in the grate, low but still burning, and the trivet on which the cooking was done.

Some time later, Sam and Dick came in from their shopping.

'What is that, master?' Sam asked.

'Dinner. But it won't go in. The *entrée* will not enter.' He was trying to fit a joint of meat into a saucepan.

'But there's enough there for ten men.'

'The sheep's heart yesterday wasn't enough for the three of us, so I thought ... I wonder, could we fry this?'

'Fry a whole leg of mutton? No, Mr Cowper, we could not.'

'Do you know, Sam, it really is a matter full of perplexity. I never knew before how to pity poor housekeepers, but now I cease to wonder why they always look so harried. '

After eating the mutton – boiled – he went out to look at the river. The Ouse was the most agreeable circumstance in that rather flat part of the world and he meant to swim in it, but not today. Today, standing on the bridge at sunset, he was a little depressed.

Could it be that he was simply bored? Considering what he had been through, to feel boredom was scandalous. Overcome with contrition, he rested his head on the parapet and prayed.

'I say, are you all right, sir?' A young man was hurrying towards him.

'Oh, yes, thank you, I'm quite all right, I was, as you can see ...' and he began to dismiss imaginary dust from his hands as if that were an explanation.

The man paused. 'You're Mr Cowper, sir, if I'm not mistaken.'

'Well, yes, I am.'

'My name is Unwin, Mr Cowper. William Unwin. I've seen you in church and, if you'll excuse me saying so, I thought, now there's a face, there's a soul, and I wanted to speak to you, but I was too shy.'

'It seems we're kindred spirits.'

'Why so?'

'We share an affliction and, you know, it is affliction that makes us Christians.'

'How true, Mr Cowper. How wonderfully true. Tell me, have you read Mr Taylor's book *Holy Living and Dying*?'

'Yes, I cherish it, book and thought. Have you read *Meditations among the Tombs*?'

Not only had young Mr Unwin read the *Meditations*, he was studying them at Cambridge, where he would soon be taking Holy Orders and becoming, like his father, a minister, but more on the Methodist side of things. Father's rectory was but a hundred yards away; Mr Cowper must come in immediately and make himself known to the family.

The rectory was in the middle of the High Street, terraced, not detached, and it had tiny *trompe l'oeil* windows in the top storey, a deception which one could not approve of, even for the sake of proportion, but, with its rose-red brick front and white-sashed casements, it was in its way beautiful, and Cowper had admired it since his arrival in Huntingdon.

'Mother, Mother,' William called out in the hallway, ushering him into a drawing-room. 'This is Providence, sir, I assure you. Resist it not.'

A young woman, who had been reading by the window, rose to

greet the visitor. 'Susanna, this is Mr Cowper. Be kind to him.' He went out, calling, 'Mother!'

'I hope I'm not disturbing you,' Cowper said.

'No, not at all. We rarely receive at this hour, but if William should bring someone home, I know the unusuality of it will be justified.'

'Unusuality? That's a most unusual word.'

'Isn't it? I heard a tax-collector use it in town the other day and determined it should be saved for posterity.'

'It will prove, I am sure, an interesting and perennial plant in the language.'

'Do you like flowers?' Susanna asked.

'Yes, very much.'

'Which is your favourite?'

'I'm very fond of night-scented stock. But I think my best favourite is mignonette.'

'Oh, they're very good choices. Mamma will be pleased.'

An old man, carrying a sheaf of papers, came in, looked at Cowper and said, 'Oh really, this is too tiresome.'

William returned, saying, 'Mother will be along directly.'

The old man said, 'Your mother shouldn't involve herself in these affairs.'

'Papa, Mr Cowper is a visitor,' Susanna said.

The Reverend Unwin put on his glasses to inspect Cowper, then shook his hand.

'Oh gracious, I mistook you for one of my parishioners. Unhappy people. Always complaining. About what I don't know.'

'You won't talk to them, Papa, that's why.'

'I preach to them, is that not enough? Do you have daughters, Mr—?'

'Cowper, sir.'

'Cooper, eh? As in barrel?'

'No, sir, as in cow.'

As Susanna and William burst out laughing, the door opened and their mother came in. Behind her a servant stood with an oil-lamp; the light from it glowed about her head.

'Mr Cowper, forgive me. I delayed to order up the light.

Welcome to our home. William tells me you're shy. You mustn't be shy here.'

Mary Unwin had heavy eyebrows and a domed forehead, but her too-wide mouth was at once kindly and commanded respect.

'I am reminded of Diogenes,' the Reverend Unwin said.

'What's that, Morley?' Mary took her husband's arm affectionately – and Cowper thought, Why, she can hardly be seven or eight years older than myself.

'Diogenes was a kind of cooper, you know, or at least he lived in a barrel. An odd way to carry on, but he was a most excellent fellow. Don't you agree, sir?'

'I do, I do indeed.'

Cowper smiled. And when, two hours later, he left the rectory, after taking tea, he was still smiling.

13

Dick Coleman had seen grown-ups diving into the pool at the old quarry in St Albans, but this was not a dive. It was as if Mr Cowper, who was such a fusspot he'd spend half the morning taking the top off his egg and the other half pecking up the crumbs of his toast from the tablecloth – why, he even walked in a pernickety way, lifting his feet up and putting them down carefully, like an old hen – it was as if he was flinging all the bits of himself, unjoined, up into the air and did not care where they came down. But he swam like a duckling – no, he was more like an old spaniel, with his head held up and a worried look on his face, wondering how quick he could get back out and shake the frightened drops of water off himself. Only, he did not get out quick but went paddling up and down for an age.

Another thing amazed Dick and he had asked Sam about it: when the master was swimming, why did he wear his breeches? Sam had said it was because Mr Cowper was a gentleman, but there were gentlemen in St Albans and they swam in their pelts, though they were not half so grand. Now he was climbing up the bank and Sam was wrapping him in a threadbare towel.

'I do wish you gentlemen would join me some day,' he said.

'We have more sense,' Sam said.

'Well, I'm sure you have. But, really, the exercise is beneficial to what sense I have.' He gazed shivering at the river. 'Oh,' he said, 'isn't this a noble stream? It reminds me of the Thames at Windsor.'

Sam said, 'It's not a patch on it.'

'Why, they're as alike at this point as, well, my fingers are to my fingers.'

'Your fingers will wither from all this swimming.'

'They are indeed well wrinkled. Which reminds me, did we iron the linen shirt?'

'We did.'

'I wonder should I wear the brown or the white wig. What do you think, my dear?'

Since meeting the Unwins, the master had become almost foppishly concerned with his appearance. He had written urgently to Joe Hill in London for money to buy a new coat; it had broad lapels, a collar fashionably high at the back and its colour was, for an evangelical, an unsuitably frivolous canary-yellow.

It was after midday when they arrived home and not yet one o'clock when Cowper set off again, best dressed and powdered. At least, Sam thought as he buttered bread for himself and Dick, the food bill has gone down.

William Unwin had returned to Cambridge; the Reverend Unwin was in his study as usual; and Susanna stayed reading in her bedroom. Cowper was glad – what he had to say was for Mrs Unwin's ears only.

'I'm sure you can understand,' he said after an hour, 'why I fear that this history, indeed my very being, must be a cause of scandal.'

'Scandal? Good heavens, no. Your scruples are – excuse me for saying so – absurd. It wasn't madness that led to your conversion. An unreasonable cause cannot produce a reasonable effect.'

'Yes, that's true. But Christianity is not reasonable.'

'That is an unorthodox opinion.'

'On this subject, Mrs Unwin, I have no opinion, I have a certainty. Christianity is a sacrifice. Only a sacrifice. And he that stabs deepest is always the wisest man.'

She laughed. 'Ah, my dear Mr Cowper, stabbing is not for sensible people. We prefer – if I may include myself in the plurality – we prefer to find in our spiritual life a degree of peace and social comfort, which, I can see from your expression, you rather despise.'

'No, no, I don't despise them at all. But my history contradicts comfort. I have committed a great crime. I feel it even now, before God.'

'You have not been criminal, sir, except once and to yourself. You do not stab, you are stabbed. What you feel is the wound. And the wound, I think, is more in your nature. But God has forgiven you. You must trust in Him.'

'Yes. I do. We are at one in this, are we not?'

'Oh well,' she laughed, 'I am merely a handmaiden.'

'No, no, do not say that. There must be no difference between us, as Christians.'

'It appears, Mr Cowper, that you require an equalness for which my origins have not suited me.'

'No, I do not require. Forgive me. That would be presumptuous.'

He was just the sort of person she had long wanted as a friend: bookish, serious, amusing, devout in the advanced style, and she had absorbed without too much surprise the confession of his suicide attempt – he was too intense for there not to be an extreme explanation for his intensity. But what now disconcerted her, especially since he was so extraordinarily timid, was that there was more than a hint in his tone of voice that he did indeed mean to presume and to oblige her not to maintain a difference between them, whatever that difference might be.

That night as she lay in bed listening to Morley snoring, she could not help but be pleased. As Cowper was leaving, she had gone into the street with him and said, 'If I am the converted and you the converter, there already exists, by necessity, room for separation, which as you know from your own experience can lead to indifference. So,' she had wagged a finger at him, 'be warned, Mr Converter. I am separate and I can be indifferent.' That had been a somewhat daring intimacy, but it had struck a glancing blow at his presumption, and when she had then given him her hand, he had bowed over it silently and gone away, chastened, which was, all things considered, appropriate to the situation.

A few streets away Cowper was also listening to snoring, which came in this case from Sam in the next bed. He had just now asked him was he awake and when Sam had said 'No!' he had returned to his solitary thoughts, disappointed. After supper he had read to them from the Bible that *ten thousand worlds would vanish at the consummation of all things*, and Dick Coleman, amazed by the number, had gone to look out the window at the stars. What had remained in Cowper's mind, however, was the following verse, *But the word of God standeth fast, and they who trust in him shall never be confounded.* He did trust in God. Why then should his new-found confidence be so badly shaken? Why, when he had repented, was he gnawed by recollection? He felt himself deeply in danger of betrayal. But by whom? He could not remember; it was too far back, too much part of his essence, for memory. And then, before the image of his mother could swim up from the deeps, his brain turned, almost audibly, to calculating and imposing order on the future. He knew what he had to have, or rather what he must not lose. But possession was carnal, and therefore impermissible. It was a desire he could not give room to – but he could not help it.

14

'Make way!' Sam shouted. Passers-by withdrew to a safe distance from the gates of the livery stable and watched as an ostler led out a large and skittish horse. The ostler let go of the bridle and Sam cried, 'Hold him, sir. Don't give him his head.'

'I don't believe,' Cowper said, 'I have any choice in the matter.'

Nor did he. The horse galloped off down the street towards the open country.

'God help us,' Sam said and went back to his breakfast. It was not all that strange, he supposed, that the master should decide to take up horse-riding – in London he had had no need to learn how to ride, and it did make it easier to go to Cambridge to see his brother. But why, when the Reverend Unwin drove up there every week and they got on with each other so well, had they only travelled together the once?

Eventually the horse grew tired of having its mouth pulled about and slowed to a walk. They had gone a mile and were nearing a pretty little church. Although it was situated on rising ground, it was so close to the river that the water washed the wall of the churchyard. He still had more than thirteen miles to go before meeting John in Cambridge, but there was something he needed to pray about.

The church smelled of damp and candlewax, and in its silence there was a sense of being removed out of time. He knelt on a lumpy hassock and prayed, 'Dear God, you who know all my thoughts, help me not to think this thought. Save me from my desires, through Jesus Christ our Lord, Amen.'

The prayer was half-hearted. It was unchristian to pray for worldly things, but he could not pray against this craving with any conviction. He got up off his knees and wandered around, stopping to look at a memorial which read:

> Thou wast too good to live on earth with me,
> And I not good enough to die with thee.

As he transcribed the couplet into his notebook, a thin gust of wind suddenly blew up outside and in the renewed silence that hollowed the church, he heard faintly what seemed to be his father's voice saying, 'The Lord of Hosts will do this.'

After only two nights in Cambridge – John, irritated by continued attempts to convert him, was not sorry to see his brother go – he was back home, sitting at the dinner table lost in thought.

'Master,' Sam said, 'this can't go on, you know.' Cowper did not respond. 'Your Uncle Ashley thinks twelve pounds a month is comfortable enough and he's right – a modest gentleman could do nicely on it. But a gentleman and his lackey and a boy, it just won't do.'

'It won't do what?'

'It won't do to live on. How come you've managed to spend a whole year's money in three months? What I'm saying, master, is that if I looked after the budget ...'

'Oh yes?'

Sam put a plate in front of Dick.

'Rats' tails again,' Dick said.

'You see?'

'See what, Sam?'

'The rats' tails, master; that's what the boy calls the liver. He can hardly eat it any more and nor can I. We had lambs' hearts and lambs' legs and now we have lambs' liver. It can't go on.'

Cowper said exultantly, 'But it can! It's the will of God!'

'The will of God? Well, if you don't mind me saying so, Mr

Cowper, sir, it's a strange God that says we have to eat liver every day of the week.'

He was on his feet and there was fire in his eyes. 'It's the will of God,' he said. 'I see that now. The Lord of Hosts will do this.'

'He will, will He? Well, I won't.'

'Oh, you will, Sam. I know you will.'

Cowper took his coat off the back of the chair and went out without another word.

Susanna and Mary were reading and Morley had nodded off by the fire. He was woken by a knocking on the front door and groaned, 'Susanna, my dear, if that's a parishioner, tell him to go away.' But as she went out, he heaved himself to his feet, saying, 'Oh, very well, very well. Why can't these people die in the daytime?'

When Susanna returned with Cowper, Mary said to him, 'Is there something amiss? You look pale.'

'Do I? No, no, there's nothing amiss. Except I am somewhat nervous.'

The Reverend Unwin, glad not to be going to a death-bed, said, 'What's to be nervous about, Mr Barrel?'

'I have something to say and now I feel unsure ...'

'Calm yourself, Mr Cowper,' Mary said. 'Take a seat and be calm.'

'Yes, of course. Thank you, I am actually quite calm. I want to ask,' he said and stopped. 'I hope I don't presume on your kindness.' He stopped again. 'I wish to make a proposal.'

'A proposal?' The Reverend Unwin was suddenly on guard. 'You wish to make a proposal. Well now, propose ahead.' He had not thought of Cowper as a son-in-law, and yet it made sense.

'I wonder if you would consider me as, I mean if there was any chance that ...'

'There is every chance,' the Reverend Unwin began, but, seeing Susanna's expression, did not continue.

Cowper noticed only the encouragement and rushed on. 'Of course there's the matter of Sam and young Dick and I should not want to be parted from them but both would make extra servants if you would consider taking me in.'

'Taking you in?'

'Yes, as a lodger.'

'A lodger, Mr Cowper! Well, bless my soul, I thought you were asking—'

But Mary interrupted him. And the proposal was immediately accepted.

15

The Rectory, Huntingdon, April 16th, 1765

Dear Lady Hesketh, dear cousin, dear Harriot,

As I can name thee thrice, so am I now thrice contented, Morning, Noon and Night. At the moment I write it is the middle of these and Mrs Unwin has had a little table brought for me into the garden whence, like some indolent Caliph, I am enabled to supervise a brawny carter, assisted by my Sam, whose only affinity to brawn is the eating of it, unloading from a low dray great slabs of rock. But more of that anon.

Having begun with time, I now command you — you have no other choice — to accompany me on my diurnal round. We breakfast commonly between 8 and 9; till 11 we read either the Scriptures or the Sermons of some faithful Preacher of those holy Mysteries; at 11 we attend divine Service which is performed here twice every day, and from 12 to 3 we separate and amuse ourselves as we please. During that interval I either read in my own apartment, or walk or ride, or work in the garden. We seldom sit an hour after dinner, but if the weather permits adjourn to the garden, where with Mrs Unwin and her son, lately holidaying from the university, I have generally the pleasure of religious conversation till tea time; if it rains or is too windy for walking, we either converse within doors, or sing some hymns, and by the help of Mrs Unwin's harpsichord make up a *tolerable concert, in which however our hearts I hope are the best and most musical performers. After tea we sally forth to walk in good earnest. Mrs Unwin is a good walker, and we have generally travelled about four miles before we see home again. At night we read and converse as before 'till supper, and commonly finish the evening with hymns or a sermon, and last of all the family are called in to prayers — I need not tell you that such a life as this is consistent with the utmost cheerfulness, accordingly we are all happy, and dwell together in unity as brethren. Mrs Unwin has almost a maternal Affection for me, and I have something very like a filial one for her, and her son and I are brothers.*

When she was ill in December, quite seriously so, with a quinsy, I wrote the following little hymn. I began to compose it one morning, before daybreak, but fell asleep at the end of the first two lines. When I waked again the third and fourth were whispered to my heart in a way which I have often experienced.

Oh! For a closer walk with God,
A calm and heavenly frame;
A light to shine upon the road
That leads me to the Lamb!

He put down the quill. He would have to transcribe the rest of it from his notebook; it was quite extraordinary that he could remember only the second-last verse:

The dearest idol I have known,
Whate'er that idol be,
Help me tear it from thy throne,
And worship only Thee.

The reason he remembered these lines so well — Harriot had a very beady eye, and he wondered would she guess it — was that 'the dearest idol' was Mrs Unwin. A compassion that wanted to be greater than her illness wrote the poem, but was there not the opposite of pity in saying she was a false god? She was not a graven image. But if he fell down and adored her …

He put the thought out of his mind and went to help in the unloading of the slabs. In the letter he had said nothing about the Reverend Unwin because he did not quite know how to put it.

Morley, as he now called him, was perhaps as diligent as any clergyman in England who was not awakened, but family prayers had never been practised in his household, and now that his wife and son were praying night and day and singing hymns and sermonising to each other and the servants, Morley had seemingly decided to retire to his study and his reading of the classical authors in general and of Ovid in particular. As to Susanna, there was very little that could be said about her to Harriot; she was as close to her mother as ever, but not as often, and sometimes when Cowper came into the room, she went out.

There were other things he could not communicate to Harriot and which he did not wish to express clearly to himself. Morley Unwin had moved to Huntingdon from a place as dire as its name, Grimston, because Mary was lonely there. Despite being full of the sort of people who thought that dancing and horse-racing were compatible with Christianity, Huntingdon was also well supplied with those who were not only interested in their salvation but lively company too. Amongst them were two or three odd scrambling fellows like Cowper, and yet, since he had moved in to the Unwin house, Mary saw little of them and soon she had fewer visitors than in Grimston.

'Sam, I shall have need of a ball of twine.' Cowper had not got as far as to lay hands on a slab, and now, instead of explaining what he needed string for, he went back to writing to Harriot.

> *I have for some time past imputed your silence to the cause which you yourself assign to it, viz. to my change of situation; and was even sagacious enough to account for the frequency of your letters to me while I lived alone, from your attention to me in a state of such solitude as seemed to make it an act of particular charity to write to me. I bless God for it, I was happy even then; solitude has nothing gloomy in it if the soul points upwards. My dear Cousin! I have often prayed for you behind your back, and now I pray for you to your face. There are many who would not forgive me this wrong; but I have known you so long, and so well, that I am not afraid of telling you how sincerely I wish for your growth in every Christian grace, in everything that may promote and*

secure your everlasting welfare. My circumstances are rather particular, such as call upon my friends, those I mean who are truly such, to take some little notice of me; and will naturally make those who are not such in sincerity rather shy of doing it. To this I impute the silence of many with regard to me, who, before the affliction that befell me, were ready enough to converse with me.

Yours ever,
W.C.

He read over the last paragraph. Was it too stern a rebuke? Well, whether Harriot liked it or not, it would do. He folded the letter and put it in his pocket. Would he show it to Mrs Unwin? No, better not. Instead he would talk at tea about string, pegged out in necessarily straight lines, to plot out the curve of the new path. It was a metaphor for the Christian soul.

16

Far from the world, O Lord, I flee,
From strife and tumult far;
From scenes where Satan wages still
His most successful war.

The point of his flight was in the doubled 'far'. If he came close to the world, to John's Cambridge or Harriot's London, he felt like a cuckoo, a raw-breasted fledgling tumbled out of its nest, squawking uselessly on the wrong ground. He had, for example, written to Harriot begging to be forgiven for his priggishness, but then he could not prevent himself from also expressing anxiety about her father. At the age of sixty-six, Uncle Ashley had published a volume of poems in which the names of Christ and Mahomet were jumbled together in a manner very shocking to a Christian reader. He had mitigated this harshness by assuring Harriot that it was not the fate of her father solely that concerned him – his own father was excellent and praiseworthy, but had even he died in grace?

The Reverend Unwin was coming down the path saying, 'Mr Cowper, I require your assistance. It's a point for my sermon tomorrow. I simply cannot find the reference. You remember the two clerks who went to the tomb of Ovid to ask his spirit what was the best line he ever wrote?'

'Yes, of course.'

'Well, what was it? Can you remember?'

He quoted the line and Morley wrote it down. It was not strange that he could remember it immediately since he had himself been puzzling over its meaning for some days. What was strange was that Morley should ask him about it. Did he know?

'I suppose,' Morley was saying, 'I shall have to translate it for the brethren. "Virtue it is to abstain even from that which is lawful."' Would you say that's close?'

'Very near.'

'Which is very far, of course. Still. Isn't Ovid wonderful? So almost Christian.'

'Oh yes.'

'You don't seem quite convinced.'

'Well, I can hardly think it right, Morley, to give credence to a voice speaking from the tomb other than that of our Redeemer.'

Morley patted him on the cheek. 'Ah, my dear boy, you're so witty.' He went away a little, then returned. 'Tell me, don't you ever harbour doubts?'

'Doubts? Of course.'

'But not on the essentials, eh? Not, for instance, about the divinity of the Redeemer?'

'Oh no! Absolutely not.'

'Yes. Well. It seems to me the most absolute must be the most doubtful.'

'One can hardly doubt that Jesus Christ is the Son of God.'

'Who am I to doubt anything, my boy? It's hardly good manners, is it, to be an Arminian nowadays? It causes unnecessary pain, and we must avoid that, mustn't we? Farewell until tea-time. Splendid path, splendid.'

As briskly as his bird-like legs allowed, the Reverend Unwin hirpled back to his study. And Cowper, astonished that he should make such an elementary mistake, suddenly realised that the raw-breasted fledgling tumbled out of the nest was not the cuckoo.

It was a fine Sunday morning. Sermon in pocket, Morley was riding to an outlying church in his parish for the first service of the day. Mary and Cowper had gone ahead in the *chaise*. Susanna had stayed at home – and Morley understood why.

The previous evening, as he was adding the final polish to his sermon, she had come into the study to complain about what she was now calling 'the lodger'.

Really, it was no concern of hers that Mr Cowper's relatives were girning yet again over the cost of his upkeep; it was one thing for a man to have a lackey – and Sam Roberts was an excellent servant – but it was piling Ossa on Pelion for them to learn that he also had a half-orphan boy attending on him. It amused Morley that Mr Cowper, who was so curious about everything from the making of the world to the manufacture of a ball of twine, seemed oblivious to the commotion Dick Coleman had provoked in his family. The lad had been let go forthwith, put into an apprentice-ship with a breeches-maker, but, as happens with families, the fires of resentment continued to smoulder underground. Recently one relative, a Major Cowper, had vented his irritation by threatening to withdraw his contributions to the support of, as he put it, 'this former lunatic'.

Mary, of course, as was her wont, had taken the matter in hand, first by arranging that Mr Cowper should pay off an almost Turkish assortment of debts (including one for a splendidly suave pair of doeskin breeches) by selling off a small part of his capital, and then by cutting the rent in half – which was what had brought Susanna into his study. She was outraged that her father, whose living amounted to only £500 a year, should be subventing a gentleman who kept a servant on an income of £140. Was that fair? Was that just?

'Just, Susanna, what's just? Let's not wash our hands in that pot. Besides, this is rather a special case and one must make allowances. *Habitarunt di quoque silvas.'* Mr Unwin had uttered this line from Virgil half to himself as, taking off his spectacles, he observed through the glooming window Cowper on his knees putting the finishing touches to the new garden path. But the relevance of saying that 'Even the gods have lived in the woods' was lost on Susanna, though she had softened a little when he said that Mr Cowper, as well as being good in himself, was good company for her poor old father and he would not like to lose him, adding that he knew she would be tolerant for his sake because she was – kissing her unexpectedly on the cheek – his 'favourite daughter'.

On the other hand, it was significant that Susanna had complained to him directly. That boded ill for the future. Until now it had been tacitly understood between them that Mr Cowper had displaced her mother's affections. Well, displaced was not quite the word, but it was true that Mary could never love more than one person at a time. No, on reflection, that was not quite true either. She did love him as before, only Mr Cowper was a more interesting person, as those who have fallen a great distance usually are. There was something Luciferian about the man; he was one of those imps of darkness, very Londonish, used to knocking people aside in the street, thinking always of another distant trophy to satisfy their depravity, their deeply wicked hubris, though in this case the gentleman had debauched himself not on pride but on humility. And of course he was an entirely proper exile from Pandemonium, no matter what the gossips said behind their hands, as if Mary's constant walking abroad with him unchaperoned were tantamount to her hiking up her skirts in the High Street so that he could mount her like a dog. That had not happened; Eros had not fluttered his wings, but the thought of it being thought rankled. Actually, the perpetual praying, the constant ejaculating of the name of Jesus, the tuneless hymn-singing and the tinkling on the confounded harpsichord were even more of a nuisance than being calumniated as a cuckold.

On this fine Sunday morning, after he had gone about a mile from home, the Reverend Unwin gave his placid old mare her head and, as he often did on this familiar journey, began reading a book. The church steeple came into view and the horse, needing only the merest nudge from his heel, ambled off the turnpike and headed down a narrow rutted track. Plodding along between high banks of lacy cow parsley, the mare shook her head just once as a hungry cleg found its way into the velvety coolness of her ear.

Five minutes later, as they were rounding a bend, he looked up and saw a small golden-haired boy pissing figures of eight into the dust on the track. Just then the cleg found a vein in the mare's ear and pierced it. The mare reared up her great bulk and Mr Unwin was thrown off backwards.

The boy was seven years old. In one pocket of his ragged coat he had a crust of bread and a chunk of cheese wrapped in the scrap of red flannel he slept with every night. In the other pocket, because he was running away from home, he had stowed his best treasure, a glass marble, perfectly blue. He stood there for a moment, then ran off, still unbuttoned, back to his mother.

The Reverend Unwin's book, the *Ars Amatoria*, lay open beside a large stone, fanning its pages at the behest of the mild movements of the air. On the title page, beneath the author's name, *Publius Ovidius Naso*, was a speck of fresh blood.

17

The sky was the colour of an old bruise, grey-black and dirty lemon. In the warm eddying breezes there were occasional currents of colder air and flecks of rain. Ragged children were jostling to get a look in the window of the mud-cabin where Mr Unwin had been lying for three days, so the golden-haired boy's story of how the old man baahed like a sheep while they were carrying him to the house was old news, too often told.

When the breeze dropped suddenly, the children heard thunder rumbling in the distance and turned towards it. Behind them the sun broke through the clouds and, by its low raking light, which made the trees look feverishly tawny, they saw on the brow of a far hill the outline of a man on horseback standing out clearly against the pearl-bright horizon.

Over the three days, Susanna and her mother had swept clean the hovel's earthen floor with brooms fetched from the rectory, but the tenants, whose name was Coulter, had hens, ducks and a black sow with piglets, all of which came in and out during the day and slept in the house at night. Despite the stench and the noise, Mr Unwin was sleeping. His head was heavily bandaged and two padded blocks of wood kept it from turning. He was lying on the only bed in the house, a sort of wooden trough with a sack of feathers for a mattress. Clean sheets had been brought down from the rectory, but the local surgeon, Mr Teale, would allow them only to be draped over the patient. Morley was not to be moved, not for linen sheets, not to have a sip of soup, not for any reason.

Mary was sitting on a low stool stroking her husband's hand as if trying to draw him towards her.

'He sleeps so peacefully,' she said. 'Don't you think he's better, Mr Cowper?'

'I do, very much—'

'Mayn't we take him home?' Susanna interrupted.

Cowper said, 'It would be best, of course, but any sudden jolting—'

'Mama, it would be best to be out of this foul place.'

Suddenly Morley took in a huge tortured breath. Mary stood up and knocked over the candlestick. Her stool also fell over and broke a crockery basin of water on the floor. The candle flamed into the puddle and was quenched. At the same moment there was a sudden clap of thunder and a flash of lightning lit up the window. Without seeming to breathe out, Morley inhaled again in the same terrible way. Susanna stood clutching her waist with one hand, covering her mouth with the other.

In this gloom and chaos, the door opened and a man came in. Rain was streaming off his cloak. He surveyed the crowded room for a moment, then strode over to Mary and took her hand.

'Mrs Unwin, my name is John Newton. And this is your husband. Poor gentleman.' He bent over him. 'Calm yourself, sir. I've come to pray with you in your affliction.' He put his hand on Morley's forehead. 'Has he spoken since this happened?'

'No, sir. I mean yes. At the beginning he spoke, or rather he prayed.'

'Good, that is good. We are standing here on false ground, madam.'

'Sir?'

'But when the false ground gives under us, we find our feet upon the rock of prayer, which can never give way. Do you believe that?'

'I do, sir.'

'I see that you do. Continue steadfast, dear lady. Mr Unwin and all who believe are to be shown great mercy.' He raised a warning hand. 'Great and *undeserved* mercy. Let us pray now.'

With his potato nose and fat cheeks, John Newton was not an impressive man, but since he had come in, a hen had stopped pecking at the floor and stood with one leg raised, head cocked, wondering at him with her beady eye.

They prayed. But at midnight Morley Unwin quietly died.

The storm blew itself out before daybreak. Two days of fine weather followed. Then it started to rain steadily. On the morning of the funeral, the grave held almost enough water for the coffin to float on.

The Reverend Newton had been speaking for some time but was now concluding. 'Earth to earth,' he said triumphantly, 'ashes to ashes, dust to dust.' At the end of each phrase he fired a clod of mud onto the coffin like a man driving away a rabid dog, successfully. Then he raised the muddy hand in the air. 'From the germ of the cradle to the worm in the grave, man's life is a nothing. Nothing, brethren, nothing. But God said, let there be light, and there was light. And now Mr Unwin has gone into it. We hope. Hope is all we have. Through Christ Jesus our Lord, Amen.'

The funeral feast was held at the rectory. There had been some talk of a hotel in Huntingdon, but Newton intimated that such places were not far removed from being brothels. Intimation was not his strong suit, but since he had known Mrs Unwin only for a short time, he had limited himself to milder terms, such as bagnio and sponging-house.

Every room on the ground floor of the rectory was filled with tables laden down with provender, including an enormous goose and a barrel of oysters packed in seaweed fresh from Grimsby. For pudding there was a syllabub solid with gelatin. Many pitch-sealed bottles of old wine from Mr Unwin's cellar were opened. Newton, like St Paul, approved of 'a little wine for thy stomach's sake', and as he tore through a tumulus of goose-flesh, a fried beefsteak and a quivering mound of syllabub, he downed the most of a bottle of good claret; not that he noticed either the quality or quantity of anything he consumed – he went at food and drink like a horse going through a thick patch of brambles: rapidly and with an eye on the beyond.

Mr Teale, the surgeon, a thin, bald man with a pointy nose and a moustache that grew like moss in the shade of a stone, observed Newton's appetites and misunderstood them. He was not the only unawakened person at the feast – Mrs Unwin had even invited, though Newton did not know this, friends of Morley's who were Roman Catholic – but he was perhaps the least religious person there. Professionally, too, he avoided enthusiasm. At one stage he had considered trepanning the Reverend Unwin, but between the almost hopeless chance of his patient surviving by remaining absolutely still and the near-certainty of killing him by boring a hole in his head, he preferred to rely on inanition. As Teale was cautious medically, so also was he reticent socially, particularly in the company of evangelicals, who despised the world but were insistently polite about it, who looked down on money but assiduously gathered it up, who dismissed good works as useless and did them incessantly, who were mad for religion but sane and cold stone sober about everything else.

Normally Teale would have as soon dreamt of getting pickled with puritans as he would have of taking his bit-and-brace to the Reverend Unwin's temple. Unfortunately, an urgent amputation of a leg – two slashes with the knife, then the saw, and it was off in less than a minute, but the cat-gut stitching took longer – had kept him from the funeral, and so he had never met the Reverend Newton until he sat beside him at table. He recognised instantly that Newton was, like himself, a social upstart; the accent was a little affected, not like the born-to-the-silk drawl of the man on the other side of him, Mr Cowper (a sure rake by his fancy coat), but the affectation could not disguise Newton's origins – the man was a cockney! And he had been for many years a sailor. Well, they had that much in common: Mr Teale had served as a ship's doctor. The fact that Newton was now a clergyman did not discomfit Teale either – the church had long been a safe haven for retired tars. His appetites, too, were like those of the clergymen Teale remembered from his youth. My word, he said to himself, the parson's fond of his grog! So Teale, who had fortified himself before the amputation with half a pint of brandy, now matched Newton glug for glug.

Having garnered all this information and all these impressions,

Teale thought he would add to his store. Topping up his glass, he said, 'May I ask, Mr Newton, are you married?'

'I am.'

'And to a most excellent lady,' Cowper said. 'Mrs Newton supervised the preparations of our sad feast.'

'Well, give her my compliments. It's very tasty. I wish I was married to her myself.'

'*The wish is father to the thought,*' Newton said and Teale laughed.

'That's Shakespeare,' Cowper said.

'Shakespeare was a most licentious man.'

Teale thought that this remark, though delivered with a scowl, was also a joke and laughed again. 'Oh,' he said, 'we Englishmen are the most licentious people on earth, underneath it all.'

'We are,' Newton said grimly, 'and we will be.'

'Ho, ho, that's true, that's very true. We'll all be under the earth one day, but our wives won't; they'll be in heaven.'

'There's no sex in heaven,' Newton said.

Teale, missing the Biblical reference, said, 'You're very hard, Mr Newton, very hard. I hope you don't voice such opinions from the pulpit.'

'I do, sir.'

'Aye aye, captain! Here, let me tell you something I've just been reading in a book.'

'Oh yes,' Cowper said. 'Perhaps we should move into the parlour.'

But Teale ignored him. 'My wife gave it me, for Christmas. Mr Goldsmith's novel *The Vicar of Wakefield*. He talks there about the church being an excellent market for wives.'

'What?' Newton said in a low voice.

'Oh yes, it's comical in the extreme. You see, Mr Goldsmith has this man in his book, Moses is his name – must be a Jew – and this Moses says he knows of only two markets for wives in Europe.'

'Do I hear this correctly?' Newton said to Cowper, but Teale rushed onward to his doom, smiling, regardless.

'One market is our own Ranelagh, the pleasure gardens you know, and the other is in Spain, I forget the name of it. But, says Moses, the Spanish market is open only once a year, while in

Ranelagh wives are for sale every night. Every night! Isn't that good?'

'It is swinish,' Newton said, again in a low voice.

'What's that?'

'You're drunk, sir,' Newton said quite loudly. He was on his feet and was just about to speak even more loudly when he realised that people were looking at him and that the occasion was solemn, so he managed to restrain himself and merely bore down on the astonished Mr Teale and hissed in his ear, 'You're drunk, you swiving bastard, you poxed-up fucking son of a whore.'

Then, followed by Cowper, he stalked off to the parlour in search of Christians.

18

To the rule that every man can master a grief but he that has it, John Newton was an exception. Not only was he master of his own grief but of everyone else's. He made it his business to rescue those who were drowning in sorrow by plunging them further into it. His mission in life was Christian death, death preceded by suffering and followed by the eternal torment of hellfire, unless, that is, the sinner, by prior Election, was saved and entered heaven, but in Newton's book paradise was found not in the narrative but as an appendix.

He was, in some respects, an ideal companion in sorrow. As soon as he heard about the accident and that the Unwins were serious Christians, he hurried to offer assurances that since things could not be worse, they could not therefore be better. In his view, and God's, this was the nearest anyone could get to happiness on earth. The paradox distracted Mary from her grief; she was too sensible to believe it, but its gaudiness was a comfort. Cowper, too, was comforted; two years had elapsed since he had escaped from hell and Newton reminded him of his good fortune, as if the roaring inferno were a beacon glimmering noiselessly in the middle-distance.

One morning shortly after the funeral, Mary was sitting in her husband's chair in the drawing-room. Cowper had just brought her a cup of tea but she had taken it with only the faintest acknowledgement. He walked up and down, not knowing what to say. When the rug on her lap slipped a little, he tucked it back in place, but as he was wondering if he should dare to put his hand on her shoulder, Sam came in. He intended to announce a visitor, but he had hardly opened his mouth when Newton was striding past him as if he were invisible.

'Are you well, madam?' Newton asked, taking Mary's hand and looking into her eyes intently.

'Yes, thank you.'

'Mr Cowper?'

'Yes, we're both well, but sorrowful.'

'Well then, we are united in sadness.'

'Oh yes?'

'I have just received news of the death of my niece. My brother's daughter.'

'Oh, my dear sir, this is terrible news,' Mary said.

Newton smiled iron. 'The infant has gone to a better place.'

'Poor, poor child,' Mary said.

'She is in heaven, I have no doubt. And yet when I told my brother that this was the best place for her, he was, I fear, somewhat taken aback.'

'Not unnaturally,' Cowper said.

'You think me heartless, Mr Cowper, but we wept together and in the end he was persuaded it was God's will and that we must be glad of it.'

'Still,' Mary said.

'Still? Nothing is still, my dear lady. Faith moves! It moves, that is its business. Which is, in fact, why I am here. The moment is, I think I may say, momentous.'

'Oh yes?'

'How long is it now since Mr Unwin was translated?' Newton asked this as if death were a question of scholarship.

'One week,' Mary said.

'That's quite long enough. It's time to be up and stirring.'

'In what sense, Mr Newton?'

'In God's sense, Mr Cowper. Good Christian people, such as you are, should be joined together in community with their fellows. There are too many of the pagan sort in Huntingdon. Break free of them, shake the dust of this place off your shoes and, in short, come with me to Olney.'

19

Orchardside, Olney, November 14th, 1767

My Dear Josephus,

You will, I think, be somewhat astonished by this new address, but hardly more so than am I. And yet the gentleman responsible for the precipitancy with which our situation has been altered remains entirely unmoved by it — we are breathless but Mr Newton panteth not. Indeed, I sometimes rather suspect that he thinks he has brought us nor fast nor far enough away from the sinful world but like a lion knee deep in the cool waters of an oasis lifts his head and sniffs for new fountains beyond. He feeds on the ungraspable and what for Tantalus is misery is for him fulfilment. Whether that be true or no, it is certain that his power of decision cannot be doubted. Poor Morley Unwin was hardly in heaven when Mr Newton proposed that we should come, as he puts it, within the Sound of his Ministry. I dare say he would have taken us here within the hour had that been possible, and if in parting it was observed that the front door of the rectory had been left open he would have galloped on down the street regardless. Of places and persons he holds a view so practical it is positively Berkeleyan: as soon as he decides to turn his back on them, they, like the late Bishop of Cloyne, cease to exist. This establishment, however, could not be detached so swiftly from the ties that bound it to Huntingdon; it was three months before Mrs Unwin turned the key in the lock of the front door for the last time.

It took all of that fine October day — an exact month ago as I now see — to travel the thirty-odd miles to Olney, but for Mrs Unwin and myself the journey was considerably shortened by the presence of Mr Newton and his Mary, a helpmeet whose sometimes mildly astringent patience and abidingness, like the lanthorn of Faith in the whirlwind, are as remarkable as they are constant. What most abbreviated the journey, however, was Mr Newton's willingness to cast light into heretofore darkened corners of his history, not least the one occupied by his wife — but more of that anon.

At this juncture I must say that as we bowled along in our open chaise I could not help but be struck by the contrast between this sedatest part of England (Greek pastoral without the mountains) and the fume and flame of Mr Newton's narrative (Greek drama with added volcanoes). If I am the Englishman I take myself to be, this is what Englishmen like: a quiet amazement in a sober place.

Quietude of any kind never figured large with Mr Newton. For instance, he told us that at the age of fifteen, on reading Beattie's Church History, *he stopped speaking! And why? For fear of saying something that might offend the Deity, a silence that lasted all of three months, during which time he ate no meat. (For the why of that see below.) His mother, a Puritan of the old school, intended him for the church, but she died young, and this calamity (like unto my own) almost instantly made of him a violent atheist. Having been then sent to sea by his shipwright father, he racketed around the oceans of the world, indulging in every vice known to mariners and cursing the God whom he once adored. Extreme in blasphemy as he had once been in piety, when he fell in love the extremity of his fall was vertiginous — the object of his passion was a child of fourteen.*

I should say here that this point in his narrative was greeted with a cry, 'Fourteen I may have been, Mr Newton, but I most certainly was not a child!' — by which you will have understood that the infant was amongst us.

Within an hour of seeing her first, this loud-swearing tar was rendered as helplessly mute as the gentlest giraffe. Indeed, Mary Catlett, for that was her name, had such a paralysing effect on Mr Newton that the ship on which he had then enlisted, bound for Jamaica, sailed without him. And shortly thereafter he was kidnapped! Perhaps that word is too strong, but what other describes abduction by a press-gang? This happened at Harwich Dock and he says it was his sailor's check shirt that tempted the miscreants — how different our life would have been, quoth his spouse, had you been in good white linen.

Attired by compulsion though he now was, Mr Newton not only wore the badge of his fate with equanimity but soon rose into being a midshipman. However, on his ship being posted to New Guinea and realising that on his return Miss Catlett would have reached the age of nineteen, he deserted, was caught, brought back, stripped and flogged most savagely. Maddened by this punishment and by the tropical heat, he planned self-murder or the murder of his ship's captain, or both — and was only prevented from these final crimes by the thought of Mary.

Released at last from this captivity, he then found himself a greater: he became a slave! What began as service on a plantation soon became the grossest servitude, apparently because his master had a black mistress who conceived a violent hatred for him. Worked to the bone, clad in rags, fed on husks and draff, infected by tropical fever, he sank into dumb beastliness. For two years his only consolation was a book, a tattered Geometry and — picture this — when night fell he would repair to the beach and trace out on the sand Euclid's ideal forms by the pure light of the African moon.

He then managed to escape to a group of nearby islands, the Bananoes, where he became foreman on a plantation. It was a less servile existence, but as he had given up all hope of ever returning to England, he now became as African as the Africans themselves and if anything even more superstitious, a man afraid to sleep beneath that brilliant moon which had but shortly illuminated his old Geometry.

At last, after two and a half years, he boarded a ship bound for England. What a sight he must have been! A ragged and reckless skeleton burnt black by the Afric sun, and so profane and blasphemous in his speech that the captain feared he would bring down the judgement of God on his vessel.

The which in part, and very nearly in the whole, Mr Newton did. During a violent storm, which raged for two days, the masts were torn away, the holds were flooded and a number of men were *swept overboard. As Mr Newton watched them weltering in the mountainous waves he realised with a great thrill that he too was about to die. Then, while labouring desperately at the pumps he found himself crying out, 'If this will not do, the Lord have mercy on us!' The import of which exclamation, uttered unthinkingly, he understood at once, and it was followed immediately by the thought that, 'If He really exists there will be very little mercy for me.' And at that moment he was saved! First the soul was saved and then the body — the latter only mattered insofar as it allowed the saving of other souls, a purpose to which he has devoted his life ever since.**

My dear Joe, I must call a halt here. This epistle is already too full of excitement, and excitement, as you know, is bad for me. But, though I now see that what I have written is shot through with a quiverful of exclamation points, a reprehensible and disgusting thing in a prose style, I assure you that the archer's hand trembles not. I am, in fact, calm, and who has made me so, amid all this whirl and breathlessness, is Mr Newton. All my life I was afraid of last things and fled what I was convinced was my damnation, uselessly. Mr Newton has stopped my fear by bringing me right into it. For this I love him. As for you, dear friend, I shake your hand

Affectionately,

W.C.

*Post scriptum. 'Ever since' is somewhat of an exaggeration. Having married Miss Catlett, he returned to sea and became a slave-trader . . .

Newton had been reminiscing all day. As they neared Olney he was explaining why, after six years, he had decided to quit the sea: not because slavery was inhuman, though he did begin to wonder were the chains, the thumbscrews and the tongue-wedges quite in the tradition of Christian kindness, but because it was all too human.

'A temptation to the flesh?' Mrs Unwin inquired. 'I don't quite see how that could be.'

'He was exceeding vile, but not a cannibal,' Mrs Newton said.

'No, madam, but the consumption of flesh came into it. There were occasions, you see, when the slaves I carried were female.'

'This, you will understand, was in the past,' Mrs Newton said brightly.

Newton ignored this remark and went on: 'It is my experience that the consumption of animal fats arouses animal lusts. Beefsteaks lead to beastliness, and even the rancid salt pork which constituted our diet contributed to the risk. At such times, therefore, I ate no meat.'

'You were very wise,' Mrs Newton said, adding under her breath, 'then'.

'Indeed I was wise, for some of these women, the Nubians especially, had such magnificent black bosoms that I had to mortify myself most severely.'

'Oh look,' Cowper cried. 'Journey's end!'

The cry was not of joy but embarrassment: there were times when Newton seemed unaware of the impropriety of touching upon certain subjects in the company of ladies – bosoms for instance, however magnificent and black they might be.

The journey's end was not magnificent. Olney High Street was long and broad, a straggle of low houses and poor shops which widened into a triangular market square.

'That's the Round House, the town prison,' Newton said, pointing. 'And there is Orchardside.'

Cowper's heart dipped. To his eye the Round House, a six-sided building overshadowed by three great elm-trees, looked less like a prison than did Orchardside, with its mock-Gothic battlements louring over a red-brick façade. But did any prison ever have as many windows? Eight in the top storey, then eight more, double the size, in the middle, and five more on the ground floor. This disproportion was explained by there being three front-doors – really, it was three houses in one, except that the low door through which Sam now came out to greet them had obviously been a window once upon a time. The whole place – and they were only to occupy half of it – was as confusing as it was depressing.

Then, as they were alighting from the carriage, they heard a strange sound.

'Mr Newton,' Mrs Newton said, 'kindly ignore them.'

The sound was coming from the Swan Inn on the far corner of

Market Place. A group of men, young and old, who had been lounging on benches drinking jugs of beer in the last rays of the setting sun, had now turned their heads towards the new arrivals, and the sound issuing from their mouths was a hiss. A wench, who had been emptying a pail of slops into the gutter, crooked a finger at Newton invitingly, bent over, pointed the finger at her backside and made a loud farting noise. The drinkers cheered.

'John,' Mrs Newton said, 'mind your own business.'

Newton growled frustration, like a lion tormented by arrows from pygmies on the other side of a just too wide river. Then he went into the house, saying, 'This is a low and dirty town.'

20

Orchardside was not ready. When they entered the door that had been a window, they found themselves in a surprisingly spacious hall with a cupola ceiling, but there were gaping cracks in the plaster and the floorboards were rotten. They went down a dank passageway into a drawing-room.

'Oh, what a sweet little fireplace,' Mrs Unwin said. But the room itself was little and not sweet at all.

They went out into the back garden. It, too, was poky – a long, narrow wilderness bounded by high brick walls – but it led to a gate which opened on the wide and pretty orchard that gave the house its name.

'The wild boys from Silverside,' Newton said, 'come over and filch the apples, but I let them for they're hungry.' He turned and pointed. 'And there, you see, is the back of the Vicarage – if it weren't for that wall, we could walk over there.'

'One day you shall blow your trumpet and it will fall down,' Mrs Newton said. 'But in the meantime let us go round by the road.'

So they drove to the Vicarage, and when she saw it, Mrs Unwin said, 'Now this is pretty.'

The Vicarage was built of stone; there were three dormers in the slated roof, five windows in the first floor and five in the ground floor, a repetition nicely interrupted by a panelled hall door. The setting, too, was pretty: the house looked out on a broad water-meadow, an old mill, a wide bridge arching over the Ouse and, straight ahead, the church, its tower and steeple soaring high above an ancient grove of elms.

'Is this not grace?' Newton said. 'Let us go in now and say a prayer of thanks to the Lord our God.'

'And to the Earl of Dartmouth,' Mrs Newton said.

'There is no comparison,' Newton barked – if there was one thing he disliked about Mary it was her habit of jesting about the Deity. Even worse was the way she had of picking at the scab of an old annoyance. When, after supper, he opened a bottle of vintage port, she tasted it and said, 'Well, bless me, this is excellent wine. Thank God for the Earl.'

'Why do you say that?' Mrs Unwin asked.

'Because it's a gift from him, like the house.'

'The house is not a gift,' Newton said.

'The Earl built it for you and gave it to you. If them's not gifts, I'm sure I don't know what is.'

'It was not done for me, it was for my Ministry.'

Cowper said, 'Dartmouth obviously esteems your abilities highly. This house, for instance, is much too good for the living one would expect in such a parish.'

Why, Mrs Unwin thought, he's jealous.

'Much too good for an old slaver and a Surveyor of Tides,' Mrs Newton said.

'Forty is not the slightest bit old,' Newton said.

'Forty-two,' said his wife.

'Surveyor of Tides?' Cowper said. 'We have not heard of that before.'

'John far prefers to reminisce about the Nubian bosom, don't you, sir?'

Newton growled, but all of a sudden indulgently, as if the lion had realised a toothsome pygmy was on his side of the river. 'Mary knows all my faults, not the least of which is I paint too bright the black. Yes, I was the Surveyor of Tides at Liverpool for a number of years, and it was there that I learned not just to love but to idolise this wife of mine.'

'*Thou shalt not have graven images before me*,' Mrs Newton said.

She was contented. It was sad not to have children and some-times it was wearing to have to listen yet again to the African saga, but though John could be depressed or disgusted – the Jezebel pointing her farting arse at him was what had made dinner so, relatively speaking, gloomy – there was no doubting the depth of his love for his Mary, even if the idolatry was a typical nonsense, a variation of the superstitious foolishness that had driven him to buying ticket after ticket in the lottery, or that consumed him with guilt when the earthquake destroyed Lisbon, for not doing anything to help the people of Liverpool prepare for a similar disaster. First fate, then God had enthralled him – but it was she who had magicked him, body and soul. No wonder Mr Cowper, who was talking now about the danger of adoring persons, was so taken by him that he had altered his life almost in an instant, though she could not yet work out why John himself seemed to have fallen under the sway of this embarrassed nobleman. With his long sensitive nose and hurt mouth, he looked and behaved like a grief-stricken greyhound, or some sort of nocturnal animal, a mole perhaps, that as soon as you come near contracts in a flash back into its den. On the other hand, when you poked John he burst snorting out of his stall like a bull that scents a heifer in heat. Oh, it was so easy and so amusing to goad him then.

'The only person we are permitted to adore,' Newton was saying, 'is Jesus Christ, the son of God.'

Mrs Newton leaned back in her chair, kicked off her shoe, put her foot up into her husband's lap, unseen, and said, 'John Wesley wouldn't care for that sentiment.'

'Mr John Wesley,' Newton said, goaded, 'Mr John Wesley is a very troublesome man.'

'Really?' Cowper said.

'Of course. Not to believe that Christ is the Son of God, what else but trouble could he expect to bring upon the church? In this he is almost as culpable as Mr George Whitefield.'

'Really?' Cowper said again. 'I thought Mr Whitefield was a hero of yours.'

'He used to be, but then the scales fell from my eyes. He has disseminated more false doctrine to the nation than he should ever be able to eradicate.'

'You'll do it, John,' his wife said. 'You'll eradicate their errors.'

'God help me,' Newton cried, in a congested voice, 'between Whitefield and Wesley I am blinded, but I shall see to their confusion.'

'Isn't it fortunate that you weren't obliged to depend on either of them to be ordained?' Mrs Newton asked sweetly.

Newton clamped her foot even more tightly between his thighs. This remark was deeply provocative: it had taken so long to get into Holy Orders because no bishop would accept him, on the grounds that he was debarred by not having been at Oxford or Cambridge or some other university, even a Scotch one, whereas the real and scandalous reason was that they regarded him as a Methodistical ranter.

'I am obliged to no one, Mrs Newton, and I am only too well aware that you are trying to grig me.'

'Oh, I wouldn't dream of it.'

'Of course you would, but I'll say this to you, ma'am. If the Earl built me this house and if he got the Bishop of Chester, an obscure and unsavoury person, to ordain me, he may well have been guided by Providence.'

'The Providence of the Lord is indeed a mystery,' Mrs Newton said.

Then she, who was an adept at the contrarieties of love-making, put her foot back into its shoe – that was enough of that – and at the same moment finished off her husband with a flourish. 'May we,' she said, 'have another little glass of his port?'

The next morning, while they were taking their first walk alone by the river, Mrs Unwin said, 'I rather thought at some stage you would say you had been at school with the Earl.'

'I resisted the temptation.'

'Temptation?'

'Yes. You remember when I asked your son to call on my relations in London?'

'Of course, and they treated him so hospitably.'

'What do you think my motive was in doing that?'

'Motive? Did you have one?'

'I did not suspect so at first, but on looking into my heart, I discovered I had yielded to a temptation.'

'Oh yes? And what was it?'

'Credentials. I wanted to establish my credentials. To prove that I was not a mere vagabond. To prevent people describing me as *that fellow* Cowper, which I heard more than once in Huntingdon. I wanted, vile as it sounds, to show that I had splendid connections, to give an ocular demonstration of them and by doing so to assert my gentlemanlihood.'

This recital was punctuated by Mrs Unwin saying, 'How bizarre! How bizarre!' and when he had finished she said, 'But, my dear, I'm a draper's daughter, from Ely.'

'Well, such is pride. It pretends to walk erect, but really it crawls.'

'What a comical creature you are.'

'It twists and twines itself about, but it can't get out from under the Cross.'

He said this so seriously and yet so comically, doing such a strangely accurate imitation of a snake walking upright, that she did not know whether to laugh or cry, and for that reason laughed helplessly.

'Which is why,' he said, 'I am resolved that the name of Dartmouth will never issue from these lips.'

But he, too, was laughing, and she thought, My God, he is proud.

21

*M*ary woke with a start to the sound of Newton bellowing, each word accompanied by a blow of his fist on the lectern.

'*Time flies, death urges, knells call, heaven invites, Hell threatens.* These words, brethren, are from the *Night Thoughts* of Mr Edward Young, and dark are they and gloomy, for Hell indeed threatens us all.'

'What hour is it, Mr Cowper?' Mary asked. He took out his watch and showed her. 'Good gracious,' she said.

'Wonderful, isn't it? Six hours preaching and every moment full of fire.'

'Wonderful,' Mary said.

Newton's main purpose was Sudden Conversion, but though he gloried in what he called the Moment, he believed that when the tomb was opened, those who rolled away the stone should already be well and truly exhausted by prior Experiment. And then, having been arrived at, the Instant required prolongation. When he was not preaching – and six-hour sermons were not unusual – he was visiting the sick, teaching the local children, distributing charity to the poor or writing letters of exhortation and complaint to evangelicals all over England.

And sometimes he entertained.

One of these occasions coincided with the arrival of Susanna Unwin to her new home. Although she had yet to announce it, she was engaged to be married to the Reverend Matthew Powley. He was from a very decent family in Huntingdon with whom she had stayed while her newly widowed mother whirled off to Olney with the lodger, neither of them apparently the slightest bit concerned that it would take three months for their accommodation to be made habitable, during which time they had had to live, most irregularly in Susanna's opinion, with Mr and Mrs Newton.

Susanna's engagement would not have come as a surprise to Mrs Unwin had she known about it, but she did not need to be told – one look at the happy couple was enough for her to realise that they were made to be bound together for life. Happy was not quite the exact word to describe Susanna's state of mind; it would have been more precise to say that she was determined to be satisfied. Satisfaction, however, was hardly the epithet to apply to Matthew Powley: he was large, heavy, muscular and yet, Mrs Unwin thought as she watched him walking in the garden of Orchardside, and exchanging monosyllables with Cowper, beyond emotion, somehow immaterial, too solid for description.

'The Newton house is pretty; this is ugly. That's the top and bottom of it,' Susanna said.

'Yes, dear, but I'm fond of ours already.'

They were standing at the gate to the orchard, comparing the two houses.

'When is William coming?' Susanna asked.

'Next week, I believe.'

'Is there room for him?'

'I haven't quite made up my mind yet where to put him. I had thought of the top room, but that would involve moving Sam.'

'And Mr Cowper?'

'Yes?'

'You've given him the nicest room.'

'Well, as far as niceness goes here, yes.'

'It's next door to yours.'

'Meaning?'

'No meaning, Mother.'

'Susanna, I don't care for your tone.'

'It is not my tone; it is the general opinion.'

'About what?'

'Oh, Mother, really, it's too shaming.'

Mary paused, lowered her head, then raised it again. 'Mr Cowper is my friend, Susanna. I will say no more than that about the matter. Now or at any other time. Is that understood?'

'Yes,' Susanna replied meekly. She had never seen her mother so angry. But just as she was about to say something conciliatory, she saw Cowper coming towards them.

'My dears,' he called out, smiling, 'we ought to go in and dress for the feast, oughtn't we?'

Susanna turned away and walked off into the orchard.

It was a rather harassed-looking Mrs Newton who opened the door of the Vicarage that evening. 'At last, at long last,' she said. 'I'm so glad to see you. Forgive me, I'm breathless from cooking. What a lovely dress, Susanna. And this must be your young man. May I call you that?'

'Good evening,' Mr Powley said.

Mrs Newton brought them directly in to the dining-room. Newton rose from his place at the head of the table and hurried to greet them. His other guests also stood up. The man nearest the door wore a magnificent uniform decorated with a glittering array of medals; the others were dressed identically in black.

'Hurrah!' Newton said. 'Our party is complete. Welcome, welcome everyone. What do you think, Mr Cowper: thirteen Baptist Ministers all in a row?'

'It's a very comfortable sight.'

'But none of them, I dare say, as pious as my brave Captain Scott. He's come over from Northampton to escape the races there.'

'It's not so much the horses,' Captain Scott said grimly; 'it's the gambling that goes with them.'

Mrs Newton took Mrs Unwin by the arm and whispered into her ear, 'Who could deny my husband has a sense of humour?'

'A sense of humour? Well, I thought, that's the most preposterous thing I ever heard in my life,' Mrs Unwin said to Cowper the next day. 'But, you know, it does make a peculiar kind of sense.'

They were taking an early walk by the river. Newton had sent over a message to say he had been called away urgently to Bedford. Mrs Unwin said that if it were anyone else but Mr Newton, she should say Bedford was a euphemism for a thick head.

'Have you ever noted his laugh?'

'Frequently.'

'It's not really laughter, though. It's an expected noise, a trick he's learned to perform, like a dog in a circus.'

'You're very hard, Mrs Unwin. Our friend is more than a hound.'

'Of course, my dear, but there is something theatrical about him, is there not?'

They were standing on the bridge. Autumn was in the air and the river was starred with early fallen leaves, hardly moving on the slow current.

'Well, the theatre is a fountainhead of vice and I'm glad I no longer have to enjoy it as I used to.'

'Oh, you poor wretch.'

'That reminds me,' Cowper said, taking a sheet of paper from his pocket. 'He thrust this at me as we were leaving.'

They stood together reading. A few corrections had been made, lines scored out so forcefully that the nib had almost penetrated the paper, but otherwise the thing was clean, set down with Newton's usual urgency.

'The first two words are mine,' Cowper said. 'They come from an early poem. It's a wonder he remembered them. And the scansion is rather awkward. But it's nothing that can't be fixed.'

22

Amazing Grace! How sweet the sound,
That saved a wretch like me!
I once was lost, but now I'm found,
Was blind, but now I see.

He was standing out of sight of the congregation behind the pulpit, trembling uncontrollably. It was not the singing that made him nervous – he heard it only as a muffled roaring, like waves on a distant ocean.

Newton began to speak even before the congregation had resumed their seats. 'That little hymn, my dearly beloved people, was composed by myself with the assistance of our brother, Mr Cowper. You know him to be a Christian gentleman, his goodness matched only by his shyness, but as I have prevailed upon him to sing to the Lord, I have also now persuaded him to speak to you in testimony.'

The steps up into the pulpit were carved from an almost black mahogany and, as he ascended them, Cowper felt that the rest of the world was wooden too, but denser. Then Newton, smelling of fresh sweat, was embracing him and whispering, 'Smite them hard, hip and thigh.'

As Newton left the pulpit, Cowper took some sheets of paper from his pocket.

'My text is taken from the Book of James, Chapter ... Excuse me ...' His hands were shaking so much, he could not read what he had written, and when he looked up, the congregation was faceless, monumentally silent. But then the verse from the Bible came back to him — *Every good gift and every perfect gift is from above, and comes down from the Father of lights* — and he began to speak without reference to his notes.

In what he had written, using an ancient device of rhetoric, he had begun from a small point of biblical scholarship and built on it a larger structure. The original text of the verse and the English translation both agreed that God was the father of plural lights and not, as might be expected, the father of one light, but Cowper forgot what the Aramaic word was, mixed it up with the Greek version, then confused King James with William Tyndale and stopped again.

Then a line of what he had written came back to him and, with a terrible grin, he uttered it. 'In any event, it is wonderful, is it not, that the lights are many? But that is because the dark is singular.'

Newton, standing at the communion table, called out, 'Mr Cowper, it is your father in heaven who is listening. Speak to him.'

A thought came into his head: I hate this black smiler because he wants to kill me. The words were so shockingly loud in his mind that for a moment he was convinced everyone must have heard them, but then rage and guilt overcame his embarrassment.

'Our father,' he said, 'our father in heaven is listening, yes, we know that and we believe it, or rather we believe it because we cannot know it. We do not know if the father can hear us, that is why we cry out unto him. We do know that the dark is singular and we are strangers in it, each of us solitary in our affliction, which is the fear of death. All fears are the fear of death. Our entire being then is all a wound, never to be healed. Human life is, in small, our absence from God, and that absence, when it is deliberate, an act of the will, is a kind of slaughter of the self. It is as if a man should murder his own son, as Abraham was willing to murder Isaac, which seems cruel to us, but what was Abraham without his God? He was as nothing, lonely as a grain of dust. Is the son to destroy the father? Is he to make a sacrifice of him who is the origin of all things? No, he durst not do it. And yet, such is pride, man does so dare. We call pride a deadly sin because it kills the gift of life, which is given down from the heavenly father. This is why we make proper sacrifice. To make sacrifice is to make an offering of our own guilt. But in our communion we do this as a commemoration, not as others do in theirs, which is wicked, ignorant and prideful. There was only one sacrifice, that of Christ on the cross, and it happened only once. Once and once only the Son took on the burden of death without the father. Never before or since was there such loneliness, such abandonment, such absence. We durst not feel it, and yet feel it we do in our own loss.'

He stopped speaking. What he had said was so plainly the case that he felt his weakness become a power beyond himself.

'I am here and am a poor and vile and sinful man, but a man who was a child once and had a mother and a mother's love, a well of consolation, a fountain in the midst of a wilderness of troubles that I know, and that everyone here knows, is as wide as all the world. But the well is dried up long since and the desert is dry. And yet, we look up and see the father of lights shining in the singular dark, and the heavens are no longer empty but filled with the sun and the moon and all the stars, the ten thousand worlds, and then we look at each other and are amazed by grace, the grace which Mr Newton has so recently and so freshly sung of. That grace is the source of the love we have for each other, and because of love, we go through fire and flood, and they do not overwhelm us.'

He stopped again. Mrs Unwin was looking at him.

'Where we are is lost, but God is love and he will open to our eyes a better country where there is no more death, neither sorrow nor pain, and he shall wipe away the widow's tears and all tears forever. I grieve for you, I pray for you. Could I do more, I would. But God must comfort you, not I, and he will comfort you, out of love. Amen.'

As he stumbled down from the pulpit, there was a silence, then Newton called out, 'Amen!' The word was taken up and repeated throughout the congregation. As Cowper passed him, Newton reached out his hand. Almost angrily, he ignored it and hurried down the aisle. He had to get out into the fresh air. At the door an old man stood up from his bench and embraced him, whispering, 'I've heard many men preach, but none like thee, my son.'

The daylight dazzled him. I have ventured out of the tomb, he thought, and an ancient has called me his son.

It was too much, too high a price to pay. He had forgotten himself. He had spoken of God as if he knew Him. There were no words for such presumption.

23

The parlour doubled as dining-room, and the dining-table also served for desk. Originally it had been designed for card games; at each corner were shallow recesses for counters, and when the table was covered with a cloth, they were easily forgotten. The table was also very low and, in order to be able to write more easily, he had taken to heaving a thick atlas onto it to raise the level.

Mrs Unwin, examining a bill, said, 'Mr Cowper, how on earth could you spend two pounds and ten shillings on hosiery?'

'I blush to think, ma'am. I must have iron feet. Saint Augustine says that God has woollen feet but iron hands.'

'Does he indeed? How very interesting.'

'You don't sound very interested.'

'Forgive me, it's this bill I'm thinking of. How is it to be paid?'

'Paid? Oh, I couldn't do that. My budget won't rise to it.'

'Mr Cowper, please be serious.'

'I know. I'll write to Joe Hill.'

'Again? Oh, very well, I will lend you the money. But in future I shall knit your stockings.'

'I should like that. Oh, damn!'

Hearing Newton coming through the back door – a frequent occurrence now that he had knocked a hole through the orchard wall – Cowper had put down his glass on the edge of a recess in the card-table and it had spilled. As he was swabbing up the milk with his sleeve, he knocked over the inkwell.

'Damn it, this is too much. Not now, not now. I can't bear it.'

And he ran out of the room, down the passageway, out the hall door, into the street and across the square before realising he had not put on his overcoat. Winter was drawing in and it was cold, but he went on walking, agitatedly muttering to himself, 'It's damnable, damnable. I'm twice damned, Newton, because of you.'

The words had come out of his mouth unbidden. He stopped in the middle of the road and prayed to be forgiven. And as he prayed, he heard the sound of a trumpet.

But it was only the postman approaching on horseback blowing his tin horn.

'Ah, Mr Post, it's you,' Cowper said. 'I thought it was the angel Gabriel.'

The postman shook his head wordlessly and fished a letter out of his satchel.

The next day Cowper left Olney before the sun had risen and took the diligence to Cambridge to visit his brother John.

The counterpane on the bed was scattered with papers and books and when Cowper, clearing them away to sit down, came across John Ford's *'Tis Pity She's a Whore*, his face fell.

'It's only a play, William,' John said. 'No need to be scandalised.'

'I'm not at all scandalised.'

'I can see you are.'

'Truly, I'm not. I know you think me a frightful prig and indeed there have been times when I've behaved like one, but now ...' His voice caught in his throat.

'But now what?'

'John, you're so much better a man than me.'

'Better but damned, isn't that so?'

'No. I am simply glad to be with you.'

'Here, but not at home.'

'What do you mean?'

'Pagans aren't welcome in Olney, are they? Isn't that why you stopped inviting me? I embarrassed you.'

'It wasn't my embarrassment, John. It was yours.'

'Oh yes?'

'You know that not being one of us, you couldn't have joined our prayers, and so I didn't want to hurt your feelings.'

'Well, you did save me then, if only from an awkwardness. How very kind.'

'Please, John, don't mock me. This is too serious for mockery.'

'Indeed it is.' John, trying to laugh, was convulsed with retching. Cowper turned away. He did not want to see what his brother was spitting into the enamel cup he had taken from the bedside table. Could it really be, he wondered, that John Cowper was less deserving of his hospitality than John Newton? And the preaching, although he had done it several times to please his mentor, had been a dreadful mistake. The pulpit had ruined him, exposed him as a fraud and his faith as false hope.

John was cheerful, convinced that he would soon be well again, but then the college physician, Dr Strick, arrived, and when he had bled the patient a little, he took Cowper aside. It was an imposthume of the liver. Imposthume meant an abcess.

Abcess and absence, Cowper thought, are not a rhyme but close to it. Absence was what he and John had had in common all their lives, but in recent years they had become strangers at heart. Now John had shrunk to a skeleton, his loose yellow skin tented by stick bones, his eyes too bright for life. He was dying, and if he died without being saved, he would go to hell for all eternity.

'*Corvus timidus!* The gypsy is at the gate.'

The sound of John's voice in the darkening room woke Cowper as he dozed in an armchair by the window.

'John?'

'Oh, William, I was dreaming and no one was there.'

'Was it a bad dream?'

'No, but it was all brown. As in a great library. And I was somehow a black thing searching in a book. It was very amusing.'

'Yes?'

'In the book, a sort of dictionary but with animals for words, it said *corvus timidus* was the Latin for scarecrow, which I knew was quite wrong, so I said, *Nec timidus nec terribilis non sum.* Then the book squawked and flew away and I woke up. Isn't that strange?'

But when William asked about the gypsy, John was startled. There had been no gypsy in the dream. And yet he became anxious and did not want to be left on his own.

Three days later John had a violent fit of asthma. His best friend in the college, Richard Gough, was there at the time and he ran to fetch Dr Strick. When Strick arrived, John was almost unconscious, but as soon as a foul-smelling bottle was passed beneath his nose, he revived. The bottle contained hartshorn, a tincture made from the horns of deer.

He slept for most of the day. Then, as the room darkened, he awoke screaming as if possessed by a demon. Afterwards he subsided into sobbing, broken by an occasional high-pitched mewing when the pain returned. Strick was again summoned. The imposthume had, he said, attached itself to the spine. He prescribed laudanum, but when the effect wore off John again gave way to helpless screaming.

Ten days later, after one of these bouts, he said, 'I feel this is a judgement on me, William, for having judged you.'

'You never judged me, John.'

'But I did, I did. I thought of your madness as a kind of diabolic pride and I considered that your sufferings were a judgement on you.'

'Which they were.'

'But also that my inability to alleviate them was a judgement on myself.'

'How strange we humans are, to blame ourselves for no fault but that of not being lost too.'

'William, I wish I had been closer to you.'

'We are close now.'

'If only you knew what comfort I have in this bed, miserable as it is. Brother, I love to look on you.'

'And I on you. But how weak our love is compared to God's love.'

'As for that, I take leave to doubt one can be loved and judged at the same time, particularly in this way. Oh, listen.'

Outside they heard the sound of an owl hooting mournfully.

'That's down by the river,' John said. 'How I wish I could walk on its banks once more.'

'You will, John, and you'll come to Olney too and walk by the Ouse.'

'You have a good river there, William. Better than all the rivers of Damascus.' He paused, his face changed and then he said fearfully, 'Oh, what a scene is passing before me.'

'What is it?'

'I can see the gypsy at the gate.'

'Is it a dream?'

'No, it's a memory. A memory I'd forgotten. And I forgot because I chose to.'

He was upset, but after some minutes he composed himself and said, 'I had my fortune told once. I think I was fifteen or so, a schoolboy in Berkhamstead. The fortune-teller was a gypsy, and he wore a soldier's red coat, all tattered and torn. The point is, just before I got ill, I was walking in the college gardens when I saw him again. He was at the gate, peering at me through the bars. The same man, the same coat, the same age. No change in him at all. I went to speak to him, but before I could say a word he vanished.'

'You could have been mistaken.'

'No, I'm not mistaken. Or rather I am all a mistake and it's too late.'

'Why do you say that?'

'In Berkhamstead the gypsy said he saw nothing for me beyond thirty. Which I now am. I have no future, William. I am a dead man.'

'But you can have every future, John, and every true happiness in heaven.'

'True? What's that? There's no truth to my life, nor ever has been. I see it now. Everything I did was simply an avoidance of living.'

'Which is only to say an avoidance of death.'

'Yes.'

'Which is what all men do.'

'But not you, William. Above anyone I've ever known, you have always been the most completely serious.'

'Me? Do you mean me?'

'I mean you, William. I believe you have been marked out.'

'If I have been marked out, it is because ... It is because I am not a complete man, nor ever have been.'

'Oh, that.' John shrugged.

'You know?'

'Of course.'

'But how?'

'Father told me. It is of no significance.'

Cowper remained sitting by the bed until the first grey light of dawn made the yellow glow of the oil-lamp seem insignificant too.

That afternoon Dr Strick arrived with a Mrs Perdue. She was a large raw-boned woman with red chapped hands and the imperviousness to pain of someone used to the relief of it. Without bothering to take off her coat, she threw back the covers, rolled John onto his side, folded the under-sheet in half, heaved him over onto his other side and whipped it away. Then, as he lay whimpering on the mattress, she dragged off his nightshirt. When she saw the bedsores crusted on his back, she muttered loudly enough for Strick to hear, 'I'd have washed them before this, but it's too late now.' Then she swiftly dressed John in a clean nightshirt, again flipped him from side to side, and when she was finished, there were clean sheets under and over him, his head rested on a fresh pillowslip and he was bound up as tight as a baby in swaddling clothes. Cowper was revolted by a savour of gratuitous cruelty in what she had done, but he was also awed by her almost divinely indifferent – the word came to him with a shudder – motherliness.

Mrs Perdue installed a camp-bed for herself in the drawing-room and set about cleaning everything in sight. That night and all the following day John alternated between agony and silent melancholy. As the evening darkened, he asked, 'How long can this go on?'

Cowper said, 'Only as long as God in his mercy wills it.'

John cried out, 'This mercy of his is torture. Your God hates me and I hate him.'

Pursing her lips and shaking her head, Mrs Perdue slashed the covers straight with the palm of her hand and said, 'You should save your breath, Mister John, for nothing hates you or any of us. There ain't no malice in it. A scholar like you should know that. Now then. Do you want the bedpan?'

'No, I do not want the bedpan,' he snapped. Then his voice changed and he said, 'I only want to die. Can't you see that?'

Mrs Perdue smiled. 'I see said the blind man, when he couldn't see at all.' Then she ruffled his hair and added gaily, 'Well, Mister, I believe a small tot of spirits wouldn't go amiss now, would it?'

She brought brandy. John sipped a little, slept briefly, then woke. His eyes were opened wide in ecstasy. The room was flooded with moonlight. 'Oh, brother,' he said and grasped Cowper's hand, 'I am full of what I could say to you.'

'Do you need the laudanum or the hartshorn?' Mrs Perdue asked.

He smiled faintly and replied, 'None of these things will serve my purpose.'

Cowper said, 'But I know what would, my dear, don't I?'

John said, 'You do, brother.'

Mrs Perdue left them together and went off to bed. She reckoned, having seen many a happy death, that there would be no more screaming, but that the final moment would be a fair long time coming yet.

Cowper had arrived in Cambridge on the sixteenth of February. It was now the tenth of March and he had hardly set foot outside the sick-room. Over the next six days, John, made strong by his new faith, grew weaker but painlessly so. On the sixth night he took Cowper's hand and said, 'Brother, you suffered more than me before you believed, but our sufferings, though different in their kind and measure, are directed to the same end.'

After that he slept and did not wake again. Two days later he lay so still it was hard to believe he was not already dead, but every now and then Dr Strick held a mirror in front of his mouth and it misted over slightly. When it showed clear, he took a little silver box out of his pocket.

'This is the last sign,' he said, taking a pinch of eiderdown from the box and placing it on John's upper lip. After a moment an unnoticeable breath floated it away. Replaced, the down floated again, then settled of its own accord. Cowper began trembling. This was not salvation by experience; this was death by measurement.

'John!' he cried out. 'I'm with you, John!'

'Mr Cowper, please, this moment requires absolute stillness,' Dr Strick said.

But he could not be still and he could not stop saying John's name.

'Mr Gough, would you be so good as to take Mr Cowper into the other room?' Dr Strick said.

'Come along, man,' Gough said.

'No! John needs me!'

For a moment everyone except John was struggling, and Cowper felt chaos invading the room. But then Mrs Perdue put her hands on his face and kissed him repeatedly, saying, 'Now now, Mister William, you must be good and do what your old mother tells you. Go in with Mr Gough and I'll call you when the time comes.'

He did as he was told. But she did not summon him until she had washed the body.

Then he said, 'My poor dear brother is dead and I'm so glad. I don't believe I have ever felt such joy before, except in the moment of my own conversion.'

Gough whispered to Dr Strick, 'What a fellow!'

Soon the Master of the college and a flock of the Fellows crowded into the room to pay their respects. Cowper was asked to say the Lord's Prayer, began, forgot the words, giggled and could not continue. The Master took him to his rooms and gave him a large glass of whisky, but he spilled most of it. The Master then ordered up his own coach and had him driven back to Olney. There was plainly no question of him attending the funeral.

24

$\mathcal{M}$rs Unwin had said, 'Give me your hand.' In considering
that, it was important to bear in mind the journey from
Cambridge, pitching about all afternoon in the Master's second-
best carriage, and then arriving at Orchardside to find her standing
in the doorway as if she had been long installed there, like a statue
in an alcove. It was nearly dark, the last of the light was raking into
the market square low from the left, but that could not explain why
her face stood out so clearly, as if it were that chrysanthemum
which had survived the winter, turning from white to a golden
bronze without decay, against the rough brick wall in the back-
garden. Nor could the light or any other image explain, as she
watched him get down from the carriage and approach her, the
look of avaricious pity in her eyes.

'Give me your hand,' she had said and he had given it, saying,
'How do you do?' and when there was no response, added, 'To that,
it's best to say it back.' She had looked at him intently and then
said, 'How do you do?' and he had replied, 'Very well, thank you.
And then everything goes on as before.' And they had smiled at
each other, linked in the eye, connected by hand. At that point Sam
had come hurrying up the passageway with a smoking oil-lamp
held aloft, seen them smiling and said, 'Is the news good then?' and
when it was not, had said, 'Oh, master, master,' and had tried to
embrace him, which was awkward because of the lamp. Mrs

Unwin had held on to his hand still, and for a moment the three of them were one disparate thing, Sam crying and Cowper saying, 'Don't be silly, don't be silly.'

The house, after so long an absence, seemed unfamiliar, the rooms smaller, as if looked down on from a height, and colder, though Mary had built a great fire in the parlour. She had prepared his favourite dish, halibut with capers, and he ate voraciously, drank almost the whole of a good bottle of Rhenish wine; and when Newton came over from the Vicarage, they had stayed up late drinking port and laughing again about Euclid in Africa. That night he slept deliciously and dreamed that on the shore of a tropical island Mrs Unwin was holding in her hand the moon – or was it Mr Halley's comet? – and using its beam to draw glowing circles in the sand.

For some weeks he felt like an invalid who realises he is on the mend. The March winds still blew cold but the afternoons were crisp and clear and he walked with Mrs Unwin to the water meadow to see the already budding poplar trees. For the rest of the time he sat by the fire in the parlour or stayed in his bedroom. There was a reason for this seclusion. Everything that was joyful, or at least without sorrow, in his childhood was coming back to him unbidden. He remembered the verses his father had composed, in the old ballad form, and which John sometimes sang for guests. 'On Miss Roper Having the Toothache' was one, hardly suitable for a clergyman but amusing and quite neat, after the manner of John Gay. It had even been published in a miscellany, which he took down and read through from cover to cover. Then, too, he felt irresistibly drawn to the classics. Since his conversion he had hardly dared look at them. Homer, somehow, remained undreadful. Virgil too. But Horace still had to be guarded against. He looked into the Satires and they were too sharp a joy.

For Mrs Unwin it was not unpleasant of an evening to be read Homer in Greek, which she could not understand, 'for the sound of it', nor was it particularly worrying to hear him up in his bedroom singing the songs his father had sung so long ago. But when she remarked that Horace seemed a very pagan sort of person, he had put the book back on the shelf, saying he was 'glad to be relieved of that burden'. The weakened eagerness of convalescence then gave way to lassitude. He absented himself from prayers and made excuses to stay away from church or see Newton. This, Mrs Unwin knew, could not continue without embarrassment, so she went and spoke privately to Mrs Newton, who in turn spoke to her husband. His forbearance was already wearing thin, but his wife prevailed upon him and, instead of brushing Sam aside and bursting into the parlour at Orchardside, which he had planned to do, he wrote a letter. This, because it required guile, unlike the writing of sermons, took the most of a week.

'Well, it is a dreary task Mr Newton proposes, but perhaps dreariness is what I am cut out for now,' he said after reading the letter.

'What does "now" mean except self-pity?' Mrs Unwin said, more sharply than she intended.

He looked at her closely, but then smiled and said, 'Yes, I stand corrected. This is a bastard deserves the rod.'

Mrs Unwin knew the reference was biblical, though not where it could be found. In a way that was the point. Like Newton, he knew the Bible inside out, and copying and editing a commentary on the first chapter of St John's Gospel, which was the task proposed, was undemanding work, but time-consuming. So it was begun. And soon Newton was back in Orchardside again.

'It is curious,' Mrs Unwin said to Mrs Newton as they walked in the orchard, 'that praise of his handwriting should so much gratify our friend.'

'Mr Cowper is a born boy,' Mrs Newton said.

'Yes, he does like to be patted, which is why when he refuses to do something it is such a cause for concern.'

'I'm sure, my dear, that Mr Cowper would refuse you nothing under the sun.'

'My daughter thinks the opposite is the case.' And Mrs Unwin told her what had happened while Cowper was in Cambridge.

That night as Mrs Newton watched her husband on his knees praying at his side of the bed she considered whether or not she should tell him the story. Susanna, with her thick braid of auburn hair which she twitched from side to side like a young mare, was such a fierce girl when she was galled. Had Sam heard the shouting and had he told his master? Probably not. No, certainly not, since the dispute indirectly concerned the cost of his own upkeep, as well as many other minor and major outgoings. This was all to be expected in a family that kept a lodger as improvident as Cowper, but for Susanna to have said to her mother, 'You didn't love my father, you betrayed him, you traded him for this squire' – well, that was bound to cause shouting.

You'd think she would have told me before this, Mrs Newton thought, and wondered would they ever really be close friends. After telling her about Susanna, Mrs Unwin had hurried away, as if ashamed, down the path and into the parlour where the two men were poring over the Bible on that absurd little table. She was, no, not a snob, but a man's woman; though with that curt way of speaking, cold and yet warm underneath, and that white satin gown, the blue quilted petticoat, and the fallen swell of her bosom, you felt like putting your arms around her.

Mrs Newton stretched out her foot beneath the bedclothes until the tip of her toe just touched Mr Newton's clasped hands on the eiderdown. He raised his eyes to hers. She had decided as usual not to say anything to him about what had been said to her. It was simpler to be lonely. And there could be pleasure in it too, being made love to by an ignorant man. When Newton threw back the covers, she was lying face down and her nightdress was already drawn up.

25

$\mathcal{N}$ ewton was always out in the world, whatever the weather, and now, having completed the commentary on St John, Cowper was out in it with him.

It had been a busy autumn, visiting the sick, teaching Sunday school, leading prayers at the mid-week meetings in the Great House, and several times they had gone on preaching expeditions into the countryside – 'lighting fires in the wilderness', Newton called it. For Cowper these were exquisitely shy-making occasions. In one of the poorer farmhouses they had even had to share a bed, but Newton merely launched himself into it, as if sleep were another form of Christian endeavour, and was snoring before Cowper had decided how to take off his breeches modestly. In the grander houses of the lesser gentry, adherents of the Earl of Dartmouth, he had to put up with impertinent inquiries about his seed, breed and generation and the suspicion, no, the certainty, that this noble knight or that honourable lady knew all about his career in crime. Luckily, Newton had been put on notice by his wife to allow no probing of anything to do with Parliament which might lead to Mr Cowper's role in it. Prohibition of any kind was no hardship to Newton, so if someone mentioned the House of Lords, he simply said, 'Those gentlemen are plural. There is only one Lord. Let us cleave to Him.'

But on one occasion a trespasser got over the fence. It occurred at a place called Cross-in-Hand, near Lutterworth, in a house built when Cromwell was Protector. The heir to the manor was a fervent young evangelical, but his father was sly, wry and irreligious, yet glad of any company at dinner. It turned out that a cousin of his was the barrister who had taken Cowper's rooms in the Inner Temple. This was embarrassing enough in itself since, apart from his stepmother's inheritance and a few hundred pounds in stocks, which never produced more than five per cent, the £20 a year rental was the cornerstone of Cowper's income, and Joe Hill, who managed his affairs, had been obliged to go to endless trouble to collect it. It then emerged that the defaulting barrister had spent some time in a lunatic asylum in St Albans, and there he had become acquainted with an inmate called Theadora Cowper. Was she any relation? Newton answered this question with a disquisition on fraternity in Christ, and in the middle of it Cowper got up, muttered, 'Excuse me', and went to bed.

Next morning, leaving Newton to his prayer-meeting, he rode off alone on the long journey back to Olney. Cross-in-Hand was the last call on their tour and Newton would catch up with him that night in Northampton. It was one of those stopped days in early October. The roads were dry. The sky was bright blue. The air was so still that when a leaf fell off a distant birch tree, he could hear it fall. The birch stood isolated on a hillside in a grove of larches, already stripped bare by the winds of September. Seen from afar, its wiry branches were invisible and each small golden leaf stood out on its own. Above the slim silver trunk they gathered together in a halted shower, like a single candle with many flames. He had wanted to write to Theadora when he'd heard she had imitated his descent into the Avernus of St Albans, but that was impossible. How could the disease explain the contagion? He shook the reins and rode on. That was the past. He must not think of it. This landscape was the glory of England. Really, it was why he went out with Newton on these theatrical pilgrimages. He was thirty-nine years old, oaken-faced from riding about in the sun, strong from digging in the garden. He was healthy.

Mrs Unwin did not think so.

Then it was winter. Now they only visited locally. An iron-hard frost, weeks thick, had reduced everything in the countryside to black and white. As they rode out of Olney in the morning, the hooves of their horses clanged sparks from the road. Even the cattle that mourned together in a corner of a field seemed petrified, only the steam of their breath showing they were not made of stone.

'But you do seem resistant, Mr Cowper, on human composure?' Newton said – he was referring to the writing of hymns that did not adhere strictly to the divine texts.

'The Psalms are, of course, infinitely preferable unsung. On the other hand, it can hardly be denied that the actual practice of singing has improved since the days of Sternhold and Hopkins. One note per syllable was too dogged to be natural.'

'Yes. We used to howl like dogs.'

'But natural is a large word. As soon as Tate and Brady brought in the common metre and above all the rhyme, we had human composure and the world was changed. To me it's like a horse cantering in iambics, four feet and three, four feet and three, which, though it pleases the ear, reduces the divine to the animal.'

'Oh, yes?' Newton was mystified and irritated. In his own hymns he used the common metre, but he was impatient and often bludgeoned the syntax into its harness. Anyway, the hymns had to be written, and it did not matter a fig how it was done.

'It's quite simple really,' Cowper was saying. 'Take, for example, the first Psalm in the King James version: *Blessed is the man that walketh not in the counsel of the ungodly, nor standeth in the way of sinners, nor sitteth in the seat of the scornful.*'

'Blessed indeed.'

'Now in Tate and Brady that becomes:

How blest is he who ne'er consents
By ill advice to walk;
Nor stands in sinners' ways nor sits
Where men profanely talk.

That, I grant you, is not unmelodious. However, while there is walking, standing and sitting in King James, the hymnodists introduce talking, which is only there for the sake of the rhyme.'

'You will allow that the sense is nearly the same.'

'A drowned man won't thank you for telling him he was near to being saved. Or, to put it another way, a man's spectacles are so near to his nose that a philosopher might well wonder whether the spectacles were made for the nose or the nose for the spectacles. Human composure inclines to the latter.'

In the distance a dog, hearing Newton's laugh, barked in return.

'We're nearly there,' he said, thinking that for a sensible woman Mrs Unwin could sometimes be remarkably foolish – according to her, mornings were the worst time for Cowper's depression, whereas in his experience it was in the mornings that his friend was most cheerful, especially if they faced an uninterrupted journey together. Then he could not be stopped from talking.

The dog that barked had come down the road to greet them and was now running broken circles around the horses' legs, wearing a supplicant expression, its ears humbly sleeked back and its belly dragging along the ground, as if they were deities, steaming, from a world before frost. They had arrived at the lace-school. From the windows of the cottage, pale girls peered out.

The day did not pass quickly. To protect the lace against smoke and smuts, no fire could be lit, and as a result the room was bitterly cold. Even Newton, who was usually brought to fever pitch by the heat of his own words, had to halt his homily on Holy Poverty after an hour because his teeth were chattering. He was given a crude terracotta jar filled with hot ashes, which caused a general disturbance as the pupils rearranged themselves around what they called, with screams of laughter, their dicky pots. He tried to continue his sermon while straddling the pot, but the heat did not rise beyond his knees and he had to sit down and tent the skirts of his coat over it before he could go on.

Lunch was bread, mouldy cheese and buttermilk. Cowper had brought a big bag of sugar-plums and these were greeted with joy. Eventually the dicky pots, along with the body-heat of two men, four women teachers and twenty girls, overcame the cold. Newton grew drowsy and rested for a while. It was already growing dark. A tall stool was taken out of a cupboard. In a hole in the seat a candle was inserted and around the candle five bottles were placed – Cowper asked what they contained and was told 'snow-water' – so that the light was magnified and spread onto the lacemakers' pillows and the patterns of golden pins around which the flying bobbins wound the threads. The four teachers and the oldest girl who sat closest to the candle were called First Lights, the second row of younger girls were Second Lights and so on out to where Cowper was sitting with a set of twins, who were the Fifth Lights. He knew the girls from Sunday school: they were nine years old, broad-faced and pale-eyed like their parents, descendants of Protestants who had fled persecution in Flanders. At first there was silence, except for the clicking of the bobbins and the head-teacher counting down from twenty-five, but when they reached nineteen, as was the custom, the girls started chanting one of their tells:

> A lad down at Olney
> Looked over a wall.
> He saw nineteen small girls
> A-playing at ball.
> Golden girls, golden girls,
> Will you be mine?
> You shan't wash the dishes
> Nor wait on the swine,
> But sit on a cushion
> And sew a fine seam,
> Eat white bread and butter,
> Strawberries and cream.

The 'golden girls' were the pins in the pattern, and when the tell started again, they were down to eighteen, then seventeen, and so the chanting went on. The bobbins clicked and the room grew darker, lit only by the candles shining through the bottles of snow-water.

Cowper's heart felt heavy. Where had he seen this before? These lovely, half-starved girls who were ungolden and counted only as pins, what did they remind him of? They reminded him of no memory, of the time before sin, which was unknown. The chanting ended when there was only one girl left to marry the lad from Olney. It was time to go. It would not do for the horses to be caught out on the ice after dark. As he said goodbye to the twins, he noticed that on their bobbins, now empty of thread, words were scratched into the wood.

'You haven't written this yourselves, have you?' he asked them.

'We have,' they said together, alternating their sentences. 'Our father wrote it down for us. He has a pencil. And we pricked it out with our needles.'

One bobbin was inscribed 'Do not steel.' The other said, 'Jesus weept.' The misspellings made his eyes prickle.

Outside a thaw was beginning to set in and a gusty wind was blowing from the south. The pupils were hurrying home, heads down, clutching their shawls around them. The twins were running as fast as they could. He had slipped them a silver sixpence each.

As they rode back to Olney, Newton returned to human composure. Raising the subject in the morning had been no accident. In their recent endeavours Cowper had proved a willing assistant, but with the utmost passivity, as if he were a beast of burden, a blinded horse going round and round the threshing floor. Newton had not seen this for himself – Mrs Unwin had told him that she saw and feared it, and on reflection he had agreed with her.

'These girls, now, Mr Cowper, is it not remarkable that the most of them are unable to read and yet they know their old tells backwards?'

'I should rather say that they know them by heart. I think I never understood before today what that phrase means.'

'The experience has affected you, my dear?'

'Yes, it has. You know, Mr Newton, you have often reminded me that our religion comes not from the top of the mind but from the bottom of the heart. Well, I believe these girls spoke from there.'

'But how much more affecting they would be were their rhymes directed to a higher purpose.'

'They seem already high to me.'

'High and dry, Mr Cowper, high and dry. There is a deeper fountain, which is the love of God.'

'I wonder.'

'Do you? How can you?'

'I don't doubt God, Mr Newton, because I cannot. All that I wonder at is being so submerged and yet so dry in myself, as if Tantalus were beneath the water and yet still thirsty.'

'That is the old world, Mr Cowper. That is the mindful world before Jesus.'

'Yes, so it was and so it is. But now I hardly ever experience faith, except in a nursery rhyme.'

Newton, although he had been warned by his wife against doing so, gave in to his instincts, reined in his horse and roared, 'Are you a child, mister? Are you a baby snatched from the bosom, squawking and squalling?'

Cowper, who had not been roared at since Westminster School, said meekly, 'No, sir.'

'Wake up then! Wake up and come out into the world like a man!'

'What is it you want me to do, Mr Newton?'

He already knew what the plan was – Mrs Unwin had told him. To write hymns and help Newton with his own awkward compositions and make a collection of them and publish it. She thought human composure would be good for him. But it was unfair to say he was acting like a baby. If only Newton knew how hard he had to work to repress his panic. No baby, no set of twin girls, had to do that.

They were still halted on the road. Where the sun was going down, the thick, torn clouds had turned a ruddy colour. Near the river a solitary silver birch, naked and wasted, was scraping its leafless branches on the pitiless wind.

'Very well,' he said, 'I will do what I can.'

26

How could it be that as he grew ever more timid, he had also become so stern?

Mrs Unwin was puzzling at this question as she lay in bed. Dawn had not long broken and yet already she could hear a continuous underground rumbling, sudden panicky tramplings, heavy collisions, the explosive gasps of frightened cattle and the curses of drovers beating them. It was market day and horribly wet. She pitied those poor men driving their beasts all night through the downpour, and the women with their few eggs in baskets, half of them rotten, and their skirt-clutching children, bright-eyed and placid from hunger. At least there were no summer flies to cluster around the flayed heads of the sheep that the butchers hung up on hooks on their stalls; and the stream, banked with scrubby willows, which used to run down the middle of the High Street, had been paved over and would not be slopped crimson with gore and guts. But she would have to post one of the maids at the door of the house to stop people making water against it. Sometimes, along with the usual salt cod and herring, there would be halibut all the way from Grimsby, probably gone off and stinking of ammonia. No, she would buy an old hen from one of those countrywomen, make a good soup and then a *blanquette* from the breast with plenty of nutmeg.

Today he would have to stay indoors out of the spilling rain.

Often on market days he went off walking in the countryside from morning till night to escape the clamour. Once he had met a pedlar on the road to Tovey and had bought a Spanish tortoiseshell comb to keep up her hair. He was always buying her things, as long as they were small, a thimble or a jade button, and of course he always expected the money for them to be in his pocket. Susanna said scornfully, 'You end up buying presents for yourself,' which was less true than it was exasperating.

Joseph Hill had sent two notes for £30 in September, one for £20, the arrears of the Inner Temple rent, in November, and his Aunt Judith Madan had given him twelve guineas at Christmas, a sum of £92 and twelve shillings, and now here it was, February, and all gone. He could sell some stocks. She had already decided £400 worth would remove the subject of money from his attention for at least five years, if he was careful. Or she could sell something – the little dower-house in Grimston perhaps.

The important thing was steadiness. Calm at all costs. But then in recent months he had taken to solitary walks, and not just on market days, ducking into an alley if he saw someone coming who might stop to talk before he could get out of the town. Mr Geary Ball, who always seemed to have nicked himself shaving, had noted the habit and made it a joke among the town's many mockers. Was Ball malicious because Mr Cowper had seen him, a supposedly upright Methodist, rolling out of the Royal Oak tavern in the middle of the day? The answer to that question was yes. Mr Cowper had become almost as censorious as Mr Newton, but unlike Newton, he was stern from timidity, for fear of the loss of restraint that went with the disorder, the anger, the wildness of sin. Any sort of violence horrified him. He could not bear the cattle being beaten. It was curious, though, how soldierly, almost exultant, he was when the gypsies and the drovers, maddened with gin after the market was over, fought in the square. It was as if these bloody riots were some kind of dreadful theatre show, swirlingly lit by smoky torches, watched by screaming gypsy women who kept on throwing their shawls out wide and then wrapping them tightly around themselves, like black wings applauding, urging the men to stop and yet to go on too.

But the terror of the gypsy children frightened him. That was because they were helpless, like the cattle who did not know they were headed for the slaughterhouse and the axe. That was why, although he ate meat, he preferred fish: there was no blood.

She sat up suddenly in the bed. No, it couldn't be that, surely. She was forty-seven years old; her courses were long over. Well, they had come back a few times. Did he know anything about such things? Once – it was in Huntingdon – they had been out walking in the country and she had had to hurry home, it was dreadfully embarrassing, the hall-door wouldn't open, and as she struggled with the key she saw him looking at the white cotton stocking on her instep where a fresh drop of blood had just landed, startlingly red, and then another. The look that passed between them, what did it say? One ought know in such circumstances, but with William one didn't. His politeness was unfathomable. Had he been kinder to her that day? She couldn't answer that either, because he was always kindness itself, so kind that sometimes she felt utterly – utterly what?

It was time to get up.

In the next room Cowper, lying stiffly in bed with his fists clenched together on his mouth, opened his already startled eyes. Through the thin wall he had heard, was it a cry or a laugh or a groan? He did not know that the sound, which was anyway indeterminable, had been caused by Mrs Unwin coming upon the word 'helpless'.

The new hymn was on the little desk but he did not need to get up to read it: he had it in his head.

> There is a fountain filled with blood
> Drawn from Emmanuel's veins,
> And sinners, plunged beneath that flood,
> Lose all their guilty stains.
>
> The dying thief rejoiced to see
> That fountain in his day,
> And there have I, as vile as he,
> Washed all my sins away.

*

The idea for the hymn had come to him in Newton's study in the Vicarage. On the sash of the window a butterfly, a Red Admiral, had been opening and closing its wings, fanning itself. Then it stopped and rested, wings spread wide again. It had been there when he came in and this was the first movement it had made in two hours.

Sometimes, when Newton was away on church business, he had the use of his study to work on the hymnal. On that day Mrs Newton had gone with her husband to Bedford. He had been alone in an empty house. The window was painted white. Its eight panes of glass squared off the view as if it were a cartoon for a painting: a meadow starred with daisies in the lower half, trees clustering towards the middle and rising out of them the church steeple, which touched the top sash – he moved to make this happen – with the tip of its lightning-conductor. It was a silent afternoon late in May and any season beyond the coming summer seemed unimaginable. As he went back to the desk, he stopped to look at the inscription written in Newton's own hand over the fireplace.

> Since thou wast precious in my sight,
> thou has been honourable.
> BUT
> Thou shalt remember that thou wast
> a bond-man in the land of Egypt,
> and the Lord thy God redeemed thee.

The 'BUT' charmed him. Newton hardly uttered a sentence without a 'but' in the middle of it. He was a contrary creature; careless too, not to say slipshod. One would have thought a sea-captain would keep his quarters ship-shape and Bristol fashion, not like this midden of books, pamphlets and letters. They had been cleared off the desk and arranged neatly on the floor, and in their place were Cowper's various notebooks and the record-book where completed hymns were entered. He counted them: fifty-three so far. What a paltry amount for almost eighteen months' work. Not much more than two or three lines of verse a day. The difficulty was that the form was so simple, the metre so regular, the rhymes so unavoidably obvious. Sometimes he did dream the words but mostly they had to be worked at, fretted into mortices and tenons, like carpentry, or cobbled together, stitched and welted on the last. That reminded him. He turned back to the beginning of the record-book. Was this movement obvious?

> Heal us, Emmanuel! here we are
>   Waiting to feel thy touch:
> Deep-wounded souls to thee repair,
>   And, Saviour, we are such.

Newton had exclaimed, 'You've made us a shoe, Mr Cowper!' delighted at how quickly he had seen the sole and heel of it. But he had no conception of the labour that had gone into the first line, the sacrifices involved in accepting the extra syllable and beat for the sake of 'Heal' and 'here' sounding off each other. Why, he wondered, am I so angry?

As he dipped the pen into the inkwell, he noticed that his hand was shaking. It was a familiar tremor, born from an excitement that could be only borne by indulging in it. He wrote, 'I thirst, but not as once I did,' and put down the pen. In his head the possible rhymes laddered down the alphabet and returned to 'forbid'. Against his will, his eye was drawn back to the record-book.

> She, too, who touched thee in the press,
>   And healing virtue stole,
> Was answered, 'Daughter, go in peace,
>   Thy faith had made thee whole.'

The memory of her touch was vivid. They had walked through the colonnade of shivering poplars and were entering what they called 'the mossy alley', a long tunnel of yew trees which was shadowy at the best of times and now in this March afternoon was almost pitch dark. He trod upon a dry stick, and at the sound of it cracking some crows cawed, threw themselves up into the sky like a handful of ashes and then settled back down into the branches.

'In my part of Norfolk,' she said, 'they say crows cawing means rain.'

'Well, it's not far-sighted to make that prophecy beneath these skies. Shall we turn back?'

'Oh no; not unless you want to.'

'I'm quite content to continue, if you are.'

'On we go then.'

'On we go, Mrs Unwin.'

'We agree about everything, Mr Cowper. We are the most agreeable pair of old crows in England.'

'You are neither old nor a crow.'

'Thank you, sir.'

'I should rather think of us as an amphivena.'

'And what might that be?'

'A creature with two heads. It's mentioned in the bestiary and in Milton. Apparently they can hold on to each other and bowl along like a hoop.'

'How very convenient!'

'And their eyes shine like lamps.'

'Wonderful for this place.'

'The crow, on the other hand, is a prophetic bird. Your people in Ely were following an ancient tradition, Mrs Unwin, when they said it foretells rain. It has long been associated with foretelling the troubles of men and in particular disclosing the paths of treachery.'

'It can't be right to believe that God entrusts his secrets to birds.'

Cowper laughed. 'What would I do without you, ma'am? You're a fountain of good sense.'

'Do you think so?'

'Of course I do.'

'In any event,' she said, her heart lurching in her breast, 'in any event here is no path of treachery, except underfoot. The more emerald the moss is, the more one is inclined to miss one's footing, haven't you noticed?'

And as she spoke she took his arm. He was startled. After a moment she said, 'I think this is my favourite part of our walks, this place.'

'The poplar colonnade, that's mine.'

'Oh yes, aside from that. But do you know why I like it here?'

'The moss, is it the moss?'

'Yes, the moss, and the stillness, it's always so still here, and we can be private. I like that, don't you?'

'Yes.'

'We can be alone and private, the monarchs of all that we see. It is most agreeable, don't you think?'

Neither of them heard the other properly. She had taken his arm spontaneously, but not entirely so. While her husband was alive, such a thing would have been unthinkable. Morley had been jealous, but he had had no reason to be, and it was monstrous of Susanna to imply otherwise. But once he had come upon them when they were walking by the river near Huntingdon and laughing immoderately, and that evening sitting at the fire after prayers he had become jolly, yet wistful too, and then at last said, 'Do you know, Mr Cowper, I have been thinking of the last things. It's rather difficult in this house not to now, since our devotions have grown, thank the Lord, so fervent. Personally, of course, I'd find it most inconvenient, but if I should chance to die, do you know I think you might still dwell with Mary.' Cowper had laughed and said, '*Absit omen*, Morley, *absit omen!*' and she had changed the subject. In bed that night she had told Morley she was really quite vexed, it was such a silly thing to say, but then she laid her head on his chest and after a few moments he had stroked her cheek and found his hand wet with tears.

She was too sensible to feel guilty about her husband's death. She had no reason for guilt, although when she remembered him now, she linked his dying with his wistfulness, of which she was the cause. Moreover, but at a deeper level than memory, she could not help but feel that Providence had played a part in the sequence of events: that Cowper had been sent to her and that what followed, even Morley's accident, were not merely happenstances. Had any of it been wished for, it would have been sinful, but since it was not, it was magical. There was also a kind of magic coincidence of opposites between the characters of Cowper and Newton which seemed providential.

Recently, while they were dressing for a special occasion, she had said to Mrs Newton, who had grown near to being her confidante, 'You'd think, Mary, the one was the other, only turned inside-out.' Mrs Newton had said, 'They're more like this hairbrush, my dear, and your side has the silver on it.' They had laughed, but the conversation had ended there – Mrs Unwin's reserve had been too deeply penetrated by 'your side'. She was not, unlike Mrs Newton, a sensual woman, except in relation to her hunger for an idea beyond herself, which had never been satisfied by her husband or by any of her intellectual friendships, though there once had been the prospect of it with the novelist Samuel Richardson, who was attracted by her enthusiasm for his genius, and with Arthur Devis, who had painted her portrait, now stored in the attic. Then she had cared about clothes and it had been very pleasant, even slightly thrilling, to discuss with him what she should wear for the painting. He had decided on a white satin gown with long hanging sleeves over a blue quilted petticoat, belled out with a hoop, and a stiff eau-de-Nil stomacher which pushed her breasts up high. He had done a watercolour sketch of her wearing a fashionably flat hat, but in the painting she was sitting under an imaginary tree that had a circular bench around the trunk, and she was holding the hat in one hand while the other pointed towards a distant golden town and the spire of a gloomy church, all invented. She had not forgotten how he had looked at her when he'd said, 'Well, madam, which will it be, heaven or earth?' It was an impertinent thing to say, and absurd too, but then he was an itinerant artist and could go off on his travels whenever he liked, not a twenty-six-year-old mother of two small children. And he did go off, leaving behind the oil painting but with the watercolour in his portfolio.

The portrait had hung over the mantelpiece in their bedroom in Huntingdon until one day Morley had idly remarked how *outré* that old style of dressing now seemed. When, some days later, she replaced it with a hand-tinted *veduta* of Roman ruins, he hadn't noticed, or if he had he hadn't mentioned it – that was Morley's way. So the years went by and she forgot the painting, almost leaving it behind in the attic when they removed to Olney. That she should remember it now, wrapped up in the blue petticoat in a trunk under her bed – in Orchardside the attic was too impossibly high to get up to – was, she thought, a sign of how far she had fallen. A fallen woman? That was an absurdity, like the choice Mr Devis had imagined for her, which couldn't be made, and yet the idea of being a fallen, an abandoned, woman had quickened her, so that she sometimes felt as if she were living out one of those dreams she had had when she was a girl, of walking in a crowded street naked but visible only to herself, or that hot summer night in Cromer when she had pretended not to know that the lovely young fisherman she adored but refused to kiss was watching from the garden as she splashed her breasts with water so cold she could feel it still, but she was only sixteen then and wild, and that wildness hadn't lasted long, only for a little while with Morley before Susanna and William were born.

But then another William — really, it was absurd to be still calling him Mr Cowper — had burst into her life, a birth without a pregnancy, painless too, until now. Of course she wasn't beautiful, but then she never had been, and yet there was a certain freshness about her in the portrait that was as good as beauty. And now it had returned, she could see it in the mirror. Of course Mr Cowper, when he wrote to relatives or friends and mentioned her, which he rarely did, always referred to her as his second mother and a blessing from God, but she only ever heard these things back from others, never directly from him, and they talked about everything under the sun, like two people who had lived most of their lives in a foreign country and meet and hear themselves speaking, at first haltingly, their native language. Of course she was motherly, in the sense that she calmed his fears and redirected them, and he obeyed her, but only because he needed to be obedient. There was a side to him, too, that was far from being child-like when it came to anything to do with knowledge or ideas. More than once she had seen him silent in company, reclining in his chair with his legs stretched out, heel on toe, almost seeming to be asleep, and then, if someone started an idea that excited his attention, he would deliver a few sentences which illuminated, and often enough decided, the question.

She remembered an occasion when a rather grand visiting bishop, taking a second glass of port in the afternoon, had quoted David, *The Lord is aroused as if he had been sleeping, mighty as if he had been refreshed with wine*, and Mr Cowper, opening his eyes, said, 'That "refreshed", you know, is rather curious. In the Latin the phrase is *crapulatus a vino* and one would be inclined to take from it that the psalmist looked mildly on crapulence. Our own Sir Thomas Browne has quoted a number of pagan authorities on the subject, including Avicenna, Seneca and Averroes, though the last, being a Mussulman, had a faith of sorts, and they all seemed to favour what Sir Thomas calls "a sober incalescence and regulated aestuation in wine". But as for drunkenness, I do rather doubt that our Lord was inebriated, don't you?'

There had been silence for a moment, but when Mary said, 'Can you say that again?' even the bishop laughed. That was the point: authority sat easily on him when he was least conscious of exercising it. That, perhaps, was his aristocratic inheritance. Although he was terribly shy with strangers, the shyness had nothing to do with social awe – if, instead of this bishop, the king had come to call, then, unless George had something to say for himself, his heel would still have rested on his toe. But even when he was at his most authoritative or ironic, and the two qualities coincided in him, she was not the slightest bit overawed, unlike Newton. In his dealings with Cowper, he mingled overlordship with an underlying submissiveness, not so much in relation to intelligence or Cowper's superior class as to the fervour of his sincerity. And Newton knew – if only because his wife told him – that they were more than substitute mother and pretend son, and more, too, than perfect friends who, as Morley foresaw, might dwell together, like the earth and the moon, revolving about each other and never touching.

'How perfectly absurd!' Mary said aloud. It was market day. The rain was bursting against the windowpane. After counting to seven on her fingers she slipped her cold hand back under the covers and between her warm thighs. She had taken Cowper's arm for the first time seven years after he had been born into her life in Huntingdon. The absurdity made her happy. How demeaning, she thought. Then, and for a very long time afterwards, the idea of being happy and demeaned at the same time so surprised her that she confused it with her awareness of being the subject of gossip in Olney and farther afield. It felt like that old dream of being naked in the street, but not now being invisible. It was a shameful feeling, yet pleasurable too. She abandoned herself to it.

*

It was dusk when he let himself out of the Vicarage and walked home to Orchardside. Apart from opening the window to send the butterfly fluttering off towards the river, he had done nothing except write four lines of verse:

> I thirst, but not as once I did,
> The vain delights of earth to share;
> Thy wounds, Emmanuel, all forbid
> That I should seek my pleasures there.

He had started out with the idea that he needed to drink again from the fountain of God's love, but the thought of drinking blood had prevented him from developing the image. It was still there, though, in 'vain' and in 'wounds'. That he should pun on words in this fashion was an irresistible compulsion, hard to explain but impossible not to visualise. It was a very, very small opening which he could somehow pass through. No bigger than the tip of his finger, with a hole in the end of it. Dust and blood and a spider. This wasn't a dream. He could close his eyes and see it, an entirely unabstract conception. But the worst of it was the betrayal of Mrs Unwin. She was the delight forbidden by the wound. The thought stopped him abruptly in the street.

When she had taken his arm in the mossy alley, it had been so natural, but he would never have dared to take such a liberty, had never even dreamt of it. He looked at the familiar inkstain on his second finger and thought, 'Even our hands are alike, neither a man's nor a woman's.'

Mr Geary Ball saw Cowper standing in the street staring at his outstretched hand and doubled back the way he had come. The longest way round, through the yard of the Royal Oak, into Dropshot and past Wagstaffe's tannery, was in this case the shortest way home. But his companions, Henry Butcher and Ned Beryl, who were drunker, pimpled and aged sixteen, waltzed a complete puzzled circle before they realised what had turned Geary around so quickly.

'Well, if it isn't Sir Cowper,' Henry said.

'Hen, Hen, Hen,' Ned implored, but Henry wasn't for imploring. 'It's the squire,' he said. 'Say hello to the squire, Ned.'

'Don't mind Henny, sir; he's a tosspot.'

Cowper did not mind and passed by.

'Where's Lady Cowper then?' Henry called. 'She warmin' the bed for you?'

Cowper stopped, then came back to them.

'You're a Christian, sir,' Ned said. 'You should give him a good slap.'

'I'll give you a slap, Ned Beryl, I will.' Henry tore off his coat and threw it on the ground. 'And then I'll kiss you, squire, 'cos you're the nicest gentleman in Olney.'

'Kiss him, will you?' Ned said. 'You should be down on your knees, Henry, like Lady Cowper sayin' her prayers.'

'Oh, you mucky pig,' Henry said and they both laughed.

'Gentlemen,' Cowper said.

'Who's a pig?' Ned said. 'Am I a pig, squire?'

'Gentlemen,' Cowper said, 'there's no need to be kind to me, but do please be kind to Mrs Unwin. She doesn't understand our despair.'

As he was letting himself into Orchardside, the two boys were still standing outside the Royal Oak staring at him. Later that night they met a burly man called William Pearce and in exchange for half a bottle of Dutch gin allowed him to fondle them, which was exciting. Eighteen months later, in front of witnesses, Ned Beryl offered to take an oath that he and Mr Pearce were lovers. Because one of the witnesses was Mr Pearce's wife, Pearce's reply was a fist and a thrust that knocked Ned into the street.

But now it was market day. Cattle and men were bellowing in the square, Mrs Unwin was getting out of bed and Cowper was pressing his tight-clenched fists against his ears.

27

$\mathcal{S}$he used the finest needles. He told her he had never seen their like, flashing and gleaming thinly as her fingers flew through the stitches. It was an activity he associated with winter evenings by the fire, but now it was midsummer and they were sitting in the yard between the back-door and the wash-house. She had a candle to count the stitches by, though it was hardly needed – she had been knitting his stockings for so long now that, whether in worsted, cotton or silk, she knew just where to start turning the heel. By the light of another candle he was reading aloud from *The Spectator* a report of the imminent departure of Captain Cook for the South Seas.

'Do you know, Mrs Unwin,' he said, 'of all occupations in the world I should prefer to discover unknown lands and savage peoples for the first time, and yet here I am, as far from the ocean as one can be in England.'

'I liked what Mr Newton said about our own savages, didn't you?'

'Oh yes. But I rather doubt he'll be invited to preach there.'

Susanna had just sent bad news about her betrothed, but on hearing it Newton had said, 'To be sent down from Oxford is no disgrace, but for the barbarians to send down Mr Powley for holding a prayer-meeting in St John's College is grace positive.'

Mrs Unwin said, 'One is better off staying at home. Give me the use of your hands, please.'

He held up his hands and she looped over them a skein of worsted and began to wind it into a ball. He enjoyed this task because he had once done the same service for his mother, a memory so vague it might have been false but which over time had become clear and true. Mrs Unwin enjoyed it because it gave her some chance of looking into his eyes and gauging his mood. His shyness was such that in speaking, even to her, he usually looked off to one side as if trying to discover the whereabouts of a door, like a boy-criminal.

'Susanna seems confident that Mr Powley's expulsion won't affect their wedding calendar, but I've written to say they had best wait until he has secured a living.'

'Which must be sooner rather than later. The fame of his dissent is bound to bring forward a curacy, if not a parish.'

'God willing.'

'Amen. Still, early or late, I will be sorry to see her go. I shall miss her about the house.'

Mary bent to pick up the ball of wool which she had dropped in order that he shouldn't see her smile. He thought of Susanna in almost exactly the same way as he thought of money: causeless, evanescent, mysteriously good. He would indeed be sorry to see her go, though he might not notice.

As if to confirm what she had been thinking, Cowper said, 'As you picked up your ball of wool just now, it occurred to me to wonder have you ever been in Worsted?'

'Many times. Why do you ask?'

'Well, Mrs Unwin, it's one of the nuisances of writing a great deal of rhyming verse. One is always rolling odd pair-shaped words around in one's mouth. And Worsted is not only the name of a thing and a place but also a verb.'

'Oh yes?'

'As in battle. And, when uttered in the proper Norfolk accent, it rhymes with disgusted. I wish I could forget these things. Once upon a time your own home town gave me similar trouble.'

'Ely?'

'As in eel. The adverb of. Which is hardly a word at all. Do you remember when we first met, you showed me that print of the cathedral?'

'Of course I remember.'

'I was greatly struck by how tremendously it rises from the plain.'

'The reality is even more tremendous. I intend taking you there some day.'

'I should like that,' he said vaguely. 'But do you know what I thought, what I could not prevent myself from thinking, when I saw the print? That the steeple was like an enormous eel standing up straight.'

'Really?'

Although Mary had not intended the pun, she joined in Cowper's laughter, but his lasted longer than hers, and when he did manage to stop, it was only to take out his handkerchief, which started him off again, giggling now and waving it helplessly around his face like a white flag, trying, and unable, to say, 'Really, I surrender, I surrender.' He stumbled into the dark kitchen to re-emerge in a couple of minutes restored to seriousness, angry and penitent.

That night she found it hard to sleep; even with only a sheet for covering, it was too warm. He was awake too; she could hear through the wall the scratching of his pen and once what sounded like an exclamation, probably a prayer. That did not concern her. It was usually when he fell asleep early that the dreams woke him. She got out of bed and opened the window wider to let in some air. The moon was high and Market Place was lit up. Out of the printed shadows of the elm trees in front of the Round House a fox loped into the middle of the square, leaped onto the side of the horse-trough and drank from it, but then a dog barked nearby and the fox darted off into Silverside. So frightenable, Mary thought, and so like Mr Cowper. She decided then that she would say what she had to say the following afternoon. As she went back to bed, a floorboard creaked; she stopped, turned her head and saw herself in the mirror, a ghost in a mob-cap, ridiculous and watchful. In the morning she would be tired and pale. She would make sure to do her hair neatly. And she had recently bought a little pot of rouge in Newport Pagnell; it was not a thing she approved of, but she would use a little beneath her cheekbones, to stop her looking like death.

Next door Cowper had snuffed out the candle and fallen straight asleep. In his notebook, from amongst many false starts and crossings-out and a faint memory of a conversation with Mrs Unwin, four lines had emerged:

> Bastards may escape the rod,
> Sunk in earthly, vain delight;
> But the true-born child of God,
> Must not, would not, if he might.

The next afternoon Mary halted their walk at the poplar colonnade. She had thought of continuing on into the Mossy Alley but she chose the brightness over the gloom from nervous impatience and because there was a place to sit, a grassy bank that Cowper liked to call his sofa. The river moved slowly past them like molten glass, and the hedgerows and fields on the other side of it sloped up mildly towards the low horizon and the spire of a remote church.

'What one sees daily,' he said, 'and daily pleases one, that must be the best of what we call beautiful, don't you agree?'

'You are well contented then?'

'Oh, me!' he laughed, 'I wasn't thinking of me. I think too much of that person already.'

'Well, I wonder. Would the place be beautiful without you to look upon it?'

'Oh, more so, I'm sure. Olney could go on very well without my enchantments.'

'One can think of the self without being selfish.'

'I'm sure you can, Mrs Unwin, but in my case the self is like a fish in that river, incapable of distinguishing its limits from what surrounds it.'

'That sounds sorrowful.'

'Yes, I rather suppose that is why baptism is by water.'

'But baptism is freedom, Mr Cowper.'

'Yes, of course. The promise is secure. Only ...'

'Only what?'

'I do wish I did not have to think about it all the time.'

She laughed. 'Well, I see you are ironical.'

'Irony is often, alas, the armour of an empty heart.'

'Oh, no one could doubt your seriousness, my friend, which makes your wit all the more sensible and indeed, to me, wonderful.'

'Well, we are friends, Mrs Unwin, and I suppose in friendship it is allowed to estimate the other person higher than he does himself, or than he deserves.'

'And vice versa?'

'And vice versa, but less than you deserve. On this I can speak with authority.'

'And without irony?'

'Of course. That goes without saying.'

'But it is pleasing to hear it plain sometimes.'

'Well, hear it plain then now, Mrs Unwin. You mean the world to me.'

He was looking at the river.

'And you mean the world to me.' She put her hand on his arm, he bent his head and they sat in silence for a while. Then he looked into her eyes for as long as it took him to say, 'I am, you know, an unfortunate.' It was not a question. He lowered his gaze and said haltingly, 'This is something I can say beyond self-pity. I learned it when my mother died. Perhaps I knew it even before then. I believe it has been set out for me. And not just for me.' He smiled at her sideways. 'We are a tribe, you know. The unfortunates.' Again he dropped his eyes. 'For someone of our sort, grief is a constant, as the water is for the fish. And yet it can happen that such a wretch is led to find in all the world a person who loves him and whom he loves in return. That event is then for him more than the greatest of good fortune; it is a blessing. And that wretch is me.'

'Give me your hand,' Mary said and was surprised at the harshness of her command, almost, she thought for an instant, as if she was angry at his being so – she did not stop to find the right word among so many – unmanly. And he did quail before her, but when he unknotted his tightly knitted hands and turned over the right one to her, she took it so gently that the gentleness shocked him, silk to the bone.

They walked on then out of the poplar grove. There was a good deal that Mary needed to tell him, even if he knew it already. William had become the rector of Stock in Essex and Susanna would soon be leaving home to get married, and without their presence in the house the gossip would become insupportable. Already there were righteous people in Olney and elsewhere who were saying it was scandalous that a widow and a single man should be living together so openly.

At last they arrived at another favourite haunt of his, the Peasant's Nest, a derelict cottage high up in a stand of scrub-oak trees, a hidden viewing point for the whole countryside. When she had explained all the reasons to him and all the financial, social and domestic advantages – but hurriedly, because both reasons and advantages were immaterial in such a risky circumstance – she asked him to marry her. He agreed and she kissed him. The kiss was intended for his cheek, but his lips were offered and so she kissed them, briefly.

28

'Give me your hand.' She had said that before. The first time his brother died; the second time she proposed marriage. She gave orders and things happened. It signified.

A movement startled him. It was a tiny spider right in front of his eyes, jerking downwards on an invisible filament. Did a spider so small have eyes? Of course, and they were so small they could see into his soul. Once upon a time he had killed spiders because they frightened him. Now he could not bear to do it, no matter how big the spider was. He opened the window and let this baby out, flapping his hand to free himself from the imperceptible thread.

It was November. The town and the house were sleeping. He could not sleep. He was afraid even to attempt it. The night before he had had a kind of premonition, just as he was drowsing off, that he would have a nightmare about falling asleep, and in a few minutes he was awake again and dreaming it, suffocating.

Then he was walking up a hill towards the glow from a candle shining in the distance. When he arrived at the summit he saw, instead of the candle, the first rays of the sun striking up from the horizon. He turned and ran along the brow of the hill, watching the light sideways. Now it was lying there in his record-book, already old. A postmonition. Was there such a word? It was a warning after.

I see, or think I see,
A glimmering from afar;
A beam of day, that shines for me,
To save me from despair.
Forerunner of the sun,
It marks the pilgrim's way;
I'll gaze upon it while I run,
And watch the rising day.

He had a nagging pain in his right side, as if some object were lodged beneath his ribs. The pain made him weak in the legs, and in bed he could not lie on that side, which prevented him from sleeping. Was it an imposthume of the liver? Dr Strick had told him the liver was 'a silent organ', the pain arose from what it hung on. In his mind's eye he saw himself in Mr Carroll's butcher shop and there, pierced by a hook, an enormous beef-liver was hanging, dripping blood onto the sawdust. He could tell from the way Mr Carroll's white moustache bristled that he despised him. Mr Carroll had sought advice because his wife, who owned jointly with her brother some rents in Newport Pagnell, had died intestate, and there was a question, the rents being payable half-yearly, about the amount and who was entitled to what, since she had passed away in the middle, more or less, of the period of payment, namely between Lady Day and Michaelmas, although Mr Carroll seemed only to require Cowper to issue rebarbative threats, entirely unfounded in law, against his unfortunate widow's brother. It was a confusing case. But Mr Carroll was at heart a good man, and it had been very kindly of him at the end of it all, instead of a fee, to make a gift to Mrs Unwin of a parcel containing a dozen of his best chump chops.

Mrs Unwin was the epitome of mildness, which made it all the more surprising to see her so unaccountably angry when Susanna said with regard to the meat, 'Every little helps, Mr Cowper, every little helps.' Perhaps the anger was due to the stain the parcel left on the tablecloth, but that wasn't Susanna's fault; it was his for putting it down so carelessly. The incident nagged at his mind, like the pain in his side. Both were inexplicable. Sam had been upset too; he had turned pale, and when he had snatched up the parcel to take it into the kitchen, the wrapping-paper had come undone and the chops had tumbled onto the carpet. Susanna had gone up to her room, followed by Mrs Unwin. It had all happened at once, so he had the impression, as Susanna swept past him, that the chops were flying through the air, like a covey of bizarre birds scattering from a gunshot. And Sam juggling with them somehow seemed like a memory. Yes, of the pharmacy in Lambeth and the bottle of laudanum falling.

And then the author of this chaos, himself, William Cowper, was left standing alone in the room, bewildered,

But that night Susanna had been very sweet and had apologised, which he told her she had no reason to do because the offence was his for being such a dunderhead. Supper had then been eaten peaceably, indeed with even more cordiality than usual as mother and daughter chattered quite gaily and entirely without any sign of strain from their *contretemps*.

Thinking of this tenderness, he fell asleep smiling.

In the mirror Mrs Unwin did not see how worried she looked. It was not the prospect of marriage that was depressing Mr Cowper's spirits but the writing of his poems and the attention they attracted. Recently he had been disturbed by the sinful pride he had taken in hearing the congregation singing his words. So she had advised him to reduce the amount of time he spent writing. Which, of course, and with signs of relief, he had immediately done.

She turned away from the mirror and looked at herself in the portrait. It was the third time she had done this in the past week. On the first occasion she had dragged the trunk from under her bed hurriedly, feeling as if she were doing something both exciting and wrong, a sensation strangely intensified by the sight of the blue petticoat wrapped around the portrait. Nearly twenty-three years had passed and the woman in the painting was an auburn stranger. But she had prepared herself for regret and hardly felt it, because, despite the dulled steel in her hair, she was still the same person and, more, she was actually improved, at least in the sense that she now knew what she wanted, which then had been something only imagined from reading novels. What she wanted now was so near that the imagination of it was superfluous, a non-existent hindrance, like closing a gate on a flooded field.

Although in the portrait she was pointing at the distant town and steeple, the central subject was herself, a woman who did not realise she was desirable, even though Arthur Devis had painted her swelling breasts as if they were an offering to desire. It was a shameful thought, and yet a shameless one too, and so she had stood up, closed the lid with an unintentional bang and shoved the trunk back under the bed.

Now she was looking at the portrait again, but with more calculation. It was not possible to be what she had been, although she had one night half-crazily imagined presenting herself to him dressed up in the old style, and the next morning had even opened the trunk for the second time to find the white satin gown, but as soon as she delved into the depths and saw a corner of it, faded to cream and crinkle, not by light but simply by the years, she had drawn back. Involuntarily she closed her eyes and was walking through the poplar colonnade on a hot summer afternoon and felt her breast against the sleeve of his coat. Surely he must have noticed the fullness of it and the stiffness of the nipple. But if he had, he had given no sign. A sign was all she wanted, and if it had been given, she would have paid no further attention to the yearning, but now, like herself in the portrait, it had become a physical ache. True, since the engagement, when they parted at night on the landing outside their rooms, they had developed a kissing ritual, but that was so like the kind of kiss one exchanges with a hostile kinswoman at a funeral, she almost dreaded it.

At supper that evening she drank three glasses of wine and afterwards put a saucepan of water to boil on the fire for a punch of port and lemon with honey, a stick of cinnamon and a small dash of brandy. While they were sipping the second glass, she said, 'Do you know, this couch has begun to irk me.'

The couch was really a day-bed, with nothing to lean back against except a sloping wooden frame at one end, and its horse-hair cushions, covered in threadbare gold silk brocade, were thin and lumpy.

'Oh? I thought you were fond of it,' Cowper said.

'I was, but I'm weary of it now.'

'Being weary of what one rests upon is, I suppose, a poetic conceit. Rather sad though.'

'Well, I can bear the grief of parting with it, my dear, particularly as I was thinking of buying a proper sofa.'

'A sofa! Do you think that's wise?'

'I do.'

'Your boldness never ceases to amaze me, Mrs Unwin. Indeed, it's almost Turkish.'

'Sir, I'm determined on it. Besides, you need something more comfortable than that old chair of yours. Don't you find it too straight-backed?'

'I've grown rather used to it, actually.'

'You look like a judge in it.'

'Oh, hardly a judge, Mrs Unwin. Let us say an extinguished lawyer. Quite invisible in fact.'

'Well, I see you clearly.'

'Yes?'

'You are in my eye as you are in my thoughts: constantly.'

'Oh dear, to be always looking upon a cloud, especially one so very nebulous, must be dismal. But I thank you for the attention, though I deserve it as little as I do a sofa.'

'I wouldn't class the purchase of a sofa among the deadly sins.'

'No? Perhaps not. It is a fine point.' She laughed loudly. 'Really, Mrs Unwin, you are very cheerful this evening.'

'I think the punch has gone to my head.'

'If it has, I shall keep your secret.'

'Will you?'

'Of course.'

She looked at him for a moment, then said in a low voice, 'Come here.'

'Pardon?'

'Come here.'

He unwound his entwined legs, stood up like a disturbed giraffe, crossed the narrow defile between them, and sat down beside her on the chaise.

'Give me your hand. Now. There it is, my secret. But you must know it already.'

'Must I? I don't really.'

'Of course you do. I want a sofa so that I can have you close to me. You know that mystery, don't you?'

'Oh, yes, I suppose I do.'

'And with the mystery comes a command.'

'Yes?'

'I command you to call me Mary. I am tired of Mrs Unwin. Let me hear you say it.'

'Mary.'

'Isn't that better?'

'Yes.'

'And I shall call you William.'

'But that is the name of your son.'

'And the name of my father. All the men I have most loved have been called William.'

'I hardly know what to say. I am not worthy of it.'

'If I say you are, you are. Henceforward it's William. Are we agreed?'

'Yes.'

'Goodness! You look pale, as if a spider had alighted on your shoulder.'

'A what?'

'You know what a spider is? An ugly little creature, but she spins silk.' She paused. 'You are required to say, "Not ugly at all, Mary," and I am required to drop my gaze and make a little *moue*. But we shan't pretend, shall we?' She gave a strange little laugh. 'Oh, you're lost for words. Accept your fate, my dear. It is God's will.'

'What is?'

'That we sit here together in front of the fire, you breathless and me with my heart beating fast. Look, don't you feel it?' She pressed his hand against her breast. After a moment she went on, 'It's been such a long time, you know. I thought I'd forgotten these feelings. As I should have. But now, well, now I feel such a tenderness for you, I could almost weep for it. Isn't a woman easily moved, especially when she's lonely?'

He raised his head and looked at her. His expression was beyond reading, but his mouth was open and he began to pant, like a child too young to understand that it has been struck a violent blow by its mother. Ice-water showered through her veins. She stood up in confusion, put her arms around his head and pressed it into the folds of her skirt. Then she said something – about the fire, or the lateness of the hour, or the new sofa – which she could never remember, and the moment passed.

29

That night he slept dreamlessly and in the morning woke with a feeling of profound relief and anticipation, as if his long fever had broken and there was work to be done. When Mary came down for breakfast, rather late, her eyes smudged with tiredness, he jumped up from the table, toasted bread for her at the fire and talked about the weather. He had been out in the garden, which was so white with frost it might have been snow, and the air was so utterly blue and fresh that he was minded to go off for a walk into the country. Would she mind if he went alone? Mary did not mind. There was a deal of house-cleaning to do for Christmas.

Then, just as he was about to leave, still putting on his coat, she said, 'William, are we to say nothing to each other about last night? Speak to me, please. Have I offended you in some way?'

'Me offended? On the contrary, you have bestowed on me a great gift.'

'A gift?'

'A very great gift. Do you know, I have never seen the truth made so manifest, at least not since the Lord's mercy was revealed to me in St Albans.'

In the street he was gladdened by the way the frost had reduced every colour to black and white. The pavement winked millions of tiny ice diamonds. Every person he passed he knew, and each had a particular way of greeting him. It was very gratifying. A small boy said, 'Good day' in the exact fashion of his father, who was a vestryman in the church, and Cowper answered, 'Good day, Simon.' The boy was wearing a bright red scarf, the colour of Christ's blood. It was humbling to think that no one but himself and Simon understood that Mrs Unwin had called him by his proper name, Will I Am.

Then he was striding across a white field of crackling grass and it occurred to him that he had been granted the gift of no victory in life, which was the meaning of Unwin. Why had he, alone in all the world, been given access to this place of power, and why by her? The answer that came to him stopped him in his tracks. Shortly after their first meeting, she had told him the old form of her husband's name, originally Flemish, was Onwhynnes. The disguise was so slight that it was obviously intentional: On Why-ness. Also, Mary was the mother of Jesus, and she had borne the Child who explained at last the world's whyness, the only issue of its being. It was plain and wonderful. To be chosen was humbling, and yet one could, if only for the merest moment, glory in it, glory in saying to one's sinful self, Will, I Am the Victory of Whyness.

'Oh, I am mad,' he said and laughed joyfully. Then he went home, shaking his head, amused by his own foolishness and the world's ignorance, went straight up to his room and wrote a letter.

Olney, December 13th, 1772

My Dear William,

You know me of late to be a dilatory correspondent, but no more, I am resolved, will I make the ancient excuse of fatigue. Put this down to punch! Last night your mother concocted a cauldron of the stuff and whether it was the elixirical steam or the pleasantness of our conversation concerning the ordering of a new sofa — what the Italian calls a <u>casapanca</u>, literally a belly house — I slept more deliciously than I have done this twelvemonth and woke refreshed, then made breakfast for my dear Sam, the extent of whose astonishment was only matched by the heartiness of his appetite for my poached eggs and toast.

Since the above was written most of the afternoon has passed —

excuse the hiatus — though I suppose you should not know of it had
I not told you. The passage of time in writing, I mean the awareness
of it in the reader, is a remarkable subject — but I leave that for
another occasion. Mr Newton has again attempted to persuade me to
preach, but he soon relented when I informed him that my
sermonising was like unto a scarecrow uttering forth from a whited
sepulchre. Something was strange however. When I turned around, I
realised that in all the whiteness of the morning the boy was wearing
a really bright red scarf, worsted, the colour of Christ's

At this point he stopped writing, read over what he had written
and tore the paper into many pieces. It was almost midnight.

Mary, too, was awake. She was thinking about what had happened during the day. Nothing really. In the morning he had been
very cheerful, which was perhaps surprising considering the night
before, but she was inclined to think she had misunderstood his
sobbing. Had she not wept when Morley had first made love to
her? As for his making breakfast, he was helpful about the house,
and Sam told her he had sometimes cooked, dreadfully, in the
lodgings they had shared in Huntingdon. Nor was it particularly
novel that he should go off on his own into the country — he often
did. But one thing was strange: when she was helping him on with
his greatcoat, he said, 'The Lord's mercy is in my name.'

So he had gone out. And when he came back he smiled at her,
and from time to time during the day she caught him smiling at
her, almost paternally, as if they shared a secret known only to
themselves.

It was well past midnight. He knew something was wrong. The
pieces of the torn-up letter told him so. The offence was in its
ungainliness of style. Now he had to teach Mr Newton a lesson
for asking him to preach. At dawn he finished the last four lines in
a rush:

> Banish every vain pretence
> Built on human excellence;
> Perish every thing in man,
> But the grace that never can.

The following Sunday Newton used the hymn, and in particular the line 'Cast your idol works away', as the starting-point for a sermon on the Christmas festivities. He had, he said, noted with horror that not a few of the congregation were indulging in idolatrous practices wholly incompatible with the sobriety that should have marked the birth of the Chastiser. But more than a few of the few resented the rebuke, and when he described their Christmas as a Feast of Fools, they sniggered. Hearing this sniggering, which was begun by Mr Geary Ball, who had come to the service under the influence of three glasses of gin, Newton waxed wrathful.

'Holly!' he thundered. 'A Christian can bear the hanging up of holly, since the thorns remind him of the nails that crucified the Saviour. But mistletoe! Mistletoe and the practice of kissing beneath it are pure lechery, an invitation to tongue the greasy maw of Satan!'

Cowper heard this, but not consciously. He was listening, instead, to a creaking sound. It was trochaic, strong and weak. The last four lines of his hymn had the rhythm of wings, a strong down-beat followed by a weaker one on the uplift. The sound was metallic, and the wings were those of the brass eagle that perched on the pulpit with the Bible on its back. For amusement he imagined golden wings sprouting from Mr Newton's clavicles, lifting him inches into the air. Then what he imagined became real, but the wings were black, those of a great bat, far too big for the small man who bore them, and the creaking was leathern. He shook his head and the image went away.

Mrs Unwin had noticed his fist beating on his knee, but paid it no attention. Now when he gave a little whinnying laugh and lowered his head, tinily shaking it, she thought he was amused by the sermon and whispered to him, 'Really, it's too absurd.'

He drew back to look at her and said, 'Oh, absolutely absurd. Did you see it too?' But he said it so wonderingly and in such a loud voice that she blushed and shushed him.

The social part of him was aware of the embarrassment caused by speaking in a normal voice in church, but there was another part that found it hard not to laugh at Mrs Unwin's cleverness. It was intriguing to realise that she too had seen Mr Newton rising up those inches as an eagle. Every so often he would steal a look at her face and was reassured that it was growing fainter and fainter in the dimming marsh-light of the church, frail as the weak beat of the trochee 'banish', soundless as the 'h' of her 'shush'.

Christmas passed peacefully, Mr Newton said afterwards, but even at the time his wife did not think so. She had gone over to Orchard-side early on the morning of Christmas Eve with the gift of an embroidered pin-cushion for Susanna, who was taking the post carriage to Huntingdon to be with the Powleys, but on coming out of the Vicarage she had found under the door-knocker a sprig of mistletoe and, attached to it with thread, a rolled-up scrap of paper covered with pencilled Xs and hearts with arrows through them.

'Mr Cowper will interpret it for us,' Susanna said. 'Is it an educated hand?'

He examined the note and said, 'I rather think not. There are no words.'

'It's those dastardly children from Silverside,' Mrs Unwin said.

'They want whipping,' Sam said, 'but I think it's Geary Ball that's behind it.'

'Oh, Sam,' Mrs Newton said, 'you are an old calumniator.'

'Well,' Mrs Unwin said, 'Ball is a vile gossip, so Sam may not be far off the truth.'

'Mr Newton will be greatly shocked,' Cowper said.

'Body o' me,' Mrs Newton cried, 'I'd as soon show this to Mr Newton as I'd throw myself in the river.'

'Oh, but you must,' Susanna said. 'And then afterwards come and tell us about the splash.'

'Really, Susanna, you are a poisonous creature,' her mother said. 'Sam, give the master a cup of tea.'

'I'd pay sixpence to see Mr Newton's face, wouldn't you, Mr Cowper?' Susanna said.

'No!' he said in a low but vehement tone.

'Really,' Susanna said, 'I was only jesting.'

'In bad taste, too, my girl,' her mother said.

'No, no, don't mind the taste,' Mrs Newton said. 'It is an amusing conceit, but I wonder do I dare.'

'Oh, do,' Susanna said.

'Well, perhaps I will,' Mrs Newton said, 'but I should need more than a sixpence for my courage.'

'Are you all agreed then?' Cowper asked.

'Agreed on what?' Mrs Unwin said.

'Or is it only you who obliges me to do this?'

'I think I hear the horn for the carriage,' Mrs Newton said.

'I can't,' he said in a weaker voice, 'I simply *can not* pay the price.'

'Well then,' Susanna said, 'Mother will make you a loan.'

'Susanna!' her mother said. 'Now, I do believe that the carriage is at the door.'

Mrs Newton stood up and said, 'Yes. It's time to be going.'

Cowper said, 'Forgive me, I misunderstood you all, especially you, Susanna. Do forgive me.'

'Yes, of course,' Mrs Newton said.

'What's to forgive?' Susanna said bitterly.

'Look, then!' he said, raised the cup of tea to his lips and drank it all down, hot and milkless, although he knew it was poisoned.

30

He threw away the mistletoe but kept the scrap of paper with the kisses and the pierced hearts on it. When he returned to Orchardside he found it in his Bible, smoothed out and flattened by the weight of pages that had not been lifted for a year. On it were written words that he had forgotten adding then: This is Mr Newton's portion, their Hatred of Him.

The festival had indeed passed over peacefully. On Christmas day they had dined at the Vicarage. Mrs Newton served a roasted goose and Mr Newton broke open a case of champagne which the Earl of Dartmouth had sent as a present. Despite misgivings about its name, Dom Perignon, which smacked of Roman monkishness, Newton drank the most of two bottles and talked about Africa. He did so as fiercely as ever, but when Mrs Newton said, 'You might better have stopped there, sir,' he only laughed and pinched her on the upper arm.

Mrs Unwin, who had also drunk quite a lot of champagne, because she felt there was nothing else for it, said, 'Ah, Mary, he could only stop where you are.'

'That reminds me,' Newton said, 'I propose to begin reading the banns on New Year's Day. Is there anyone, Mrs Unwin, who might cry halt to your nuptials?'

'Not a soul that I know of.'

Cowper said under his breath, '*Caecus amor sui.*' But whose love was blind he did not say, nor was he asked, because Newton had not, unlike Mrs Unwin, heard him, and Mrs Newton, who had heard, had no Latin but more sense than to inquire. He, too, had drunk champagne and now felt sleepy because, on top of the wine, he had devoured a great deal of goose and potato stuffing, the first food he had touched since the previous day.

It was late when Sam led them home through the orchard by the light of a torch. A faint wind was sighing through the apple-trees. Mrs Unwin, holding Cowper's arm loosely, looked with forgetful gladness at the wavering flame and tried to hum the childhood song that Mrs Newton had sung earlier, but could not quite remember it.

'Well, Mary Catlett, I see you still the child,' her husband had said. 'You in a bib and me with my back-hair in a queue.'

'All thick with tar,' his wife said.

'Aye, I stank of pitch. My head was as black as my soul. But you were well used to the whiff of shipmen before I came alongside, were you not, sweetheart? Oh, you were, you were.' And he began to sing a sea shanty, some of the words of which were indecent.

When he had finished, his wife said, 'The good people of Olney would not like that, Mr Newton.'

He had raised his glass high over his head and cried, 'A foutra to Olney!'

It was the word 'foutra' that Cowper was thinking of as they walked through the orchard. The meaning was obscure but plainly obscene, and therefore probably French. It was at this moment that Mrs Unwin said, 'I think our friend is wistful for the sea, don't you?'

'Mr Newton wistful?'

'Oh yes. By the minute. The older he gets. Don't you sense it?'

'I hadn't thought of him as old.'

'Well, he is a youth still, in his joys. But imagine if he hadn't been saved, what he would be like now.'

'What would he be like?'

'I'd be afraid to say. But if it weren't for Mrs Newton, oh, Africa and the black bosom.'

The brim of her bonnet hid her eyes, but the pulsing flame of the torch lit up her mouth. Out of it came a little laugh, like a sob, the same noise twice. To him the repetition sounded mechanical, magnified and deliberate, like the movements of a clock, and somehow he was in it and yet it was directed at him, too. At the same moment he felt that he had trodden on something soft.

Sam doused the torch in a bucket of dirty laundry water which he had left at the back door for the purpose. There was a loud hissing; a cloud of steam and smoke enveloped Mrs Unwin; and vestiges of it clung to her as she lit the lamp in the parlour. It was cold in the house and she wanted to make him a nightcap. He said, 'I will drink whatever you want me to.' Then he made for the door, muttering, 'But really, I'd prefer on Christmas night that the cup should pass from me.'

She did not catch this because she was crying out, 'Oh, look what you've done now! You've brought dung into the house. Look, it's all over my best rug.'

There were brown smears on the carpet. She picked up the nearest paper to hand, a copy of *The Spectator*, tore off the cover and began to scrub at the dirt.

'Oh, it's my fault,' he said, 'my fault entirely.'

'Sam,' Mrs Unwin cried, 'bring me a basin of water this instant.'

But then, to his horror, she dipped her finger in the mess, sniffed at it, stood up and came towards him with her hand held out, saying, 'Smell! Smell that! Smell my finger, you monster!'

That night as he went to sleep, he saw Newton falling through darkness, turning over and over, and his cry was visible, a pinpoint of fire that sang, 'A foutra, a foutra, a foutra,' as it fell, extinguished, into the pit.

Then he was a man, but unnaturally small, boy-sized, dressed in a red velvet cloak, going rapidly down a steep staircase into a huge featureless hall where a woman was sitting on a dais. Her skirt was voluminously bell-shaped. Beneath the bell, one shoe moved as if squashing something and he heard a crunching sound. Then the shoe lifted very slowly, the heel remaining on the ground, and he saw a shattered snail stuck to its leather sole. Then he was even smaller than before and the snail was above him, rearing up languidly so that he saw its slimy underside, frilled around the edge. Then, as the snail came down on top of him, glutinously, he woke up, unable to scream or to remember.

What he did remember, indistinctly and obscurely, a year later, as he rolled the scrap of paper with the kisses on it into a ball before throwing it into the fire, was a faintly sharp, faintly rotten odour. But he did not remember Mrs Unwin's finger twitching at his nose or her voice saying triumphantly, 'It's only a windfall. You trod on a windfall.'

Boxing Day was a blank. But Mrs Unwin understood his reasons for not eating or drinking anything touched by her hand – she was, after all, intent on poisoning him. That this was entirely proper he accepted; it was his fate. To be proud about it would be yet another sin to add to the listing cargo of his faults. Listing! The word came to him in the garden, and it seemed appropriate that when she called him in for lunch he tacked towards her with a slight compensating lean to the left, which he thought was an adequate signal – he had told her about it often enough – that the nagging pain in his right side was worse than ever.

She stood at the door drying her hands on her apron and said, 'I hope you're hungry, my dear. I've made you a fish pie.'

The smile he managed only bared his teeth. 'A pie? Don't you think a pie is going rather too far?'

'What do you mean?'

He saw her fear and tried to comfort her. 'Believe me, I mean no offence. After all, a pie is classical. Procne did it and she turned into a nightingale.' Then tears came into his eyes and he added, 'Which you always were to me. And always will be.'

Then he ran through the house and out into the street. There, Mr Carroll, the butcher, who was passing said, 'That's a grey day now, Mr Cowper,' to which, stopping only briefly, with his head thrown back, he replied, 'Hopeless! Hopeless!'

It was a grey day, but somehow the fact of the widowed Mr Carroll saying it so cheerfully slowed his racing mind and made him feel sorry for the weather and for Mrs Unwin. After walking repentantly around the town for a quarter of an hour, he returned to sit at the luncheon table, where he behaved as if nothing had happened, talked amusingly about his shortcomings as a lawyer in dealing with the butcher's estate and, when Mrs Unwin was not looking, managed to transfer most of his portion of fish pie into his handkerchief.

Mrs Unwin did not have to look to see. She spoke to Mrs Newton, who did not have to be told to understand. They went up to Mr Newton in his study and told him the story. He saw and understood differently. Their friend's lack of appetite was due to a spiritual hunger for eternal life and a fleshly hunger to be married. The former could never be satisfied except by holy dying, but the latter ought be dealt with immediately by the vow that only death can unbind.

However, on New Year's Day, obeying his wife, Newton did not begin to read the banns.

'There he is.'

The words, said twice almost simultaneously, startled Cowper. He and Mary were going up the aisle when he heard them. It was the twins from the lace-school who had spoken, though for a moment he did not recognise them in their Sunday-best pinafores and little mob-caps tied under the chin. They had come in from the country with their parents and were excited by the town, by the church and by seeing 'the sixpenny man' with the lady he was going to marry. When he told Mrs Unwin who they were, she turned round in the pew and fluttered her fingers at them.

'What adorable babies,' she whispered. 'I should like to kiss them for an hour.'

Newton then made his entrance, somewhat belatedly, carrying a basket of apples, to which, having placed it on the communion table, he paid no further attention. This was curious, since if he brought an item on to the altar, which he did often enough, it got plenty of use – the congregation had once spent an acutely interesting period contemplating a butcher's knife employed to illustrate Abraham's putative sacrifice of Isaac, a performance brought to a premature end after only two hours when he sliced the top off his index finger. What Cowper was never to know, and Mary only to learn much later, was that the basket of apples had opened a rift between Newton and his wife. Mrs Newton, who usually gave her husband free rein in religious affairs, had on this occasion adamantly refused to allow him to preach on the Psalm *They shall bring forth fruit in old age; they shall be fat and flourishing*, even though he insisted that his proposed reference to Mrs Unwin's barren womb being quickened was not to be understood literally. He was deeply offended by his wife's grossness and had only relented at the last minute when she said she was going home and he could play the organ himself. Instead, he had improvised a sermon from Isaiah:

> They trust in vanity, and speak lies; they conceive mischief, and bring forth iniquity. They hatch cockatrice's eggs, and weave the spider's web; he that eateth of their eggs dieth; and that which is crushed breaketh out into a viper.

That evening, revisiting the text in his room, Cowper heard the voice that had begun to speak to him, to instruct him, since Boxing Day. It seemed to come from high up in the corner of the room, where a small spot of damp had stained the fine shavings of silk that made up the flock of the wallpaper, rose-coloured roses on cream. The voice was mechanical and when he had first heard it he thought it came from the pump in the yard, because it had the same rusty clank. But now from out of the maculated flower it said with Isaiah's voice, 'Better forever to be hid.' This was true because in the drawer of his desk – he opened it as he had known he would be obliged to – there were pieces of the shell of an egg, no trace of albumen adhering, sucked clean, and a crust of bread, both of which he had stolen from the kitchen in the middle of the night when she was asleep, or pretending to be asleep. It was wonderful to be alive and hungry.

But now, as he mumbled the crust, Isaiah spoke again from the iron rose:

> Their webs shall not become garments, neither shall they cover themselves with their works; their works

are works of iniquity, and the act of violence is in their hands.

He could not read any further. It was settled.

In the kitchen he had worn his dressing-gown, which had a belt of gold. She had given him the gown as a gift. Probably in all deliberation. As a sign. Sinfully avoided then, but settled on now. On the braided golden cincture. That was the choice.

But he slept well that night, for the reason of decision, and in the morning he said to Mrs Unwin, 'I would be very obliged if you could present my apologies to Mr Newton for my absence from Divine Service for the forseeable future. I believe he will understand, if anyone can, my unworthiness. Apart, of course, from yourself.'

Whereupon he made a small, formal bow and went out.

Some hours later he found himself in the Mossy Alley. Here the truth was simpler. It had to do with the frown of appearance. The plain winter silence. It was a mine of unfathomable darkness. This was the truth on which he had been advancing. What smiled was necessarily hidden. For a long time he stood in the yew-tree gloom. Then he returned home, went up to his room and completed, or almost, the new hymn:

> God moves in a mysterious way,
> His wonders to perform;
> He plants his footsteps in the sea,
> And rides upon the storm.
>
> Deep in unfathomable mines
> Of never-failing skill,
> He treasures up his bright designs,
> And works his sovereign will.
>
> Ye fearful saints fresh courage take,
> The clouds ye so much dread
> Are big with mercy, and shall break
> In blessings on your head.

Judge not the Lord by feeble sense,
But trust him for his grace;
Behind a frowning providence,
He hides a smiling face.

His purposes will ripen fast,
Unfolding every hour;
The bud may have a bitter taste,
But sweet will be the flower.

Blind unbelief is sure to err,
And scan his work in vain;
God is his own interpreter,
And he will make it plain.

Six weeks later they brought him his manuscripts and immediately he changed 'But sweet will be the flower' to 'But wait, to smell the flower'. To be able to call a halt, even to the Lord's purposes, was, still, wonderful. Then he looked directly at Newton and said, 'It's the calculus, you see. That's the poet's sin.'

31

$\mathcal{I}$n the days after he had written the hymn, the house was as tight as a drum. Then Susanna came back from Huntingdon and that evening made a scornful noise when he absented himself from prayers; and the next day when a bill came in from London for shirts she cried out, 'Well, mercy me!' But after her mother spoke to her, she said no more. Susanna's silence towards him was organised, yet ragged. But she had a great deal to report about the Powleys, and the old routine of the house was re-established, for a while, after a fashion.

In the drum-tight house his shoes beat out a swooshing tattoo on the floor of his room, like two opposing armies marching in counter formation. Swoosh and bang, swoosh and bang. So he took off his shoes and stole around in his stockings. Still, though shod with wool, his feet were iron.

Then it was very late. Down the stairs he sidled. In the yard, drinking cold handfuls from the rainwater barrel, he raised his head and caught a glimpse of moonlight reflected from Sam's window. That was the border of the upper world. To find the border of the lower, he went farther into the garden and threw himself onto the ground. The fall was a shock. Shocking, too, was the icy wet grass against his face. He was free, or nearly, so he lunged towards the final freedom, with the armless heavings of a walrus making for the waves. But then, just as he was about to make the last dive with his head, he saw two eyes staring at him, chips of moon-silver, and heard a hiss. It was a cat, and she was short-stabbing the cobwebbed air with one paw. Oh, he knew her! He could not go any farther; she was the guardian of the gate. Feeling foolish for not realising that a tortoiseshell cat could be the three-headed dog of hell, he got to his feet and went back to the barrel and washed his muddied face and hands. Each dash of the water woke him the more into his foolishness and ordinary tiredness. Chastened, he crept up the stairs to his room, burrowed under the bedclothes and fell asleep, rolled up into a hedgehog ball.

He was awake. Again he was descending. This time there was no creaking staircase but a tunnel, huge yet tight, the artery of a worm walled with the words of the clanking voice, blurred, peristaltic, pumping him slowly towards the centre of the earth, towards more compactness. But because he could not arrive, the journey could not end. Instead, the tunnel became a tube, a cannula stuck down his throat and spine, a hollow column. And there she was again, this time with no head. And her skirt was barrel-hooped, holding in black water. Then the dream became matter-of-fact. He was with his father in the Temple and they were discussing the arrangements. There were a great many fine details to be dealt with, and Father did not seem to mind that a rat was sitting on the table worrying with her front legs around the region of her mouth, worrying with little boxing motions. 'The main question is,' Father was saying, 'will she have a needle to pinch it out of its shell? There will be a bill, of course, and you will be impeached for it. That goes without saying.' Then he was naked before the bar of the House of Lords and Mrs Unwin was the Lord Chancellor, laughing and pointing at him. But before she could announce the verdict, Father was drawing out of the rat's mouth a long length of seaweed that braided into a golden cord. 'Oh, this will have to do, I suppose,' he said. Then he was knotting the cord, which was the belt of his dressing-gown, around his mother's neck and Mrs Unwin's tobacco-black tongue was extruding slowly from her mouth and it waggled, attempting to utter his secret. But he rapidly wound the cord more tightly around her throat. And she was dead. And the door of the featureless hall swung open, and Father's godly voice was booming, '*Actum est de te, periisti!*'

Mrs Unwin screamed.

The tortoiseshell cat, sitting on the garden wall, saw Sam running in night-shirt and bare feet through the dawny grey orchard, his arms flailing.

The cat jumped down from the wall and went off into Silverside. There she caught a pygmy shrew, played with it for a while, then killed it. It was the coldest part of the day and the greyness was beginning to develop edges. The cat dropped the shrew in the long wet grass, raised one paw and turned her head when she heard the voices hurrying through the orchard.

The mirror in Mrs Unwin's bedroom was broken and Susanna was crying as she and her mother tried to undo the cord that was knotted around the madman's neck. It had not been a continuous endeavour. Nothing was continuing. One minute he was sitting on the bed, the next he was swimming across the Turkish complexity of the carpet, then he was trying to loop the golden belt over the coat-hook on the door. But he was not violent, and all his actions were punctuated with apologies for creating such a nuisance. At one point he banged his shin off a chair and kicked out at it but managed only to get his legs tangled up with its legs and both fell over, fighting and threshing. Other than that and getting to the coat-hook, his one intention seemed to be not to touch Mrs Unwin, to keep close to her, to avoid her eyes, to stare at her.

She kept saying his name and the word 'please'.

On the chest of drawers, where the starred mirror leaned at a universally drunken angle, the delph ewer had been knocked over and from it water was dripping comets onto the rug.

He was cowering in a corner, driven there by Newton, who had burst in shouting, 'Good Lord, Mr Cowper, what is this I hear? What in heaven's name are you doing, sir? You've frightened everyone. Have you gone mad?'

Newton's wife brushed past him, muttering, 'Pick up the chair,' went to Cowper with her hand held out and said, 'You're tired, my friend. Will you walk over to our house and rest there a while?'

A year had passed and he had come back to Orchardside. The difference was that now he was never left alone. On this occasion

Sam was outside on the landing, the door had been left slightly ajar and at the sound of any unusual movement he looked in. Today the only sound – and it was unusual – was the scratching of pen on paper.

After throwing the message with the hearts on it into the fire, he caught sight of his haggard face in the mirror. On the advice of Dr Cotton, whom Newton had travelled to St Albans to consult, they had more than once opened a vein and watched him bleed into an enamel bowl. But the loss of blood had not bled him white. Not yet.

'Not yet!' he had cried out one night in the Vicarage as Newton sat by his bedside watching the invisible battle.

'What is it, my friend?'

'Twice lost, twice lost,' he answered, but when Newton turned to follow his gaze, all he saw was the door. He did not realise that Mrs Unwin was outside preparing for the night watch and that Cowper could see the tiny gleam of her candle through the keyhole. She was the Twice Lost. Then he cried, 'They've arrived! They're coming through!'

'Who is it, Mr Cowper? Is it the evil spirits?'

'No! No! Not both of them.'

'One is a good spirit?'

'Oh yes,' he said resignedly, 'but the other one wins.'

'Then look to the good,' Newton said. 'Good is salvation. Reach out to it.'

Cowper said weakly, 'If I could reach that far …' But then he gathered up his remaining strength and said, 'If all my sufferings could be banished with a wave of my hand, but without God's approval, I would not do it. And I will not! Instead, I welcome them.'

'Your faith amazes me.'

'They're as alike as my fingers,' Cowper said, 'so let them in,' and he meant Mrs Unwin.

When Sam heard the cry, he looked in, but the master began writing again and he decided to let him be.

> Hatred and vengeance! my eternal portion,
> Scarce can endure delay of execution,

Wait, with impatient readiness, to seize my
                    Soul in a moment.

Damned below Judas, more abhorred than he was,
Who for a few pence sold his holy Master,
Twice betrayed Jesus me, the last delinquent,
                    Deems the profanest.

Dante found Judas in the lowest circle of Hell. He, William
Cowper, was lower still; his pride was beneath commerce. 'Twice
betrayed Jesus me' was the furious bedrock pride and protest of his
suffering. The God of love, he hated him. The God of hate, he
loved him. Both were entitled to the meat of his soul, to eat of it
forever. To those who loved him, he had shown only hatred. And
they in turn despised him. An agony of loneliness imprisoned his
heart. And yet it was contemptible to try to escape it.

Man disavows, and Deity disowns me.
Hell might afford my miseries a shelter;
Therefore hell keeps her ever-hungry mouths all
                    Bolted against me.

Hard lot! encompassed with a thousand dangers;
Weary, faint, trembling with a thousand terrors;
I'm called, if vanquished, to receive a sentence
                    Worse than Abiram's.

He wrote swiftly now, trembling and thinking of a cruelty
greater than that which Moses had called down on Abiram the rebel.

Him, the vindictive rod of angry justice
Sent quick, and howling to the centre headlong;
I, fed with judgements, in a filthy tomb, am
                    Buried above ground.

Was it finished? No. In a final burst of rage that was also a plea,
he underscored the words 'Him' and 'I'. Then he wrote out the
poem again and changed 'filthy' to 'fleshly'. He was, as ever, capable
of calculation.
And then he was back in his mad body again.

32

*W*ild hares came bounding through the wall. Their names were Tiney, Puss and Bess. The breach in the thick masonry between kitchen and parlour he had opened with Sam's help, but he alone had carpentered the little doors.

Puss nibbled a leaf of lettuce from her master's fingers; Bess leaped up onto the sofa, crept into a fold of Lady Austen's wide skirt, turned round three times and gazed up at her; and Tiney, after throwing himself against the wall for a few frenzied moments, deposited at Mrs Jones's feet a little mound of shining black-currants, then went on gambolling at a more leisurely pace. Sam came and removed the dung with a brush and dust-pan, but the ladies, who were sisters, hardly noticed – there were too many other animals in the room distracting their attention: a bulldog, called Mungo, two spaniels, Beau and Marquise, a litter of kittens and a linnet, which had been let out of its cage for a while and was whisking around the room chirruping until the lights were lit. The lamps would have been more dangerous to the bird than was the devilish mother cat occasionally batting a paw at its swooping flight.

It was a place, Anna Austen felt, where the lion might lie down with the lamb, but while it was all settled, genteel and refined, it was also quite shockingly wild – no one, she thought, no one else in England lives like this.

Being summer there was no need for lights until late, and as the gloom slowly gathered, so too did the scents of the flowers that Mrs Unwin had filled a basket with as they walked in the garden before supper. Such a neat, well-ordered and yet profuse garden it was, Lady Austen thought, better-ordered in fact than the indoors. It had shaven lawns and fences of flowers, mignonette, roses, honeysuckles, wild olive, silk cotton — too many to name — and in the greenhouse, along with pineapples and a most unusual and tender flower from New Zealand called Broallia, there were melons.

'This one,' Cowper said, 'we shall have after supper, because it is cleansing to the palate. Cantaloupe is the name our American rebels have for it, but they are wrong for once, the dears, since the rind is not netted as theirs are, but wrinkled, unlike the varieties we are familiar with, which are smooth-skinned. But this variety I doubt they have. The Crenshaw it's called, after, I suppose, the gentleman who first cultivated it, which is as English as anything Persian could be.'

Lady Austen was impressed by the melon, but even more so by the greenhouse, which was, she said, 'as neat as a bandbox'.

'Mr Cowper is glowing,' Mrs Unwin said. 'He built it with his own hands, you see, and cut the glass with a diamond pencil, which item is not easily acquired in Olney, and therefore, as I know, rather expensive.'

'In another, more fortunate life,' he said, 'I like to think I might have been a wandering glazier, hefting his fragile castle upon his back. It is a pleasant craft, but then all hand-work is pleasing, don't you think?'

'Oh yes,' she said. 'I have myself a positive passion for lace-making.'

'Well,' he said, 'you have come to the right place.'

And she had. Immediately Lady Austen had liked the man, drooping there on the sofa, anxious heel on nervous toe, but the first going had been a hard slog, even with her sister Maud, Mrs Jones, rattling on nonsensically and Mrs Unwin politely helping her. Then the subject of poetry came up, which, Anna said, she had heard he dabbled in.

'About verse I can say,' Cowper said, 'that I go into it to get out of something worse.'

'In what sense?'

'Well, the pursuit of a pretty image, or a pretty way of expressing it, draws me in, and then I'm drawn out of myself, the which is irksome.'

'Not at all irksome,' Mrs Unwin said and set about pouring more tea from her best silver teapot.

'Oh, more than some,' Cowper said. 'But with scribbling I'm like a boy who plays truant, determined to be amused now and to forget that he must soon go home and be whipped.'

'No one deserves whipping less, I'm sure,' Mrs Jones said.

'But there is – is there not? – more to poetry than truancy,' Lady Austen said.

'Oh yes?'

'More, too, than prettiness and a nice noise, don't you agree?'

'About poetry, Lady Austen, I should be afraid not to agree, but I prefer to think of what I do as verse. And as for the niceness, verse diverts me rather as a rattle does a baby – he likes the noise, even if it drives others to distraction.'

'But you're not a baby,' Mrs Unwin said. 'You only act like one. Now and then.'

'You see how kind she is,' Cowper said.

'Mrs Unwin is the soul of kindness,' Mrs Jones said. 'Everyone knows there's not a kinder soul in Olney. I told you so, didn't I, Anna?'

'Nonsense,' said Mrs Unwin.

'And she's as polite as a duchess,' Cowper said.

Lady Austen laughed, showing little ivory-yellow teeth, pointed like a cat's. 'I have met duchesses in my time who would bullock one out of the way for the prospect of an almond biscuit.'

'Mmmmm,' he said.

'Indeed I fear that the higher one goes in society, and in my experience this is true also in France, the more necessary it is to keep one's elbows well pointed.'

'Really?' he said. 'How thrilling.'

It was thrilling, and he knew it would be as soon as he had seen her and Mrs Jones coming out of the draper's shop across the square that afternoon. Maud Jones was a familiar sight in Olney, along with her rather beastly husband, the Vicar of Clifton, who had been a barber until Mr Newton apprenticed him to Christ, but the stranger was obviously, by her lustrous grey silk dress, a cut above blood-letting. There was, too, something about her demeanour as she strolled up and down waiting for Mr Jones's carriage, an energy, both nervous and indolent, that reminded him of someone, like a faint perfume made sharper in the memory by reason of its faintness.

So he had run down to the parlour and said, 'Mrs Unwin, you do, do you not, believe in Providence?'

She was not given time to wonder why her belief in something so mysterious should preface a request that she go across the square and invite Mrs Jones to tea. She had to act immediately.

'Before,' as he said, 'the barber's cart arrives and takes her away.'

Later that night Mrs Unwin did wonder why; and she wondered, too, at the slightly indecent sensation she had felt approaching Lady Austen outside the draper's shop while he, hidden and not smiling, watched from his curtained window. Now he was hiding still, but in sleep, and she was watching over him at his bedside.

It was not true to say, although she had once said it to Mrs Newton, that she had slept in her day clothes for longer than any vagabond in England. But it was true that she had kept up the custom for more than eight years, though she did not actually sleep, only sometimes dozed, and then, when he was safely down, went off, slow-footed, to her own room. Nor did she wear her day clothes, except sometimes in the depths of winter, when the bedroom window was starred with frost and his fears were too starless to leave him. Otherwise she put on a night-dress and a shawl, always the same shawl, which her father had long ago given her out of the shop in Ely, a heavy cotton-silk wrap from India, embroidered with roses and fringed with tassels, which was unsaleable because there was the faintest water-stain on its whiteness, brown-edged. She had tried to dye it scarlet, but it had turned out a deep rose-madder pink, and somehow the blotch was more visible than before.

She always wore the shawl because one night in the Vicarage – it was after Mr Newton had returned from St Albans with Dr Cotton's instructions on the bleeding procedure – she realised that he was looking at her not as a harpy intent on poisoning him but as a woman in an imperfectly pink shawl, and instead of crying out for help to be saved from her, as he had done for months, he reached out and took hold of a handful of the tassels.

But now it was too humidly warm for the shawl. Lady Austen, having sent Maud home with comical peremptoriness to mind her children, had stayed on almost till midnight. They had eaten supper and drunk two bottles of wine, many cups of coffee and a very small glass each of brandy, the effects of which now made Mrs Unwin feel uncomfortable and, somehow, disconsolate. She slipped off the shawl and plucked out the front of her nightdress to let some cooler air in at her bosom. It was a happenstance, but a fortunate one for conversation, that the wine had come from Sancerre, where Lady Austen had lived for years with her late husband, Sir Robert, who was twice her age when she had married him. Was she forty now, or more? She didn't look it, even if she said, quite meaning it too, that she was the ugliest of women, which she certainly was not – no, while she wasn't strictly beautiful, she was freely lovely. And it was exciting to have a guest who had lived in Sancerre, a part of France stocked with Jacobites yearning for their Bonnie Prince Charlie and the destruction of England. It was curious the excitement this information engendered in Mr Cowper: he had a horror of such people and yet he thrilled to hear of Anna living amongst them, as if she were, almost, one of their gang. Perhaps it was because of the sensationalism of Lady Austen's past – it was sensational though she had not actually done anything – that he had tried to impress her by reading aloud some lines from *Retirement*, telling her that the poem, along with other pieces, was to be published in London. Lady Austen had said immediately she would subscribe to the volume, adding that, of all the gifts of genius, to be a poet was in her opinion the greatest. He was, of course, pleased, but said, 'Really, you know, I have no more right to the name of a poet than the maker of mousetraps has to that of an engineer.'

Lady Austen had laughed, prettily but strangely, saying, 'I would pity the mouse who strayed into your engine, sir.'

There had followed a silence that lasted only a moment. Mrs Unwin had not understood the remark. But now, half-asleep, she half-realised it was an explanation for why she sometimes felt her pity was, underneath it all, almost savagely submissive. She was the mouse in his trap. Or was it other way round? Whichever it was, no one could ever appreciate that the tenderness she felt for him was so great that it amounted occasionally to rage. And she only felt it. It was a feeling that could have no name, that was too womanly to share with its engineers.

33

. . . The very next day Lady Austen's lackey and a lad that waits on me in the garden drove a wheelbarrow full of eatables and drinkables to the scene of our fête champêtre. A board laid over the wheelbarrow served us for a table; our dining-room was a root house lined with moss and ivy. At five o'clock the servants dined under a great elm on the grass at a little distance, boiled the kettle, and the said wheelbarrow served us for a tea-table. We then took a walk into the wilderness (a designed one, by Capability Brown) about half a mile off, and arrived home again a little after eight. We had spent the day together from noon to evening without one cross occurrence or the least weariness of one another – a happiness few parties of pleasure can boast of.

The lad who waited on Cowper in the garden had, however, a different view of the day than that communicated to Joe Hill. He had never seen the squire in such a flurry and flap, giving orders, laughing at himself for giving orders, running in and out of the house, changing his wig, chivvying and harrying poor old Sam about putting on a clean neckcloth and – it was the talk of Olney for a week – washing the wheelbarrow.

The lad – his name was Crouch and he looked like a squat fox – was only just thirteen, so wheeling the wheelbarrow along the river to the big house at Weston Underwood, with its lawns and statues and fountains, was an important responsibility, and at the picnic he got to taste things he had never tasted before: a banana, a marzipan cake and a drink that tasted like piss.

But when it came to actual pissing, Lady Austen's lackey, Murdoch, and her maid, Mistress Jenny – a maid called Mistress was a grandness Crouch had never heard of – had a falling-out because the lackey twigged Sir Cowper wanted to relieve himself, did not know how to make his excuses to the ladies, walked up and down faster and faster and then at last sidlingly bolted off into the bushes.

'In France,' Murdoch said, 'gentlemen piss in the street right in front of their doxies. Shows them there's pork for supper, I suppose.'

'You oughtn't to talk like that in front of the boy,' Mistress Jenny said. 'And besides, gentlemen in France do no such thing, or in England for that matter, not true ones.'

'Not this one any road,' Murdoch said, indicating Cowper emerging from the bushes. 'Look at him! He looks like a bum-bluffer to me, but milady fancies him, from what I hear her saying to the skin and blister.'

'The what?' Crouch asked.

'Skin and blister? Her sister. Mrs Jones the bag of bones. She says Lady Anna heard about his book of hymns down in London and came up special. Well, Jenny, what do you say? Does she fancy him?'

'Fancy, fancy, fancy,' Mistress Jenny said. 'Some people aren't vulgar, you know.'

'Like you, you mean. Stuck-up little trollop. Here, boy, try this,' and he gave Crouch a mug of white wine. 'What's he like, your master? Has he got cash?'

But Crouch gagged on the wine, spat it out, everyone laughed and the question was forgotten. He would have said that the squire was, of course, rich, because he paid him sixpence for one day's work a week, the most of which the squire did himself, unless he was walking around the garden holding old Mrs Unwin's hand or sitting in the glasshouse writing with the feather of a goose. Crouch might have said, too, that the week before Lady Austen arrived, the squire had given him a shilling to go home because he preferred not to see anyone just then, and that he once saw him leaving a meat-pie on the windowsill of the Widow Mitcham's house over the garden wall in Silverside, unbeknownst to anyone, or so the squire thought, but Crouch was not a fox for nothing, and he had dug a good handful out of it before making himself scarce.

'Sincere and candid persons' were the only kind the Reverend William Bull judged worthy to speak to, but since that included almost everyone, and as he was, besides, somewhat short-sighted, he inclined not to notice individuals at all, unless, that is, they were remarkably interesting, like Mr Cowper, or remarkably bumptious – amongst the latter he did not, strangely enough, include the Reverend Newton.

'This is nonsense, Mr Bull,' Newton had said on their first meeting.

'Do you think so?'

'Absolute nonsense. A fantastical affectation.'

'Actually, I find it places a limitation on fantasy.'

'What do you mean, sir?'

'I mean that I see only what I need to see. It is a kind of adequacy.'

'Adequacy! You would be better off knocking down the entire wall and letting the Lord's light shine in upon your ignorance,' Newton had said.

The cause of his ire was an eye-wide aperture Mr Bull had had pierced through the garden wall at the Vicarage of Newport Pagnell Independent Church. He sat there for lengthy periods observing the countryside, left to right, right to left – from a viewing point of view it was entirely adequate. Newton had also criticised his daily five-mile walk around the garden, each lap marked off with a piece of lead shot moved along a groove in the wall. To dub this ingenious regulation an eccentricity rather puzzled Mr Bull. As a result of their meeting, Newton had formed a low opinion of this large man. But seven years later, when he chanced to hear Mr Bull preaching at a funeral service, he had been reduced to silence.

'Which was remarkable then and, indeed, occurred so often thereafter that Mrs Newton used to say Mr Bull was her husband's pope,' Cowper said to Lady Austen. It was Wednesday and Mr Bull was lunching at Orchardside, as he did every fortnight.

'On the whole I should prefer to talk about cucumbers,' Mr Bull said. He tasted the iced soup, which Mrs Unwin had made with cucumbers from Cowper's garden, and pronounced it excellent.

'And yet,' Lady Austen said, 'it was a further six years until you gentlemen met. Why so?'

'You see, *mon cher Taureau*, how closely she listens.'

'Well, the delay was not my doing,' Mr Bull said. 'It was quite mortifying to think that so wonderful a monument to the power of divine grace should stand within five miles of me and yet not to be able visit it.'

'What kind of monument?' Cowper asked. 'Am I an obelisk?'

'No, not an obelisk,' Lady Austen said, 'that's too funerary. If you were an Egyptian, I should say a Sphinx. Not the famous one with the nose knocked off. No, no, if you'll excuse me, definitely not noseless. But since you are not a pagan, I should say from reading the Olney hymnal that you are a lighthouse for the faithful, who are, the majority of them at any rate, as well as being simpletons, not far off being blind.'

Cowper laughed out loud – the loudness was an unusual sound to Mr Bull's ears, which were more used to mild giggles, and somehow the display of it, like this black-eyed woman showing her silken bosom, made him feel ill at ease.

'A lighthouse for the blind,' Cowper chortled. 'Am I meant to be flattered or insulted?'

'The wine is going to our heads,' Mrs Unwin said and poured more of the gift of Sancerre that Lady Austen had brought over from Clifton.

'I despise flattery,' Anna said, 'but my question remains unanswered: why the delay between kindred spirits, being only a five mile off?'

'Perhaps,' Cowper said, 'it was that Mr Newton adjudged I was not fit for the excitement of imaginative company.'

'I must see about the fish,' was all that Mrs Unwin said, and she went off to the kitchen – they were eating out in the garden beneath an improvised awning.

She did not like the implied rebelliousness of what he had said.

'I had a letter from him yesterday,' Mr Bull said. 'He tells me the delay with the printers means he is no longer correcting your proofs.'

'Yes, I am saving him the trouble of finding fault with me by doing so myself.'

'It can only be right that an author correct his own work,' Lady Austen said. 'Anyone else to do so must be merely mechanical.'

'Nothing is mechanical with Mr Newton, my dear lady. He will change a sentence as quick as a comma, and while Mr Bull may be his Pope, I am still a clerk and need his imprimatur.'

'Perhaps you are too much a Roman and not enough a Protestant,' Anna said.

'In one way yes and in another way no,' Cowper said. 'I have always been inclined to be Roman in submission to authority and yet I also recently find myself quite willing to be strict in favour of the relaxation of strictures. I am hard about being soft.'

'Does that make sense?' Mr Bull asked. It was unusual to hear Mr Cowper speak so much about himself – it must be, he thought again, the bosom.

'It makes sense in the sense that I have in the last year produced a good deal of stern stuff, three or four thousand lines, I suppose – some of which even Mr Newton held was too acerbic – and now that the printers have gone to sleep, I am determined to take off my Methodist shoes and tiptoe up to the public with a sugar-plum or two to sweeten the pie.'

Mrs Unwin returned with a silver platter on which were laid four large fat trout, fresh from the Ouse, dredged in flour and fried crisp in butter, with a slice of lemon and a sprig of parsley on each.

'We have the loaves and the fishes,' said Cowper; 'now all we need is the miracle.'

'Oh, this is wonderful enough!' Lady Austen trilled.

But Mr Bull lowered his great head and, when he raised it again, Mrs Unwin saw that a tear stood in his eye. He was often overcome by an unexpected allusion to the life of Jesus, but usually what he choked over were thoughts, memories really, of the Passion – it was the shock of realising that another preacher felt the misery of Christ's death on the cross more so than he did himself which had reduced Newton to silence.

Mrs Unwin raised a disapproving eyebrow at Cowper, and said, almost but not quite gaily, 'Sufficient unto the day,' and left it at that.

She was not surprised, however, that some fortnights passed before Mr Bull came to lunch again.

34

'Newton played with fire and now he is being kept by a woman in London. Why, even without the mistress, shouldn't I be seen there too?'

They were sitting in the greenhouse late on a September evening. The only light came from a single candle – Mrs Unwin had taken the oil-lamp and, pleading exhaustion after another long social day, had gone off to bed.

Even on the basis of an acquaintanceship of seven weeks, Lady Austen understood the significance of the decision they were now discussing: on the title page of his first proper book of poems he wished to be described as William Cowper Esq. of the Inner Temple.

'Well, you astonish me,' she had said at first. 'It's as if Lot were to give his wife's address as the Pillar of Salt Street, near Sodom.'

He had, of course, no intention of going back to the sinful city, but it was – or when the book came out in the spring it would be – a sign to those who once knew him, for instance Ned Thurlow, now Lord Chancellor, that he belonged within, indeed owned a piece of, the Temple. More importantly, it was a declaration of independence from Mr Newton – she realised this as soon as he explained that it was Newton himself, after all, who had said he was being kept by a woman in London: St Mary Woolnoth, at whose church in Hoxton he had become parish priest.

'Ah well,' Lady Austen said, 'my hopes are dashed.'

'Hopes?'

'Well, I immediately thought how, as it were, *rounded* it would be if the sailor who served the naked black mistress in Africa should end up slave to another in London.'

'Serviced would be more accurate,' Cowper said.

Because I speak my mind, she thought, he speaks his, but he would not be so lewd in front of Mrs Unwin.

'That's enough of that,' she said. 'This title page accords with your wishes, but there is, don't you think, evil, a childish evil, in everything we wish for?'

'I will think about that.' He laughed a little. 'Indeed, I go so far as to say I will wish myself to think about it.'

'Not for my sake, I hope.'

'Of course yours. Whose else? But it was, remember, your hopes that were dashed.'

How Newton had played with fire took longer to explain. It was an intricate story, 'curlier', Cowper said, 'than a pig's tail'. Afterwards she felt faintly shocked, not so much by the comic absurdity of the figure he described as by the dispassionate hauteur of the description. But there was something else in Cowper's manner that she was not able to put her finger on until she was jogging back to Clifton half-asleep in the barber's cart.

The curly story had reached its climax on Guy Fawkes Night three years previously. According to Cowper, Newton was obsessed with the vestiges of paganism remaining in the hearts of the people of Olney. 'I rather suspect,' he said, 'that he believed in magic as part of a more general conspiracy. In any event, on the Sunday before the commemoration of the Gunpowder Plot, he preached a violent sermon against the black arts of – can you guess what?'

'Fireworks!' Newton had roared at his flock. 'Fire works for the devil! And placing lighted candles in windows? What else can they do but show the way home to the infernal spirits? And bonfires? Bonfires are lit for the sons of Belial!'

'Whereupon,' Cowper said, 'almost every window in the whole of Olney – but not of course in Orchardside – was on the night of the fifth of November illuminated with candles. The whole rebellious town glimmered like the interior of the basilica of St Peter's in Rome and an enormous bonfire blazed in Silverside. And eventually a mob, incandescent with gin and *eau de vie*, set off for the Vicarage brandishing flaming torches.'

'The Vicarage, though, is still standing.'

'But it mightn't be, indeed I think it wouldn't, if Mr Newton had had his way. At the breaking of the first window –'

'Windows broken?'

'A hail of stones, pebbles really, and a howling as of wild beasts woke the household. Mr Newton was all for routing them, like the archangel, but with a fire-poker for a sword.'

'Heavens!' said Lady Austen.

'It must have been an awesome sight, though rather diminished – no, enhanced – made biblical even, by Mr Newton being clad only in his night-shirt.'

'Delicious!'

'Well, yes, but in any event common sense prevailed over heroism and Mrs Newton, a woman of heroic practicality – how I miss her! – put her foot down, dragged her husband back from the front door, delivered him a fearsome scolding, opened her budget, pressed into his unwilling hand an unconscionable amount of coinage, copper, silver and gold, and thrust him into outer darkness where he paid the sons of Belial to go off and get drunker. Which they did, singing his praises. But that was all of Olney that Mr Newton could take.'

Love! That, Anna realised with a jolting of her heart, was the something that she had not been able to put her finger on. He loved Mr Newton, but not – she ran through the variations – as a close friend simply, nor as a brother, nor as father loves son, or the other way round, but – she paused here – rather as a young and inexperienced wife loves an older and wiser husband. Well, perhaps not. She had played that role with Sir Robert and he had learned soon enough that the mistress was the master. There was something of the disappointed slave in Cowper. She had never been a slave. She had bettered herself, though hardly by marrying money – her husband's estate was heavily mortgaged – but she had paid a price for being an angel to a man more than twice her age, for beating her wings over his weariness, slumped at his desk, and kissing his forehead. She had played muse to a non-poet. What other word was there to describe Sir Robert?

Other women did what she had done, and the world at large deemed it a suitable and sensible way to establish a family and, given a fortunate natural ordering of things, a comfortable widow-hood to look forward to. But even at the age of nineteen, when she married, she had chosen, even half-calculated, her independence, in order to be free to think and, above all, to read.

It had not been exactly *un mariage blanc*, but it was – and here fortune and nature had played their part, by way of miscarriages – without issue. And now here she was, going on for forty-six years of age, *une jolie laide*, full of life and free. Mr Cowper, too, in relation to Mr Newton, and much else, was a rebel. Already they were, she felt, in league with each other, like America and France against England. As she was a woman who would not be just a woman, he was a Christian who would not enter a church, or even say grace before meals, only bowing his head *pour la politesse*. How proud he was in his meekness!

The carriage was drawing up to the Vicarage, darkened except for a lantern, left out for her, hanging over the door like an almond of light.

Well, if he thought he could be cruel to her in the same way as he was to Mr Newton, he would be making a very grave mistake. She was his match, easily. It was a mouth-watering prospect.

By the time she was obliged to return to London, Lady Austen had decided to buy a house in or near Olney.

The decision refreshed Cowper's view of his surroundings: abandoned buildings that he had grown accustomed to seeing as if they belonged to the weather – the shuttered-up hulk of Clifton Manor for instance – now stood forward differently to his eye. Why not, they seemed to ask, live in me? Speculation could become actually physical – that was Anna's glory. Living in France had developed her instinct to imagine that a beautiful ordering of things is possible. It was a sense, unlike the English desire to seek comfort in necessity, that was both abstract and material, the purpose of which conjunction was elegance. To be elegant, as Lady Austen lived it, was not a matter of mere style but – as the origin of the word indicated – of election, of philosophical and moral choice, of conducting oneself *comme il faut*.

'What on earth is going on?' Mr Newton said, throwing across the breakfast table to his wife the letter he had just received from Olney. She read it silently:

> *I have heard before of a room with a floor, laid upon springs, and such-like things, with so much art, in every part, that when you went in, you was forced to begin a minuet pace with an air and a grace, swimming about, now in and now out, with a deal of state, in a figure of eight, without pipe or string, or any such thing; and now I have writ, in a rhyming fit, what will make you dance, and as you advance, will keep you still, though against your will, dancing away, alert and gay, till you come to an end of, what I have penned of; which that you may do, ere Madam and you are quite worn out with jigging about, I take my leave, and here you receive a bow profound, down to the ground, from your humble me – W.C.*

'It rhymes,' Mrs Newton said.
'I know that,' Newton said, 'I know that. That is not an answer to my question. What on earth is going on in Olney, pray?'

Mrs Unwin knew what was going on. But Anna, for all her intelligence, imagined the dance as more of a *pas de deux* than a three-handed jig, though of course she knew it was that too. She could not affect to be a provincial, but she was careful not to be too *à la mode* – Sancerre, after all, was not Paris – and she was careful, above all, not to outshine Mrs Unwin. Instead of dazzling, she dulled; she put herself in the way of learning, as it were, how to damp down a stove in summer (a lot of coal slack mixed with a little soapy water). The fourteen-year difference in their ages she ignored – they were sisters, simply. And William was their brother.

That he managed at the same time to be also Mrs Unwin's son was, Lady Austen said when he first told her this, 'rather magical'. And that Mrs Unwin's real son, William — it sometimes seemed that almost everyone in England was called William — as well as being Mr Cowper's ideal brother, was also his ideal son, well, though it titivated the tip of her tongue, she never uttered the word 'incest'. Really, so much did her William love the William who was now the Vicar of Stock in the wastes of Essex — the distance between them was less a barrier to affection than its means — that she almost felt jealous of him, and would have been were it not that their intimacy was to be perfected by constant correspondence.

This was decided late one October evening while they were sitting in the candle-lit greenhouse. On the morrow she was going back to London.

'Well,' he said, 'I did not intend to say the receipt of a letter, or the reading of it subsequently — in themselves they are quite distinct pleasures — I did not intend to say that either is a more perfect pleasure than this is.'

'Whatever this is.'

'In the law this is what we call direct evidence, my lady.'

'You swear to that?'

'I do.'

'On your oath?'

'Well, now, an oath is a serious thing.'

'You hesitated.'

'Did I?'

'You did.'

'One does, you know.'

'One does, does one? And why does one do that, pray?'

'Well, the case has only just begun, hasn't it?'

'That's true. That is a material point.'

'And I hardly know what I am charged with.'

'It's a capital offence. And you've already confessed to it.'

'I have?'

'You have. You said *my lady*. You said I was your lady. Am I?'

But when he paused, she thought, Oh, I've gone too far. For that reason she let the pause last only long enough to be sweet and then

– I do have, she thought later when she considered how swiftly she had chosen the tone, a sort of theatrical genius – she hissed at him, 'Answer me, you dastardly person.'

And he said, 'Can I send you a letter?'

So they stayed on in the greenhouse until midnight, and she would go home to Clifton only on condition that he allow her to cut off a lock of his hair as a keepsake.

'It's your punishment,' she said, brandishing her nail-scissors at him, 'and you know what for. Now, turn around.'

He did as he was told and, after she had clipped off the curl from his neck, just above the collar of his elegant shagreen coat, she kissed the spot.

35

*H*e did send a letter. But since it was written in verse, it took some time to compose and arrived when she had been back in London for two months. 'I suppose,' she said in her reply,

> *that you think your delay is justified because of your fit of poetic jingling. How proud you poets are to set a rhyming scheme above the wants of ordinary mortals, such as women, like myself, must be! Well, I snap my fingers at you! And if I forgive you now it is only for revenge later! And because, my dear, one of us at least should be sensible of the prospects of our future felicity!*

'Prospects?' Mrs Unwin said. 'What did you say to her, Mr Cowper, that she should talk of prospects?'

'Nothing very much,' he said, but his anxiety was all the more anxious for being so long anticipated – Anna's letter was a week old and he was only now showing it.

'Nothing,' he added, 'that I can recall at any rate, or that was intended to mislead her.' He truly did not know which was the worse lie – that he did not recall what he had written or that he had no intention of leading Anna on. In his mind both were confused, but in his notebook there were drafts of the letter and no confusion at all.

Dear Anna, between friend and friend
Prose answers every common end,
Serves, in a plain and homely way,
To express the occurrences of the day –
Our health, the weather and the news,
What walks we take, what books we choose,
And all the floating thoughts we find
Upon the surface of the mind.
But when a Poet takes the pen,
Far more alive than other men,
He feels a gentle tingling come
Down to his finger and his thumb,
Derived from Nature's noblest part:
The centre of a glowing heart!

To think that he should claim to be 'Far more alive than other men' when he was actually far more dead – his soul withered like a leaf in a flame. And yet was it not, after all, true? Those who would sneer at him up in London, let them write decent light verse or even a passable letter – Anna's, with its multiple, ungainly exclamation marks, was more disappointing than she would ever understand. He had concluded the epistle by saying that their chance meeting

Produced a friendship, then begun,
That has cemented us in one;
And placed it in our power to prove,
By long fidelity and love,
That Solomon has wisely spoken –
'A threefold cord is not soon broken.'

He had already told her that there was no attachment in the, well, romantic sense between himself and Mrs Unwin. So in all honesty he had not thought that what Lady Austen said then – that they might live in a *ménage à trois* – had any indecent meaning. Oh well, perhaps he had a slight inkling, but the daringness of the notion, which was almost practical, was thrilling, especially with those huge black eyes of hers so close.

Anyway, Mrs Unwin knew almost everything about him, and could guess the rest, but there were ways and means of sharing their knowledge without speaking of it, of knowing how not to know, and he could count on her to find them out.

Already she was aware of the fact that he had not told her son about the publication of the book. He had written to say he was making up a collection of poems 'not for the Public but for Myself', which was childish enough – since there would soon be, he half-hoped, an advertising blast blown through every newspaper in the land to the effect that 'the Poet is coming!' – but which also had had the consequence of Mrs Unwin having to write many letters to Stock that amounted to, well, a deception.

And then there had been the publication of the *Anti-Thelyphthora*. This was a deception that was, Mrs Unwin told him, almost devilishly mischievous. Of course, it was Mr Newton who had put him up to it – they were like two demon schoolboys lobbing a firework through an open window and making a run for it – but Mr Newton at least had the shred of an excuse: the window didn't belong to a member of *his* family. Because, after all, Martin Madan was Mr Cowper's cousin, and if Martin had known when he visited him at the Collegium Insanorum that his kindness was to be repaid in such a manner, would he not have been entitled to say, 'Sir, you are a moral imbecile and you belong here and I bid you good day'?

Of course, Martin was himself eccentric, one of that breed of Englishmen whose extreme innocence leads them to believe that things can be set to rights by certain *very simple* reforms: the restoration of the Long Parliament, the decimalisation of time, the teaching of Epicurus to infants, the introduction of wooden money, the legalisation of polygamy. This last was Mr Madan's panacea. He had published, anonymously – not from shame but shyness – a long poem called *Thelyphthora or a Treatise on Female Ruin, Considered on the Basis of Divine Law*, which was based on the observation that the male of the species was by nature incorrigibly concupiscent – 'Why doesn't he come straight out with it,' Mr Newton roared at his wife, 'and say that we men are fucking animals?' – and as such would, if the opportunity presented itself, despoil a maiden of her virginity, wherever such a cherry might be found. The consequences, Madan maintained, were plainly set out in the Old Testament: the couple were married in the eyes of God, and the man was thenceforth responsible for his wife's upkeep and should cleave to her always – which was something of a conundrum when one considered that many of these former maidens had become, as a result of that illicit but divine act, common prostitutes. The transition period between the present state of rampant fornication and a wider, more responsible form of wedlock was likely to have social consequences that would be temporarily embarrassing – why, some of the drabs might *claim* to have hundreds of husbands, the poor girls, and establishing the identity of the original cherry-picker could be a matter of some forensic delicacy. Madan had discussed this puzzle with Mr Newton, who had advised him that the entire thing was blasphemous nonsense and instructed him not to publish it.

But the truth must out, and out the poem had come.

And being published it was duly noticed, mockingly, in the *Monthly Review* by a critic called Samuel Badcock.

'The name,' Newton said, 'suits the business.' It was a scandal and something had to be done about it.

Whereupon, Cowper, at first reluctantly but then gleefully, had written the *Anti-Thelyphthora*, a two-hundred-line allegory in which poor Martin, alias Sir Airy, a kind of Don Quixote, was comprehensively windmilled by Sir Marmadan, alias Badcock. Worst of all, the satire was published – anonymously, of course, because he did not want Martin's mother to know – and praised by Badcock as 'an elegant fancy'.

Newton was pleased: the poem was morally impeccable – they had hurled their firecracker through the window, after all, of a putative pimp – and therefore it could not be hurtful. He was, however, soon to discover what it felt like to be a hurt author.

The keeping of William Unwin, Martin Madan and John Newton in their varying states of ignorance was a complicated business. It was all the more so because the book of poems, delayed by the printers, was swelling like a pregnancy by the day. Mrs Unwin, who was transcribing the manuscripts twice, one copy for Newton, one for Mr Johnson, the publisher, could hardly keep up with him.

'It's all too dark,' he said to her one morning in December. 'All these moral satires – they're too moral, not sufficiently satirical.'

'Have you finished the letter to Lady Austen?'

'I've finished with *Heroism*,' he said and handed her the product of his morning's work. 'I fear it is,' he added, 'an even more sable effusion than the others.'

'Well then,' she said rather grimly, 'that should prove suitable. I look forward to reading it.'

She did not mean the poem, which was about the recent eruption of Mount Aetna; she meant the letter to Lady Austen. And he knew it. But the poem began:

> There was a time when Aetna's silent fire
> Slept unperceived, the mountain yet entire,
> When conscious of no danger from below,
> She towered a cloud-capped pyramid of snow.

It was, as he had guessed it would be, prophetic. Aetna and Anna were more than similar sounds. Not infrequently in her life Lady Austen had exploded, but never with the ferocity that melted her snows when she received his letter. She broke a valuable vase, pulled Mistress Jenny's hair and beat Murdoch repeatedly about the head with an embroidered cushion.

'Get me a frank,' she cried. 'I told you before, I must have franks when I need them. And fresh pens! Where are my pens?'

Even before Murdoch had returned from buying postage, she had composed her reply.

> *Dear Mr Cowper,*
>
> *I note your apology for my thinking highly of you. The mistake obviously was mine and it is I, therefore, who should be sorry. But I am not. Far from embellishing your portrait with colours taken from my own fancy, as you put it, and turning you into an idol to be adored, which would be absurd, I was quite simply impressed by your qualities as a gentleman, and it was to him that I opened my heart. As I am, of course, still convinced of the truth of that impression, it follows that I cannot apologise for it.*
>
> *Please convey to Mrs Unwin my warmest good wishes for the New Year.*
>
> *Yours sincerely,*
> *Anna Austen*

'Well,' Cowper said, 'what should I say to her now?'

'Say?' Mrs Unwin said. 'You could not possibly say anything. Indeed, I am alarmed, Mr Cowper, to think you could possibly consider replying to such an impertintent communication.'

She spoke sternly, but during the day she found occasion to praise him for his work and even, unexpectedly, to kiss him, like a mother compensating a child for momentarily forgetting his bleeding knee. Of all the transactions between them, this kind was, she knew, his favourite, and so she used it sparingly.

He, however, though wounded and pleased, went up to his room, lay down on the cold bed, rejoiced in what he had made of himself – the reedy boy had stiffened into an iron man – and began, a little resentful of Mrs Unwin's role in making him do what had to be done, to regret it. He stayed up late that night and when he came down the next morning handed Mrs Unwin a new poem without saying a word. It was entitled 'Verses, supposed to be written by Alexander Selkirk' and began:

> I am monarch of all I survey,
>   My right there is none to dispute,
> From the centre all round to the sea,
>   I am lord of the fowl and the brute.
> Oh solitude! Where are the charms
>   That sages have seen in thy face?
> Better dwell in the midst of alarms,
>   Than reign in this horrible place.

The poem was signed 'Robinson Crusoe'. Well, Mrs Unwin thought, I may be his Man Friday, but he wants a Thursday too.

36

Anna Austen was mercurial. As soon as she had been feline, she wanted to be friendly. She wrote again, many times, but words failed her – the tongue that had rasped wouldn't lick – and the letters were not sent. At last a wordless solution suggested itself; once, when he had been complaining about the dinginess of his neckcloths, she had promised to sew some lace ruffles for him. So she worked three sets and sent them to Olney. But Maud refused to be the go-between, to play, as she put it, 'the Pandar to a person who could write you such an odious letter'. Then, behind Maud's back, Mr Jones had delivered the gift – and subsequently regretted it, frequently.

Mrs Unwin was not mercurial. But she was capable of change when necessary, and in this instance she had little choice: he would not stop harping on about the cruelty he, but of course meaning she, had inflicted on Lady Austen. Then the ruffles arrived, and in gratitude he had sent her an advance copy of his book.

Mrs Unwin then tried another tack. Was Lady Austen really quite respectable? When she spoke of 'prospects', did she not mean, to put it bluntly – but not to Cowper – that she had no money? Discreet inquiries were made and it was discovered that she owned her house in Queen Street, that she was the residual legatee of her father's estate and when certain minor legal difficulties were resolved, she would be quite comfortable. Then William was sent to interview her in London and he, knowing how to take a hint from his mother, found her 'unattractive, cold, stiff, strange'. But Cowper was furious – Anna was never stiff and the only thing that was strange was that anybody, especially William, should find her so.

Mrs Unwin sighed; he was becoming as wilful as he had once been shy.

The shyness had also variegated into slyness.

Newton had made room in his mind, rather as he knew God would in His, for Cowper not going to church – the conviction that he was destined for hell was mistaken but commendable; if only more people were as serious, the Pit would not be so densely populated. Newton was also satisfied with the rigour of Cowper's Protestantism, all the more so when others, not triflers like Martin Madan, but considerable persons, William Unwin for one, found it too rigorous. Of the poem called 'Truth', for instance, Unwin had complained that it was a little too stern, even dismissive of the value of doing good deeds. But the poet had defended himself:

> *I wrote that Poem on purpose to inculcate the eleemosynary Character of the Gospel, as a dispensation of Mercy in the most absolute Sense of the word, to the Exclusion of all claims of Merit on the part of the Receiver. Consequently to set the brand of Invalidity upon the Plea of Works, and to discover upon Scriptural ground the absurdity of that Notion which includes a Solecism in the very terms of it, that Man by Repentance and good works may deserve the Mercy of his Maker.*

When he read that, Newton clenched his fists by his ears and cried out to his wife, 'Isn't that splendid? Isn't that wonderful? I could hardly have put it better myself!'

But then, with a suddenness that astounded him, Newton's preface to the book was dropped. And why? Because the publisher, Johnson, thought it was too Methodistical! In his opinion, few lovers of poetry would spend their five shillings on what Newton promised them: not being entertained. He would 'infallibly pre-judice the critics against the work before they have read a line – and their judgement has no small influence on the success of poetical composition'.

But before Newton could snarl, 'Critics! What have the

Badcocks of the world to do with the success of a Christian poet before God?' the preface was effaced and he was reading from Cowper a delicate screed of brutal consolation:

My Dear Friend,

I can only repeat what I said some time since, that the world is grown more foolish and careless than it was when I had the honour of knowing it. Though your preface was of a serious cast ['What else did he expect?' Newton cried. 'Saltimbanques? Dancing bears?'] *it was yet free from everything that might, with propriety, expose it to the charge of Methodism, being guilty of no offensive peculiarities* ['Guilty?' said Newton. 'He means innocent'] *nor containing any of those obnoxious doctrines at which the world is so apt to be angry, and which we must give her leave to be angry at* ['Must we indeed?'] *because we know she cannot help it. It asserted nothing more than every rational creature must admit to be true, that divine and earthly things can no longer stand in competition with each other, in the judgement of any man; and that the moment the eyes are opened, the latter are always cheerfully relinquished for the sake of the former. Now I do certainly remember a time when such a proposition as this would have been at least supportable, and when it would not have spoiled the market of any volume to which it had been prefixed, ergo — the times have altered for the worse.*

'Oh, the market! Oh! Oh!' Newton groaned. But the upshot of it all was that, as the letter concluded, 'I have reason to be very much satisfied with my publisher.' The book stood alone.

He wanted Lady Austen alone, too. This was where she made yet another of those mistakes that led to the vomiting up of her will. She thought, the ruffles having been sent on before, that it would be easier to follow them behind the shield of company. She thought wrong. On hearing of her plans, he wrote to William Unwin:

Lady Austen is to spend the summer in our neighbourhood. Lady Peterborough and Miss Mordaunt are to be of the party: the former a dissipated woman of fashion, the latter a haughty beauty.

Retirement is our passion and our delight. It is in still life alone that we look for the measure of happiness we can expect below. What have we, therefore, to do with characters like these? Shall we go to the dancing school again? Shall we cast off the simplicity of our plain and artless demeanour to learn — and not in a youthful day either — the manners of those whose manners are at the best their only recommendation, and yet can in reality recommend them to none but the people like themselves?

Well, Mrs Unwin thought, 'plain and artless demeanour' is a bit rich. Anyway, it was not he but she who would have to write to Lady Austen and, as it were, put her own stamp on it. Which she did, gently, but with some satisfaction.

Sam, who knew all this because Cowper had told him, was not, therefore, surprised when he opened the door one afternoon in July to find Lady Austen standing there in the rain, all on her own and looking it. But he was surprised when he showed her into the parlour.

'There was the missus in her best black dress,' Sam told Sal the cook that night, 'stood to attention like a soldier on parade, except she was sittin' on the sofa, and there was Lady Austen dressed in black too — like a pair of nuns they were. And there was the master, you know the way he has, with the one foot on top of the other, heel and toe, only he was swingin' it from billy to jack. So help me Jesus, I could have laughed, and I had the time for it too, she stood that long in the doorway, casual-like, shakin' the umbrella and the drops of the rain flyin' off it. Well then, Lady Austen, says the missus, like a judge she was, you'd think she was goin' to put on the black cap, Well then, says she, you're very welcome, very sincerely welcome, and right then − Clap! − milady drops the umbrella and off she gallops across the room and throws her arms around Mrs U's neck and bursts out into tears, bawlin' that she was so glad to be back and so very, very, very sorry. God's truth, I thought I was goin' to bring up my porridge!'

Sal laughed and kissed Sam. He told her things he never told anyone else, and not long afterwards they got married.

✻

Anna's tears were soon dried – 'the threefold cord' had not been broken, though she refrained from quoting the line or mentioning the letter it had come from, or indeed from saying anything very much directly to him. There was too much ground to be made up with Mrs Unwin, and after tea she felt it only decent to beat an early retreat.

But the next morning, as soon as she had arrived, he took her out through the spilling rain to the greenhouse to see the new mahogany cage he had made for the hares – three interconnecting compartments, each with the name of its occupant, Bess, Puss and Tiney, inlaid in rosewood.

'Well,' she said, 'it is divinely clever, but not as stiff as my lace,' and they burst out laughing, so loudly that he indicated, with a barely perceptible lift of his chin towards the house, that they should contain themselves, while at the same time saying in a low voice, 'I am capable, you know, of doing almost anything with mahogany.'

'I know, I know,' was all she could say.

From then on the weather improved dramatically. For two weeks not a cloud was seen in the sky, and the sun, using the moisture in the air as a magnifying glass, burned away fiercely at the rampant greenery, but nothing wilted or failed; everything was lush and glut and swollenness.

Mrs Unwin retired into the shade.

They talked like people who discover, by the illumination of the spark between them, that the world is at least two kinds of idiot, and not the one blue fool they had imagined it to be on their own. Anna felt their meeting had been designed by Providence, and on the day before she went back to London, she told him so.

They were strolling along the bank of the river, and he said, 'Yes, it is providential, rather in the manner of that incident in Captain Cook's narrative when he was sailing through the Pacific on a pitch-black night and suddenly a tremendous flash of lightning revealed that there, right alongside, was another vessel – do you remember the passage?'

'Of course,' Anna said. 'Reading it made me shiver.'

'We shivered mutually,' he said. 'But what struck me as most wonderful was the thought that in an ocean where all the ships in the world might gather and none see another, these two should not only meet but be saved from mutual destruction by a bolt of lightning.'

'Exactly,' she said, 'but the strange ship passed on unscathed and yours, William, yours almost swamped me, didn't it?'

'Oh look,' he whispered. 'A kingfisher!'

What a transparent deception, she thought, just because he doesn't want to admit causing me pain. She was right, but he had also not been deceiving her: in line with the tip of his pointing finger she saw the bird, a compacted drop of the spectrum, arrested for a second on a rock in the stream before it jewelled off into invisibility.

While pointing out the kingfisher, he had taken hold of her upper arm and now as they went off again, walking down the bank of the river, he still held on to it. It was the first time he had deliberately touched her, and the deliberation of it excited her. At some point in the previous two weeks he had planned it, just as the lightning had decided to charge down upon the sea, as it were to satisfy itself, and without at all caring whether the ships dashed into each other or not.

She leaned against him and said, truthfully, 'Oh, my dear, I feel faint from all this sun. Let's move into the shade for a while.'

For an hour they sheltered beneath a weeping willow that trailed its branches into the hardly moving river. While they ate their picnic of bread, cucumber and radishes and drank a bottle of old cider, wrapped in straw and still cool from the cellar, they talked about a bewildering variety of subjects – it was the king-fisher speed with which they flitted through each other's store of knowledge that delighted them most: the war in the West Indies, Admiral Rodney's victory and his boastfulness, the greatness of Queen Boadicea, the discovery of the planet Uranus, the prospect of his becoming a star in the firmament of poetry (she knew all the reviews by heart – they had been mixed but generally favourable), and the fact that it was Virgil who for the first time in literature had used a parenthesis.

'Hoc nemus, hunc,' inquit, 'frondoso vertice collem
(Quis deus incertus est) habitat deus.'

This had a peculiar elegance, but writers who used the device frequently had not properly arranged their matter and were cloudy in their heads. Having said this, he closed his eyes and began to nod off.

And when he woke she was gone.

He sat up, breathless, desperate, certain, as always on these occasions, which were the experience of every evening on the sofa after supper, that he had gone to Hell and that only terror had restarted his heart and sent him scrambling against the torrent back up into life. He tried to call Anna's name, but it was as if the Styx were in his throat, and the only sound that came out was a stony gargling. She must have heard, though, because she was instructing him, seemingly from a great distance, to keep away, keep away. He could, as ever, only disobey prohibition. Stumbling through the bushes that grew thick by the river, he came to a great boulder, an erratic deposited by a glacier, and saw her. She was sitting in a peculiar position on the riverbank, her skirts drawn up, one leg in the water, cooling her bare breasts with a wet neckerchief. Standing on the other side of the boulder, near enough almost to touch, was an old man, bald and bearded, wearing the tattered red coat of a soldier, and in his furiously working hand was a brown and purple rod that oozed a gluey sap. And the man smiled at him the smile of conspiracy.

Afterwards he thought, although he tried not to think, that it was all a dream, and he had the faintest recollection of seeing once an engraving of the subject of Susanna observed at her bath by the elders, one of whom was a bald man. But whether he dreamt it or not, he did faint, and when he returned to consciousness a few seconds later, Anna was bending over him, her hair was loosened, and he could not see her face.

37

'*Une singe sur un âne? Mais, c'est drôle, ça.*' Claude said, but 'a monkey on a donkey' had no comic sound to it in French, and the pathos of the image, if that was what Anna intended, well, for Le Comte Tardiff du Granger it was something less than pitiful; in fact, the *drôlerie* was nearer to a *grotesquerie*, degrading to the dignity of his wife, even if she was inclined, as the English were, to allow the comic and the ugly to be confused. However, because they were spending the winter at his villa on the island of Djerba in Tunisia, which they often did now since the Terror, these distinctions, as well as manners in general, mattered less than they did in France – still, just about. All the same, the slight strain of English eccentricity added to her *cachet* as the wife of the poet which, though not as highly regarded as she said he deserved to be, he undoubtedly was.

Five years on from their marriage, which had happened in the same month of 1796 as Napoleon married Josephine de Beauharnais, Anna was still vivacious, although her figure had thickened and her features, now that he thought of it, had taken on a faintly monkey-like appearance. As he looked at her, reclining on a chaise amidst a scatter of books and journals by the fountain in the courtyard, he thought, I will have to speak to her about this constant sipping of brandy and soda, and the affectation of the purple djellaba worn by the native women, and the even more absurd patterning of her feet and hands with henna. One had to be careful, however, in case she flew into one of her tremendous rages, though these were rarer now than her sadnesses, and, besides, she was amusing, interesting, generous of spirit and so passionate and tender, almost insistently tender, in her love-making, as if she was — what were the English words for *plein de reconnaissance?*

'Very grateful,' Anna said. 'And I am, you know.'

As for the man whom she had loved, what could he say? Apparently he was regarded as the outstanding poet of his generation, but as far as France was concerned, Monsieur Cowper's chief claim to fame was that he had translated Madame de la Motte Guyon. Why anyone should bother with such a Jansenistic nobody was beyond the Count's understanding. Seemingly, Anna herself had been directly responsible for his most popular poem, which every schoolboy in England knew by heart. It was a sort of *ballade* about a man on a runaway horse. Apparently she had told him the story one night at dinner and the following morning he had come down to breakfast with the entire piece, pages and pages of it, ready for publication. The count had looked at it, but it was full of mock-ancient English —

> John Gilpin was a citizen
> Of credit and renown,
> A train-band Captain eke was he
> Of famous London town

— which made no sense to him; and moreover what he could understand of it seemed to him not at all comical but to glory in the helplessness of its hero. But that was the English way: kind to animals, cruel to each other.

'Lo, she comes!' Lady Austen cried. 'A monkey on a donkey!'

That August, when she returned to Olney from London, was the wettest that anyone could remember. Morning, noon and night it rained and the road between Clifton and Olney was a river of mud. Sensible people stayed indoors, but Lady Austen had requisitioned a donkey and now here she was crossing the square, perched on its back, like Christ riding into Jerusalem, crying out from beneath an umbrella to her friends huddled at the front door of Orchardside. As Sam helped her dismount – swinging her sodden-skirted leg over the animal's head was an inelegantly parenthetical manoeuvre – she cried out again, 'And the monkey has news!'

The news was that Mr Page, the present parson and tenant of Mr Newton's former Vicarage, had agreed to lease it to her.

'Oh, my dear girl, I am so glad,' Mrs Unwin said. But her gladness was like Anna's crying out: genuine but too glad. And, as she spoke, the donkey, all of a sudden, shook its ears, kicked out with its back legs and bolted across the square, with Sam chasing after it. But Cowper did not see the end of the pursuit because he had, without a word, gone up to his room.

The women were glad because they needed each other, but neither of them was able to say why.

When Lady Austen had returned to London, he had sunk into silence, which made Mrs Unwin, who had not been told of his fainting at the river, even more jealous than she already was. But when Anna came back, though he was attentive and tried to be cheerful and amusing, he was like an actor afflicted by stage fright who only succeeds in making his audience uneasy. And now he had suddenly quit the stage.

When he came down from his room two hours later, he said nothing about the donkey's bolting or his own. Nor was any further mention made of the renting of the Vicarage – Lady Austen felt she had somehow committed an indecency. Instead, while tea was taken, he read aloud from his favourite book, Clarendon's *History of the English Rebellion*, and afterwards he and Mrs Unwin played battledore with a shuttlecock across the little room. Then, after a decent interval, Anna went back to Clifton.

Two more days passed in a similar fashion. Lady Austen felt increasingly uneasy, as if she were being – all at once – ignored, watched, avoided, judged.

On the third day she cornered him in the greenhouse, but he said he needed some twine from the kitchen and went out. She followed him, saying, 'No, William, you must speak to me first. Please, I beg you.'

She thought for a second that he was raising his hand to strike her, but then she saw what he was looking at: on the threshold of the wash-house the biggest viper she had ever seen was hissing and darting its tongue at three of the house kittens, which did not appreciate the danger. He ran into the house and came back with a long Dutch hoe to find the mother of the kittens, known only as the Old Cat, boxing at the intruder with her paw in an inquisitive, almost philosophical, fashion. With a slash of the hoe he decapitated the snake. Then, while the body coiled and uncoiled upon itself and the eye in the head looked on at its own death, he flung the hoe across the yard and, crying out repeatedly 'Aaah!', kicked out with his legs and flailed his arms about as if trying to rid himself of some filthy, oozing, gluey substance.

What Anna found most extraordinary, however, was that by the next morning he had composed a poem on the event, accurate in every respect but, as it were, in reverse: the viscous horror was turned into a fluid amusement. And when she read the last lines –

> Filled with heroic ardour at the sight,
> And fearing every moment he would bite
> And rob our household of our only cat,
> That was of age to combat with a rat,
> With outstretched hoe I slew him at the door,
> And taught him never to come there no more.

– she laughed at the schoolmasterly way he had decisively underlined, as if correcting an unruly pupil, the words 'never to come there no more'. But then a thought that had struck her before, a mixture of nameless fascination and dread, feline and female, struck her again, though differently: If he does this to a serpent, would he not do the same to me?

She had good reason to feel that she was being watched. Some days after the beheading of the snake, Mr Jones, driven by Murdoch, went to London on business. No sooner had they left than Clifton was visited, first by tinkers wanting to mend pots and pans, but with no implements, then by an old Redcoat begging for alms. That evening shadowy figures were seen in the garden. Around midnight a speechless maid brought Maud down to the kitchen where a pane of glass had been taken out of the window, but because it was nailed tight to keep out draughts, the villains had not been able to get in. Then Anna heard somone trying the front door. There was no doubting the danger they were in. Anna, Mistress Jenny, Maud and her daughter Esmeralda, along with the two maids and the pot-boy, fled out the back door, scrambled through a gap in the hedge near the privy and ran across a field of lodged barley in the teeming rain to the nearest farm. The alarm was raised, men with firearms were put into the house and the robbers beat a retreat.

But Anna would not go back and insisted on being taken to Orchardside.

There, at dawn, she was woken by the sound of voices. She went out anxiously onto the landing and, looking over the banisters, saw Mrs Unwin coming out of Cowper's room, yawning, stretching with satisfaction and going into her own room.

38

She began retching violently as soon as she saw him, but nothing came out of her mouth except yellow bile and a flood of saliva. There was nothing she could do to prevent it, bent over, paddling with her lace-gloved hands at the fluids blackening the grey silk of her skirt. Worst of all, she felt she was losing control of her bowels, a hot liquid squirting and staining. The hares were leaping, the dogs barking, the linnet flying desperately, thump thump, against the window. Mrs Unwin and Sam, yelling for the servants to come and help, were trying to prevent her from falling.

And still, when Lady Austen raised her head she saw him standing there, looking at her with that same look, that mouth set in thin pity, unforgiving.

It was Sunday and she had been at evensong. When she suddenly got up from the pew, it was frustration, irritation, a desire to speak her mind that drove her out of the church. She was even happy, almost. It was only after she had knocked on the door, was kept waiting and then, when it was opened, brushed past Mrs Unwin, strode down the hallway, turned back, threw her arms around Mrs Unwin's neck, sobbing, 'Oh Mary, Mary', tore herself away and saw him coming out of the parlour, dark with the light behind him – it was only then that she began to stagger.

Now she was on her knees with her hands planted on the Turkish rug, retching into a greasy enamel basin from the kitchen, chipped on the edge, and the locket containing the lock of his hair had come out of the neck of her dress and from it was hanging a long thread of glutinous saliva.

Later that night, having been put to bed in Mrs Unwin's room and left alone there for some hours, Anna began screaming. At first, shame made her speechless. What could she say to the door opening, somehow formally, and the two of them ceremoniously entering to stand at the foot of the bed, like judges, like examining magistrates? She had, or rather her body had, already given them the evidence they needed: her soiled clothes, stuffed under Mrs Unwin's bed, reeked of her guilt, or so Anna thought. She had willingly taken the nightdress Mrs Unwin had given her, but she had refused to undress in front of her.

'Anna?' Mrs Unwin now said. 'Anna?' But Anna did not reply.

'Will we summon the physician?' Cowper asked.

'Anna, did you hear Mr Cowper? Do you want me to send for the doctor? I will send for him this instant, if you want me to.'

The tone of her voice had been neutral, but the sharpness of the way she had pronounced 'this instant' frightened Anna. There's no pity from that quarter and why, she thought, should there be? She sat up, looked at Mrs Unwin dumbly, shook her head, a gesture that was more than a 'no', and then rested it, still shaking from side to side, on her knees.

'What ever can be the matter?' he said.

'It may be a colic,' Mrs Unwin said.

'Could a colic come on so suddenly?'

'No doubt. Perhaps some brandy will settle her stomach. Anna, will I fetch you some brandy?'

But Anna only shook her head harder, disbelievingly.

'Perhaps she may have eaten something that didn't agree with her.'

'She ate what we ate.'

'Those herrings were high. I said so at the time.'

'That was Friday, Mr Cowper. Today is Sunday.'

'No, no, Mrs Unwin, it was Saturday. Perhaps it was the herrings.'

'Well then,' Mrs Unwin said, 'I shall get you both a brandy.'

Anna thought she was going to laugh, but instead she began to sob and then the sobbing turned into the screaming. Then she was flailing around on the bed, past shame, breathing as if she was going to die from lack of breath. What brought an end to the fit was, she thought afterwards, even more embarrassingly laughable. Mrs Unwin wrestled with her, then bestrode her like a man on a spirited horse and pinned her wrists to the pillow on each side of her head, saying, 'Now then, my girl. Stop this nonsense.' So she had stopped. And when she did, Mrs Unwin, exhausted from the struggle, collapsed on top of her for a moment, during which Anna saw him looking down at them and heard him saying, 'Poor, poor creature.' But she did not know if it was her he meant or Mrs Unwin. And the expression on his face – could it really have been both pity and triumph?

39

Yield to the Lord, with simple heart,
All that thou hast, and all thou art;
Renounce all strength but strength divine,
And peace shall be for ever thine –
Behold the path which I have trod,
My path, till I go home to God.

'Well, Taureau, is that well done or ill?' Cowper asked, but Mr Bull, too near to tears to speak, merely nodded and began to knock the dottle out of his pipe on the heel of his boot.

'But you, madam, you, I see, are amused.'

'Yes,' Lady Austen said, 'I am, a little.'

'And why, pray?'

'Oh, it's the notion that you and Madame Jeanne Marie Bouvier de la Motte Guyon should be confused one with the other, as far, I mean, as Christian doctrine is concerned.'

'I think I have guarded against that in my translation. She is indeed sometimes guilty to a degree of—'

'Guilty?' Mr Bull cried. 'What do you mean guilty? She is as innocent as the day is long.'

'Oh, Taureau,' Cowper said, 'I beg of you, don't charge at me here. The place is far too small.'

'But what is the fault you find in her?'

'Well, she does incline occasionally to treat the Deity familiarly—'

'As if she knew Him personally,' Anna said.

'—and without paying due attention to His majesty—'

'Which could never be said of *Notre Seigneur.*'

Mr Bull frowned and thought, I really do not care for this lady.

'Well,' Cowper said, 'it is a wonderful fault for such a woman to fall into.'

'Oh!' Lady Austen said. 'Oh, really, such a woman!'

'She's French, isn't she?' Cowper said sharply. 'That's an adequate explanation for most failings that I know of.' And then, because Mr Bull was beginning to rake the floorboards with his hoof, he added, 'But I venerate her piety most tenderly, you know, almost as much as I value our friendship.'

'Well,' Mr Bull said, half-mollified, 'I admit some peculiarity in her theological sentiments, but to infer that you share them, why that would be almost as absurd as to suppose the inimitable translator of Homer to have been a pagan.'

'Inimitable!' Cowper cried. 'You can't mean Pope, can you? The man was a machine, a disgusting machine!'

And they would have been off again, but for Lady Austen putting her hand under Cowper's elbow and whispering into his ear, 'Snuff is upon us.' And there was indeed the sound of footsteps and then the door was torn open.

He had built himself a little house at the bottom of the garden. It was made of clay daubed thick on a wattle frame, lime-plastered. He had needed help with slating the roof, a trade, unlike carpentry, he did not know. The sash window, which occupied most of the wall opposite the door, he had acquired from a derelict house. The door and the window dictated the size of the building: tall enough to walk through without bending, tall enough to look out of while standing. But walking from door to window was not possible: to get past the table you slid along one of the benches that faced each other. There was space for two people comfortably, and that was how he preferred it, but sometimes Lady Austen squeezed in beside him when Mr Bull called.

'I built this palace for you, Mr Bull, and don't you forget it.'

'For me, sir? You do me a great honour.'

'I do you no honour at all, *Bos Bovis*. It is merely that I cannot have you stinking up the greenhouse with your damnable tobacco. Who wants to see or to smell brown flowers?'

But sometimes Anna also squeezed in beside him when there were just the two of them. It was easier to pore over the dictionary, to make corrections, to compare translation with original and so on. She did this, however, only when she was pretty sure Snuff was not on the prowl.

'It was the worst case of colic I ever witnessed,' Mrs Unwin said to Maud Jones as Anna was being settled in the barber's cart before being taken back to Clifton.

Maud said, 'Anna could never bear ... Really, don't you know, her spirits are so mercurial, she can't abide to be the cause of embarrassment to others.'

What Maud had been about to say was that Anna 'could never bear to be crossed'. And when she was in bed with Mr Jones that night, she said, 'I was so furious, I'm sorry I didn't say it.'

'That would have been a mistake.'

'I know that, you imbecile.'

'What have I done now?'

Maud could have replied that he knew very well what he had done – carrying Anna's gift of ruffles for a start – but they had been over that ground before. Instead she said, 'Really, to have that old witch condescending to our family in her so Christian fashion, it's too galling. And to think that I had to drag Anna out of her bed, like a cuckoo out of the nest, my head aches, it positively aches. The whole of Olney is guffawing at us. I have a good mind to never speak to her again.'

'Oh, Maud, in the name of Christ Jesus, I beg you. Don't, Maud, don't. I beg you.'

It was not the possibility of his wife never speaking to Anna again that was now exciting Mr Jones. It was the fact of what she was about to say and do this instant. For downstairs, Lady Austen, as if nothing had happened, had begun playing on her harpsichord the twenty-fifth of the Goldberg Variations by Johann Sebastian Bach. The piece was, she often said, an exact expression of the liberation of her spirit. Mr Jones's entreaties were futile. The confrontation, however, that then ensued in the drawing-room, with Maud in her nightgown screaming at Anna that she was waking the children and making a skit of herself in the entire county, was utile, in the sense that the sisters were freed from speaking to each other until the day Lady Austen moved to Olney, and not very often or warmly thereafter.

Anna was quicksilver but also sensible. In the days after her fit of hysterics, she reviewed the situation: it was true that she had been rejected, betrayed, investigated, humiliated, interviewed, ignored, avoided, besieged by robbers, that she had surrendered her identity to her desire, like a schoolgirl, that she had been disgraced, soiled by her own body – ever since she was a child and her mother would say, 'Have you done a soil?' she had hated that word – but it was not true that she had gone mad. She was not deranged, just extremely temperamental, and only very occasionally. It was a trait that allowed her to be acute, and to give voice to her acuteness immediately, sometimes too immediately, because she didn't care what other people thought of her, and, after all, she was a woman, and a woman couldn't get people to notice her if she didn't make some kind of *réclame* in society, which was so full, anyway, of dull women and even duller men. Mr Cowper, despite all his versifying about Retirement, was far from dull. He was the only person she had ever met as intelligent as herself, and his intellect was em-otional, of the heart, and for that reason he was – she recognised this before any of the idiots in London – a poet of genius. To her, genius was a desert island and she wanted to land there, to leave her footprint on its sands. That Cowper's outpost of enchantment, Olney, was inland, in the middle of England, was immaterial. Actually it was the very middlingness of it that, being chosen, had become the new and deliberative symbol of his genius. He was making an exploration out of, or rather into, the ordinary – like Captain Cook, but in reverse. To this compliment he said, 'You flatter me, madam,' but she could tell he was pleased. Also, he was very attractive, sleek as a greyhound. Actually, the attractiveness was more than an also.

So, all in all, she decided that since she had made her bed, she had better lie in it, even if it was Mrs Unwin's.

Besides, when she moved into the Vicarage the bed was hers. In the first gloriously still mornings of that October, following her colic, he visited her after breakfast to pay, as he said, his respects. They met in the drawing-room and she dressed with care, but as time passed she began to come down in her dressing-gown, and they laughed more. And then, as the weather turned cold, she received him in bed, propped up by many lacy pillows, saying, 'Well, if old King Louis can have his *levée*, I can have mine too.' By the time the summer heat arrived, it was too warm for a dressing-gown and she was more and more *déshabillée*, showing more and more bosom. She had not been mistaken in thinking that he liked to look at it. And he so particularly liked the fact that she always wore the locket with his curl of hair between her breasts that one morning he gave her a pellet of paper and told her not to unfold it until it was time for her to go back to bed that night. Which instruction she obeyed, because the pleasure of yielding, she had learned, was in the delaying of it; and when she did tease it open by the light of a candle, the delay was well worth the wait:

> The star that beats on Anna's breast
> > Conceals her William's hair,
> 'Twas lately severed from the rest
> > To be promoted there.
> The heart that beats beneath that star
> > Is William's, well I know;
> A nobler prize and richer far
> > Than India could bestow.

✻

'Is this a special occasion?' the Count asked. The Countess was wearing a gown he had not seen before: grey silk, fine but a little démodé, and on her bosom a diamond locket glittered.

'No,' Anna said, 'I felt like dressing up, that's all.'

She had joined him for dinner on the terrace, rather later than usual. The sky was heavy with stars; boats with lanterns on their masts tented the sea with lights; and the air was so still that the flames of the candles on the stone table burned up without wavering.

'The little jewel,' he said, 'is very charming. Is it new?'

'No,' Anna said, 'it's an old thing, an old mistake.'

But she would not say why it was a mistake. She could have told him that she had been given it by Monsieur Cowper, but that would have been only half-true. She had asked him to get it for her, as a present, to replace the old spit-soiled one, something really bijou to keep the poem in, and she had given him the money for it, too. But the greatest mistake had been not to have kept the whole thing to herself, petto in pectoris, like the Pope did with the names of cardinals he wanted to keep secret.

In any event, the star-shaped locket, set with diamonds, disappeared in the furious sadness of the night, though whether it was thrown off or snagged on a pointing finger Anna could not remember. The next morning, before anyone else was awake, one of the Arab servants, an eagle-eyed boy, saw it winking at him from the bottom of the fountain in the courtyard. He fished it out, threw away the lock of hair and the soggy pellet of paper and, some months later, sold it to a dealer in the bazaar at Sousse, a little town on the mainland, further up the coast.

Mrs Unwin had reasons for jealousy, but she also had cause to be thankful to Lady Austen. By the time she had ensconced herself in the Vicarage, the winter was upon their lord-and-servant. But January had passed over almost without incident, as had February and March, all thanks to Anna. For Mrs Unwin, managing her companion was like trying to sew tearing silk, darning by day what had been torn by night. But now she had help, she did not feel that Lady Austen was a cuckoo in the nest.

Anna was, though, a magpie of ideas. When she said, 'Misery usually stands in the way of creation, William, but in your case it opens the road. The dejection of spirits that stops many a man from setting out makes you to start, because you know that composing puts off your being decomposed' – when she said that, she was only singing back, with her own trills and grace-notes added, what she had heard him say months earlier. This was flattery of a high order. The lower order variety was merely an irritant. 'Lady Austen says that you are the most elegant woman she has ever seen,' her son had reported. Anna had started her own warm correspondence with him – yet another way of worming herself into her lover's confidence. The compliment was nonsense, gallingly hypocritical, but on reflection, for a draper's daughter who knew good dress-making when she saw it and who had her own proper plain style, it was positively pleasurable nonsense, like being caressed by a human-thinking cat. But, when it came to verse, he told Anna – it was at an important moment, too – that he set Mrs Unwin's opinion above anyone else's, because she was a critic not by rule but by nature, and it was, he said, part of her nature to be right about matters of moral beauty.

'Well then,' Lady Austen said – and it was almost the last thing she did say to them – 'I shall leave you to distinguish which one of you is better than the other, for I can't work it out.'

When it came to intellectuality, however, Mrs Unwin readily admitted that she could not keep up with Cowper and Lady Austen. Sometimes she suspected that Anna did not really know what she was talking about; that her intelligence, like her manner in company, relied on challenge for its authority. Still, there was no contesting the speed of the exchanges between them, and Mrs Unwin was far too sensible to try.

'These Goldberg Variations by Herr Bach that you're so fond of,' he said to Lady Austen one day as the three of them were out walking, 'I was thinking about them last night.'

'Well, they are night music.'

'But not a cure for insomnia. I can vouch for that.'

'They were not meant to cure, but to make the sleeplessness more bearable.'

'It seems to me a curious form of medicine that is efficacious only in not curing the disease, making it worse in fact.'

'Well, yes, that's true,' Anna laughed, 'but the best music requires the most attention.'

'Perhaps, but you'll excuse me if I resist wearing the red coat and appearing always on parade.'

'That's a Protestant fault.'

'By which you mean?'

'I mean the resistance to order.'

'Well, I am hardly a Protestant then.'

'Of course you are. It's what, at least in English terms, makes you a Whig and not a Tory.'

'You accuse me of disorderly conduct – me of all people.'

'But of course. That's why you so misunderstand my Bach, than whom there is no artist more Protestant.'

'I can see his merits, Lady Austen, but, religion or no religion, he ticks; he ticks like a watch. It's all too perfect a performance.'

'That,' she said, 'is exactly the accusation you level at Mr Pope:

> But he (his musical finesse was such,
> So nice his ear, so delicate his touch)
> Made poetry a mere mechanic art,
> And every warbler has his tune by heart.'

'Well, the devil can quote Scripture,' Cowper glowed. Anna's ability to recite his own work back to him was one of her most endearing qualities. 'But perhaps there is something in what you say.'

'There's no perhaps about it.'

'And the solution then? More dissolution, I suppose.'

'No, of course not. You are far too orderly for that, at least in the moral sense. No, you must go on as you do now, but you are free, you know, to indulge those continual zigzags you already half-approve of, and you have, too, perhaps more than any poet now alive, all this.' Anna indicated with a wave of her hand the sweep of the landscape. 'This is a divine machine. This is clear, this is plain.'

'Nothing could be less clear, less plain.'

'Oh, but it is! To your poet's eye it is.'

'Well, forgive me, my dear Anna, you could hardly be more mistaken, certainly about my pride as a creature. After all, what the God of Scripture has seen fit to conceal, he will not as the God of nature publish.'

When Mrs Unwin arrived home, she sat down straight away and transcribed this last sentence. It made sense to her in itself, but what Anna had said about Protestantism, Whiggery and so on, that was all, oh, just fog and flash. Straightforward people, Mr Bull for instance, could not abide this sort of display, and they took the manner of it for arrogance, an outward defect that makes more enemies than many worse but inward sins. Yet, while it was true that Anna had an edge of contempt in her thought for the un-enlightened – which was almost everybody – Mrs Unwin under-stood that she was actually the opposite of cocksure. At heart she was generous, kind, fearfully needy. But that was before the business with the locket, which came at the end, and the poem about the poplar grove.

Without notice, he had taken Anna there. Resentment at not being informed, Mrs Unwin realised, was irrational – there were walks everywhere, so why should he announce this one? But he knew that the grove was their place, that it had an unshareable history. Absurd as it was, she felt Anna had somehow violated and plundered her memory, as if she had, as it were, pulled out of a private drawer an intimate garment and was saying, 'You don't mind if I wear this thing, do you?' But what really galled her, what hurt her so scaldingly, was the simultaneity of feeling betrayed and receiving the news of the fate of the trees.

He came back from the walk, looking stricken, and said, 'My dear, you will never guess what has happened.' And behind him, standing in the doorway, was Lady Austen – it was strange, Mrs Unwin thought, how a room can be made to appear darker by opening it to sunlight. Then the next morning he showed her the new poem:

The poplars are felled, farewell to the shade,
And the whispering sound of the cool colonnade!

The winds play no longer and sing in the leaves,
Nor Ouse on his bosom their image receives.

Twelve years have elapsed since I first took a view
Of my favourite field, and the bank where they grew;
And now in the grass behold they are laid,
And the tree is my seat that once lent me shade!

My fugitive years are all hasting away,
And I must ere long lie as lowly as they,
With a turf on my breast, and a stone at my head,
Ere another such grove shall rise in its stead.

'Mrs Unwin,' he said, 'please don't weep so.'
'I can't help it,' she said. 'It's the word *fugitive* I can't bear.'

But it was not the fugitive word; it was the real absence of herself in the poem that compacted all her feelings together into a pellet and fired them at Anna. Whose years were the twelve? Whose favourite field was it? Where was I? Where were we? Nowhere. And in my place another woman, still young, still sheath-shaped, a poplar.

However, the 'continual zigzags' that Lady Austen adored had to be kept under strict control. And he knew it. It was, also, how he wanted things to be: invariable. Or as invariable as the insomnia and the nightmares that followed would allow.

So every morning before breakfast, he wrote verse or letters; then he went across to the Vicarage for one hour; then there was a walk; in the afternoon more writing, and gardening, carpentry, watercolours, reading aloud, battledore and shuttlecocks. Lunch and supper were taken either at the Vicarage or Orchardside, in strict alternation; and every evening Lady Austen played the harpsichord. Some days, particularly in the winter, were set aside for the distribution of charity to the poor. There were so many thousands of them around Olney that only the starving who were also industrious and churchgoing could be considered. And every second Wednesday Mr Bull called. So every day was various but the same, and the three companions parted only to go to bed. What happened then Lady Austen could only guess at, inaccurately; and what happened in the hours before breakfast, when Mrs Unwin, if she was lucky, was asleep, was only known when, occasionally, uncontrollable despair sent him wild-eyed out of his bedroom.

The only day in the week that was different was Sunday. The ladies kept it holy by going to church together. On Sunday he saw only Mrs Unwin and – eventually he looked forward to it – he did not have to see Anna.

It was not just that she called Mrs Unwin 'Snuff' and even 'dear old Snuff'. Mrs Unwin had always taken snuff, and there was a time when she chewed tobacco, a pastime for which ladies in Ely had a great fondness; but she had given up that habit long ago in Huntingdon, although Cowper had rather liked to see her spirting the juices halfway across Morley Unwin's garden. Anyway, no matter how Lady Austen mocked her, she would not relinquish the pleasure of a delicious snuff sneeze.

Anna then took to making fun of her knitting. 'Do you know,' she said one evening, 'if you joined up all the stockings you've made in this illustrious career of yours, I believe they would reach half-way to the moon,' and she went on to develop the conceit, after the manner of a Rowlandson cartoon, portraying Mrs Unwin as a kind of giant Mother Hubbard standing on the earth with the moon tied to her thread and Cowper shinning up it. He laughed and Mrs Unwin smiled indulgently, because he was still happy then. But when he said about his own role as human spool, sitting with his hands up as Mrs Unwin wound thread off them, 'Thus did Hercules, and thus probably did Samson,' Lady Austen missed, as perhaps she shouldn't have, the implications of the reference to Omphale, the slave-keeper, and to Delilah, the hair-cutter.

She was also inclined to make verbal mistakes and to miss noticing them. On three occasions she referred to him as 'your wife'. The first time was a slip of the tongue but the second time made them think of the first time, and sure enough, when it came to the final icy meeting at the Vicarage, there was no doubt about the hurtful deliberation of the third.

'You seem to think,' Anna said, 'that I want to deprive you of your wife … I beg pardon, your husband. Nothing could be further from my mind. I have had a husband and one was quite enough, thank you.'

But he was not present on that occasion. He was back at Orchardside, wondering what was going on but knowing some decision was being taken for him. No, the reason Lady Austen's tongue slipped so deliberately was because she had been provoked.

Of course she had heard a good deal about Susanna Powley, but in all her eighteen months in Olney, nothing she had been told had prepared her for meeting with Mrs Unwin's daughter in the flesh.

Mrs Unwin herself was very reluctant to involve Susanna in anything to do with, well, anything really, but in particular with Mr Cowper, especially because what he seemed to be inclined to drift into – some kind of marriage with Lady Austen or at least a removal to the Vicarage – was quite acceptable to Susanna.

'If I were you,' she said to her mother, 'I'd be glad to be shot of him. You've been caught in his mousetrap long enough. Let her ladyship try it for a while. Besides, he's after her money. The man's a sponger.'

Mrs Unwin was prepared to put up with a great deal, but this was going too far. So Susanna did not repeat the remark. She did not have to; once was enough.

Nor when she arrived in Olney did she dawdle. Immediately she went with her mother to interview Lady Austen. It soon became clear that, while Anna did not require a husband or, for that matter, a wife, she felt she had acquired certain rights on Mr Cowper's heart, and she intended to exercise them, because she at least genuinely loved the man and he loved her, as Mrs Unwin well knew, because the previous week Anna had snapped the locket open in front of her.

It was, Susanna said, 'quite amazingly disgusting that you have actually shown that stupid, stupid poem about *your* titties to *my* mother'.

But even if he had leched after them, what had poetry to do with anything in the real world? She wouldn't, Susanna said, give one little pork-chop for the whole lot of it.

The meeting ended in tears, with Mrs Unwin and Lady Austen

embracing each other apologetically and hurriedly, while Susanna looked on. But by the time mother and daughter had made their way back across the orchard – a path well trodden – the way forward was clear. And it was made plain to him, blindingly so: either he dismissed Lady Austen, or Mrs Unwin was going home to Huntingdon with Susanna.

That was in May. Two months later, William Unwin received a letter.

Olney, July 12th, 1784

My Dear William,

You are going to Bristol. A Lady, not long since our very near neighbour, is probably there. She was there very lately. If you should chance to fall into her company, remember if you please, that we found the connexion on some accounts an inconvenient one; that we do not wish to renew it, and conduct yourself accordingly. A character with which we spend all our time should be made on purpose for us. Too much or too little of any single ingredient spoils all. In the instance in question, the dissimilitude was too great not to be felt continually, and consequently made our intercourse unpleasant. We have reason to believe however that she has given up all thoughts of a Return to Olney.

Your mother is well and sends her love, as do I mine,
W.C.

But he was wrong. At the end of 1785, long before she married the Count, Lady Austen did return, not to Olney but to Clifton, where she stayed until 1790. During that time they would occasionally meet on the road, but Anna had a fine carriage and a black horse as spirited as herself and she would crack her whip over the animal and bowl past her former friend without a second glance.

40

Now stir the fire, and close the shutters fast,
Let fall the curtain, wheel the sofa round,
And while the bubbling and loud-hissing urn
Throws up a steamy column, and the cups
That cheer but not inebriate, wait on each,
So let us welcome peaceful evening in.

'That's enough of that nonsense,' Cowper said. John Johnson closed the book, disappointed – he had been about to ask who had been sitting on the sofa that evening? And if, as he had heard, Lady Austen was there, was it on this occasion that Mr Cowper said he had nothing to write about and she replied, 'You can write about anything that catches your eye. Look, here's the sofa, write about that.'

He knew, however, that Lady Austen was a delicate subject. Still, she had been the prime mover of the enormous poem which began, 'I sing the Sofa', and, well, he would risk it.

'When I wrote it, nobody was there,' Cowper said. 'Would be so kind as to help me out of here?'

He hauled the old man to his feet, helped him up the stairs and put him to bed. Hearing him mutter 'Poor India' as the curtains were drawn, Johnson thought he understood, and when he went back down to the fireside and reopened *The Task*, he was certain of it.

Is India free? And does she wear her plumed
And jewelled turban with a smile of peace,
Or do we grind her still?

'The dear, dear soul!' he said aloud, and his heart glowed to think that Mr Cowper, despite his dejection, could still find time to lament the crimes of the East India Company. On the other hand, the man who was guilty of the grinding, Warren Hastings, he still had a soft spot for, because they had been at school together. How impressed Lady Hesketh had been by the passion with which he had railed at the others responsible – 'We should unking the tyrants!' he had cried. That was a brave thing to say in front of her, whose devotion to the monarchy was so vehement, she jibbed at the use of the word 'unking' in any circumstance. But then, as the letter he had just got from her showed, emphasis was Lady H's way; she spoke as she wrote:

To see the Royal Family parading under my window half a dozen times a day and the dear King looking so well and so happy, was to me, Mr Johnson, a pleasure almost unimaginable. Nor do I blush to say that my well-known Loyalty was rewarded. As soon as they became aware of my presence in Weymouth they never ceased to pay me every attention – Concerts, Tea parties etcetera. I have been in one week at two Balls, to one of which (given by his Majesty) He invited me himself. But nothing, Mr Johnson, nothing amidst all these gay doings was so truly flattering to my Family as the Tête-a-Tête I had with the Queen in her Dressing room last Thursday which lasted for three hours, at the end of which she showed me Princess Amelia's travelling case wherein her favourite books were placed and amongst them two volumes of my dear Cousin's poems of which her Highness said 'Them's Amelia's favourites'! Now I am well aware, Mr Johnson, that Mr Cowper Once spoke in favour of the appalling Mr Tom Paine and his soi-disant Rights of Man – you only need to look at this Present Pickle in France to see where Rights lead one to – and I know too that he did take it upon himself to criticise His Majesty's First Minister, Mr Pitt, for the candle tax, because the poor people would be barking their shins against the furniture – not that they have much in the way of Chippendale – but though he and I used

to argue about such things, to <u>divert</u> ourselves from <u>other matters</u>
— I need not mention a <u>Certain Person</u> — yet he is at bottom, like
myself, a <u>Lover</u> of Liberty and would never <u>Publish</u> anything that
could reflect on the character of the <u>Executive Power</u>!

That was very true: even if the Certain Person, Mrs Unwin, used to insist that Mr Cowper was a secret Jacobin, Lady Hesketh knew where her cousin's deepest sympathies lay, and she had even prevailed upon him to prove it in — what was the year? Johnson took down the volume where the piece was printed and read:

> O sovereign of an isle renowned
> For undisputed sway
> Wherever o'er yon gulf profound
> Her navies wing their way;
> With juster claims she builds at length
> Her empire on the sea,
> And well may boast the waves her strength
> Which strength restored to thee.

It was an oddly circular thing, but then Mr Cowper did incline to circularity, swooping back again and again to the same fatal convictions. At least the title of the poem was straightforward: 'On the Benefit Received by His Majesty from Sea-Bathing in the Year 1789'. Goodness! That was nigh on ten years ago. Well, perhaps it was not a very good poem, but it certainly had not deserved the scorn heaped on it by Mrs Unwin.

'Whatever else I may be accused of,' she had said, 'it could never be said that I made of Mr Cowper a toady.'

To this remark, Lady Hesketh, being far too naturally superior by breeding, would not deign to reply. All she did say, after a long silence, was, 'Well, Johnny, it's not plated anyway.' And she gave the silver teapot a rap with her wedding ring that made it ping.

Cowper said, 'Oh, Harriot, really,' and went up early to bed.

'I've always been fond of the bells of Olney,' he said, 'but I must say I was never more pleased with them than I was yesterday.'

'Well, I thought I must have interrupted a funeral,' Harriot said.

Mrs Unwin laughed. 'Oh surely not, Lady Hesketh. It was such a joyful noise, and people do not usually applaud at funerals, do they?'

'They might at mine,' Lady Hesketh said.

But she had to admit to being gratified at her reception. In Italy, where she had spent a good many years, because of her husband's health, the people had not rung bells for her, coming or going; and at Cheltenham, Twickenham, Bath and the other watering holes she had been flurrying through since the death of poor Thomas, persons of quality were so numerous that the ringing of bells for their arrival would have created an incessant din, which she would not have put up with, even if it required strangling the bell-ringer with his own rope. On the other hand, as Olney was, to be polite about it, somewhat short in its bloodlines, it was not perhaps surprising that even someone as humble as herself should be the cause of a carillon.

'But then,' she said to Mrs Unwin, 'perhaps my reputation has gone on before me – I am well-known in London for cleverness and conversation. Why, Mrs Thrale, who is a judge of such things, being the friend of Samuel Johnson, the greatest talker of the age after all, once told me I was one of the three women she liked best in the world, with more beauty than almost anybody, as much wit as many a body and six times the quantity of polite literature – *belles-lettres* as we call 'em.'

'I know the term,' Mrs Unwin said.

'Mrs Thrale has a very distinctive way of paying a compliment. "Oh my dear," she said to me at the same *soirée*, "you are so round, so sweet, so plump, so polished, so red, so white – you have every quality of a Naples wash-ball!" Well, to be compared to a soap (and not even the best, which comes from Bologna) might have been regarded as *troppo assurdo* coming from someone other than Mrs Thrale, but I made allowances for her, because, you know, she is really quite ugly.'

Actually, Harriot, who was well-used to the velvet-edged challenge of London literary conversation, had merely responded to the compliment with one of her horse-laughs, a neigh of pleasure and incredulity. But she would not have felt so equable about it had she heard what Mrs Thrale said to the company later that evening: 'Lady Hesketh is wholly neglected by the men – why is that? If it were age that stopped her progress, well, I'd accept that *volontierre*, but many as old are caressed, admired and followed. I never can find out what that woman does to keep the men from adoring her.'

Had she said this to Lady Hesketh's face, she would have got her answer very quickly: 'Followed, Mrs Thrale? Am I to be followed like a harlot? Any man that follows me will get a good cut of my whip!'

Cowper, however, had never been afraid of her, partly because it had always been she who followed him, but mostly because they adored each other. And if she had drifted out of his life, well, so had the whole of London, and now she had sailed back into it with a flourish, still beautiful and still stamping her lovely little Italian boot.

'Now then,' she said the next morning as they inspected what were to be her new quarters, 'since we have been speaking of funerals, this here Vicarage – Dartmouth built it, you say?'

'Not with his own hands, Harriot. He had it built.'

'Dreary little man.'

'My dear, you've never met him.'

'That doesn't prevent me from knowing how dreary he is. The entire place could do with a lick of paint.'

'Don't you like it?'

'Of course I like it, Mrs Unwin. I wouldn't be here otherwise. Or rather, I am here because there is nowhere else suitable. For the moment. Look at this now. What is this?'

They had arrived in the study and Harriot was goggling at what Newton had pencilled on the wall over the mantelpiece. She waved the back of her hand at the inscription, as if instructing it to go away.

'It's from the Bible.'

'Well, I can see that, William. But what is it for? I mean, this could be quite a pretty little room for me to read in, but surely I cannot be expected to sit here and be admonished all day, can I?'

'No, Harriot. That would be asking rather a lot, even from the Bible.'

'What do you mean, sir? What do you mean?'

But before he could reply, the two women caught each other's eye and burst out laughing. Harriot took Mrs Unwin's arm and dragged her out of the room, saying, 'Come along, madam, I'm glad to hear you are not such a Puritan after all.' And as they went down the stairs, he could hear her saying, 'I hardly spoke to him for eighteen years because of all of this Methodistical cant, and now I have a good mind to do the same thing for another eighteen.'

He was relieved that Harriot had hit it off so quickly with Mrs Unwin; it might well have been otherwise, especially because, prior to her arrival at Olney, she had required him to explain the nature of his association with a woman not his wife.

'Tell her what you like,' Mrs Unwin had said. 'She is your cousin, not mine.'

'But it's not an unreasonable question, is it? It is quite natural, after all, don't you think, that she should want to know.'

'Oh, very natural. Very reasonable.'

'So what shall I say, Mrs Unwin?'

'Well, let me put it like this, Mr Cowper. Tell Lady Hesketh that if she asks me I will give her her answer.'

'Oh good!' he said.

And so he had replied to Harriot:

> Your question, your natural, well warranted and most reasonable question concerning me and Mrs Unwin shall be answered at large when we meet. But to Mrs Unwin I refer you for that answer: she is most desirous to give you a most explicit one. I have a history, my dear, belonging to me, which I am not the proper one to relate. You have heard somewhat of it — as much as was possible for me to write; but that _somewhat_ bears a most inconsiderable portion to the whole.

Harriot was mollified. It was not true, of course, that she had cut William out of her life because of his religion; she was herself religious — one could hardly not go to church: the King went, he was the head of it after all, and what was good enough for Him was good enough for her. On the other hand, the idea that William, a Cowper, should have allowed himself to fall under the sway of Mr Newton, a ranting sea-captain, was repugnant. But then, the balance of his mind had been disturbed, partly by the Clerkship business and partly by the engagement to Thea, who was too whimsical to be married to anyone. So here now was Mrs Unwin, quite cheerful, even gay, and such an aged little body, well into her sixties, that the idea of her marrying William, let alone wantoning with him, was absurd.

Still, having been invited to ask the question directly, Harriot, after a few days, did ask it.

'Well, Lady Hesketh,' Mrs Unwin said, 'I had intended to tell you to mind your own business, but now that you have come to Olney and I see that you love Mr Cowper as much as I do, I have changed my mind. The fact is, you and I have both been married and we are both now widows. I cannot, of course, speak for you, but for my part I have no intention of ever repeating the experience. Is that a satisfactory answer?'

'Splendid, my dear. Splendid. And do you know, if you had told me to mind my own business, you would have been quite within your rights. I am, I need hardly tell you, a person of very decided character, very troublesome and very impertinent – it seems to be the way I am made, so I have to keep it up – but when I come upon someone, like yourself, who is not only firm in character but also essentially benevolent, why my heart melts.'

'Well, we are both melted then. We could be spread on toast and eaten.'

'Oh, my dear Mrs Unwin, you are such an amusing creature, but, if you don't mind me saying so, I can see you have suffered as a result of all that you have done for my poor cousin.'

'Can you see that?'

'I can. Not in your person, of course, but in your eyes. One cannot surrender one's will to a man without it leaving a trace there.'

'Really? Is that what you think I have done?'

'Of course it is. And how, you might say, do I know all this?'

'How indeed?'

'Because I have done it myself. All I need to do is look in the mirror and there it is, looking back at me. The same eyes. The same submission.'

This was an unusual intimacy to come from Lady Hesketh. Most of her brusqueness was really shyness, the Cowper vice, and if her shyness was marked by irritability, that was because of jealousy. Without knowing it, she had always been jealous of Theadora's, well, glory was the only good word for it. But there was no need to be jealous now. He had written to say, very prettily, 'I love you, my very roses smell of thee.'

But love was one thing. The state of his mind was another. Harriot had asked him about that too. He had told her that while he still suffered occasionally from dejection, he was not afflicted by the extraordinary elevation of spirits that commonly occurred in the absence of, as he put it, Mr Bluedevil. Moreover, he was certain that she could lift his burden and perhaps bring him an abiding peace of mind. 'Every day I think of you,' he wrote, 'and almost all the day long; I will venture to say, that even you were never so expected in your life.'

And so she had come clattering into the market square on a sunny June day, like Juno in her chariot, to a pealing of bells and a clapping of hands. But instead of springing forward to catch her in his arms, he had turned pale, kissed her as if she were a corpse and preceded her into the house as if leading a funeral procession into a mausoleum. She had the oddest feeling of being both uninteresting and invisible, a boring ghost.

'But that was me, darling,' he said the next day. 'Really, it was just that under the pressure of so much joy, I went flat and dark. But then, as you've known this many a year, sable was always my suit.'

So he had become, and remained, cheerful all during her stay. Well, she thought, the state of his mind is perfect, but life is not entirely mind, and his physical living is not at all satisfactory.

'Now then, this place,' she said some days later, shaking her fan at the parlour, 'while it is most agreeable and curious and very suitable as a menagerie – I don't believe there is a hare in England as well-housed – nonetheless it is hardly a proper habitation for gentlefolk. In fact, excuse me, my dears, for saying so, but it is my opinion that this house has the aspect of a place built for the purposes of incarceration.'

'Mmmmm,' he said. 'You're always so vague, Harriot. What do you mean by incarceration?'

'I mean the place is a prison!'

'Ah,' Mrs Unwin said, 'I've heard that word spoken before.'

But Lady Hesketh, without asking when 'before' was, went on directly, 'And being the horribly presumptuous personage that I am, I have done something about it.'

What Harriot had done was to get up very early in the morning, drive out to Weston Hall, give a good rat-tat-tat to the door with her silver-handled stick, introduce herself to the Throckmortons and make it clear to them that an invitation to dinner would not be refused.

Nor was it.

As his guests took their places at table beneath the glimmering chandelier in the great dining-room, Sir John said, 'Well now, at this juncture we usually have our chaplain in to say grace, but as he is such a frightfully Roman creature, I have banished him temporarily to the priest's hole – I believe you will remember me showing it you, Mr Cowper – and so, instead of praying aloud, all I ask is that we bow our heads for a moment to thank the Lord for what we are about to receive.'

Mrs Unwin had always liked Sir John; not only was he adept at self-mockery, as any commonsensical Roman Catholic had to be in society, but he was also sensitive – he had heard about Cowper's inability to be present at prayers, which explained the silent grace – and he was very willing, in fact only too delighted, to rent Weston Lodge to his friends.

'Good man!' Lady Hesketh said.

41

I know that dog, Mrs Unwin thought, stopping to listen for a moment as she got into bed. It always barked when the baker passed by on his way to start work, but since this was the last time she would sleep in Orchardside, the sound made her sad. A body would think, she thought, that it would have learned the baker's smell by now, yeasty and fermenting. Harriot has similar smells – she comes into a room with a waft of that perfume she gets sent up from Grasse in France, attar of mimosa, but when she goes out, she leaves a reek behind her, like opening an old handbag smelling of damp talcum powder. Poor creature.

Mrs Unwin felt sorry for Lady Hesketh, but that did not mean she was not also irked by her.

'Why does she bellow so?' she asked Cowper. 'You'd think I was in the next parish, or deaf, or a simpleton, or all three.'

'It's not just you, Mrs Unwin; it's everyone. All the same, I do think her *basso profundo* is quite musical, don't you?'

'She doesn't listen either.'

'Oh, I find her very attentive.'

'Or she chooses not to.'

'Chooses?'

'I had heard the word prison before, you know, and I expect she knew that I had.'

There was a pause, during which he pursed his lips half-resentfully and half-guiltily. Mrs Unwin relented: 'You two are very alike,' was all she said before changing the subject.

If only Lady Hesketh had responded, 'Of course you have heard the word, I certainly have. William has been writing me for months groaning that the house you have laboured to make a nice home for him is a jail.' If she had said that, it would have been all right, because ever since Lady Austen's departure he had been complaining that Orchardside was a prison. I suppose, Mrs Unwin thought, he's looking for some kind of reward for giving Anna up, though it's me that should get the reward since I got her to go, because he was bored with her. But Harriot not being straightforward was a kind of stupidity, because it implied that Mrs Unwin was too backward to realise that he had put Harriot up to it.

The stupidity saddened Mrs Unwin, but it also made her smile. He had a gift, when he didn't get his way, for getting other people to get it for him. Poor Harriot was his proxy. Really, she thought, he's just like my own son. As a boy, William had had the same brazenly sly way of sending Susanna in to do his persuading for him while he sauntered around the garden like a grown man, examining the length of his fingernails – she had often felt like giving him a good slap for his guile. He was also, now that she thought of it, as feckless about money as Mr Cowper. No, that wasn't quite true: William was embarrassed by the subject – he was hopeless about getting the farmers in Stock to pay their tithes – whereas Mr Cowper had a very sociable way not only of putting his hand in your pocket, but also of making you feel that it was somehow good for you. She chuckled as she remembered approving the letter he had sent to Lady Hesketh:

Since Mrs Unwin and I have lived at Olney, we have had but one purse, although during the whole of that time, till lately, her income was nearly double mine. Her revenues indeed are now in some measure reduced and do not much exceed my own; the worst consequence of this is that we are forced to deny ourselves some things which hitherto we have been better able to afford, but they are such things as neither life, nor the well-being of life, depend upon. My own income has been better than it is, but when it was best, it

would not have enabled me to live as my connections demanded
that I should, had it not been combined with a better than itself.
Now, my beloved Cousin, you are in possession of the whole case
as it stands. Strain no points to your own convenience or hurt, for
there is no need of it, but indulge yourself in communicating (no
matter what) that you can spare without missing it, since by doing
so you will be sure to add to the comforts of my life one of the
sweetest that I can enjoy — a token and proof of your affection.

All this was true, but all of it was also false: it was her income that
had been reduced, by him spending it; the things that life did not
depend on were books, books, books and silver buckles for his
shoes, which absolutely had to be bought; and if there were
connections demanding he should live otherwise, she did not know
who they were — they were ideal persons living in his head, but then
all the Cowpers were ideal to themselves.

Mrs Unwin drifted off to sleep, still smiling and thinking,
'Well, irksome as she is, I had better give her the credit. After all,
she has paid for the privilege.'

42

Weston Lodge, November 26th, 1786

It is my birthday, my beloved Cousin, and I determine to employ a part of it, that it may not be destitute of festivity, in writing to you. The neatness and snugness of our new abode compensate all the dreariness of the season, and whether the ways are wet or dry, our house at least is always warm and commodious. O, for you, my Cousin, to partake these comforts with us! Come back soon! You will know that the best house has a desolate appearance unfurnished. This house accordingly, since it has been occupied by us and our <u>meubles</u>, is as much superior to what it was when you saw it as you can imagine. The parlour is even elegant. When I say that the parlour is elegant, I do not mean to insinuate that the study is not so. It is neat, warm, and silent, and a much better study than I deserve, if I do not produce in it an incomparable translation of Homer. I think every day of those lines of Milton, and congratulate myself on having obtained, before I am quite superannuated, what he seems not to have hoped for sooner:

And may at length my weary age,
Find out the peaceful hermitage!

For if it is not an hermitage, at least it is a much better thing, and you must always understand, my dear, that when poets talk of cottages, hermitages and such like things, they mean a house with six sashes in front, two comfortable parlours, a smart staircase,

*and three bedchambers of convenient dimensions: in short, exactly
such a house as this.*

*Wintry as the weather is, do not suspect that it confines me. I
ramble daily, and every day changes my ramble. Wherever I go I find
short grass under my feet, and when I have travelled perhaps five
miles, come home with shoes not at all too dirty for a drawing-room.
I was pacing yesterday under the elms that surround the field in
which stands the great alcove, when lifting my eyes I saw two black
genteel figures bolt through a hedge into the path where I was walking.
You guess already who they were, and that they could be nobody but
our neighbours, the Throckmortons. They had seen me from a hill at
a distance, and had traversed a great turnip-field to get at me. You see
therefore, my dear, that I am in some request. Mrs Throckmorton,
Frog as I call her, is also daily transcribing my labours. Such a team
of helpers I have — and I drive them too!*

Good night, and may God bless thee,
W.C.

Weston, Nov 30th, 1786

Dear Harriot,

*In great haste — the Diligence is at the door — Mrs Unwin's son
has died, at Winchester, of a putrid fever. I feel as a father does that
loses a son, and doubly, as a brother a brother. And yet this is
imagined loss. His real mother, she did not cry, only looked at me as
if I were a ship in a great storm which she had fallen overboard from,
passing helplessly on.*

W.C.

He rarely wept. He often wanted to but he simply could not do it.
'I think men's eyes must be made differently from women's,' he said
to Mrs Unwin on their first night at Weston Lodge. 'We don't
seem to be able to open the fountains of our grief as you do. I
wonder why that is.'

'Well, you don't mean me, Mr Cowper. You've never seen me
blubbing.'

They were discussing the subject because he had wept as they drove away from Orchardside. He had looked back over his shoulder at nineteen years of his life, and when he turned away and again became aware that he was sitting between two monumental women, one booming, one silently staring ahead, tears had welled up, but even then only a few drops had managed to escape from his eyes.

On that first night in Weston, he had wanted to cry again, but this time with relief, because Mrs Unwin had come in to see him off to sleep as she did in Olney. There, they had had only the thickness of a lath wall between them and she was near if a nightmare woke him. Here, their rooms were the length of a landing apart and the distance had seemed ominous. Another thing that was significant, though Mrs Unwin did not know it then, was that as she crossed the landing in her nightdress and badly dyed shawl she was seen by Mrs Eaton, Lady Hesketh's personal servant.

'It was a strange sight, milady,' Mrs Eaton said while they were driving back to London the next day. 'She was holding a candle down low, trying to see the door-handle I suppose, and the flame coming up made her look like a witch.'

'Mrs Eaton!' Harriot said reprovingly, but the image, as well as the impropriety, lodged in her already teeming judgement box.

In the first days after her son's death, Mrs Unwin did not cry. She had not been able to attend the funeral – by the time the letter arrived he was, for fear of contagion, already buried. Still, there was a great deal to do – letters to write, sympathisers to meet – and she was kept busy. Cowper, she insisted, should also keep to his routine as much as possible. Habit was his oxygen. Homer morning and evening and a walk in the afternoon, that was how he passed the hours. At night she came and sat by his bedside as usual, but she did not want to play nocturnally the Roman matron of the daytime. The stillness of Weston Underwood was preferable to the perpetual bustle of Olney, but now at night it seemed hollowed out, as if the womb that had borne her son had somehow been emptied into a hole in the ground – ground, moreover, that she had never stood upon. Stock in Essex. She was almost inclined to search for it on the map now that it had become William's permanent address on earth. But it was not these feelings that made her weep at last.

On the morning of the fifth of December she sent Cowper into

Olney to buy some of the baker's almond biscuits to serve to the Throckmortons with their tea when they came to pay their condolences in the afternoon. It could have been an awkward occasion, but the Frogs had the most exquisite manners, and they brought gifts: a brace of partridges, a Greek dictionary, a box of Egyptian dates and an ancient bottle of sherry. The almond biscuits reminded Maria Throckmorton of the convent in France where she had attended school; the nuns invariably served them with sherry to visitors. Thereupon the bottle was opened and emptied, and there ensued quite a gay conversation about the enclosed orders. It was curious, Maria remarked at one point, that many of the nuns in her convent were the daughters of Irish wine merchants.

'Speaking of curious affinities,' Cowper said, 'I learned today that our old house in Olney is to be taken one half by a publican and the other by a cobbler. Such, it seems, is what we were the measure of.'

That night they returned to the subject. She was, she thought, so unsentimental about Orchardside that she was about to say, 'I suppose, Mr Cowper, the gates you made for your hares, this publican will now pass tankards of ale through,' but she bit her lip, and then without warning tears were flooding silently out of her eyes. After staring for a moment, he gave her his handkerchief from under the pillow, then got out of bed and poured her a glass of water, which she refused, though she did not intend as a refusal the waving of the handkerchief.

'No, no,' she said, 'this is, it's all, this is too ludicrous. Please, get back into bed. Please, you'll catch your death.'

Trembling, but not from cold, he got back under the covers, lay on his side with his head propped up on his hand and watched her.

'Oh, you poor thing,' she said after she had collected herself a little, 'you look just like ...' But she did not finish the sentence and instead blotted away the tears, then held out her hand to him. Staring up at her sideways from the pillow with his paw extended, he looked even more like Beau, his spaniel, which is what she had been going to say. That started the tears again.

'I'm sorry, my dear,' she said. 'Forgive me.' Then she kissed him and went off to cry in her own room.

He had not told her how he had learned that their old house was to be let. There was nothing to conceal, but something had been, if not revealed, forewarned. Prefigured.

He had been crossing the market square when he noticed that the door of Orchardside was ajar. It was a cold and gloomy day, but in the house the gloom belonged to an order of things out of time, and the cold, as if taking revenge for the withdrawal of human heat, was starved, perished. The rooms looked smaller, yet they sounded bigger, echoing to his footfalls. It was all the more startling then that, as he turned away from looking into the grate in the parlour, where there still remained the delicately balanced ashes of their last fire, beige and bone-blue, he saw a man standing only a few feet away.

'Oh joy!' the man said, advancing with his hand out. 'You have come amongst us again.'

'Mr Teedon. You startled me.'

'Dear heavens, squire, you are the last person on earth I wish to startle. Do forgive me.'

'Of course.'

'That is munificent of you, as always and ever. And how is Madam?'

'As well as can be expected.'

'The informations concerning the recent fatality are grievous, most grievous. Please convey to her my solicitations.'

'Yes, yes.'

'And yourself, squire, how is your own dear self?'

'I am well, Mr Teedon, but rather in a hurry.'

During these exchanges Teedon had been bowing over Cowper's hand, which he held in both of his and was stroking as if it were a miniature infant Jesus who had fallen out of the manger and needed consoling. He was wearing a rabbit-skin hat, which stank of rancid meat, and the jet-black hair that hung down from under it onto his dandruff-drifted shoulders also reeked, but of ancient sebaceous fats. Both stenches now wafted into Cowper's nostrils as Teedon suddenly raised his head.

'The Lord,' he said, 'is cognisant of your welfare. It has been delineated in one of my recent notices.'

'Oh yes?'

'I call them that. They are signs that require to be read, you see.'

'I see. Very interesting, but —'

'Mammy and Eusebius are waiting *dans la place des marchands*. Shall we go out to them? Mammy has some intelligence to impart of a domicilary character.'

So they went out into the street where Mammy told Cowper what she had heard about the new tenants. She was almost as talkative and frowsty as her son, but whereas he was tall and thin, she was small and ball-shaped. On the other hand, Eusebius Killingworth, who was Mr Teedon's assistant in the local school, had no visible physical characteristics, owing to his body being encased in an ankle-length overcoat and his head and face being swathed by a woollen muffler at all seasons. Worthy, as the townies called him, was as dirty as his master, but his hands were clean, because he spent hours every day washing them.

After listening to Mammy's news, Cowper gave the trio some biscuits — they were, like many in Olney, hungry — and went home. Apart from Teedon irritating him, as always, with his obseqious-ness, he forgot him. Or almost.

After Mrs Unwin's first night of weeping, the same thing hap-pened the following two nights, but in a more orderly fashion: she cried, held his hand, kissed him and stumbled off to bed.

On the fourth night, as they were going up the still uncarpeted stairs accompanied by their huge candlelit shadows, she stopped and said, 'This is too much for me, Mr Cowper. I cannot bear the prospect of watching over you at the moment. Let me be alone tonight. I am tired, so tired. Please forgive me.'

He forgave her. And every rational part of him understood that she needed to be alone in her lonliness. But he did not sleep. At four o'clock in the morning, he went across the landing to her room and tentatively opened the door to a shocking blaze of moonlight — shocking because his room, on the dark side of the house, was not in its path — to discover her fast asleep, lying on her back with her mouth open, hardly breathing, still as stone.

The next day after lunch he fell asleep in the study, and as he gasped back to wakefulness a wheedling voice spoke to him, saying repeatedly, 'I will promise you anything.' It was the voice of God the father and what it said was a deliberate, malicious, mocking lie.

Mrs Unwin, who heard him shouting, came running. At first he could not make out what she was saying, her words had a horribly frantic drone to them, like a fly buzzing in a bottle, and for a dreadful instant, when he understood that she was asking him would he take some tea, he saw her as the poisoner of the past. But then he did hear her clearly, saying, 'Oh my God, if you cannot think of my welfare at this time, then think of your own!' She was desperately angry, and instantly he submitted.

It was many months later, after he had tried to hang himself again, that he unconsciously associated Mrs Unwin's use of the words 'God' and 'welfare' with what wheedling Samuel Teedon had told him in the ashen parlour at Orchardside.

For now all he could think of was the shame of standing in the way of her grief. So he resumed his daily habits and nightly went off to bed on his own. He managed to go on like this for six weeks, partly because he derived strength from a perverse kind of resentment, like a boy punishing his mother all day for not remembering his birthday first thing in the morning, and partly from the pleasure of Mrs Unwin appreciating the effort he was making. But the strain of his being good was too much for her and eventually she knocked on the bedroom door and asked to be let in. The next day he wrote to Lady Hesketh:

> Last night, quite contrary to my expectations, the fever left me entirely, and I slept quietly, soundly and long. If it please God that it return not, I shall find myself in a position to proceed with Homer. I walk constantly, that is to say, Mrs Unwin and I together; for at these times I keep her continually employed, and never suffer her to be absent from me for many minutes. She gives me all her time, and all her attention, and forgets there is another object in the world.

There was to be a perversity, too, about the suicide. John Throckmorton had shown him the priest's hole at Weston Hall, a secret room where recusant Catholic clergy, such as Campion the Jesuit, hid during what the Romans called their persecution. As soon as Cowper saw it he thought, 'This is where the Pope would want me dead,' and for months afterwards vivid images came irresistibly into his head of the scene, and he even imagined Mrs Unwin, with a moonlit knife held aloft in her hand, crying out that she would rescue him while she charged across the lawn towards the great house, as if attacking it. But it was from the stairs of the landing in the Lodge that he attempted the hanging, though there had been, as there always was, a kind of prefiguration in the imagining, since Mrs Unwin did have a knife, which she used to cut the cord, while Sam, naked from bed, clutched his legs to take the weight.

43

And now with nerves new-braced and spirits cheered
We tread the wilderness, whose well-rolled walks
With curvature of slow and easy sweep –
Deception innocent – give ample space
To narrow bounds. The grove receives us next;
Between the upright shafts of whose tall elms
We may discern the thresher at his task.
Thump after thump, resounds the constant flail,
That seems to swing uncertain, and yet falls
Full on the destined ear. Wide flies the chaff,
The rustling straw sends up a frequent mist
Of atoms sparkling in the noonday beam.
Come hither, ye that press your beds of down
And sleep not – see him sweating o'er his bread
Before he eats it. – 'Tis the primal curse,
But softened into mercy; made the pledge
Of cheerful days, and nights without a groan.

He interrupted Johnson's reading. 'Tell me,' he said, 'what was the name of that man, the omnipotent magician, he who planned the gardens at Weston?'

'Mr Capability Brown.'

'Yes, the very creature. Imagine designing a wilderness! I never approved the man's haughty tamperings with nature and yet I seem to have approved of the Weston deception.'

'The deception, as you say, was innocent.'

'Not on my part,' Cowper said. 'I always knew what I was doing. But what reader could know the wilderness was a gardened place?'

'A what?'

He ignored the question and went on. 'Indeed the whole poem is like reading Homer: to understand him properly, you need the assistance of a clavis, an almanac and an ancient of the age who remembers everything. You have the ancient, sir, but, alas, he forgets even his own production.'

'A clavis, Mr Cowper, what is that?'

'A key.' But then he said no more, since Johnson pretending not to understand Greek, though he had taken Holy Orders, was another deception.

From the beginning he had his suspicions that there was something uncanny about his cousin. He had arrived in January, a year after the death of William Unwin, a season not made any less terrible by Lady Hesketh, who had arrived in September, being still at the Lodge.

One pitch-black night Sam had found a letter lying on the hall table. No one in the house could say who had put it there or who had brought it. It said:

> J. Johnson, a grandson of the Rev. R. Donne, late of Catfield, in Norfolk, is just arrived at Olney, and with the greatest pleasure will pay his respects to Mr Cowper in the morning, if he may be allowed that happiness. Mr Johnson reflects with satisfaction on being so near a gentleman whom he has long had the greatest desire to see, and for which sole purpose his journey to Olney has been so long premeditated.

'He speaks of himself in the third person,' Cowper said. 'That's suspicious.'

'Oh, nonsense, man,' Mrs Unwin said. 'It's shyness, that's all. It runs in your family.'

'Not on the Cowper side,' Lady Hesketh said. 'You may be assured of that.'

'Well, he may be a grandson of my Uncle Roger, for aught I know, but he may also be a butcher-like man, the very sight of whom will be enough to kill me.'

'And Sam maybe is Vulcan and John Frog is Aristophanes. Oh, give me patience!' Mrs Unwin said and went off to bed. Lady Hesketh shook her fan furiously.

The next morning Cowper waited in his study while Mrs Unwin interrogated Johnson. The interview took much longer than expected, and when Mrs Unwin came in she was shaking her head. 'Oh,' she said, 'he's just a wild boy, a wild, lost, downy boy. Take him out with you on your walk, Mr Cowper, and be kind to him.'

He did take him on his walk, all around the polite wilderness of Weston, and afterwards said, 'He is, Mrs Unwin, a shred of my mother. We had better put him up for the night and give him meat, else he will make his nest in a bush and feed only on berries.'

Johnson was indeed bird-like, very slight, thin-boned and, though he was twenty-one years old, still as downy as a nestling. He was wild too: during their walk he had suddenly broken away and, with a cry halfway between a screech and a chirrup, had leaped over a high yellow ragweed for no apparent reason that Cowper could see, except perhaps joy that he had found his famous relative. The Johnsons had lost touch with the Cowpers and none of them knew where he lived, so Johnny had simply arrived in London, a city he had never been in, knocked on the door of Cowper's publisher and sought directions. He had been given a bed for the night – grown-ups often felt they had to shelter him from the storm – and the following morning he had been put on the coach to Olney.

Some days later, as he was being shaved, Cowper said, 'Sam, that little pile of linen I've put out there on the dressing-table, could you contrive to transfer it into Mr Johnny's room? Without being seen?'

'Yes, sir.'

'Did you see that satchel he has? There is nothing in it save for a family tree. The boy knows more about my family than I do. Every Cowper and Donne that ever walked the earth is in it, back to the Dean of St Paul's and beyond.'

'He wants to belong, sir.'

'Indeed he does. And do you know why, Sam? The boy – it

took me an hour to get it out of him – the boy is ashamed that his father made his living out of tanning hides. Trade, Sam, trade.'

'Some people that doesn't have any thinks he should eat in the kitchen.'

'She didn't say that!'

'Well, sir, she likes Mr Johnson, but she still thinks it's where he belongs.'

'Oh, give me patience!' Cowper said.

Apart from Sam, only Mrs Unwin could speak plainly to Cowper on the subject of Harriot, but only Sam got an opinion back. In the struggle that was developing between the two women, Cowper, being the *causus belli*, could see no other choice than to be, like any field of battle, dumb and trampled on.

That night after supper, Johnny, dressed in a clean shirt, laid out the family tree on the table. He was particularly keen to point out that, after extensive researches, he had established a link between the Donnes and Thomas Howard, the first Duke of Norfolk.

'A Roman, of course,' Lady Hesketh said, 'but the best of them. A most loyal family. The present Duke—'

'Charles Howard, the eleventh in the line,' Johnny said.

'Yes, Mr Johnson, yes indeed. But I was about to say that Charles is held in the highest regard by the Monarch.'

'I happen,' Johnny said tremulously, 'I happen, you know, to be acquainted with him, personally.'

'You? My dear boy.'

'But I do know him, truly.'

'*Incroyable!*'

'Well, Mr Johnson, I believe you,' Mrs Unwin said.

'No one disbelieves the word of a gentleman,' Lady Hesketh said, 'or of a gentlewoman for that matter.'

'How did this come about, Johnny?' Cowper asked.

'Well, sir, to begin with, I simply wrote to his Grace informing him of our family connection.'

'And he replied?'

'Oh yes. In fact we then engaged in a rather wider correspondence which the Duke apparently found so interesting that he saw fit to invite me to visit him in Saffron Walden, at the family seat, Audley End.'

'Your origins, of course, are very respectable,' Lady Hesketh said.

'I'm obliged to your ladyship. As it turned out, he and I discovered we shared a mutual passion for the muse of poesy. Needless to say, the Duke, whilst a very great personage, is not half the poet my cousin is.'

'Prettily spoken,' Lady Hesketh said.

'As it happens,' Johnny said, delving into his satchel and fishing out a sheaf of papers, 'I have here an example of his verses. They resulted from a discussion we had concerning Audley, the countryside thereabouts being, as I observed to his Grace, remarkably suited for an eclogue. Whereupon he composed this, after the manner of Theocritus.'

'Is it an autograph?' Lady Hesketh said. 'Let me see it please.' She seized the poem, examined it and exclaimed, 'What a noble hand. I must invite him to one of my evenings. And you can come too, perhaps.'

'That is most kind of you, milady. I am indeed overwhelmed by your kindness. But as regards the Duke, well, you know, he harbours a peculiar reserve in the matter of authorship. In fact, he holds a deep-seated aversion to it being bruited abroad that he has put on the poet's mantle.'

'The rogue,' Mrs Unwin cried involuntarily, and whispered into Cowper's ear, 'Don't embarrass the boy. Change the subject.'

Meanwhile Lady Hesketh was saying, 'Really, madam, I can hardly think it proper to describe a belted earl as a rogue, even in jest. William, what are you people whispering about?'

'Whispering, Harriot?'

'Not speaking aloud is whispering. What are you saying there?'

'I don't know.'

'What do you mean you don't know?'

'I can't remember.'

'Of course you can remember.'

'I can't, really.'

'I,' Mrs Unwin said, 'asked Mr Cowper to change the subject because it is one which in my opinion is mortifying, and Mr

Cowper said he would do so. And if he can't do it, then I will. Is that plain enough?'

'Well,' Lady Hesketh said in genuine puzzlement, 'it's not plain to me. Is it plain to you, cousin?'

'Aaaaah,' Cowper drawled, 'I would say that on the one hand it appears to be, but on the other hand it seems there may be a certain lack of, well, clarity.'

'Not on my side,' Mrs Unwin said.

'Nor on mine,' Lady Hesketh said, just to be different.

'Well then,' Cowper said, 'I suppose the truth must lie somewhere in-between. What do you think, Johnny?'

'I'm not quite sure,' Johnson said, 'what it is we are talking about.'

At which point Mrs Unwin laughed heartily, Lady Hesketh huffed and Cowper emitted a sort of huffing giggle. But it was enough to change the subject and to make the remainder of the evening even more uneasy than usual.

The next day he took Johnson into his study and subjected the eclogue to close critical scrutiny. As Mrs Unwin had twigged immediately, the Duke of Norfolk was not the author of the poem. Nor had he invited Johnny to Audley End. In fact, he had been driving up the avenue to the house one afternoon when Johnny had hopped out of the shrubbery and run alongside the Howard phaeton waving a large scroll of parchment and crying out, 'I've brought your tree, sir.' The duke had accepted the gift, invited his kinsman into the house, given him a cup of tea and allowed that, yes, a poem could indeed be written about the estate.

'You weren't too hard on him, I hope,' Mrs Unwin said after the interrogation.

'I was actually. I don't think I was ever as stern in my life. Really, to be so given over to deception at such an early age is quite outrageous.'

'The boy needs a father,' Mrs Unwin said.

This was true. Johnny needed a father and he was dimly aware of it. The one he was ashamed of had died five years earlier. But he was in greater need of a mother and did not know it at all: she had died when he was a year old. The boy's history, as far as Cowper was concerned, was too similar to his own to be mentioned. Nor was it.

But Johnny, while remaining the only person in the world he ever felt he could be stern with, was also serving another end.

He belonged to the Prefigured Types, a large, perhaps infinitely large, intricately organised and pervasive order of beings who, while they appeared to be human, were not. Their essence was other than human. They were messengers, heralds from the dark world. In the past these Prefigured Types appeared fleetingly: a man with a pigtail; a Mr Nunally from Didcot; an apothecary purveying laudanum; an old soldier, sometimes balding, sometimes not, in a ragged red coat. Now, here was John Johnson, a boy who went on a pilgrimage and stayed at the shrine forever. His purpose was to step forward out of their ranks and be visible, to serve the seen, Cowper, and report back to the unseen. To this end he had, within a matter of months, followed his new-found father's advice and given up the study of mathematics at Gonville and Caius in Cambridge to become a priest – what, after all, were numbers in eternity?

Another of the Prefigured Types was Henry Fuseli. He was serving a dual purpose and it was for the reason of duality, Cowper suspected, that he never met the man. Fuseli's role was simple, because it was literary, but its very simplicity made it complicated.

After Lady Austen had departed – women, by their nature, could not belong to the order – and he had finished *The Task*, all six books of it, he had stopped writing poetry. At first Mrs Unwin was relieved; she had been his guide, but if the way that he went seemed to be a garden path, it was one that wended down to hell. The fact that he was at the same time achieving a kind of fame had also brought him self-confidence, and the result of fame and self-confidence had been wilfulness and ambition. To a degree he had sensed this himself; he felt that further large-scale composition would be too Luciferian for his pride and that the little occasional poems, which readers liked so much, were too small for his talent. So he had given over his will entirely to Homer, the greatest of all poets, in competition with Alexander Pope, whose translation, in his opinion, had only produced a rhyming Greek in knee-breeches. Putting this botch to rights was a task for which Cowper was sure *The Task* had uniquely prepared him.

This was where Fuseli came in.

Joseph Johnson, the publisher, began to send to Weston anonymous, scholarly and highly detailed commentary and criticism of the translation. Cowper was pleased, mortified to be corrected and puzzled – here was someone not only with Greek as good as his own but with a knowledge of both the mechanics of English prosody and, more astonishingly, of the soul of poetry. And, as he found out, the man was Swiss; English was not even his native language. Even more humbling was the fact that Fuseli was doing Homer in his spare time, making a few shillings as a jobbing reader. In his full time he was an artist of genius. And it was in this capacity that he belonged to the order of invisible beings. Cowper only ever saw two engravings of Fuseli's work, but two was terrible enough. The first was a self-portrait in which the artist, arms folded, chin on left wrist, left hand splayed on right forearm like a spider-weapon, crouched over an open book and a little round container, perhaps for wig-powder, on the side of which was written – so small that Cowper had had to get a magnifying glass to read them – the words 'His T.C box'. This was terrifying – how did Henry Fuseli know of Theadora Cowper? The second engraving showed exactly the dream – the by now almost forty-year-old dream – in which Harriot took a snail from his hand and leaned into the mouth of a cave, offering it to the darkness. That the figure in the drawing was not Cowper but Perseus, and that the object offered to the god by Athena was not a snail but an eye only made the coincidence the more awful. Fuseli was a messenger, prefigured. He had been sent.

Sent, too, was Samuel Teedon.

44

'Send for Mr Teedon, Sam,' Cowper said, 'I need to see him urgently.' But before Sam could speak there was Teedon, standing in the doorway to the study, hat in hand and a mournfully aggrieved expression on his face. The hat was new, or rather new second-hand, and it was not rabbit but Canadian beaver, a high-pointed helmet with earmuffs which stuck out like floppy wings. The aggrieved expression was soon explained: 'Oh, squire,' Teedon said, 'I have been most dreadfully wounded.'

But then much the same could have been said of Lady Hesketh, and a hat also played a part in her anguish.

'Send the bitch away, William,' she had said. 'She is the most scandalously extravagant little bitch I have ever had the misfortune to come upon in my entire existence.'

'Oh, Harriot,' Cowper said, 'it's only a hat.'

'Only a hat! A white satin turban exactly as worn by the Princess of Wales only a hat! Really, it is quite, quite inappropriate for an item worn by a member of the Royal Family to be sported by a kitchen maid.'

'But Hannah is not a kitchen maid.'

'Indeed she's not. That is very, very true.'

'Anyway, Harriot, the hat is bought, so really there's nothing to be done about it.'

'Nothing to be done about it? Why indeed there is, or rather there was.'

'Was?'

'There was something to do and I did it.'

'What did you do, Harriot?'

'Of course I would much prefer not to have to tell your dear sweet self about such matters, but if I don't *Someone Else* will.'

'Harriot, what did you do?'

'With the hat? I confiscated it.'

'Oh?'

'And gave it to Johnny.'

'Harriot, may I ask you a question?'

'Yes?'

'What possible use could Mr Johnson have for a white satin turban as worn by the Princess of Wales?'

'Oh, William, I do so love to see you smile.'

'That pleases me, cousin, rather as the image does. But—'

'But of course I didn't give him the hat for himself. Actually, I had the rather bright idea of sending him over to the Hall to present it to Catharina Throckmorton. A noble gift for a noble girl. Much more fitting for her than a common slattern.'

'Really, Harriot! Miss Hannekin is not a slattern.'

'William, the girl is a bitch, and I call her that because that is what she just now called me.'

'Oh, she didn't, did she?'

'She did indeed. You should send her away out of here. She is a bitch, and worse than that, I believe she is next thing to being a whore!'

At Weston, as at Olney, where there had been less room for them, there were always plenty of female servants coming and going. Most were local girls who lived out, but some lived in, and either way they got little more than their keep, which was a lot in times of near-starvation. When Lady Hesketh came to stay – it was usually in the winter, but the present terrible season was to last for twenty-one months – she brought her body-servant, Mrs Eaton; her cook, who was called Cookee; and her driver, Daniel, a handsome youth. Mrs Unwin, who did many of the household chores herself and supervised all of them, was run off her feet. Lady Hesketh, who did no menial work, appreciated how wearying were Mrs Unwin's labours – 'The poor, dear woman,' she said to Cowper, early on, 'looks even older than her years' – and endeavoured to help by taking command, which she would have done anyway, even if Mrs Unwin had been as spry as a spring chicken. One of the first things she did was to suggest that space should be made at table for Mrs Eaton, who was a gentlewoman, by sending Hannah Wilson to eat in the kitchen. On her arrival at Olney, Lady Hesketh said it was 'charmingly rural' that Hannah should be dining with her betters; then at Weston it was 'extraordinarily eccentric'; then 'unheard of'; then 'outrageous'. But Mrs Unwin would not budge, and nor would Cowper, though for different reasons.

When Lady Hesketh discovered the facts, she was, being a woman of the world, only mildly astonished. Hannah was the daughter of a bastard, and the father of the bastard was also the father of Mrs Unwin. 'After all,' Harriot said, 'men is animals, especially in that department,' and she was prepared to allow that even the Prince Regent had sired a byblow or two, here and there, thither and yon, up and down the country. But that William should be so taken with Miss Hannekin, as he called her – what possible explanation could there be for such an unseemly infatuation, except that it was yet another way the Witch had of keeping him under her spell?

When, much later, Lady Hesketh said this to her face, Mrs Unwin was deeply offended, partly because it was partly true. But the charge of witchcraft was typical of Harriot – like her cousin, when she could find no earthly reason for something she always turned to the nether world for one. It was also absurd of Harriot to say on the same occasion that she had acted the Pandar for Cowper with Lady Austen. She had merely allowed his passion to work itself into exhaustion, much as she had allowed Mr Newton to whisk them out of Huntingdon, and Lady Hesketh to hurry them out of Olney – 'Have you ever remarked,' she asked Cowper once, 'the similarity between that pair of generals?' – and much as she had allowed Samuel Teedon to take over the direction of her man's spiritual life.

The reason Teedon had come into the study hat in hand was not out of deference but because it was heavy with money. It was a slight to his dignity to burden him with three golden guineas, four crowns, four half-crowns, ten florins, five shillings, six sixpenny pieces, five fi'pences, three groats, four thruppenny bits, twenty-four pennies, five ha'pennies and four farthings.

'Mr Teedon,' Cowper said, 'there is no need to count the sum. I take your word for it.'

'Ah, but there is, squire,' Teedon said. 'I must be mindful of imputations.'

'Imputations?'

'Of malfeasance. On my part. Relative to the exactitude of the sum. Rendered unto me.' Each pause marked an addition to the ramparts of coin he was building on Cowper's desk.

'Who would impute that to you?'

'Ah!' Teedon said, lifting his head to inspect the ceiling as if the imputers might be up there. 'Ah, there are persons of such ilk, alas.'

'Do you mean Mrs Unwin?'

'Oh no, squire. The madam is always correct in that regard.'

'Lady Hesketh then?'

'Oh heavens, no.'

'Who then?'

'It would be invidious to say, but let me inform you, my highly honourable sir, of the circumstance which I encountered as I was progressing in this direction today. I had paused on the other side of a hedge, momentarily, for a reason which I need not go into, when two persons – let us only say they appertained to her lady-ship's household – came into my audition. They were engaging in *disputatio*, choleric in character, as to whom should say what to whom about a certain matter.'

'Yes?'

'Ah, squire, I can divagate no further, and I have gone so far merely to illustrate what Mammy said to me yesternight. There are, she observed, more voices contending in that house than in any other house in the county.'

'But, Mr Teedon, what do your Mammy and something you heard through a hedge have to do with this heap of money?'

'Heap?' Teedon cried. 'There is, even in this new situation, a wanting of two and a half pence!'

'What new situation?'

'Heavens, squire, can it be that you are *incognito* of it?'

'Of what?'

'Oh Lord,' Teedon cried and cast his eyes again to the ceiling. 'Oh Lord, sir. Well, well. What can I say? I do believe it would be circumspect of me to retire to consider the case. But I am distraught. Mammy will be distracted. And what Eusebius will do is beyond prediction.'

As he spoke, he was disassembling his castle of coins and transferring them into various pockets. Now he put on his beaver and made for the door, where he paused, remembering his function.

'By the by, squire, how is the state of your soul?'

'Very well, thank you,' Cowper said politely.

There was a difficulty in being polite to Teedon, but Cowper was not paying him £30 a year for the sake of politeness. The difficulty arose from the fact that Teedon's mind, like his person, was spider-like, and the webs it spun out of words had a quality of engineering no spider, no known spider, had ever contemplated attempting with silk: strands of each web – and it was impossible to define which strands – were capable of hanging in the space of the whole without touching any other filament of it. Teedon was, moreover, conscious of the mystery of his genius for disconnection and tended to exploit it. In this case, hearing through a hedge Mrs Eaton and Daniel the handsome driver arguing about Miss Hannekin was best left unsaid, and it did not at all connect with Cowper not knowing that Mrs Unwin had reduced his quarterly emolument from £7 and ten shillings to £6 and ten shillings, paid, slightingly, in coin, and tuppence ha'penny short of what it should have been, even in the new situation.

Teedon also inclined not to take offence, especially where

offence was meant. Just now in the kitchen Mrs Unwin, emptying out the tea-caddy in which she kept her small change, said, 'Oh, you're discomposed, sir, are you? Well, for the life of me I cannot think of any other school-master in England that gets paid for transmitting fraudulent notices from the deity, and if you don't like it, you're at liberty to go and do better elsewhere.'

'Oh heavens, madam, I wouldn't dream of such an excursion. Who would the squire write his letters to if not poor Samuel? What would he do without me? He'd be lost. Lost forever. And all for the want of tuppence ha'penny! Could you not find them somewhere, madam?'

But madam could not and would not find them, not least because she was desperately short of pennies and shillings and pounds.

If Teedon provided notices from God the Father in heaven, Hannah Wilson brought messages from the maternal earth. Fatherliness was in Cowper's character. William Unwin and Johnny Johnson were ideal sons; they shared his nature, which was that of a child whose maleness depended on being bereft. Hannah, on the other hand, while being lost and abandoned, was not at all bereft – she was her own mother, perfectly found in herself, and yet, especially when she first arrived, as a neglected, knotty-haired and grubby ten-year-old, she was not the slightest bit motherly or even girlish in manner. She was a tomboy and remained one, even when, it seemed overnight, she became a beautiful young woman.

Before that happened she would fly in for supper from the Market Square, where, as Lady Hesketh said, 'She appears to me to be engaged from morning till night in playing with all the dirty boys of Olney,' and fling herself onto Cowper's lap and kiss him passionately and yet disinterestedly, as if he were an old human dog. She kissed Mrs Unwin in the same way, but as if she were an old human doll. Otherwise she treated them as if they were her grandparents. She was quick-brained, imaginative and a cool judge of character – her eyes were brilliantly grey, like clouds with the sun bright behind them, but some people, Lady Austen for one, withered under their gaze and avoided her. She was also illiterate, and though Cowper taught her to read a little and how to write her name, which intrigued her intensely for some days, as if she had found a key to a secret room, she hesitated only briefly before rejecting book-learning as a way to knowledge – keys and locks interested her as little as did mirrors or her own looks. This straightforwardness, or lack of vanity, when combined with the simultaneous arrival of beauty and sexual passion, made of her an irresistibly attractive young woman, and a troubling one. She troubled all the dirty boys of Olney and she troubled Daniel the driver – although his handsomeness had inured him to the beauty of others, he could not withstand the fire of Hannah's dull-bright eyes. He kissed them one night, and Mrs Eaton, who saw him do it, threatened to tell their mistress, which was what Teedon had overheard behind the necessary hedge. But what Teedon did not hear or see was Mrs Eaton kissing Daniel, which, as far as Daniel was concerned, was not as exciting as kissing Hannah, but stimulating enough and a great deal less troubling, because Hannah had told him she would be damned if she had to be stuck with one stupid man only.

But Daniel, like any dirty boy, Ely draper or Prince Regent, was in Lady Hesketh's eyes only a spark from the male hell. What infernally troubled her was Cowper's perpetual staring at Miss Hannekin's brazen half-apple breasts and, worst of all, how he kissed her. He was a Saintly Creature and if he was now panting like an old human dog in heat that could only be because Mrs Unwin could not get her own hands on him and instead had trained up and set loose the bitch to satisfy her desires at second hand and keep him under her leash and whip him, whip him, whip him in. Harriot had seen this kind of horrid behaviour in Naples, but in Buckinghamshire, really it was perverse beyond belief. And worse than perverse was how Mrs Unwin hallowed Hannah, set her up as as an idol, treated her each coming and going – she was hardly ever in the house – as if it were the passage of Pallas Athena from or to the Eleusinian Mysteries.

'Actually, Johnny,' she later said to her ally, 'there was something more than Greek to that relationship. It was Egyptian. It was deathly. And it made me shiver.'

Had she heard these words, Mrs Unwin would have scoffed. But she recognised, with a pang of regret, her role as vestal, made virgin by age, in the ceremony of his adoration of the bosom of Anna Austen and its replacement by that of Hannah Wilson. The regret, though, did have a slightly guilty tang to it: she had dwindled from robust middle age to frail old age almost as swiftly as Hannah had flared from thin child to full woman, and her physical desire for Cowper had faded away almost as quickly, being unsatisfied its strongest memory, lodged in her own neglected breast like the musty stone in a wrinkled peach. It was true that she did take some faint pleasure, some faintly perverse pleasure, in seeing her desire transferred towards Hannah, but the perversity, the pleasure and the desire were considerably less powerful than those she had experienced observing Lady Austen lying back and being looked at in her bed in the Vicarage – one morning she had crept up the stairs to spy on them, to see what was actually happening. It was these feelings as much as fear of him being taken over that led in the end to Anna being driven away. But – and this made Mrs Unwin almost want to strike Harriot with her fist – none of these sexual urges was acted on, ever, for the simple reason that they could not be. As far as the act of connection was concerned, Cowper had only ever reached the point of being a calf butting its mother for milk. Did Harriot not know that? Had Theadora not told her? But perhaps Thea had not known. His father and his brother John knew, but it would be typical of the Cowpers, so convinced of their own wholeness and uniqueness, not to tell Thea, even if it cost her a lifetime of grieving.

As for the kissing, had Harriot never noticed a simple peculiarity about her cousin that almost any woman who ever kissed him noticed? He kissed not on the cheek but on the mouth. When a simple social kiss was called for, cheek to cheek and just a noise, he pursed his lips and offered them to be kissed directly, experimental as a baby. Often enough in the social flurry, the woman would automatically turn her cheek, but more often than not he would get back what he was offering. For Mrs Unwin the trait was childish and unmasculine, like a receptacle that could not be poured from. But it was also endearing, and Hannah, who noticed such things even more acutely than Mrs Unwin did, had adored it from the time she had first arrived in Olney. She would dash in late for supper, kiss him ritualistically on the mouth, as if he were an inanimate object that could only be made to live by force, then draw back and look at him as if to say, 'Now, that's what it's like to be me,' and then purse her lips out and when he pecked them briefly, she would give him a look that said, 'Oh, dearie me, is that what it's like to be you?' and lay her head on his chest, mockingly sorrowful, before gobbling down her dinner like a savage and running off into the street to torment the dirty boys again.

No wonder Lady Hesketh called her a bitch: it had been painful to be young and not Thea, but now to be old and not Hannah, who was the spirit of the aging Mrs Unwin in the body of a childish whore, was excruciating beyond jealousy.

45

He was alone and looking through the window of a strange room where preparations were being made for his execution. The men in the room were stiff in their movements, certain and monotonous, monotonous and certain. The equipment they were arranging in place included baskets of appropriate sizes in which to put the various parts of his body after it had been taken down from the gibbet, drawn and quartered and the head cut off. But if only that would happen! If only it could be over! But that was the point of the torture: never to be done with, always to be looking in the window, under sentence of death and always waiting, waiting, waiting. He was guilty, guilty as charged, of some unspeakable, nameless crime. Against a child. Against his beloved Hannah. She was standing behind him but he could see her clearly, dressed in rags, her hair knotted, and a long thick viper of excrement was slowly extruding itself from her mouth.

He woke suddenly as if his heart had been wrenched round in his chest, and he forgot everything about the dream except the room and the preparations for his execution and the certainty that he was guilty. Everything in him that was most pure and good and tender was being turned against him, turned somehow into a crime, a crime that he could not fail to commit; and the highest blank wooden wall of it all was that the charge could not be answered, there was no defence – the defence of love was the crime itself.

It was dark. But he had to work. From six o'clock to eleven.

Only then was breakfast justified. He went down through the sleeping house to the study, a ghost with a candle but not mad. Having survived the night, he knew that the voices, now that they were silent, were only delusions. But as he crossed the study to draw the curtains, a voice spoke to him.

'Lo!' it said. 'The bard awakes!'

He dropped the candle, but before he could pick it up, the curtains were swished back and William Hayley, delighted with himself for finding a rhyme, was crying out, 'And lo, the dawn, it breaks!'

'My dear sir,' Cowper said, 'you startled me.'

'But of course, darling, is that not what I am here for? Did I not promise I was coming to carry off not only your Mary, but your castle, your garden and even your River Ouse with its poet – what was William the Conqueror to this?'

'Well, yes,' Cowper said, 'but actually I had forgotten you were here.'

'Only,' Hayley said joyfully, 'only a true genius could do that.'

'No, no, Mr Hayley,' Cowper lied, 'I had forgotten you were here, that is, in the study.'

It came back to him now: they had gone into the study after dinner to drink some more port and look at the extensive revisions he was still doing, well after publication, to the translation of Homer. Hayley had vowed to stay up all night if necessary to finish reading them. Which he had not done. He had instead polished off the bottle of port, read some very disturbing notes describing dreams and voices, purloined an early draft of the last page of *The Task* as a souvenir, thought sorrowfully of his wife, dispelled the sorrow by fantasising what he would like to do with his mistress, and fallen asleep on the rug in front of the fire. There was a rank and yeasty smell in the room.

'Would you take some breakfast?' Cowper went on.

'Breakfast? Wonderful! Do you have eggs?'

'I think so.'

'Let us go and fry some eggs, drink a great quantity of tea, then sally forth immediately to investigate the Ouse. Oh, this is going to be a glorious day. Glorious!'

And it was glorious, up to a point. But they did not sally forth immediately, for when Mrs Unwin came down at nine o'clock, which was late for her, they were still in the kitchen. The servants were going about their business, casting sidelong glances at the visitor, but the novelty of the experience was too much and occasionally one or other of them would cover her mouth with a corner of her apron and run out the open door into the garden to laugh – it was like having a large, rosy, slightly bald bullock in the kitchen, except the girls knew from the way he winked at them that he was not a bullock.

The door was open because it was one of those May days when the air is so fresh, warm and sparkling that doors have to be opened, and if in the afternoon, after the bustle of the morning, the house goes quiet enough for a bee to be heard in an upstairs room, and if then a sudden breeze blows in and slams a door, it only comes to show that full summer has not yet arrived but is on its way, soon. Even Hannah, who was restless in this kind of weather and who normally did the minimum of chores before disappearing off to Olney, took over the job of kneading dough in order to observe Hayley's performance; and when Mrs Unwin came in and had her hand kissed, the two women made small movements with their eyebrows at each other to signal astonishment.

Although Hannah had been at supper the previous night, she still could not quite work him out. Of course he was a fraud and a fool, but he obviously knew it, or at least he knew it as much as a fool could, and yet, far from withering under Hannah's grey-starred gaze, he had at one moment suddenly looked her in the eye and said, 'The mystery of some young beauties is that they have no mystery, and some young blades when they see this are apt to supply the lack, don't you find it so, miss?' It was a remark which Hannah, who had only recently learned to look in mirrors, found oddly unsettling.

He also had an odd way of belittling himself. Here he was now, striding up and down the kitchen, pausing only to take one of Mrs Unwin's breakfast rashers from the frying pan half-raw and nibble at it, the while saying, 'My own verses, such as they are, and they are numerous, are widely read, tremendously so, not least because their subjects are hugely interesting to themselves and to the populace at large. When I was – what age was I? – sixteen I believe – I published an ode on the birth of the Prince of Wales, confounded little man that he is, which is not to say I do not adore his royal person, but, do you see, I started at the top! Ha ha! Yes, and I made damn sure – excuse me, dear Mary – certain sure as damnation that I did not subsequently go much below the top. Mr George Romney, the great artist, who is a friend of my bosom, and Mr Edward Gibbon, the great historian, also a friend but a dull dog and costive, as who would not be after so much prose, almost as interminable as the Roman empire itself, but wonderful – both these gentlemen I have written poems about, or rather poetical essays. But when it comes to quality, alas, the quantity is scant. Why, if my verses were a sheep and the sheep's coat were shorn, I fear the production would not make a golden fleece large enough to load a mouse with.'

'Oh, Mr Hayley, you are too modest,' Cowper said, thinking what a pity Hayley's verse was not as interesting as his dismissal of it.

'Modest?' Hayley said, sucking the rind of the rasher. 'I'm not in the slightest bit modest. On the contrary I'm a proud little mouse because, you see, I know the art. I know it as well as any man in England, because I have worked at it, and I have made it my business to be close to those who have worked at it better than I could. I am acquainted with all the best geniuses in this poetic isle and, if I may say so, when it comes to genius, I declare by the Almighty God who gives it out so sparingly that I esteem yours, Mr Cowper, far above anything that I ever thought myself possessed of in my vainer days. You are a great soul and, more than that, a wonderfully kind man. Am I not right, ladies?'

Hannah burst out laughing, and the servant girls, who had not the faintest idea what a genius was but who had an instinct for the praise of champions, laughed too and clapped their hands with delight, and one of them, a rowdy fat creature, beat the bottom of a tin basin with a spoon.

Mrs Unwin said, 'Hannah, give the man a cup of tea.'

Cowper said, 'I believe Mr Hayley has had too much tea, just as I have had too much praise. Let us go for our walk.'

So they went for their walk, down to the Ouse and into Olney, where Hayley took his new friend — they had been exchanging letters for only a few weeks — into the Royal Oak, which Cowper had never set foot in, for a pint of ale, which was needed, Hayley said, to counteract the saltiness of the otherwise excellent bacon and because, anyway, he sweated so profusely, his fluids required to be replaced frequently.

'And if I do perspire,' he said, not just to Cowper but to the regulars of the Oak, amongst whom was Mr Geary Ball, looking dropsical, 'then what amazes me is that it's only water and not drops of blood that bead my brow, for, gentlemen, I have one advantage over your great, great poet here. He may, and indeed he has, secured an eternal place in history for the town of Olney, but I, William Hayley, I will go down the ages as having surpassed him in one particular.' He paused. 'Well, is no one going to ask me what it is?'

'What is it?' Mr Geary Ball asked.

'Calamity!'

'What's that?'

'Calamity, sir? Disaster. Catastrophe. Though that should be plural. Calamities! I flatter myself in having endured calamities which even Mr Cowper's imagination, powerful and sublime as it is, could never approach, never mind reach.'

But the regulars were not to hear what these calamities were, because Cowper, knowing that there had already been planted more than enough seeds for gossip, whispered to Hayley that they must leave immediately or they would be late for lunch — the pint of ale had become three pints, though Cowper had drunk only a thimble-full of sherry. Outside, however, instead of going straight back to Weston Underwood, they crossed the bridge and inspected the other side of the Ouse. This afforded Hayley ample time to explain his calamitous history, which involved separation from his wife, Eliza Ball, who was insane; the hatred of him by her father, the Dean of Chichester; the birth of a son, Thomas Alphonso, by another lady, a Miss Betts, which was catastrophic since Thomas Alphonso still thought Eliza Ball was his real mother, a tragedy which was worse confounded by the lad being confused at the presence in his father's bed of a charlady, a Miss Cockerell; and finally, as he said, 'to sting me in the heart, Eliza, the hornet, has now announced that she wants to return to the nest. What do you think of that, sir? Isn't that calamities?'

'You poor man,' Cowper said, 'I don't know how you can be so cheerful.'

'I'm cheerful because I'm hungry, and I'm hungry because I'm cheerful, and this instant I am famished.'

They were going up Weston High Street, which at this hour of the afternoon was usually deserted, but now there were women gathered at the gate to the front garden of the Lodge and when they saw Cowper and Hayley coming, they lowered their heads like cattle and shyed away a little. Then the local pastor, the Reverend Samuel Greatheed, came out the front door, took Cowper's hands in his and said, 'Be warned, sir. Mrs Unwin has taken ill. She has had, I think, a stroke against the brain.'

Cowper pushed him aside, ran into the house and up the stairs.

Hayley, who had seen the expression on his friend's face and been reminded of a thief he had seen about to be hanged at Tyburn, went down into the kitchen and ate a loaf of bread. As he tore chunks out of it and stuffed them into his mouth absent-mindedly, he examined his audience, chose the most intelligent-looking girl, who was Hannah, took her aside and spoke to her. Then they went out together. When they returned, it was nearly dark. Hayley, exhausted and sweated dry, climbed the stairs and, because it was unmannerly to intrude, waited on the landing in the gathering gloom.

At last the door opened and a little old man, who was Cowper, came out. When he saw Hayley he shrieked.

'The sound was,' Hayley told Lady Hesketh afterwards, 'like one of his pet hares being torn to pieces by hounds.'

And what he shrieked was, 'There is a wall! There is a wall of separation between me and my God!'

Hayley answered promptly, 'So there is, my friend, but I can inform you I am the most resolute creature on earth for pulling down old walls, and I can declare by the living God I will not leave a stone standing in the wall you speak of.'

Cowper stared at Hayley for more than a minute and in that time he thought a great many thoughts, but chief amongst them was an unanswerable question – if this man is indeed a Samson and will pull down this hellish temple about my ears, how is it he smells of half-raw bacon, sweat and stale ale? The whole thing was a trick, another stroke of irony, and only God could have played it on him.

Nonetheless, very sincerely, cordially and, considering the circumstances, with appropriate formality, he offered Hayley his hand and said simply, 'I believe you.'

46

'Socket, ma'am, is this gentleman's name, Thomas Socket. What age are you, Thomas Socket?'

'Fourteen, sir.'

'And you are familiar with Signor Galvani here?'

'Yes, sir. I turn the wheel for my father.'

'Well then, let us just pretend that I am your father.'

For Cowper, who had been awake all night, the scene was dimly reminiscent of the room he had dreamt was being prepared for his execution. For Mrs Unwin it was even more frightening – there was a man in his shirtsleeves whose name she could not remember except that it had something to do with straw, and there was a tall, very pimpled boy in a butcher's apron, and there was a machine. The machine did not frighten her greatly because it stayed in the one place at the left side of the bed and its cylindrical frosted-glass column was cool to her fevered eyes, but when she looked at anyone in her line of sight, at Mr Cowper now, for instance, who was standing at the end of the bed with the palms of his hands pressed together in front of his mouth, he was divided in half, vertically. It was terribly puzzling, but not as nauseating as seeing everything upside down, which had happened when her sight first came back. She knew clearly what she wanted to say – 'Please be so good as to tell me what on earth you are doing' – but all that came out of her mouth was an over-boiled cauliflower mush of sound.

Hayley, who had been saying, 'I could have, and indeed I would have, sent for my own device at Eartham,' now broke off from his preparations, which involved the adjusting of brass springs, copper wires and a variety of rubber bands and pads, and said to Mrs Unwin, 'Eartham, ma'am, in Sussex, my home you know, is a delightful spot. We will have you down there within the week. Oh yes. Hale and hearty and dancing a jig, if I have my way. Yes indeed! Now where was I? What was I saying? Oh yes.'

But instead of speaking, he set silently to clamping the rubber pads onto the column of glass. What he had been going to say was that, while he had been chewing chunks of bread in the kitchen, he had thought it prudent, before ordering a horseman to gallop off to Eartham, to go out, with Hannah as guide, to inquire if by any chance someone in the neighbourhood would happen to have one of Signor Galvani's electrical machines. That someone did should have astonished Hayley as much as it astonished everybody else, but he was not surprised: he had a feeling for these things; and he rather thought, too, that fate had arranged for the absence of Mr Socket in London – why, if the man had been at home, he might have tried to relegate him to turning the wheel: people with machines of their own were frightfully selfish, even if they were only galvanising a dead frog.

'Thomas, you may give the wheel a gentle turn.'

Thomas turned, the glass drum revolved, the pads were applied and a crackling blue spark leaped between the wires Hayley was holding in his rubber-gloved hands.

'Come here, Mr Cowper, and thrust your finger into the flame. It won't hurt you, sir, I assure you.'

Cowper did as he was told. The current made his legs twitch and he cried out, 'My God!'

'And indeed it might well be all our God,' Hayley said. 'But now, to the business at hand. When I am in position, Mr Cowper, will you kindly take a firm hold of Mrs Unwin's ankles?'

His position was to get astride Mrs Unwin on the bed, and when he was in it, to clamp the rubber pads to her temples. This done, he cried out, 'Now then, Mr Socket, whirl your wheel! Whirl it around like billyo!'

Nine days later, on the first of June, Hayley went home to Eartham.

ALL'S WELL

Weston, June 4th, 1792

Which words I place as conspicuously as possible, and prefix them to my letter, to save you the pain, my friend and brother, of a moment's anxious speculation. Poor Mary proceeds in her amendment still, and improves, I think, even at a swifter rate than when you left her. The stronger she grows, the faster she gathers strength, which is perhaps the natural course of recovery. She walked so well this morning that she told me at my first visit she had entirely forgot her illness; and she spoke so distinctly, and had so much of her usual countenance, that, had it been possible, she would have made me forget it too.

Returned from my walk, blown to tatters — I found two dear things in my study, your letter, and my Mary! She is bravely well, and your beloved epistle does us both good. I also found your kind pencil note in my song book as soon as I came down on the morning of your departure; and Mary was vexed to the heart that the simpletons who watched her supposed her asleep, when she was not; for she learned soon after you were gone that you would have peeped at her, had you known her to be awake. I perhaps might have had a peep too, and therefore was as vexed as she; but if it please God, we shall make ourselves large amends for all lost peeps by and by at Eartham.

W.C.

What he did not say to Hayley was why Mary had been in his study: Hannah had helped her hobble down the stairs because she could not believe he was not in the house, and when Hannah at last convinced her that he had only gone for a walk, she was still dismayed.

47

$\mathcal{M}$ary was amused. Why, she thought, he's trying to bully me.

'It's the Cowper strain in you,' she said.

'Beg pardon?'

'Coming out at last,' she said, but the words were slurred and he could not make them out.

'Right foot, right foot,' he said, 'lift your right foot. Oh, that's excellent.'

She had managed to swing her foot over the threshold and now they set off for yet another walk around the garden.

'Good path,' she said. And it was good: he had ordered in a cart-load of sand to cover the gravel and a roller to flatten the surface so that she would not stumble. Before that, he had remembered seeing an old sedan chair in the Throckmorton's coach-house, and for a few days she had been ceremonially carried around the garden, nodding her head and waving her left hand to the servants like the Pope of Rome. But then he had insisted that she walk, first leaning on his arm, now on her own.

'Look,' she said. 'Shoe loose.'

'Oh, that's good!' he said. 'Now, you sit down here and I will be back *instanter*.'

He lowered her onto a bench and dashed off to the house. Her feet had become so swollen that her own shoes would not fit, and he had immediately suggested that she wear a pair of his, and now the swelling had gone down and the shoes were slipping off. Well, she thought, that's good – the next thing I have to do is cut up my own food and feed myself. That was another of the cruel tests he had set her, but using a knife was difficult because her right hand was almost useless. Also, though she did not tell him this for fear of upsetting him, eating was inexplicably frightening: she simply could not see what was on the right-hand side of the plate.

When he came back and was kneeling, trying to get her feet into a pair of her own shoes, she put out her hand, straightened his chamber-cap and said quite clearly, 'You need a new hat. Write Hayley. Say we will go next week.'

He was looking up at her with such a spaniel-like expression that she felt like saying, 'Are you satisfied now?' But that, she knew, would have been unfair: he was desperately concerned for her welfare, desperately upset by her suffering, desperately afraid that she would die and leave him alone in the world, and he had turned all this desperation towards dragging her off to the God of Eartham, who was a buffoon, and his infernal machine, which was little better than a circus trick. But perhaps it had done her good, and Hayley was amiable and, above all, kind.

So, off they went, along with Johnny Johnson, Sam and Beau the spaniel, who followed the carriage tethered on a long string.

Weston, September 20th, 1792

Dear Lady Hesketh,

I have just now arrived home and hasten to meet your request for a report on our cousin's sojourn at Eartham. I need hardly say that these observations are for your eyes only. Of the house what can I say? It is built next a ruin and is at first I thought large, but for so many visitors, constantly coming and going, it must be considered cramped. It is also rackety and worn out, not very clean either. On this occasion, invited no doubt to impress Mr Cowper, the guests were Mrs Charlotte Smith, the authoress, and Mr George Romney, the artist. She has a great many children, is constantly poor and is writing a book, it is called The Old Manor House *or such like, and in the evening what she had written in the day Mr Hayley would read to the company. Our cousin did it himself one night, with his* sweet low voice, it was very moving to all, except Mr Hayley, as he is jealous of all voices except his own. In the evening they would spend some time in translating from the Italian a play about Satan! Then they would play at Quoits! What can I say? Mr Romney is a melancholic person, in some respects not unlike our cousin, and in each other's company they communed mostly in silence. He did a pastel chalks portrait of him, a likeness to perfection, and one the next day, which was dashed off and made him look uneasy. There then came a Mr James Hurdis, the curate at Burwash, not far off. First he sent a letter that his favourite sister had died. Everyone cried on reading it and he was sent for. Mr Cowper said he reminded him of Mr William Unwin, except for want of vivacity, not suprising at such a sad time. It was a gloomy company, I can tell you, what with Satan and Quoits and Mr Hurdis mourning and Mrs Unwin being dragged around in her chair by Thomas Socket and Mr Hayley's son, Thomas Alphonso. The Socket boy – having attained only fourteen years! – has been employed to teach Thomas Alphonso Greek and Latin! What a strange person Mr Hayley is! Socket also helped to turn the handle every evening on the electrical machine which treated Mrs Unwin. She seemed improved by it and said as much but it is always hard to know with the lady what she intends, she is so obliging but I notice becoming betimes impatient, no doubt due to her incapacity. Our cousin too was cheerful but I know he came to find the place a melancholy wilderness and not least because Mr Hayley is keeping an alliance with the housekeeper, Miss Cockerell, who does not appear in the company but is in his bed. She is the veriest skinflint that the world ever bore. The food which she served up was stale bread, sour beer and lumps of beef roasted but almost raw. You know our cousin and Mrs Unwin like their food cooked almost till it will shake to pieces and are disgusted by blood oozing onto their plates. I cannot hazard if this meanness bears on Mr Hayley's constitution, but he says it cannot bear a fire, and therefore he used to make my poor cousin sit shivering in a great raw Library till he almost got an ague. Here also, because he says he detests Natural Light, he kept the Venetian blinds always drawn, against our cousin's wishes who craves the light always both in his soul and his eyes which are inflamed. I was also shocked to see in transcribing some translations they did of

Milton's Latin and Italian poems some of the bold and forcible language of our dear Bard crossed out and supplemented by some flimsy, tinsel lines of his Brother Poet. All in all, I was never as glad to get out of any place as Eartham, and our cousin I believe was glad too, but seemed content that his companion has had some good out of it. As we departed Mr Hayley said it was too painful to bid adieu under his own roof and he and Thomas Alphonso and Thomas Socket ran through what they call the North Wood in a storm of rain and waited on a height to wave us off. At the sight tears gushed from Mr C's eyes but soon ceased. As cease must I now, from fatigue.

Your humble and obedient servant,
J. Johnson

P.S. I forgot to include here the information that Mr Hayley is by all appearances an <u>Infidel</u>. Our cousin did not seem to mind this or indeed anything else. What can I say?

Hayley was not aware of the existence of this letter when he visited Lady Hesketh at her home in London. The letter had hurt her. She received him coldly, as befitted an Atheist, a suitable candidate for Eternal Damnation. Damnable, too, was his having been to Weston – apart from herself, no one had ever been invited there, or to Olney for that matter. No one. Ever. She had also received another hurtful letter, this time from Cowper, but obviously written at Mrs Unwin's direction. It had instructed her, very politely of course, to stay away from the sick-bed. Yet here now was this Hayley, a common person, telling her not only that he had been to Weston and ministered to the invalid with an Infernal Machine, but that her cousin, who never ever left home, had travelled to Eartham, of all places, and in doing so – most damnable of all the hurts – had bypassed her in London.

But Hayley had saved her from a further hurt, which would have been a stab to the heart. He did not say that Mr Cowper had written a poem to Mrs Unwin – a love poem no less! And years later, when it was published, it took all Lady Hesketh's ingenuity to explain away why her cousin had concealed it from her. It was, it could only have been, forged from the delusions enforced upon him by the steely lady who kept him captive. And, even then, Harriot

could not help feeling that the poem's refrain was a dagger with
which the poet had stabbed her — fourteen times! — in the heart.

> The twentieth year is well-nigh past
> Since first our sky was overcast;
> Ah, would that this might be the last,
>   My Mary!

> Thy spirits have a fainter flow,
> I see thee daily weaker grow —
> 'Twas my distress that brought thee low,
>   My Mary!

> Thy needles, once a shining store,
> For my sake restless heretofore,
> Now rust disused and shine no more,
>   My Mary!

> For though thou gladly wouldst fulfil
> The same kind office for me still,
> Thy sight now seconds not thy will,
>   My Mary!

> But well thou played the housewife's part,
> And all thy threads with magic art
> Have wound themselves about this heart,
>   My Mary!

> Thy indistinct expressions seem
> Like language uttered in a dream,
> Yet me they charm, what'er the theme,
>   My Mary!

> Thy silver locks, once auburn bright,
> Are still more lovely in my sight
> Than golden beams of glorious light,
>   My Mary!

For could I view nor them nor thee,
What sight worth seeing could I see?
The sun would rise in vain for me,
                    My Mary!

Partakers of thy sad decline,
Thy hands their gentle force resign;
Yet, gently pressed, press gently mine,
                    My Mary!

And then I feel that I still hold
A richer store ten thousandfold
Than misers fancy in their gold,
                    My Mary!

Such feebleness of limb thou prov'st,
That now at every step thou mov'st,
Upheld by two; yet still thou lov'st,
                    My Mary!

And still to love, though pressed with ill,
In wintry age to feel no chill,
With me is to be lovely still,
                    My Mary!

But ah! by constant heed I know,
How oft the sadness that I show
Transforms thy smiles to looks of woe,
                    My Mary!

And should my future lot be cast
With much resemblance of the past,
Thy worn-out heart will break at last,
                    My Mary!

48

Of all the voices, the one he feared the most was the Grumbler's. She grumbled about his inability to do anything properly – if he spilled a drop of ink, or let a candle burn down until it smoked, or made a floorboard squeak when he was tiptoeing out of Mary's bedroom after the night's vigil, she grumbled. The others, the Accuser, the Judge, the Director and the Mocker, spoke with men's voices. But the Mocker was the most persistent and detestable. He had begun to speak following William Unwin's death, saying the responsorial madness was only a sulk for notice. But he had become particularly spiteful when, after the visit to Eartham, Mary's health began to disimprove. Before this, the voice had been that of an unpleasant whispering fellow, so much so that Cowper was convinced he was hiding somewhere, perhaps in a cupboard, but after Eartham it became high-pitched, crackling, electric, and it had a being, a form, that of an ancient goblin wearing a tall conical hat and wooden clogs with turned-up toes – the image was clear, though never actually seen.

The Mocker especially liked any upset to Mary's condition that distressed Cowper. He liked the awkward way she threw her right leg when walking, the distortion of the right side of her face, the way Cowper had to go and stand on the landing, heart paper-flapping like a pigeon trapped in a bush, while she was being helped to the commode. Such indignities and mortifications amused the Mocker, but most of all when accompanied by anger. When she called Cowper a simpleton and rapped him on the wrist with her walking-stick because he had spilled down her front the hot tea he was feeding her and Lady Hesketh wept and ran out of the room – that was a scene the Mocker relished.

The Accuser's purpose was the announcement of guilt. On the night of the spilling of the tea, he said, 'Behold, you did this. All that is happening now to her is your doing, your fault, you miscreant.'

The Director, who had a note of mechanical promise in his clanking voice, told him the tasks he was obliged to perform: not to eat for three days, to stand utterly still in the corner of his bedroom for six hours, to utter repeatedly a certain obscene imprecation in archaic French – many things.

The only time the Mocker was absent was when the Judge spoke. But the Judge only occasionally uttered the condemnation in words; he was the meaning in all things, in daytime sensations of imminent collapse, in night-time dreams of execution, of being carried away, of being torn to pieces, of everlasting martyrdom in the fire – many things.

What was happening mentally also manifested itself physically. Constant diarrhoea wasted and shamed him; he was tormented by the urge to tear off his blazing skin, if only he knew where to take hold of it. Worst of all was the crushing headache which, even when it went away – and for a time chewing the bark of the willow was a help – he could sense tightening in his skull. His mind was his body, his body was his mind, there was no separation between them, no way out of their union. Except one.

As well as the voices, he had to contend with Milton. He did once have a happy dream of the poet, who appeared to be two hundred years old, taking his hand and saying, 'Well, you for your part will do well also,' but the edition of the poems that he had committed himself to doing, with illustrations by Fuseli, bulked into a mountain on his shoulders. When he came to what Milton had said about the Atonement –

wherein the just shall dwell,
And after all their tribulations long

See golden days, fruitful of golden deeds,
With joy and love triumphing, and fair truth

– the Accuser told him he would see no golden day, his home was with Satan in Paradise Lost forever, while behind him the Mocker chanted, 'And Fuseli knows it, Fuseli knows it.' So he abandoned Milton and went back to Homer, trying to wrench the English nearer to the Greek and failing. Even the writing of letters failed him. But there was one person to whom he wrote constantly, week after week, day after day, sometimes twice a day.

And now here he was.

'Ah, squire,' Samuel Teedon said, 'to be received in your sleeping chamber, that is a signal honour indeed. May I be so bold as to inquire the reason why, as it were the *ratio rationis*?'

'No, no, not now. Did you receive my letter? Of course you must have, why else would you be here?'

'Oh, sir, I sometimes arrive without being summoned, is that not so?'

'Yes, yes, Mr Teedon, but my letter now, today, have you read it?'

Teedon raised his right index finger and looked at it inquiringly, then cocked his head to one side to listen, and then, as if satisfied with the finger's reply, swiftly took the letter from his pocket and scanned through it, sighing.

'The fire, the fire, again the fire. Everlasting again. And martyrdom as always.'

'Mr Teedon, are you mocking me too?'

'Oh heavens, squire, heaven forfend!'

'What have you to say to me?'

'It is not I who says, Mr C; it is the Lord. I had a notice from Him directly yesternight. It said that there is a light greater than the fires of hell. This light will outshine the fire and latterly, at the hour of judgement, shall extinguish it entirely, and you shall enter into the bosom of Abraham.'

'Extinguish hellfire entirely?'

'Entirely and utterly.'

The Mocker hooted, 'If that's doctrine, what will we do – sleep in the ashes?'

'I hear you, I hear you,' Cowper said angrily.

'Thank the Lord,' Teedon said, 'I am glad to be of service to thee, my dear squire.'

'You have written him seventy-two letters,' the Mocker said. 'It is you who is the servant. Ask for your money back and kick him down the stairs.'

'Your notices,' Cowper said furiously, 'instead of being comforts and reassurances, are really reproaches, biting sarcasms, sharp strokes of irony, in short the deadliest arrows to be found in the quiver of the Almighty.'

'Goodness, squire,' Teedon cried, 'you seem to be upset.'

But at that moment, just as Cowper was making the decision to get rid of him forever, a knock came at the door. He opened it and there was Sam saying anxiously, 'Master, Lady Hesketh has returned.'

Behind Sam loomed a muscular man called Richard Buston, who had by now been living for a month in the Lodge.

'Watch how this is arranged,' the Mocker said. 'This is better than doctrine, entirely and utterly better.'

49

*F*or once the Mocker spoke nothing more than the truth, and he and the other voices grew silent. The house, though it was full of people, was silent too. It was a warm day, overcast, heavy, dull, still. Outside in the street two carriages waited: the horses stood listlessly in the shafts; they had come a long way and were in a lather of sweat.

In the hallway, Dr Francis Willis, seeing Richard Buston, who was his man, coming down the stairs followed by Samuel Teedon, assumed that Teedon was Cowper and offered him his hand, which was taken. Lady Hesketh, who would not have allowed this to happen under normal circumstances, or indeed any circumstances whatsoever, had been distracted by the simultaneous appearance from different doorways of William Hayley and Hannah Wilson. Lady Hesketh had not seen Hannah since the previous morning when she had arrived home after spending the night in a haybarn, at first with Daniel the driver – who had come back early in a fury of sexual frustration, which he had unleashed on Mrs Eaton – and then with an extremely shy and sincere young man called Brewster from Newport Pagnell. There had been a loud and prolonged exchange between Harriot and Hannah, from which Cowper had fled almost immediately, much to Mrs Unwin's disgust. She had warned him about the consequences of Lady Hesketh visiting them again, but while he had heeded the warning, he had also ignored it;

he needed what he called 'a cordial'; and Lady Hesketh, though her own health was failing and though she dreaded the struggle with the Witch of Weston, could supply it; and, anyway, she found it in her heart impossible to refuse him anything he asked.

So here now was Hannah in the hallway, flying her cloak around her shoulders, giving Lady Hesketh a look of fury and departing. It was at this moment, too, that Lady Hesketh saw Hayley making gestures with his mouth, eyes and eyebrows that indicated he wanted to speak to her privately in the study. In the midst of this confusion she became aware that Teedon was bowing over Dr Willis's hand and murmuring to it words which related to the fact that this same hand had very recently been laid upon the divinely appointed, melancholic and irascible person of King George the Third.

What was remarkable about these few seconds of activity was that, apart from Teedon's supplications, everything was conducted in dumb-show. Now, however, it was broken by Lady Hesketh crying out, 'Dr Willis, let go of that man's hand. Go, Teedon, go!'

Dr Willis was not accustomed to being spoken to in these brusque tones. On the other hand, he was well-used to scenes of familial chaos and he did what he always did in such circumstances: unhunched his shoulders, unhooded his eyes and stared unblinkingly at the chief offender, which in this case was Lady Hesketh, like the leathery, burnished and rather malignant tortoise that he was. The stare was famous; it was pure vision, both con- centrated and expanded, so that his entire head seemed to become an eye on a thrust-out neck. In treating the king, Dr Willis had been obliged to lower his gaze a little and to temper his authority with a certain amount of obsequiousness, which sat ill on him and which certainly was not going to come anywhere near sitting on him in his dealings with this lady and her versifying cousin.

Eventually Teedon was expelled, Dr Willis retired to the study with Buston, and Lady Hesketh and Hayley went out into the street for their talk.

There were only two questions Willis needed to put to Buston. First, had the patient taken his medicine over the past month – the answer to which was 'now and then'; secondly, had Buston found it necessary to use the strait waistcoat – he had not.

Buston had long arms and very little neck, and was useful for calming obstreperous patients; he was not entirely lacking in intelligence and he had plenty of experience of madness, but he could not explain why it was that while this patient was obviously mad, he was also quite capable of building a new summerhouse out of old floorboards, of shaving Sam his servant, of visiting the Throckmortons, of taking Mrs Unwin for slow walks and of kissing Miss Hannah Wilson on the mouth, though there were no other intimacies that Buston had been able to discern, which he had made it his business to do for professional reasons, but also because he had fallen for the girl, and when Lady Hesketh had required him to stop Hannah going out at night, he had tried, but it had only ended with him trying to kiss her eyes and getting a smart smack in the chops for his trouble.

What Hayley had to tell Lady Hesketh was that Mrs Unwin had again changed her mind and was not going to cooperate. One of the sweating horses shivered its shoulders. Harriot made a similar movement with hers.

When Dr Willis had finished his tea, Sam was sent to bring Cowper down to the study, but he had locked the bedroom door and would not come out. Lady Hesketh begged him not to embarrass the Cowper name with the royal physician; he agreed instantly, but after twenty minutes the door stayed shut and remained so until Buston burst it open with his unshiverable shoulder.

Meanwhile, Dr Willis went to inspect Mrs Unwin. The drawing-room was stiflingly hot – she felt cold and required a fire to be lit in all weathers.

When he introduced himself she said, 'How do you do?' and offered a limp left hand. He did not need the touch of plushy, satiny skin to tell him congestive heart failure was well-advanced; he had seen that immediately in the blue lips. She was wearing a pair of Mr Cowper's shoes. Lady Hesketh had told him this as if it was a felony, but there was nothing felonious in having swollen feet. Otherwise, he thought, she presents quite well, socially.

He stood for a few minutes, biting the nail of his little finger and making small talk. Whether what Lady Hesketh had said of her, that she was 'a hypocritical Sycorax', was true or not was immaterial; the lady was fully *compos mentis*. Having reached that conclusion, he said abruptly, 'Thank you, madam,' and went back to the study. Sane or not, she had no legal standing, and Lady Hesketh was next of kin – there could be no doubt about the outcome of this consultation.

He had even fewer doubts when Cowper came into the study, with Lady Hesketh holding one arm and Hayley the other. Here was just the kind of melancholic he was familiar with at the asylum in Stamford: skeletal, haggard, harried by incommunicable delusions. Nor, when they were alone, was he surprised by Cowper's reticence: it had been ironed into him since birth and, like many gentlemen lunatics, he would rather burn to a cinder than admit he was on fire. He suffered only 'a passing dejection' and 'an occasional visit from Mr Bluedevil'; he heard no voices but sometimes, as a result of sleeping badly, he was bothered by 'waking dreams'; the attempted suicide was merely 'a regrettable episode'. The only time he became agitated was in relation to Hannah Wilson; he flushed and said any suggestion of impropriety was 'monstrous'. Willis, who believed that what was most strongly denied was most likely to be the truth, and who had rarely been disappointed in this belief, said, 'Ah, Mr Cowper, if our desires were crimes, we men would all be criminals.'

'You lying whore.'

'I beg your pardon,' Willis said indignantly.

'Fuck your own mother,' Cowper said, in reply to an obscene suggestion from the Mocker.

'Ah,' Willis said, 'I see, I see. Well, I have heard enough, let us go into the company.' He was irritated with himself for not realising immediately that the lunatic was speaking to his spectre.

When Willis ushered Cowper into the drawing-room, Hayley jumped to his feet and cried out, 'Christ Almighty!'

There were two reasons for this cry. In the first place Willis had developed over the years a technique of entering a room which involved opening the door suddenly and bursting in bent double, so low that his head almost touched the door-handle. This tactic unnerved those waiting and was therefore advantageous to Willis.

The second reason followed from the first, for Hayley was already unnerved to the point of cracking.

His visit, which had now lasted a month, had begun as a mission of mercy, then rapidly developed into a series of increasingly desperate manoeuvres to avoid the skirmishing between Lady Hesketh and Mrs Unwin. After Harriot's departure to fetch Dr Willis from Lincolnshire, there had followed a day of bitter recriminations from Mrs Unwin directed against Cowper for his supine behaviour in not defending Hannah. That night Hayley had sought solace in a bottle of gin, but there had been so much traffic in and out of Mrs Unwin's bedroom, with voices raised, hers querulous, his lamenting, that he had been kept awake until dawn. Hungover and groggy from lack of sleep, he had then spent an uneasy morning alone with Mrs Unwin in the stuffy drawing-room – they were alone because Cowper was sequestered upstairs with Teedon, and it was uneasy because Mrs Unwin had taken an inexplicable turn against him.

Of course he was conscious of having surrendered his will to the awesome Harriot. She had decided to overlook his infidel tendencies, along with his adultery, his Whiggism, his disrespect for the monarchy, which was superficial, and even, most difficult of all, her own jealousy. The trip to Eartham, bypassing London, still rankled, but not half as much as the subsequent letter from Cowper in which, blithely oblivious as ever – but was he really that ignorant? – he had said, 'Hayley tells me you begin to be jealous of him, lest I should love him more than I love you, and bids me to say that should I do so, you in revenge must love him more than I do.' Love Mr Hayley! That sweating jelly? But all these sins had been set aside on condition that he support her in the battle to save the Saintly Creature from the Siren and her Idol, Miss Hannekin. And Hayley had supported her loyally, but not without attempting covertly to maintain diplomatic relations with Mrs Unwin. These deceptions had annoyed Lady Hesketh, of course, but he had managed, uneasily, to keep in with both sides – until this morning.

In all innocence and truthfully he had said to Mrs Unwin, 'The only person who has grieved my heart as deeply as our darling bard is my wife, Eliza,' to which she had instantly replied, 'My man, Mr

Hayley, is hardly to be compared to your wife.' By lunchtime this had been turned into her saying to Cowper, 'He believes you are madder than Eliza Ball,' and when Hayley said, 'Oh really, I protest, I never said any such thing,' she had added, 'And he thinks you should be packed off to the asylum in Lincoln.' Which, after all, was true.

It was still true as Dr Willis dived through the drawing-room door, right arm fully extended, left arm low to the floor, scooping Cowper onward towards the sofa as if the waters were rising and he were the last animal to be shepherded into the Ark. Never, not even in the company of Eliza and her father, the Dean of Chichester, never had Hayley experienced moments as anguishing as those he had just spent with Mrs Unwin and Lady Hesketh. Very little had been said and that little had been about the weather, the roads to Stamford, Dr Willis's house, 'very elegant', where Lady Hesketh had spent the night, and the supper he had served – 'A rack of lamb,' Mrs Unwin had exclaimed. 'Preparation for the Inquisition, I suppose' – but the silences in between the small talk had made Hayley feel as if he were a wire connecting two Galvani machines, the handles of which were being whirled around by two electrically powered Harpies. It was with a certain sense of relief then that he had sprung to his feet and uttered his 'Christ Almighty!'

'I mean,' he said to Cowper, 'that the mercy of the Lord will be done unto thee, my dear friend, and you will be brought safe out of this present danger, or quagmire, that you are in, not of course by any fault of your own, if I have any say in the matter, whether it be here or any other place where you may wish to go.'

'Which place would that be?' Mrs Unwin asked.

'Will you take some tea or perhaps a glass of sherry?' Lady Hesketh said to Dr Willis.

'Tea, please.'

'Mr Hayley, would you be so good as to tell Cookee—?'

'I should like sherry,' Mrs Unwin said, 'and I believe Mr Cowper would like a little port.'

There was a pause as Cowper made a helpless gesture with his hand.

'Oh good,' Hayley said. 'Port is good. I like port. Any port in a storm, what? What, what. Would you join me, Dr Willis?'

'No, thank you.'

'Quite right, quite right. His Majesty, I believe, suffers from gout,' Hayley added desperately. 'Port is not good for gout, I have heard tell. Is that true, I wonder. I suppose it is. *Ergo* I shall not have any.'

'Go and order the tea,' Lady Hesketh said sharply.

'Fetch the sherry,' Mrs Unwin said to Cowper, and when he made a further helpless gesture, added, 'or do you want me to fetch it myself?'

'I will do it, I will do it,' Lady Hesketh said, and went to order Cookee to make tea and Mrs Eaton to come and serve the sherry, but not to give Mr Hayley tea, sherry, port or anything else for that matter.

In Harriot's absence, which was prolonged because she felt faint and had to sit down in the kitchen, Hayley explained to Dr Willis what he had meant when he said 'if I have any say in the matter'.

'It is, of course, a delicate business, and as such it is taking rather longer than one might have hoped, and yet I flatter myself that I am not entirely without, you know, connections in high places, like indeed yourself, my dear doctor. Ned Thurlow, the Lord Chancellor, for instance, I had breakfast with him. At his residence. In Great Ormond Street. It was quite a manoeuvre to get in there, I can tell you.'

'Mr Hayley is given to manoeuvres,' Mrs Unwin said.

'For which we are most grateful,' Cowper said.

'Thank you, William, thank you, Mary,' Hayley said, looking as though he were about to cry. 'It is, as you know, the most darling project of my spirit.' He gulped and added mournfully, 'My once sanguine spirit.'

'I fail to understand,' Willis said. 'What is the project?'

'He is trying to get my man a royal pension,' Mrs Unwin said.

'It would be, as it were,' Hayley said, 'an act by the monarch of personal thanksgiving to Heaven for the gift of a wonderful and most interesting poet. Perhaps you could have a word with His Majesty the next time you see him.'

Willis, who had a horror of being used for any purpose, hissed, 'That is out of the question.'

'But I have got the approval of the Prime Minister,' Hayley said. 'The Earl Spencer told me so himself not two months since. Lord Kenyon and Mr William Huskisson worked on Mr Pitt on my behalf and now all that is needed apparently is the King's assent, his seal on the papers. Three hundred pounds a year would be a great addition to Mr Cowper's economy. Could you not see your way to a whisper into His Majesty's ear?'

For the first time Dr Willis felt alarm: £300 a year was a wretched amount of money. Lady Hesketh had told him she had only £800 a year, but he had assumed that because Cowper was the most famous poet in Britain he would be well able to afford the fees at Stamford. Now he looked around him and all at once saw that these people and their furnishings were worn, mean, genteely poor.

'No,' he said. 'Ask the Lord Chancellor.'

'That would mean stealing another book,' Mrs Unwin said.

Hayley, who had been standing up since Dr Willis entered the room, now sat down heavily.

'No, no,' Cowper said. But behind his back he heard the Mocker snickering.

'I merely borrowed the book,' Hayley was saying. 'I admit it was not quite a straightforward procedure, but the Lord Chancellor's daughter was very happy to lend me her copy of Mr Cowper's poems and when I wrote my verses therein, on the fly-leaf, for the Chancellor to see, to enourage him to take up the friendship of his youth with his old companion, how that could be regarded as theft, I don't know, since the book therefore, for that purpose, had to be given back. Is that not patently obvious?'

At this point Lady Hesketh returned with Mrs Eaton and Cookee bearing trays of drinkables. Dr Willis changed his mind and had a glass of port with a drop of brandy added, his stomach being, as he said, a little wobbly, though, actually, it was his head that was reeling, not least because a new dispute had now broken out. Mrs Unwin wanted not only sherry but also tea, and Lady Hesketh was saying she was agreeable to one or the other, but both together was unconscionable. A cold fury suddenly overcame Dr Willis's mental nausea.

'Excuse me,' he said. 'Excuse me.' Everyone turned towards him.

He glared at them violently one by one and they fell silent. Within a matter of only a few minutes he had sorted out who was going to drink what and had expelled from the room Mrs Eaton, Cookee and, though Lady Hesketh protested, Mr Hayley.

'Now,' he said, 'the business for which I have come here. The matter is, I find, plain, and the course of action I propose to take is straightforward. For a certain period of time, to be decided by me, Mr Cowper will—'

'Speak away,' Mrs Unwin interrupted. 'But I warn you, I will not be bullied. Nor will Mr Cowper.'

Three hours later Dr Willis, more furious than ever, slank into his carriage and returned to his asylum in a cloud of dust. The decisive moment had come with Mrs Unwin's declaration that, 'If the Angel Gabriel himself were to persuade me to let him go, I would not comply.' When it came down to it, Willis reflected, Lady Hesketh had seized the trumpet but she had lacked the will to blow the decisive blast. And moreover, although Mr Cowper was undoubtedly mad, he knew what he wanted.

50

There were times when Hayley could talk sense, but since they required the coincidence of his having both a crushing hangover and a clear avenue of escape from trouble, such times were infrequent. On this blindingly sunny morning there was no doubt about the hangover. One hand was pressed to the side of his throbbing head, the other was clamped over his mouth in a desperate effort to quell the queasiness brought on by the after-effects of having consumed half a bottle of gin and an entire bottle of brandy the previous night. Nor had the walk from Weston to Olney done anything to alleviate his condition. All that dizzying mile he had had to listen to Lady Hesketh complaining about the evils of the Enchantress. And yet the avenue of escape was open: the post-carriage had arrived in the market square; soon he would be on the high road to London; and he was determined never to return, even if that meant never seeing his beloved Cowper again. This saddened him, but it also lubricated his elation – he was aware that the most he could know of happiness had to be emulsified by misery, loss and general calamity.

But now, all of a sudden, hangover, escape and elation conflated themselves into a sudden outburst of insight. Removing his hand from his mouth and grasping Harriot firmly by the arm, he said, 'Oh, body of Christ, woman, of course she's a witch and an enchantress and she may well be the devil's daughter for all I know, but you have to realise that the magic lies not so much in any qualities of the lady as in the very tender heart and fancy of the enchanted one.'

In freeing her arm from Hayley's grasp, Lady Hesketh almost broke his wrist. Without saying goodbye, she stormed, slowly, back to Weston. It was impossible to credit that what he had said could be true, so she did not credit it. She thought, instead, of her beloved cousin demeaned, insulted, driven to madness by Mrs Unwin and her whore, Hannah; about how unfair it was that she had to run her household and pay her bills, and about who would have control of the royal pension when, or if, it came in – it had been extraordinarily vulgar of Dr Willis to have raised the question of paying his fees right in the middle of the discussion of William's treatment, and he had also been terribly cruel to her. All he needed, he had said, was her signature on the papers for committal and her cousin would go where his broken mind could be mended, and if that required the strait waistcoat, well, was Mr Cowper a greater man than the king that he should avoid it? But she would not, she simply could not inflict such indignity on the only man she loved in the world, especially after he had looked at her and said, 'If you do this, Harriot, I shall never forgive you.'

By the time she arrived back at the Lodge, Lady Hesketh had decided two things. First, she needed help, and now that he had taken Holy Orders, Johnny Johnson would supply it, permanently, as William's *cicerone*. Secondly, Mrs Unwin would, one way or another, have to be separated from her cousin, also permanently. Oh, if only she would die ...

51

$\mathcal{I}$t was hot and Mary had a summer cold. For days she had been snuffling and snivelling – disgustingly, in Lady Hesketh's opinion – and saying it was all Cowper's fault: he had let the drawing-room fire dwindle into ashes and she had caught a chill and he did not care. She also insisted on him feeding her regularly with highly salted beef tea, but Cookee had disappeared for a morning's gossip with the Throckmortons' cook-general and the saucepan had boiled dry, filling the house with the death-stink of burnt bones. When Cookee came back, Hannah had called her 'a fat bag of cabbage' and Mary had laughed delightedly and said she was 'a clever girl'. Even Johnson, who thought everyone was as good as himself, had realised, because Lady Hesketh explained it to him, that this remark was intended to provoke a breach of the peace, so he had been glad to be sent off to Matishall, in Norfolk, to see if Mrs Anne Bodham would welcome a visit from her cousin of, in Harriot's diplomatic wording, 'some little duration'.

Now, when Mary saw Lady Hesketh looking at her contempt-uously, she shook her head and extended her neck like an indignant hen.

'I thought your cold made you weak,' Lady Hesketh said.

'And so it does.'

'Well, madam, I should fancy that keeping your head so extremely high must be painful to you.'

'Oh, Harriot,' Cowper said, 'she cannot do otherwise with her cold.'

'Well, bless me, that is very extraordinary. It must require a deal of strength to sit in that manner, and 'tis certainly an uncommon effect of a cold.'

Mary gave another proud twitch to her head, and all that long day, whenever she caught Lady Hesketh's eye, she twitched it again.

All this prevented Lady Hesketh from raising the subject of an unpleasant communication she had received that morning. It was a reply to an almost ingratiatingly polite note she had written to Mrs Susanna Powley, inviting her to come and take Mrs Unwin away with her to Huntingdon. But Susanna, who had not seen her mother since the vanquishing of Lady Austen, had now replied that, while she could not possibly respond to such an impertinent question from a total stranger, the response, were she able to give it, would be decidedly in the negative.

When Lady Hesketh showed this missive to Cowper, he went up to his bedroom, where these days he spent much of the time, in order, he said, 'to be out of hearing of the many disagreeable things Mary says to me'. The poor man was tormented; it was heart-rending.

But now it was tea-time. Cookee had come in, banged down the tray and barrelled off back to the kitchen. The drawing-room was steamingly hot and the hot-water urn was steaming too as Cowper ladled tea-leaves out of the caddy into the pot.

'Oh,' Lady Hesketh exclaimed, 'what a beautiful teapot!'

'What?' Mary asked.

'I said, what a beautiful teapot.'

'What teapot?'

'This one,' Cowper said. 'It's the new one.'

'That isn't my teapot. Where's my teapot?'

'It's the new one, Mary. Don't you remember, the old one was leaking and Johnny took it to be repaired.'

'This isn't repaired. This is a new one.'

'That is what William just said, madam.'

'Where's my teapot?'

'Mary, I told you, Johnny exchanged it for this new one.'

'He what?'

'He exchanged it.'

'And I must say,' Lady Hesketh said, 'he did the thing handsomely. I think I never saw in my life a handsomer or a more elegant thing of the kind.'

'Is it silver?'

'Oh, yes,' Cowper said, 'pure silver.'

Mary suddenly roared, 'But is it *solid*?'

'Oh, absolutely,' Cowper said.

'But is it *real* solid silver? Mine was silver.'

'Indeed, madam, I do not know,' Lady Hesketh said. 'Plated things look sometimes very handsome, and 'tis so large one might almost suppose it is not silver, only Johnny is the last person on earth who would take a silver pot and return a plated. That is,' and here Lady Hesketh paused, 'unless you had ordered him to do so.'

'What! Me ordered him? What are you implying? What? Is it plate or is it not?'

'No, no, no, Mary,' Cowper said, turning over the teapot to show her its bottom and spilling the tea-leaves on the rug. 'Look, here is the hallmark, it is silver, solid silver, very plainly.'

'You're sure of that?'

'Absolutely.'

'Very well,' Mary conceded.

'And,' said Lady Hesketh, seeing a further opening, 'it has the Cowper crest engraved there on the front. Now who would go to the trouble of engraving a teapot if it were only plated?'

'What crest did she say?' Mary barked.

'Oh, Harriot,' Cowper said and sat down on the sofa.

'I said,' Mary said, 'what crest did this lady say?'

'I said,' Lady Hesketh said, 'the Cowper crest. Cannot you see it, madam?'

'This is my teapot, and my teapot should have the Unwin crest.'

'What does my cousin have to do with the Unwin crest?' Lady Hesketh said.

'Nothing that you would know of,' Mary said, 'but that other pot was mine.'

'Oh, our kind Johnny never thought of that I *dear* say' – Lady

Hesketh had a way of saying 'I *dear* say' which she knew was particularly galling. Cowper knew it too.

'Pho! Pho!' he said to Mary. 'What do crests signify between you and me?'

'Well,' she said after a long pause, 'well, I'm glad Mr Johnson has put your crest on my pot. I'm very glad, my man, very glad.'

The tea was then drunk. Later supper was served. By then the sun was going down. The evening grew cool and fresh, and the air was filled with pipistrelles darting soundlessly between the shadowy trees and the darkening blue sky. Hannah Wilson, who had been told as a child, and still half-believed, that bats could get tangled in a girl's hair, stole through the front door, tiptoed up the stairs, took a blanket from her bed and crept out the back door to spend the night with the sincere and shy young Brewster in a cornfield near the river under the drifts of cold silver stars. Brewster was a virgin, and though she knew very well, being a practical young woman, that he was not a suitable person for this night's adventure, she had dreamed of kissing him and of allowing him to touch again her pubic bone with the tip of his second finger, and when she had woken, she had been filled with such a feeling of longing and passionate joy that she had decided that the time had come at last to say goodbye to her own virginity.

Cowper, standing at the window, glimpsed her as she flitted through the garden. Behind him in the stifling room Mary was saying yet again what she had been saying at intervals all evening, 'I'm glad your crest is on my teapot. Very glad, my man, very glad.'

'But,' as Lady Hesketh told Johnny on his return from Norfolk, 'I gathered from her tone of voice that she was *not glad at all.*'

52

'Oh William,' Mary said, 'you have the melancholy just as you have the insomnia. Both play as many tricks on your understanding as you play on the understanding of all these others.'

It was almost midnight on Saturday. The following Tuesday they would leave Weston. He was sitting at the left side of Mary's bed, the better to hold her good hand, as he had done every night since her stroke. It was during these hours that they had their most intimate conversations. What she had resented most about Lady Austen and Lady Hesketh was that she could not end the day by talking about them freely. It had annoyed her not to have been able to deal with those entanglements as she had done with an awkward piece of verse, but to have thus analysed Anna and Harriot would have been a weakness of jealousy, which he had always played on to make people love him exclusively – it was the child in him, the demoniacally innocent child. Eventually it had driven Lady Austen away with only a lock of his hair to show for her devotion. And now Lady Hesketh had left too, and all she had in her bosom was a broken heart.

'Let us not speak of Harriot,' he said. 'Oblige me instead by unpacking what you mean by my tricks.'

'Well, as for the insomnia, I can say that you often slept much of the night, only that the sleep being frequently broken, you thought you were all the time awake. So that was a trick, a cruel trick of the mind.'

'Yes, that is probably the case, and it was certainly so when I tried those Valerian drops. I slept and yet I seemed always to be awake. But the melancholy, is that also a trick?'

She laughed. 'Do you deny it, my dear? Do you deny that these last months when you would not see your Harriot – remember when you ran away and hid in the summerhouse? – do you deny that that was a piece of trickery, a manoeuvre?'

He stared at her. In the garden a pair of bull-frogs were croaking at each other.

'Well?' Mary said.

'Perhaps it was a manoeuvre. I could greatly wish it was.'

'Oh, my man, you are not half as melancholy as you sometimes make yourself out to be.'

Mary was triumphant and yet wistful, so much so that she regretted, almost, letting Lady Hesketh go without saying goodbye to her. But rancour was truer. And besides Harriot had had her victory too, though it was hard to imagine what satisfaction she could have got from driving them out of Weston. They had fought for control of the Lodge as if it were a kingdom, and now, after a nine-year battle, no one was to rule it; they were all fleeing, never to meet again.

They went on talking until she was exhausted, and when he stood up to go off to his own room, he was so grateful that he said, 'You know, Mary, it is in you I live and have my being, far more than in the God that gave it me,' and he kissed her hand.

What Mary did not know was that he had said the same thing to Harriot.

It had happened the day he ran and hid in the summerhouse. Harriot had followed him and they had had, at last, a decisive conversation. To her, the purpose of it was simple and had been so for months: to get him to agree to unburden himself of Mrs Unwin.

But she had forgotten a conversation some weeks earlier about the way this was to be done.

'I don't suppose,' she had said, 'you would come and live with me.'

'In London?'

'It would delight me beyond measure if you would, and yet the town is such a bustle and the gaiety of my part of it, around New Norfolk Street, is so great that I don't suppose you could bear it.'

She supposed rightly. But what she failed to understand was that making his suppositions for him sounded like excuses not to have him live with her, which unconsciously they were, which in turn made him feel rejected, unworthy of being seen in London. That she did not attempt to persuade him persuaded him that she could not be adequately trained to require of him the obedience necessary to force him to do what he wanted to do, which was to go on by staying in the same place, as it were regardless, wherever that might be. Because she could not follow this reasoning, he concluded, finally, that Harriot was stupid.

'New Norfolk Street being out of the question then,' she had said, 'what about old Norfolk? You would have the society of your cousins there, the Bodhams and the Balls, and I could visit you, oh, with a tenfold more pleasure than I have in this awful place. Yes, it would be like a resurrection of the dead!'

Getting him out of Weston and into Norfolk had become an obsession with her. That move, with or without the death of the Witch, but preferably with, would see him sane again. Had he not told her how deeply he had come to despise the Lodge (where that unmentionable act with the cord of the dressing-gown had occurred)? And was not Johnny Johnson, his devoted cousin, ready to take him into Norfolk?

'But, Harriot,' he said in the summerhouse, 'Mrs Bodham seems, while I won't say alarmed, to wonder at the prospect of two invalids descending upon her.'

'God bless my soul!' Lady Hesketh said, not realising the chord she was striking. 'I do wish you would put the idea of two-ness out of your mind. It is your one-ness I am concerned with.'

There then followed the old tirade, and it only ended when he said at last that he would not go anywhere without Mary, that his life and being were in her 'far more than in Him from whom I received that being'.

Lady Hesketh fell silent. After a long pause she said, 'What power that woman possesses that she has made of you a blasphemer!'

That moment, though it did not stop her trying to get him into Norfolk, marked the beginning of the breaking of her heart. That moment, too, was Mary's triumph. But he never told her about it. It was enough to have done it.

53

There was a sudden crash as if the house had been struck by a huge hammer. Johnson leaped to his feet and cried out, 'Good God, what's that? Mr Cowper, did you not hear that terrible noise?'

'I heard it.'

'But what could it be? What could it mean?'

'I know what it means,' he said calmly. He was about to add, 'Sorrow is like the deaf adder; it hears not the voice of the charmer, charm he never so wisely,' but he stopped himself because Johnson took down in his notebook everything he said and reported it back to Harriot.

Anyway, he was by now used to thunderous noises in his head; they were cruel tricks played by his tormentors, and sometimes he managed not to give them the satisfaction of being frightened. Nor did the eventual explanation impress him: Dunham Lodge was a rambling hotch-potch of a house, and an ill-seasoned roof-beam had suddenly split and cracked along its massive length. When he climbed the ladder and was shown the damage, he said only, 'Yes, this too was waiting for me.'

Sometimes, however, he forgot that Johnson was a spy and spoke to him as if he were the Prodigal Son, albeit a prodigal guiltless of sowing wild oats. One night he had stood up and said to him furiously, 'No, no, I shall go and see to her myself.' He was angry because he had almost said, 'Go up and see how your mother is.'

She had been very ill then and so, inevitably, had he – he trailed after her, his body a shadow of hers. And yet she had got a little better after Susanna's visit, either because Susanna had come or gone; it was hard to say which.

The thing was Johnson's doing. Without consultation he had summoned the Powleys to Dunham, and he was mystified, on announcing their arrival, that a dying mother should have such an unnatural antipathy to seeing her only daughter – Mary would not allow them into her bedroom. Cowper, too, though he greeted the couple civilly enough, when asked how he was only replied with a mournful groan, then went upstairs to sit with the invalid.

'Well,' Susanna said at supper, 'Norfolk has improved his temper.'

'Oh,' said Johnson, 'I am so glad you can see that too. Our excursions have, I believe, almost wholly restored his former spirits.'

Susanna looked at her husband, but he, as he often did, stared straight ahead into a distance far beyond wherever it was he was.

'Excursions, sir?'

Twenty minutes later, Susanna said, 'Mr Johnson, you may desist.'

'Desist?'

'Cease. Halt. Stop. Write no more.'

Johnson had been eager to tell the Powleys everything that had happened in the last eight months and, despite some confusion, which required calculations with a pencil on the back of an envelope, was soon well on the way to clarity. Depart Weston July 28th 1795, one night at St Neot's, one at Barton Mills, three weeks at North Tuddenham, one day at Mattishall, then seven weeks in Mundesley – a house rented from a German apothecary, Herr Kalliere, 'a most curious gentleman' – including a visit to Happisburgh, where Mr Cowper ate an enormous meal of beans, very old bacon and, Johnny said, 'the worst apple pie I ever saw'. It was at this point that Susanna stopped the recital and never heard how, by way of Cromer, Holt and East Dereham, the happy party had arrived at Dunham.

'I believe we shall retire now,' Susanna said. 'Are the beds clean?'

The next morning Mary saw her daughter. The two women

spoke as if they had never not spoken, the subject of money was not raised and soon Mary wandered off into a confused memory of meeting Samuel Richardson and the plot of his novel *Clarissa*. Then Susanna read aloud from the Book of Job and, to her mother's mild surprise, Cowper did not leave the room.

Every morning for the remainder of her visit, Susanna read Mary a chapter from the Bible and he stayed to listen, but he did not take any notice of what he heard; it was all literally true, of course, but no longer very interesting.

'In fact,' he said to Mary the day the Powleys departed, 'given a choice between the Old Testament and *Clarissa*, I think I rather prefer the latter. Shall we go on with our reading?'

He had never cared much for fiction – he could not see the point of either the comedy or the tragedy of social life, which partly explained why he had so many tragi-comic friends – but now his nights were given over to the novel. 'So anxious is he for our evening lecture,' Johnson wrote to Lady Hesketh, 'that before the twilight is over he begins to fidget around the room, and when he thinks I don't observe him, he <u>slies</u> to the windows and lets down one of the curtains – this is a signal for me to ring for the candles – after which I go and help him let down the other curtains, and before we have finished, the candles appear, and our maidens enter with their work-bags.'

Susanna had parted from her mother for the last time undramatically – she dealt with goodbyes in exactly the same way she dealt with her meals: she bolted them – but when she got back to Huntingdon and went past the old rectory, she wept bitterly.

Now it was September. Cowper stood at the window, listening to Mary's laboured breathing. She slept much of the time and otherwise sat in her chair nodding off by the fire. Occasionally, leaning heavily on her stick and clutching his arm, she would shuffle out to look at the view. Dunham Lodge was one of the highest houses in Norfolk and from the garden miles of flat country could be seen stretched out beneath huge skies. But even on the mildest days there was a cold breeze from the sea and soon she would have to go back indoors. In Weston any such discomfort had been cause for complaint, but she had been fighting then, and now all the fight had gone out of her and she was mild-mannered, weak-willed, forgetful. The forgetfulness, though, made her sometimes plaintive.

'Hannekin, Hannekin,' she would call out. 'Where's my Hannekin?'

'Hannah is in Norwich, Mary. She's apprenticed there, to a milliner.'

'But I want my darling. Where did you say?'

Then he would read out again the letter Hannah had had written for her by a scrivener. It was a stilted thing, but the signature displayed the flourish of her personality and the sight of it made Mary cry.

'She got her way, she got her way at last,' she would say, and she meant Lady Hesketh, who had arranged the apprenticeship. It was the sensible thing to do – Hannah needed a trade for her future and could not keep dragging around the country with them. Lady Hesketh had also sent Sam back to his wife. That, too, was sensible – he was too old for this existence. In his place they had Peggy Perowne.

'Oh,' she said to Johnson, 'if you could but have seen me and Mr Cowper sheeting the old lady's bed, how nicely he spread the sheets for her.' But that was when she had first arrived and she soon got tired of the many tasks involved in minding a woman who had suffered three strokes.

It was a starless night but a small moon glowed through high thin cloud and he could see, two or three miles off, the faint speck of the flame of a torch – some traveller was walking along the road out of East Dereham, which, at least in this dry September weather, was passable. The roads in Norfolk were little better than tracks, and if this fellow, whoever he was, had any distance to go, he was likely to fall into a pothole and break a leg – one could be dead for days in this wilderness and nobody would know. Why had they ever left Weston? In the Lodge he had lived a life of infinite despair, and yet to have passed the little time that remained to him there was the desire of his heart – or that was what he had said to Harriot in one of the very few replies he had sent to her many letters. He had replied because, for once, he had to make it plain to her that she was to blame for sending them into this wasteland.

All his animals were dead, except Beau, and he was so arthritic he could hardly walk. The hares had died one after the other and he had buried them in the garden. He had torn them out of their natural life and killed them with unnatural kindness. And the last thing he had done at Weston, another murder, was to open the linnet's cage and watch it fly away into the killing world.

No, that was not the last thing. After freeing the bird, he had gone up to his room and drained the laudanum bottle. He did so because the tormentors were promising to drag him out of the carriage and tear him to pieces in front of Orchardside. But on the outskirts of the town he had interrupted Johnson's chattering to ask him to pull down the blind and, thanks to the opiate, they had rattled safely past the house and on into rich, sunlit country as if in a pleasant dream.

The problem with laudanum was what came after it. Fighting the tormentors required all his strength, the best of which was a heroically passive mental valour, and the strangeness he felt after the drug wore off was a physical thing – why, he thought, I might kill myself for a mere bodily reason, out of absentmindedness. He still took a draught occasionally, as a treat, to spite them, but he kept the bottle a secret from Mr Johnson.

In the distance he saw that the traveller had stopped. Now there were other lights. Oh, it was probably a band of gypsies setting up camp for the night. Soon there would be a fire.

He went downstairs and said, 'Mr Johnson, the winter is coming on. It must not find Mrs Unwin in this place.'

54

'Is there life above-stairs?' Milly, the servant girl, who was sixteen and, as she said herself, 'only small', was startled by the question, but she went up and in a minute returned to say Mrs Unwin was still alive. He nodded and went on reading his novel.

In more than six weeks this was the first time the gentleman had spoken to her, although once when she was making his bed he had shouted, 'Go away, you devils!' and once she had heard him sobbing while his old dog was being buried in the garden.

Going up the stairs, she had felt a kind of dizzy trepidation of opening the door and finding the old lady dead, and yet, if she had come down and told him that news, she had the feeling that he would have continued reading his book anyway.

They had left Dunham Lodge in September and returned to Mundesley because, Mary said, 'I yearn to see the sea,' but her eyesight was gone and the journey had been too much for her, so she had retired to bed and said no more.

The odd thing was that while the horror of her dying deepened, he had also found himself increasingly taken up with revising the Homer translation. 'Never in all my born days,' he told Johnson, 'did I see what it ought to have been, and how, and *how only*, Homer can be properly translated.' But that new industriousness had not survived the removal to East Dereham. Then Beau died, and after that he had closed down his mind. His thinking was as clear as the print in the book on his lap, though he could not have said what the sentences meant, and when he asked, 'Is there life above-stairs?' he was simply curious, as if inquiring about the state of the weather. He had not intended to frighten poor Milly, but there were times when fright carried less than its own weight, when the young had to understand that their fear was less important than another person's dying.

'Milly,' he said, and the girl jumped up from the fire, which she was adding coals to, stuffed a loose lock of hair back beneath her mob-cap and stood before him with her hands pressed together in front of her. 'Would you be so good as to fetch down for me the second book, the blue one, there, on the top shelf?'

When she brought him the book, he handed her his hand-kerchief and said, 'There is a smut on your forehead.'

Milly looked in the mirror, spat on the handkerchief, rubbed away the mark, handed it back to him and left the room, even more frightened than before.

He opened *The Task*. 'Meditation here may think down hours to moments' – that was the line he had been thinking of. He turned the pages idly and found a piece about dancing cows. He had once seen a herd of them gambolling at high noon in summer, uncouth in their efforts but resolved to give way to an ecstasy too big to be suppressed. It was an image of comic bliss in nature, and he had wished then for all beings who were capable of pleasure to be pleased, and for those who were not, the comfort of a reasonable joy. But cruelty was always being done to animals, particularly to those creatures – birds, hares, foxes, deer – who were hunted down and killed. Even for a good reason he could not bear brutality – the thought of the inoculation against the smallpox, for instance, though the piercing of the needle saved lives, was insupportable. And what was insupportable was wrong. The idea was foolish, and yet he had long held to it. In a way it had decided his life. Well, if he had lost the belief that an innocent form of life had existed before cruelty, he had also exhausted the certainty that there was no afterwards to it, that the garden of Eden was a scene of harmless sport but sin had marred it all. The earth still groaned beneath the burden of the war waged by desirous knowledge against defenceless innocence, but now instead of being torn in the battle between them, he had learned to remember that the loss of those he loved was the condition on which he himself lived, which was the general experience, and that the price paid for love is grief.

He returned the book to its place on the shelf. It would not do to let Johnson see that he had been reading it. Then he went upstairs and sat with Mary until supper. When the doctor said, 'Nothing will happen tonight,' he went to bed and slept.

In the morning death was in her face. She began to take long gasping breaths with greater intervals between each one. Her distress made his bones tremble, but not visibly. At half past twelve he went down to the study and read the nameless novel. At one o'clock she died.

People came and went.

Then Johnson, who had decided that dusk was better than daylight for such a tremendous sight, came into the study and said, 'Mrs Unwin is laid forth, Mr Cowper. Would you like to look at her?'

She was small in the newly made bed. After peeking at her for a few seconds, with one hand holding back the curtain, he bore himself away, stopped, clasped his hands together, threw them up violently and cried out, 'Oh God, was it for this?'

Then for six days he sat in the study, as if arrested. And for six nights he went up to bed and thought of her laid out in the next room in an embalmed stillness.

Two days before Christmas, when darkness had fallen, the undertakers came, without announcement, and as quietly as possible carried the coffin down the stairs and out of the house. It was better, Johnson thought, that Mr Cowper did not know about the funeral. But he did know.

It was a pitch-black night and so windy that many of the lanterns and torches at the graveside were blown out. No one saw him watching from the shadows – except Hannah Wilson. She came to him among the tombstones, put her arms around his neck tightly, enclosing him in her black cloak, kissed him on the mouth for a long time and then went back to the graveside – she had not spoken a word to him.

As the first clods of earth were shovelled into the hole, he turned away, and by the time Johnson came back he was sitting in the study reading the novel. It seemed as if he had forgotten Mrs Unwin. Certainly he never spoke her name again.

55

They had driven urgently to London, to one of its abandoned places, where decay obtained, to a street stopped at the end by a tall gaunt building with many long windows. They had gone in and climbed the stairs and now were standing outside a glossy black door.

'Mr Johnson,' he said, 'why have you brought me here?'

Johnson opened the door and ushered him in to a large room, uncarpeted, bare of furniture, windowless.

'Mr Johnson,' he said again, 'why have you brought me here?' But when he turned round, Johnson was closing the door and locking it. Then his footsteps were clipping down the stairs, the front door slammed and the carriage horses were clopping out of the street.

He opened his eyes. The candle he had been reading by was still tall, and that meant the night had only just begun.

Why had Johnson brought him to London and abandoned him there? Because he was gaoler, spy, torturer, liar, conspirator, the cruellest being in the universe and, worst of all, a general nuisance. Cowper chuckled. And yet Johnny minded and cared for him; it was like being looked after by a small bird, flitting around the room, batting its wings to move a boulder.

A terrible thought struck him – had Peggy been there too? The journey to London had been wind-swift, but she might have concealed herself somewhere, perhaps in the dog-box underneath the carriage, and then followed them up the stairs to witness his abandonment.

Downstairs Johnson opened his *Pro et Contra* notebook, where he was recording Cowper's daily life, wrote the date, March 19th, 1799, and stopped. Nothing remarkable had happened during the day. As usual Cowper had sat in the study, walked up and down in the garden, and in the evening drunk a bottle of port. He had eaten very little of the dish of figs and sago that Lady Hesketh believed would make him sweat, which was a cure for lunacy. She had made other suggestions for his diet, all troublesome. Peaches, for instance, were not obtainable in March, and as for three pints of ass's milk per day, there was no call for that commodity in Dereham at any time of the year. The hot baths she prescribed had certainly been good for perspiration, but the heating of all that water and the carrying of it upstairs had taxed the servants' patience mightily. On the other hand, the baths had been less distressing than the emetics – the poor man was positively obsessed with the state of his insides. But how brave he had been to sit at his desk revising Homer while vomiting into a basin. Poetry and puking were hardly ideal companions, but he engaged in this practice only once a week, whereas there had been a time when he devoted a part of every morning to scourging his naked back with a besom of birch twigs, like a medieval penitent, to cure his lumbago. But between sago and lumbago there was no easing him.

Johnson sighed and turned to the household accounts. The Earl Spencer had finally secured Mr Cowper's pension, but £300 a year did not go very far when the dastardly French were threatening to destroy the world. Was Norfolk safe? Lady Hesketh had thought not and urged them to move farther inland, but that was before Admiral Nelson and what she called 'the dear Arabs' had made mincemeat of Napoleon's navy. Nonetheless Mr Cowper seemed to think that Bonaparte was intent on coming to East Dereham personally to cut off his head with the guillotine. Something had to be done to set his mind at ease.

Johnson wrote in the margin of the account book, 'Napoleon is not interested in Norfolk.' Somehow it did not have the proper ring to it. Besides, the last time he had used the device, it had produced a disheartening result. He had gone to the most extra-ordinary lengths to make sure that Mr Cowper was kept in the dark about why a workman had been employed to bore a hole in the wall behind his bed and to insert therein a long tin tube. It was an ingenious way of conveying some comfortable sounds to his cousin to counteract the deplorable ones perpetually injected into his mind's ear by his unseen enemies. But when he had whispered through the tube, 'Here's a happy New Year coming for Mr Cowper in this very house. It will find you busy with your Homer. Here's a happy New Year coming for Mr Cowper,' and so on, the message had had the opposite effect to that intended. The next morning he had come down to breakfast to say that a new voice, a hollow echoing voice, was warning him that a time was coming, which he could only suppose meant the time of his final torment.

That was a year after Mrs Unwin's death almost to the day. It had been a black year. Lady Hesketh had been right to say that her passing was something of a relief, but it was rather insensitive to refer to the deceased as 'dead weight' and 'totally useless'. She had long assumed that Mrs Unwin was the sole cause of Mr Cowper's melancholy and was disappointed that her death had made no material difference to his condition; indeed, it was undeniably the case that, far from getting better, he had got worse – that he was, actually, insane.

Upstairs Miss Perowne felt she was going mad herself. Mr Cowper had apologised profusely for waking her, but he had then repeated it every five minutes for an hour. At last she had snapped at him, 'If you do not let me get some rest, I will be gone out of this dreadful gaol first thing in the morning.'

That had shut him up. But it was an idle threat; much as she would have liked to run away, where could she run to? What employment was there in the world for a forty-five-year-old spinster but to creep into the house of some relative and mind perhaps an even worse lunatic? At first she had thought there was something romantic in his devotion to her, but then his old servant Sam had explained it: she reminded him of Mrs Unwin when they had first met in Huntingdon, merely because she and the lady were of the same age. He had given her a shawl which Sam said was dear to Mrs Unwin, but she certainly was not going to be seen dead in it, because it was a tatty old purple thing with tassels, smelling of mothballs, and she had put it in her trunk and left it there.

Besides, it was very irritating to be followed about by an ancient moon-calf, even if he never tried to lay hands on her, although occasionally when they were walking in the garden, he would take her arm like an old-fashioned beau, courtly and harmless. He was such a child really. She could not go out into the town for an hour without him standing at the window waiting for her to return. But then he did the same thing when Johnson went to take the Sunday service at Yaxham, and when he heard the old dog down the street barking at the sound of the carriage coming back, why the old fool would almost weep with relief, even though he could not abide Johnson, quite properly too, because the boy was a booby and, if the truth be known, madder than his cousin – all these schemes he had for drawing Mr Cowper out of himself; for instance, the business of getting him to sign his name in the four hundred books he had in his library, ten books a day, what could a body do but laugh? Mr Cowper said the only reason he did it was because he reckoned he must live till they were all signed, which at this rate he would never do, because he had smuggled one book off the shelves and hidden it under his bed unsigned. Oh, he was crafty in his own cracked way, and when it suited him his memory was as sharp as a pin – only today she had been singing to herself an old song and he had taken it up and sung the whole thing through to the end. How did it go? *To all you ladies now at land* . . .

And, humming in her mind, Peggy Perowne slipped off to sleep.

56

But now our fears tempestuous grow
And cast our hopes away.

*J*t was strange that Miss Perowne should have been singing that old air by the Earl of Dorset on the very day that he was signing his name in the book about Mr Anson's voyage around the world, which he had hidden under the bed. He had not looked at it in – could it really be? – fifty years. Then he had been reading aloud to Theadora, and when he came to the passage where Anson saw the sailor canted overboard in a storm and the ship sailed on, he caught her eye and she was weeping, who never wept.

'Oh, she was always happy,' he said aloud.

All those years when the gifts came in the post, the small things that he liked so much, for instance the ivory toothbrush, and even the large and magnificent desk, which in its own way was small, being so intricately worked – all those years Mary had let on that she did not know who 'Anon' was, which was the only signature on the accompanying brief notes, and she had never questioned why he always referred to the benefactor as 'he'.

Harriot knew too. It was greatly to her credit that she had never mentioned it either – but she was a Cowper and the Cowpers did not reveal family secrets, even to each other. Setting a spy on him in the shape of Mr Johnson was, however, unforgivable, and as a result he had been obliged to sever his connection with her. But had she understood his letter?

'Adieu,' he had written, 'I shall write to you no more.' That was plain as a pikestaff. But had she grasped why? Mr Johnson had promised that they could stay in East Dereham and it was likely, in fact certain, that it was Harriot who had instructed him to make the promise. But as soon it was made, she had ordered them to flee inland from the coming invasion. Bonaparte's equally sudden decision to attack Egypt instead was inexplicable except as a way of pleasing her. They were playing cat and mouse with him. He had been terribly angry, but of course he deserved her contempt and he had finished the letter with the profoundest regret and sadness. He had spent days composing it in his mind, and yet when it came to putting the words down on paper, they had appeared there like poetry, as if they had written themselves:

> *The night contradicts the day, and I go down the torrent of time into the gulf that I have expected to plunge into so long. A few hours remain, but among them not one that I should ever occupy in writing to you again. Once more, therefore, adieu – and adieu to the pen forever. I suppress ten thousand agonies to add only –*
> *William Cowper*

That had taught her a lesson, and the lesson was a universal one: those who are cast away strike the hardest blow, and the hardest blow is the look a mother sees in her child's eyes when she murders him.

His cry woke Miss Perowne.

'Damn you!' she cried. 'Damn you, you old reprobate!'

There was a silence which lasted some minutes and she was almost asleep again when she heard him sobbing in a way that she had never heard before. She went to his bedside, drew the curtains and saw that he was sitting up with his hands over his eyes.

'What is it now?' she said, but he only mewed like a kitten. With great distaste, she put her arms around him and drew him to her bony breast. He smelled of sour port. She rubbed his back fiercely. 'Mr Cowper, this is all nonsense. Why do you weep, sir? It was a dream, that is all it was, one of your blessed dreams. Do you want me to perish from the cold? Don't go on so, I beg you.'

He drew back from her and said in a formal tone, 'Forgive me, Miss Perowne. I have been very thoughtless and selfish. Can you please accept my apologies?'

'Delighted to, I'm sure,' she said and hurried back to her bed.

Outside the March wind surged down the street; it had a booming sound, as if it had come unhindered from the middle of the ocean. He thought of Mr Anson's ship running on before the gale. It was day, obscure as night, but the clouds were lit feverishly, the sea was turquoise and he saw, as it were fixed in a rush, the castaway sailor borne up on a wave higher than the ship. I envy him, he thought, who suffered this most ignominious punishment, because his suffering was soon over and mine will never be. But it is curious that Miss Perowne should have damned me as a reprobate, because that is the meaning of castaway. Was the word not some-where in St Paul? Yes. How did it go? '*But I keep under my body, and keep it into subjection lest when I have preached to others, I myself should be a castaway.*' To be such a one and also lost at sea was a more purely physical description. And it was a new meaning for the word.

He felt his blood thicken and quicken in his heart and head. By the deliberative power of nature, which was God, he was a repro-bate, a reject, a castaway in the gulf of time, and yet the glory of it was that he had realised his fate in the language of the race. But to arrive at this glory, he had defied God's instructions to kill himself, and for that defiance God had struck at Mary, ruined her kindness and turned her against him, and humiliated her and blinded her and taken her away from him.

'Oh, God, was it for this?' he said aloud, but experimentally in order to hear again the question he had asked at her death-bed. Yes, he said to himself, it was for this.

'But,' he muttered coldly, 'I am not always mad, and it would be a great mistake to think that I am.'

In the street, the booming of the wind had stretched out into a long sustained scream, thin and shrill as tearing silk. In the chest of drawers the bottle of laudanum was concealed beneath some old shirts. He drank deeply, knowing that he would pay dearly for the indulgence, but he had to sleep soundly. All he had of the poem was the title. He wrote 'The Castaway' in his notebook. Then he thought of how Thea had wept as he read Mr Anson's book, and, amazed at his own coldness, he said goodbye to the memory. All that remained of her was a metre, that silly, silly thing he had written for her once when she was his Celia:

> No more shall hapless Celia's ears
> Be flattered with the cries
> Of lovers drowned in floods of tears
> Or murdered by her eyes.

Well, that was the old ballad form, just as it was in the Earl of Dorset's song. It would do, perhaps with the addition of a couplet to hold up the rush. The opium was beginning to work. He was sailing out of harbour into the Atlantic storm, south of Tierra del Fuego, south of the Land of Fire.

He thought of the letter he had written to Harriot and in his notebook swiftly wrote, 'Obscurest night involves the sky'.

Then he pinched the flame of the candle between forefinger and thumb and swooned into a drugged sleep.

The next day he got up as usual at six o'clock and went down to his desk. At eleven o'clock he stopped writing. His tormentors came back then and, feeding off the opium in his blood, tortured him viciously until he went to sleep that night. But when he dreamed that John Newton, standing on the sea, called him 'a damned wretch', he woke not to horror but to a profound feeling of regret. They had always kept in touch and, once, Newton had even come back with Mrs Newton to Olney to visit them. It had been intolerably sad to go around the Vicarage, which was empty and unfurnished at the time, as if it were a museum whose only exhibit was dust, and when they tried to go back to Orchardside through the gate that Newton had made in the wall, the lock had rusted solid and would not open, no matter how sailorly he cursed it. They had laughed together then in the old way. But that night Mary had cried.

And now Mary was dead and so was Mrs Newton. But while Newton was calling him a damned wretch, she was in the dream too, mocking her husband as always, because she loved him. All four of them had loved each other. And even if he alone had destroyed them, his guilt was weaker than his regret. I will sleep no more tonight, he thought, and I know it, but this is my irreducible quantity.

Six days later he handed Johnson the poem, done out very clean and dated at the end March 25th, 1799.

> Obscurest night involved the sky,
>   Th'Atlantic billow roared,
> When such a destined wretch as I
>   Washed headlong from on board,
> Of friends, of hope, of all bereft,
> His floating home for ever left.
>
> No braver Chief could Albion boast
>   Than He with whom he went,
> Nor ever ship left Albion's coast
>   With warmer wishes sent.
> He loved them both, but both in vain,
> Nor Him beheld, nor Her again.
>
> Not long beneath the whelming brine
>   Expert to swim, he lay,
> Nor soon he felt his strength decline
>   Or courage die away;
> But waged with Death a lasting strife
> Supported by despair of life.
>
> He shouted, nor his friends had fail'd
>   To check the vessel's course,
> But so the furious blast prevailed,
>   That, pitiless perforce,
> They left their outcast mate behind,
> And scudded still before the wind.
>
> Some succour yet they could afford,
>   And, such as storms allow,

The cask, the coop, the floated cord
    Delayed not to bestow;
But He, they knew, nor ship nor shore,
Whate'er they gave, should visit more.

Nor, cruel as it seemed, could He
    Their haste, himself, condemn,
Aware that flight, in such a sea,
    Alone could rescue them;
Yet bitter felt it still to die
Deserted, and his friends so nigh.

He long survives who lives an hour
    In ocean, self-upheld,
And so long he, with unspent power,
    His destiny repelled,
And ever, as the minutes flew,
Entreated help, or cried, Adieu!

At length, his transient respite past,
    His comrades, who before
Had heard his voice in every blast,
    Could catch the sound no more;
For then, by toil subdued, he drank
The stifling wave, and then he sank.

No poet wept him, but the page
    Of narrative sincere
That tells his name, his worth, his age,
    Is wet with Anson's tear,
And tears by bards or heroes shed
Alike immortalise the Dead.

I therefore purpose not or dream,
    Descanting on his fate,
To give the melancholic theme
    A more enduring date,

But misery still delights to trace
Its semblance in another's case.

No voice divine the storm allayed,
    No light propitious shone,
When, snatched from all effectual aid,
    We perish, each, alone;
But I, beneath a rougher sea,
And whelmed in deeper gulphs than he.

57

After Mary's secret burial, not only had the voices returned, many more of them than before, but the ghosts that owned them were visible even in daylight, although, as they were invariably hooded, veiled and cloaked, they were faceless. When they followed him around the house or dogged his footsteps in the garden, he could not help but speak to them, which was embarrassing because the servants shied away from him and Johnson was able to report to Harriot that he was possessed by demons. Why was it they never laid hands upon him during the day? It was as if there was torture enough in embarrassment and humiliation. But at night it was otherwise. Then he was disjointed by the rack, or let down to the bottom of the sea with ropes and drawn up again, or he saw a tree torn up by the roots and knew it was himself, or he was taken up in his bed by strange women and when he woke they were still there. And there was no doubting the reality of the monsters that lived in his stomach, half-man half-beast, fanged and fighting with each other to devour him, and finally issuing forth, dead, as excrements. He had done everything he could to stop this horror, including starvation, but then the doctor had warned him that the substance inside him would harden to such a degree that no pill would move it, and he had been obliged to feed the monsters again.

All that was no nightmare, and it was no nightmare either when he was at table eating his meal and a man came and darted a fork into his face. It signified that he was soon to be pitchforked into hell.

'Oh, Mr Cowper,' Johnson said, 'it signifies no such thing.'

'But it does, it does, and I shall have it fulfilled tonight or to-morrow morning, I know I shall.'

'No, no, my dear sir, you shan't. Really, I'm sure you shan't, because, you see, we will not permit it. We shall bar all men with forks from your presence, isn't that so, Margaretina?'

'I do not answer to that name,' Miss Perowne said, 'and I would ask you desist from employing it, especially behind my back.'

He had gone up to bed that night more convinced than ever that they were in league with each other against him – Margaretina was obviously some kind of code word. But then the thought occurred to him that the boy lacked the brains for a conspiracy, he had not got one ounce of malice in his body, he was too light for it. For that reason he had decided to tell Johnson all his dreams and visions, and although he still did not trust him, having a robin redbreast as a recording angel had relieved the loneliness slightly. And the boy certainly stank less than Mr Teedon. Actually, Johnny was, for a spy, rather amusing.

In any event, whatever about his state of mind, Cowper's physical health had improved a year after Mary's death. Food no longer disgusted him, he had begun to drink a bottle of port at night and, as a result, had put some flesh on his wasted bones.

'Why, sir,' Johnson said in his overly familiar way, 'you are master of a double chin and a ruddy cheek.'

He had even had the strength to go out riding, ambling on a hired nag as far as Mundesley. Why had they gone there so often? Eight times in the summer of 1798 was excessive. Why, when he feared drowning so much, had they rowed in a hired boat eight miles out to sea? Why, that time when they had been with Sir John Throckmorton in his chaise when it overturned on the road from Mundesley and Peggy was screaming, 'Oh murder, we're murdered!' why had he sat where he was, almost upside down and not at all frightened, until the chaise was lifted up out of the ditch? Perhaps the explanation was that what he feared in the other world was not punishment but the absence of accident. In this world accidence was the principle of everything, and when it was suddenly made plain, when a carriage overturned and a withered lady was beating her skirts down in case they went up over her head, which was really 'the murder' she had cried out against, well, then, he simply submitted to the happenstance. Submission was pure, or rather the best he knew of purity, though perhaps it was merely another word for indifference. After what had been done to Mary, he had grown tired. That was another reason for the rage of his tormentors – they hated his indifference, and they hated it even more than his decision to refuse to kill himself, because indifference was a worse stubbornness.

He was, above all, stubborn. It was stubborn not to swallow the medicines that Hayley had just now sent him, but he had no intention of eating roasted broom-seeds, and although the pulp of the tamarind was, according to Hayley, a cure for scurvy and a laxative, and therefore a remedy for the melancholy, whatever else he was, he was not a constipated sailor. Sometimes he thanked God he was mad – you could laugh out loud and not have to explain yourself. But that, too, was a despicable trait, cowardly because un-mannerly. It was not cowardice, though, that had made him refuse Hayley's offer to send up from Eartham his influencing-machine – electricity meant powerlessness and, no matter how selfish they thought him, he would not submit to it.

Poor Hayley. Such a soldier for enthusiasms. Such a dreamer and a schemer. Had there ever been in the history of the world such a combination of the two? Or such a friend? He was a deeply devoted but also, it had to be said, a remarkably absent friend – since the business with Dr Willis, he had adored him only from afar. But Hayley had bombarded him with so many kindly letters in the black year after Mary's death that he had eventually replied with a brief note to tell him of his 'perfect despair', which was true, of course, though it actually served as an excuse for not writing at greater length. But then in reply Hayley had sent him the most extraordinary communication he had ever received.

He took the letter out of his notebook – it was well worn and creased – turned on his side towards the candlelight and read it again.

My very dear dejected friend,

The few lines in your hand, so often welcome to me and now so long wished for, affected me through my heart and soul both with joy and grief — joy that you are again able to write to me, and grief that you write to me under the oppression of melancholy.

My keen sensations in perusing these heart-piercing lines have been a painful prelude to the following ecstatic vision: I beheld the Throne of God, whose splendour, though in excess, did not strike me blind, but left me with power to discern on the steps of it two kneeling, angelic forms. A kind seraph seemed to whisper to me that these heavenly petitioners were your lovely mother and my own. I sprang eagerly forward to inquire your destiny of your mother. Turning towards me with a look of seraphic benignity, she smiled upon me and said: 'Warmest of earthly friends! Moderate the anxiety of thy zeal, lest it distract thy declining faculties and know that as a reward for thy kindness my son shall be restored to himself and to friendship. But the All-Merciful and Almighty ordains that his restoration shall be gradual, and that his peace with heaven shall be preceded by the following extraordinary circumstances of signal honour on earth. He shall receive letters from members of parliament, from judges and from bishops to thank him for the service he has rendered to the Christian world by his devotional poetry. These shall be followed by a letter from the Prime Minister to the same effect; and this by thanks expressed to him on the same account in the hand of the King himself. Hasten to impart these blessed tidings to your favourite friend,' said the Maternal Spirit, 'and let your thanksgiving to God be an increase of reciprocal kindness to each other.'

I obey the vision, my dear Cowper, with a degree of trembling fear that it may be only the fruitless offspring of my agitated fancy. But if any part of the prophecy shall soon be accomplished, a faint ray of hope will then be turned into strong, luminous and delightful conviction in my heart, and I trust in yours, my dear delivered sufferer, as completely as in that of your most anxious and affectionate friend,

William Hayley

'Well, what do you make of that?' he had asked Mr Johnson, but the boy had only put his hand over his heart, lowered his head and wept. It was too wonderful for words.

Less wonderful was Lady Hesketh's reaction. 'I fear,' she said, 'Mr Hayley is a stranger to the Great Truths of Christianity,' one of which truths was that it was quite improper to announce that you have seen the Throne of God when you have not been remotely near it. On the other hand, it was a charming vision and she undertook to do what she could to help, although she foresaw certain practical difficulties, viz. convincing judges, members of parliament, bishops, the Prime Minister and His Majesty that they should be directed by a Maternal Spirit, who was not likely to be known to them, owing to her being dead for almost sixty years.

And so indeed it had proved. Lord Kenyon, for instance, did not reply, and when Hayley begged Ned Thurlow to intercede with him again, he did so rather less than whole-heartedly – 'I have been pressed,' he said, 'by one mad poet to ask you for another a favour which savours of the malady of both.'

All this had put Johnny in an awkward position. What had begun in heaven as desire had descended to earth as diplomacy, which he was no good at. He was, besides, such a bad liar.

'Where,' Cowper wanted to know, 'is the letter?'

'Letter? Which letter?'

'Mr Hayley's.'

'Oh, that one. Did I not return it to you?'

'No.'

'Peggy, have you seen Mr Hayley's letter?'

'No.'

'Oh dear, oh dear, oh dear, oh dear. I must have put it down somewhere. I will go and look for it immediately. Will you assist me, Margaretina?'

And they searched the house high and low for days until word was got to Lady Hesketh and she returned the letter from London.

Added to the embarrassment was the disappointment caused by his reaction to the few letters that did come in. When William Wilberforce sent a pamphlet on the slave trade as 'a small testimony of the high and sincere respect in which I hold you', he said, 'What have I done to deserve from a great benefactor of mankind such an obviously ironic gift?'

Worst of all was his response to Beilby Porteus, the Bishop of London. 'You must,' the bishop wrote, 'be enjoying in the tranquillity of private life, the content, the composure, the comfort of having so essentially promoted the Glory of God and the happiness of Mankind, and still more from the <u>certain expectation</u> that your patient continuance in well-doing shall, through the merits of your Redeemer, be rewarded with Glory, Honour, Peace and Eternal Life in the world to come.'

'This was written in derision,' he groaned. 'I am sure of it.'

'Oh no, no, no, my cousin,' Johnny cried. 'Say not so of Beilby, Bishop of London.'

'Well I do say it, Mr Johnson.'

'But really, can you doubt the sincerity of his saying here that you must possess the love of God in as full extent as any human being ever did.'

'Not an atom of it,' he cried. 'Not an atom!'

58

A letter had come from a Mr William Blake. He knew of the
man – Henry Fuseli had wanted him to engrave his illustrations to the edition of the poems of Milton. Satan, however,
had proved a stumbling-block to that project, and the matter had
gone no further. And then, in the first dark days of the new
century, Mr Blake had written him out of the blue.

The most of the letter was filled with a drawing of a robed and
frowning ancient with a forked beard, like two woolly triangles
blown sideways by the wind, all done in rust-brown inks and
washes of watercolour. The writing, forming an arch, ran around
the image with a large, confident, awkward childishness. It said,

> *Thou art the Son of Albion in the Evening of his Decay. I know
> this, Dear Sir, but dost thou? I see You Alone have creeped into the
> Bosom of the Abraham limned Here and Hid There. Oh! would
> that I could follow thee! But I met with Mr Hayley and he said
> you were afraid. Why are you afraid? You are hid where No One
> Other dares go and therefore are Not an Electrical Machine, which
> is Hayley's Mental Downfall, or a Steam Engine in a Mill, which
> is England's fate, and besides, in your refuge of Madness, which is
> Poetic Health, which is to see as the Risen One does, you are Free
> from Isaac Newton. I am, Sir, Your Friend in Milton,*
>
> *William Blake*

This man, Cowper thought, is obviously a revolutionary, or an agent for the government, or a plain lunatic, or all three; and he hid the letter in an old copy of *The Monthly Review*. A week later the girl, Milly, asked his permission to use the journal to line the bucket for the ashes, which had a hole in it, and the thing was burnt away. But after he had gone to bed and not been able to get up again, the words returned to puzzle his mind. He had nothing against Isaac Newton or against steam engines – no man or no contrivance of man could change the world. Furthermore, for this person to say that madness was 'Poetic Health', whatever that might be, was perverse – had he not almost committed suicide to cure himself of it? Mr Blake plainly knew nothing of real madness, which was only horror and terror and crime without joy. But had there not been in the attempts at suicide, particularly the last one at Weston, which he had imagined as being accomplished in the Priest's Hole in the Hall, an element of prideful self-gratification, which was the essence of perversity?

One morning when Johnson had finished shaving him, Cowper picked up the hand-mirror and looked at the set of his mouth. I was always a proud fool, he thought, and it may be that I was insane to spite God and please myself, so perhaps there is something in what Mr Blake said. But against that, there was always a hard part to me, a small piece that was obdurate and commonsensical and, well, cruel.

Thinking of cruelty reminded him of Anna Austen. She too had inclined to go to the extreme end of any emotion. He had loved that in her, all her contrariness, her sudden overflowing of feeling, the joy of her surrender to chance in speech. She was French to the core, romantic but cold, which is what all these revolutionaries were *au fond*. All they wanted to do was destroy the world for its betterment. On the one hand, she admired that savage Rousseau, who kicked over the traces of society, which was all very well until the horse kicked your own knee. On the other hand, she was always quoting that Jesuitical Pascal to the effect that all our troubles arise from an inability to stand alone within our own room.

'Well,' he had said to her and to Mrs Unwin one evening in the greenhouse, 'that appears to be the prevailing opinion amongst philosophers, but it seems to me more reasonable, as well as more honourable to our species, to suppose that generosity of soul and a brotherly attachment to our own kind taught us to build cities and inhabit them and welcome every stranger, which happens, I'm sure, even in France.'

'Oh, you're such an old bigot,' Anna said.

'Bigot is a stern word,' Mrs Unwin said. 'But true or not, I never until now heard you praise cities.'

'I have made him a convert to London,' Anna said.

'No, I have always been essentially of that faith, though I used to think of Olney as the bearable size for a metropolis. But the principle is the same. We do not live for the solitude of a room, but that we might enjoy fellowship with each other.'

'Well,' Mrs Unwin said, 'you keep to your chamber often enough.'

'Yes, but it is of fellowship that I think there, and what I write, if I may say so, is my own poor way out of the shyness that hinders me from indulging in what fellowship allows for.'

'What indulgence is that?' Anna asked. 'Since there is fellowship in it, therefore it cannot be the solitary vice of Onan, can it?'

Look at her, Mrs Unwin thought, leaning forward the better to show off her bosoms and every chance she gets talking lechery like a harlot to an old coxcomb.

'No, it can't, but it has the name of one of the other deadly sins, which actually we are enjoying now.'

'Sloth,' Anna said.

'No, Lady Austen, the sin, which in our case is a virtue, is called luxury. I mean the luxury of reciprocal endearments. Without them, any human paradise could afford no comfort.'

'Reciprocal endearments?' Mrs Unwin said. 'That trips off the tongue.'

She spoke so sharply that he looked crestfallen for a moment. Then he said, 'I'm not being mawkish, or puffing the extravagance of sentiment, which is the curse of our age, and indeed perhaps of all ages. On the contrary, without being any good at it, I adore the laconic, especially in you, my dear.'

'Now there's a compliment,' Lady Austen said sincerely, though its sincerity was lost on Mrs Unwin.

'But there are, you know,' he was saying, 'all sorts of characters in the world and some of them are so sluggish and their hearts such clods that they live in society without contributing to the sweets of it, or even having any relish for sweetness. A man of this stamp passes by our window continually, and as I was brushing my teeth the other morning and watching him, I thought to myself, do you know, I never saw him conversing kindly with a neighbour, though I have known him by sight these twelve years.'

'Who is that?' Mrs Unwin asked.

'Small, very sturdy of make, round belly, extremely protuberant – can't you guess?'

'Mr Geary Ball.'

'The very man.'

'He has the dropsy,' Mrs Unwin said. 'That explains the belly.'

'Yes, and as far as I can see, he considers it his best friend, because it is his only companion, and it is the labour of his life to fill it. Apart from that and the occasional adventure of buying a new pair of shoes, he shows no preference for society. He might strut about with his two thumbs upon his hips in the wilderness and he could hardly be more solitary there than he is here in Olney.'

'You never liked Geary Ball,' Mrs Unwin said.

'Like him? He terrifies me. But there are other men, you know, who have something more than guts to satisfy.'

'And there are women too,' Anna said.

'Yes,' he said and looked her directly in the eye, which was unusual for him. 'Yes, there are, and what we have in common are the yearnings of the heart, which are more importunate than all the necessities of the body and, no matter what your Monsieur Pascal says, they cannot be satisfied in solitude but require society and the pleasure of doing a kindness when we can.'

But, he mused as he watched Johnson rinsing the razor, I did not do her a kindness, and in fact, when it came down to making a choice between Anna and Mary, what I thought was, 'All this business is keeping me out of the greenhouse, where a gust of wind has loosened a pane of glass in the roof, and if it's not soon mended and there comes a late frost, I might lose my Broallia, from New Zealand, which is very tender.'

'I chose the greenhouse,' he said aloud.

'What's that you say?' Johnson asked, but he only replied, with something not unlike a laugh, 'No wonder I am going to hell.'

59

'Mr Cowper, would you like me to make you a cordial?'
Miss Perowne was asking him.

She was a vague and dusty figure, no longer threatening, so he
nodded. But, as she stood up, he felt he should say something. He
struggled to find the words. The first thing that came to mind –
'All that I ever drank was the rankest poison' – was not suitable to
the present occasion. The old extremes, like the old infinities,
seemed unseemly now. Yet she and the others who came and went
were still intent on introducing some malignant substance into his
stomach, where the monsters dwelt.

'Oh, you old fool,' he said to himself. No one meant any harm
to him. Someone had said that to him once – Mrs Perdue! – and
now he knew it to be true. And yet Mr Johnson undoubtedly did
mean harm. Only the other day he had observed the boy slying
some drops from a little brown bottle into his coffee and when he
said, 'What, pray, is that, Mr Johnson?' he had replied that it was
'only a diuretic'. Well, he had no need of such a thing. Quite to the
contrary, what he needed was something to quell the urgency, which
he had to control because they were not going to see him perform
his private business in bed with a jug. But because he was too weak
to totter off into the garden as usual and relieve himself there in
peace, he had at last used the vessel. Pudicity, private shame, public
reserve, what did they matter now? They mattered greatly – almost
as much as his best remaining defence, which was silence. Silence

had served him well these last years. Still, now that Peggy had offered him a cordial, he should say something. But what?

No one would ever know. All his life he had concealed his life. He had been created by a cruel God, joyfully feeding on sacrifice, delighting in cries and tears, to be an example of despair, to show forth the truth of its awfulness and agony, as Mr Blake understood. But he had hidden himself. How could he behold what he was and not tremble? How could he be beheld and not abhorred?

Miss Perowne came in bearing a tray. On it was a tall glass, steaming, golden. She put the tray on the bedside table and stood looking down on him.

'Mr Cowper, would you drink a little of this cordial?'

An urgent thought struck him and he said, 'What can it signify?'

Miss Perowne resumed her seat by the bedside. When she had left the room, he had been sitting up, all bones and pillows, and now he had slipped down and was lying on his back, looking up at the ceiling. You'd think that that jackanapes Johnny, who had stood in for her, would be able to straighten a sheet or plump a pillow, but of course not, he was as mean as a magpie. She had been a long time away because she had gone to her room for a private reason and when she caught sight of herself in the mirror, she had had the smallest drop of brandy from the little flask she kept in her stocking drawer; and then, while she was making the eggnog, she had taken the tiniest sip of the rum she was putting in it. Eggnog was something she could not abide; the taste was sickening to her.

He saw the light of the candle flickering on the ceiling. The time for trembling was past. He had lived his life in an ecstasy of cowardice. But really that was excessive. All along he had merely been afflicted with shyness, which was a reserved sin. Wasn't that what Roman Catholics called a sin that was unforgivable except by a bishop or – was it – the Pope himself? Maria Throckmorton had told him that once. It was the most appallingly superstitious non-sense. Anyway, a reserved sin and a sin of reserve were not quite the same thing.

When had Maria told him that? Yes, it was the night when he had gone up to the Hall with the poem he had written on the death of Bully, her bullfinch. A rat had got into its cage and eaten it, leaving behind only poor Bully's beak. It was one of those little mock-heroic pieces she liked so much, but she had given him such a strange look and then asked him to read the last two verses again.

> He left it – but he should have ta'en
> That beak, which issued many a strain
>   Of such mellifluous tone,
> Might have repaid him well, I wrote,
> For silencing so sweet a throat,
>   Fast set within his own.

'Oh, Mr Cowper,' she said, 'that makes me shiver, as if the finch in the rat should sing. But read on, please.'

> Maria weeps – the Muses mourn –
> So, when by Bacchanalians torn,
>   On Thracian Hebrus' side
> The tree-enchanger Orpheus fell,
> His head alone remained to tell
>   The cruel death he died.

It was then she had told him what a reserved sin was. No, he remembered now, it was not Mrs Frog, it was the Irish girl, Catherina Stapleton, who was engaged to George Throckmorton and who sang like a nightingale. She had sung him his own songs the next morning and then in the evening she had gone out walking with him beneath the lime trees by the river and when they stopped to listen to an actual nightingale he had said, 'Its voice is less sweet to me, Catherina, than yours was this morning. And, do you know, the more I compare you to the bird, the more highly I esteem my own poor songs – they never seemed as tuneful as when you sang them.' Oh, Catherina was lovely, and he had written her a verse to tell her so and to wish her well in her marriage.

> She will have just the life she prefers,
> With little to hope or to fear,
> And ours would be as pleasing as hers,
> Might we view her enjoying it here.

'Here' was important. He wanted her not to go, but to stay and to be, with Mrs Frog, the Queen of the Hall. And when she had married George, he had written, to the same tinkling metre, another little poem, which made what he wanted even plainer:

> Since therefore I seem to incur
> No danger of wishing in vain,
> When making good wishes for her,
> I will e'en to my wishes again:
> With one I have made her a wife,
> And now I will try with another,
> Which I cannot suppress for my life,
> How soon I can make her a mother.

Well, that edged on the lubricious, but Catherina and the Frogs had not taken offence, because they were innocent too, and anyway they knew he was not cut out to be a father, except to the boy Johnson.

But Johnson had spirited him off to London and abandoned him there in a windowless room. Was that the action of a son? And yet the boy had not been pretending when Dr Lubbock plastered him all over against the bedsores, which were open almost to the bone, and when he groaned, poor Johnny could not help but weep. He was such a cry-baby. It was like that time when he had spent all those months reading out the poems. Was that when they were at Mundesley? Yes, and they were alone in the house together, and the voices of the tormentors were so loud he could hardly hear what the boy was reading. It was the poem on his mother's portrait and in the middle of it the boy's voice had cracked. He remembered exactly what Johnson had said then: 'Oh cousin, you have written here verses that no one could read aloud to the end without tears.'

It was an absurd claim, and yet the boy had paid him a compliment the like of which any poet could wish for. To have written verses that even one person could not read aloud without tears, yes, that was adequate.

He tried to sit up a little to see was the portrait of his mother still there at the end of the bed – yes, it was – but the effort made him mew with pain.

Miss Perowne stood up. She loomed over him, but since she was blocking out the light, he could not see her face. It was blank, and she was monumental. Then, as she bent across him to plump the pillows and straighten the sheet with a slash of her hand, he smelled fresh rose-water.

He closed his eyes. It was a summer evening and he was back in the greenhouse at Orchardside with Mary. Why should he have ever envied any man? The greenhouse was a cabinet of perfumes. There were mignonettes, carnations and balsams, woodbines and jessamines. And there were roses. Dog-roses, pure white and loose-petalled, from the bush he had planted by the brick wall in memory of the one in St Albans. He had cut a huge bouquet for her, and she was holding it out to him and he was bending his face into its divine breath. And the jessamines were scarlet, the same red as the jessamines his mother had pricked out for him from the pattern on her shawl. No, no, it was a dressing-gown. The shawl was Mary's. Where was it now? He had forgotten. It was lost somewhere. But the poem he had written for her was not lost. It was out in the world, adequately too. But only because she was dead. My Mary, my Mary. Guilt and regret, like a pair of her flashing needles, knitted his heart. He had been kind to her only by letting her be kind to him. But she had approved of him.

There was something that he had forgotten, something he had to say to the boy. It arose from a time so long gone he could not remember when it was or where they had been. It seemed to be a place without furniture, a prison cell, and he had been walking around and about, up and down, for an age. Johnson was watching as always, and as always guarding him against harm.

'What is that you are saying?' the boy had said.

A spiritual voice, not that of a tormentor, had spoken to him in the night, and he had been organising the message of the voice into verse all morning, so it must have been around the time of the denial of self-murder, the time of the beginning of his final stubbornness. Yet, although he was reluctant to speak, because Johnson was bound to report it to Harriot, he had spoken.

> Sadwin, I leave you with regret,
> But you must go to gaol for debt.

'Do you know the meaning of Sadwin, my cousin?' Johnson had asked.

He had given him an answer, but it was not enough.

He should call up the boy. It was important that he be told.

Miss Perowne, using both hands to raise the glass of cordial to her lips, because it was still hot, did not notice his head rolling towards her on the pillow.

In the lamplight the liquid was golden. He could not take his eyes from the glow nor could he bear to look at it.

She sipped and sipped again quickly, and then wrinkled her nose in small disgust.

There was no need to call Mr Johnson. He was there as always. But who else was standing with him, looming over the bed? Was it Mary?

He should have told the boy that Sadwin was Mary's name, not lost, but stolen. He had made it his own. Sad and win went together. There could only be no victory. Grief was the price Mary had paid for his love. But she was still with him. Her no-nonsense hands were wiping cool his brow. Her eye was on his heart.

Did he know who Sadwin was? That was the question Johnson had asked. The answer he had given him was sufficient. Nothing could now be added.

'Yes,' he had said, 'the winner of sorrow.'

Afterword

 $\mathcal{C}$ S ome of the first chapter of *The Winner of Sorrow* is a distant variation of the opening pages of *Lavengro* by George Borrow. The description of the concentration camp at Norman Cross, written as if remembered by Cowper, copies Borrow's closely.

Works of visual art are used throughout the book, mainly, but not always, to set scenes. Some of these works are real: for instance, what Cowper sees from the window of Milligan's Chophouse is William Hogarth's *Night*; the two portraits of Cowper by George Romney are in the National Portrait Gallery in London, though the Gallery's identification of the one that shows the poet in anguish is, for some reason, tentative; the long-lost portrait of Mary Unwin by Arthur Devis was found in Knightshayes Court, a National Trust house in Tiverton, Devon in 2005. Some works are inventions: the illustrated letter by William Blake is plainly so; Mrs Unwin running towards Weston Hall at night brandishing a knife is also invented, after the manner of the great Portuguese painter Paula Rego. Many of the images are anachronistic: for instance, the giraffe that weeps in Holborn is based on a painting by the 20th century Georgian primitive Pirosmani.

When I began writing this book, the only Cowper biography I had read was David Cecil's *The Stricken Deer* (1929), which is still worth reading. A work of great scholarship, James Sambrook's annotated *William Cowper — The Task and Selected Other Poems*

(Longman, 1994) provided much useful information, as did Charles Ryskamp's *William Cowper of the Inner Temple, Esq: A Study of His Life and Works in the Year 1768* (Cambridge, 1959) and, most particularly, James King's enthralling *William Cowper, a Biography* (University of North Carolina Press, 1986).

But *The Winner of Sorrow* is a novel, not a biography. The extent of the fiction may be exemplified by Susanna Unwin's attribution of the neologism 'unusuality' to a tax-gatherer in Huntingdon, though it is actually the coinage of Mr Charlie McCreevy, until 2004 Minister for Finance in the Irish government.

The Snail

To grass, or leaf, or fruit, or wall,
The snail sticks close, nor fears to fall,
As if he grew there, house and all
                Together.

Within that house secure he hides,
When danger imminent betides
Of storm, or other harm besides
                Of weather.

Give but his horns the slightest touch,
His self-collecting power is such
He shrinks into his house with much
                Displeasure.

Where'er he dwells, he dwells alone,
Except himself has chattels none,
Well satisfied to be his own
                Whole treasure.

Thus hermit-like, his life he leads,
Nor partner of his banquet needs,
And if he meets one only feeds
                The faster.

Who seeks him must be worse than blind,
(He and his house are so combined,)
If, finding it, he fails to find
                Its master.

Translated from the Latin of Vincent Bourne
by William Cowper